Die Like Men

By Tim Kent

Maps were drawn by Chase Kent

For Chase and Timmy, a father couldn't be more proud.

Published by:
Bluewater Publications, LLC
1812 CR 111
Killen, Alabama 35645
www.BluewaterPublications.com

Table of Contents

Author's Note i

Part 1 From Alabama 1

Part 2 Race to Columbia 33

Part 3 Chessboard of War 53

Part 4 Pursuit 113

Part 5 Valley of Death 159

Part 6 Home Coming 191

Part 7 Death of a Nation 243

Epilog 303

Afterwards 304

Author's Note

I didn't put an introduction in my first book which was a huge mistake. I have so many people asking if the book is fiction. Everything in my first book is factual, only written in novel form. I thought it would make the book more interesting to people who don't enjoy reading the cold history.

I started out attempting to do the same with this book, but soon ran into serious difficulties. I wanted to keep things as close as possible to the real story. The only problem with that approach is that no one is sure what the real story is. The Nashville Campaign is full of controversies. Some of those controversies began the instant an event occurred, and others came along when certain historians attempted to change history.

It would have been easy for me to have fallen into that trap without the help of some friends who pointed me in the right direction. Daniel Mallock of Franklin, Tennessee, has written numerous articles on the Battle of Franklin and is the first person who provided me with insight. He got me in touch with Sam Hood, President of the John Bell Hood Society. Sam provided me with lots of insight on the general himself, and I've added them to the book. Eric Jacobson, the military historian at Carnton Plantation in Franklin, Tennessee, reviewed some maps with me and gave me a good bit of insight on the incident at Spring Hill.

Eric told me I had lots of freedom with a novel. I explained to him that I wanted to keep things as accurate as possible. In the end, I went with a few things that can't be proven. In other parts of the book, I had to compress a lot of the action, especially around Nashville. Although the overall story is correct, I want to be sure and point out that what I've written may differ from the actual truth.

For the best book that covers just the facts, I strongly recommend Eric Jacobson's *For Cause & For Country*. He addresses all the issues of Spring Hill and Franklin. Also, *The Battle of Franklin* by James Knight is a good book on the events surrounding Franklin.

Now I just want to address some of the controversies that surround Spring Hill and Franklin and the side I have taken. At Spring Hill there was mass confusion. I believe the confusion resulted from a good deal of miscommunication, especially between Generals Hood and Cheatham. Hood's intention was to throw Cheatham's corps across the turnpike and have them sweep southward intercepting Schofield's retreating army. He held Stewart's corps in reserve behind Rutherford Creek. When Schofield marched northward and engaged Cheatham, I believe Hood was going to have Stewart come crashing in on his flank.

I believe when Cleburne became engaged with the Federal troops to his north, Cheatham somehow decided that Spring Hill was the goal. He

i

overruled the commanding general and threatened to arrest Bate if he didn't give up on the movement to occupy the pike and move north toward town. This only started the domino effect. Things began to fall apart from here on out.

Once Cheatham's entire corps was in position, Hood wanted to attack immediately. It had grown dark at this point and Cheatham was against a night assault. General Brown, ordered to begin the attack on the right, believed he had Federal troops on his flank. He refused to move until he was properly supported.

At this point things get a bit murky. According to rumors, and evidently General S.D. Lee had heard the same thing, General Brown was intoxicated. There is no solid proof; nevertheless there is evidence that something wasn't quite right with the man that night. He had been a brave leader, and several of his subordinates became upset because he seemed to lose his nerve after his men were prepared to attack. Was General Brown intoxicated at Spring Hill? We will never know.

General Cheatham has been accused of seeing a local belle while all this confusion was occurring. Again, this was passed around and no one can be sure if it's true. There were times when he was absent from his command, and we do know that this young lady was seen standing in the road asking General Forrest to send a message to Cheatham.

Eric Jacobson made a great point when I discussed the affair at Spring Hill with him. He said the Army of Tennessee was like a pit of vipers. When General Bragg took command in 1862, there were two separate blocs within the army. These consisted of pro-Bragg and anti-Bragg factions. Wounds between the two would never heal. Eric and I both believe that is part of the reason for the fiasco at Spring Hill. No one in the army could trust the other.

At Franklin, General Wagner was accused of being intoxicated. He left his men in an advanced position that could only aide the Confederate army. Rumors abounded that he was indeed drunk, and General Wilson evidently heard the same thing. My good friend Daniel Mallock believes that General Wagner was Schofield's scapegoat. Again, we will never know the truth, but I have to apologize to Daniel for the chapter regarding Wagner.

I hope I treated General Hood fairly. I believe the man has been unjustly treated by historians. He has been accused of being addicted to opium, when there is absolutely no proof of this. He learned his warfare from two of the best in the business, Robert E. Lee and Stonewall Jackson. All the moves Hood attempted were emulations of these two great men. The Battle of Atlanta in July was a very close replica of the Battle of Chancellorsville. He attempted to get his army on the flank and rear of Sherman's army where he could force them back. The plan failed because of troop exhaustion, failures of some subordinates, and just plain bad luck.

Do I believe Hood made a mistake at Franklin? Absolutely. General Hood was mortal and subject to make mistakes. Do I believe Lee made a mistake at Gettysburg? Absolutely. This doesn't mean either of them are bad men. Some historians have declared war on Hood's character because of

Franklin. For more information on General Hood and his ill treatment by historians, I recommend going to the website www.johnbellhood.org. Again, Sam, I hope I'm not too rough on General Hood.

I tried to keep things according to the way I believe they happened. Cheatham may not have seen the local belle, Brown may not have been intoxicated, and Wagner may have been a scapegoat. Either way, this is a novel and is considered a work of fiction. I hope I haven't offended anyone with the story.

I have to thank Terri Treloar for editing the manuscript. It is very important for me to thank Angela Broyles, owner of Bluewater Publications. She liked my writing and gave me a second chance, when I had actually given up on becoming a writer. Thanks again, Angela. I truly appreciate everything.

In addition to Daniel Mallock, Sam Hood and Eric Jacobson, I would like to thank Lance Underwood for proofreading. Also, Todd Richardson for encouraging me to continue writing when I grew frustrated. My dad for telling me I can become anything I desire with hard work. My mom for all the support she gave me while trying to write during a nasty divorce.

Tim Kent
September

"But you shall die like men, and fall like one of the princes."

Psalms 82:7

The Confederates

They are all that remain of the once proud Army of Tennessee. They move north only forty thousand strong now. This army has seen little success and won few victories during the war. It has not been their fault. They have been served with inept commanders since the war began. They've fought together at Shiloh, Tennessee, and had the battle won until the attack was inexplicably called off at the end of the first day. At Perryville, Kentucky, they fought all of Buell's army with only a part of theirs and then retreated during the night for no reason. Back in Murfreesboro, Tennessee, they attacked Rosecrans's army and almost destroyed it, but again they retreated following the battle.

They won the great battle at Chickamauga in Northern Georgia, their greatest victory, only to have Bragg allow the Union army to regroup and the victory slip from their grasp. They constantly retreated into Georgia under Joe Johnston until he was relieved before Atlanta. John Bell Hood was then appointed their commander by President Davis because he wanted a general who would fight, and fight he did. He lost Atlanta by attacking Sherman's breastworks repeatedly, although the Confederate army was outnumbered. In the three months Hood was in command, the army suffered over twenty-one thousand casualties. They moved into Northern Alabama a shadow of their former selves, having been misled since the war's beginning. This would be their last chance to win the war.

The Federals

They are not even an army actually, but a group of widely scattered detachments. Sherman has taken the bulk of the army and begun his famous march across Georgia. Another part has been left to guard what remains of Atlanta. Thomas must gather these scattered units and organize them into an army before Hood arrives. If he's unable to get enough men up in time, Nashville may be lost. If Nashville is lost, Hood may prolong the war and possibly even win the war for the Confederacy.

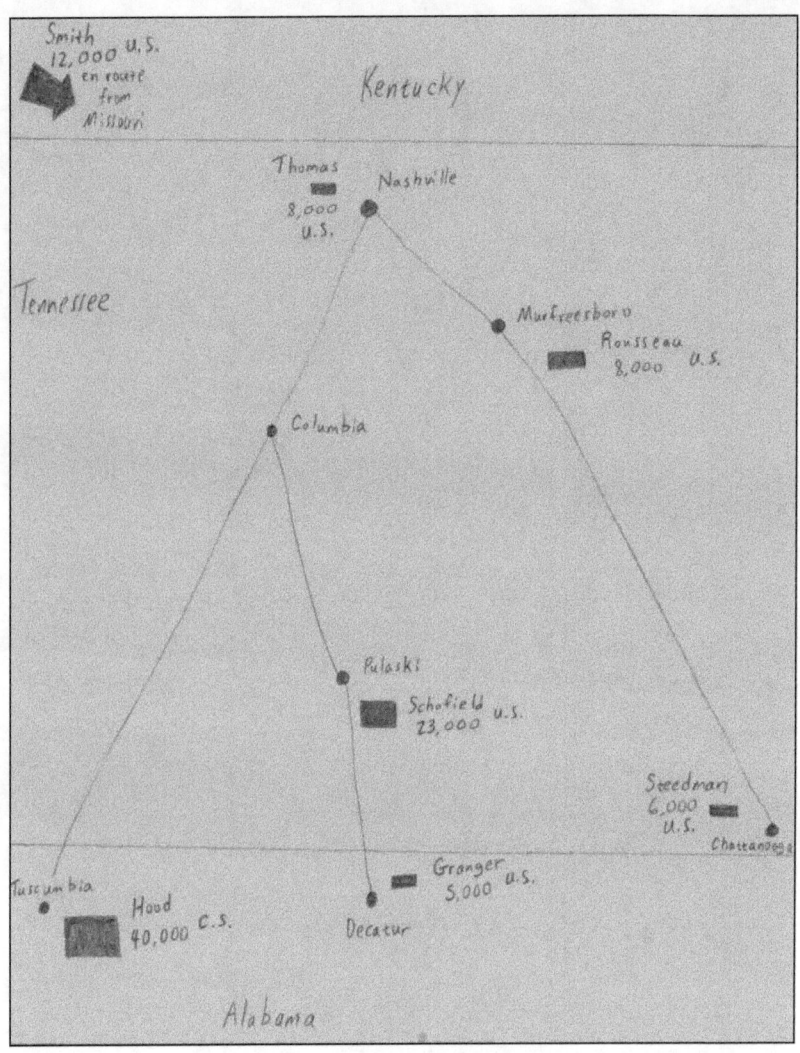

Disposition of troops. Hood's army is concentrated at Tuscumbia while Thomas's army is scattered.

Part 1

From Alabama

"Advance and do not fear the thorns in the path, for they draw only corrupt blood."

Khalil Gibran

1

October 31, 1864

CSA

He rode north through the trees, past the men of his army toward the high ground overlooking the Tennessee River below. Riding with him were the army's Chaplain, Charles Quintard, and Tennessee Governor Isham Harris. They were followed close behind by Hood's staff and escort.

Approaching the edge of the cliff, John Bell Hood pulled on his horse's reins. Quintard and Harris reined up beside him. Downstream, they could see soldiers filing across a pontoon bridge toward the town of Florence. The head of the column was disappearing into the trees on the far shore.

Governor Harris removed his top hat and scratched his bald head. He looked at Hood and asked, "How long you reckon before they make contact?"

"Any minute now," Hood said, staring across the water through sad drooping eyes.

Quintard looked from Hood to the men digging the redoubt behind him. They reminded him of ground hogs burrowing in the soft soil. The shovels were throwing dirt into the air, officers looking on, men sweating in the cool fall air. Morale had definitely improved since they had left Atlanta.

Hood turned to Governor Harris. "We'll have you back home in no time, Governor."

"Thank you." Harris was beaming at the thought. "There's nothing any more melancholy than a governor without a state."

A rifle shot echoed across the water from the direction of Florence. All three men turned their heads in unison at the sound. There was nothing to see over there but trees, rooftops, and a few of the larger buildings. There were a couple more shots, then a volley. Quintard watched Hood, but the man betrayed nothing. Soon the din across the river grew into what sounded like a lively skirmish. Quintard had heard how Hood's face would transform when battle was imminent, but he still wore the same careworn expression.

Governor Harris placed his hat back on his head and said, "Home will be nice. I hate that we left Sherman loose in our rear."

Hood glared at Harris. "Governor, we lost Atlanta long before I was given command of this army."

Quintard frowned. He knew losing Atlanta was a sore spot for the General. Once Hood had ordered Atlanta evacuated, the newspapers had called for him to be relieved of his command. Harris was shaking his head apologetically. "I didn't mean to insinuate you were to blame, General."

Hood waved his hand, cutting him off. "I know you didn't, Governor, but my point is that General Johnston lost Atlanta long before I took command."

Confederate General John Bell Hood.
Jefferson Davis's last hope for victory.

Hood felt he had to defend his honor regardless of what Governor Harris had meant. Most people just didn't understand what happened back in Georgia. He took a deep breath and continued. "General Johnston should have never chosen soldiering as a profession. The man hasn't the stomach for war. If a battle seemed to be looming, he would just retreat."

Harris was nodding his head in agreement. He hadn't meant anything when he said what he did. He was just thinking out loud.

Quintard watched Hood continue his one-sided debate. He seemed oblivious to the sound of rifle fire coming across the water. It amazed him how strong Hood looked despite his disabilities. He looked down at the wooden leg standing out at an odd angle from the horse. It didn't look natural, but Hood claimed it helped him with his balance while riding. He also wore a large gray cape and kept his useless left arm hidden beneath it.

The gunfire across the river suddenly stopped. Hood didn't seem to notice, he was still talking about the man he had replaced in command of this army. "How can you win a war when you're afraid to fight? I tell you, Governor, when I took command of this army, Johnston had the men so demoralized that I couldn't get them to fight unless they were protected by breastworks. I thought I would never eradicate this evil."

Harris continued to listen to Hood, but he was only pretending to be interested. Beside him, Quintard had his head lowered in prayer. Hood loved talking tactics, and he thought this would be a good time to give the governor a lesson on warfare. As a man of the cloth, Quintard didn't care much for war. Before becoming a man of God, he had been a physician. War destroys the physical as well as the spiritual part of man. He wondered how there could be men like Hood, men who loved war?

Hood was leaning closer to Harris now, propped against the crutch strapped to his saddle. "Under normal circumstances I would have crushed Sherman at Atlanta. But those weren't normal circumstances. Johnston abhors casualties. That's a sign of weakness in a commander."

Several of Hood's staff officers had moved their horses closer so they could hear. They were hanging on his every word. Some were bobbing their heads up and down in agreement. Hood said, "To be a good commander..." He paused and looked at the staff officers. "You men listen to this. To be a good commander, you must be willing to send men to their deaths. You can't stop and think about the cost of victory. It's all right to shed tears for the dead, but that should come later, after the battle's over."

Governor Harris had lost interest in the conversation. He was looking down at the ground, his mind a thousand miles away. *He's a politician, Hood thought. He should understand what I'm talking about. Politicians don't seem to mind asking men to join the army and go die for them.*

He was enjoying the tactics conversation and would talk tactics as long as there was anyone listening. He turned his attention back to the staff officers. "Do you men think Generals Lee and Jackson won all those battles back in Virginia by hiding behind entrenchments?"

The young men's heads were shaking, waiting. It suddenly dawned on Hood why he had begun this conversation to begin with. He turned back to Harris. "Governor, you got any idea what condition this army was in when I took command?"

Harris looked up, thought a moment, and then began to stroke his bushy mustache. Just as he was about to reply, Hood interrupted and answered the question himself. "The entire army, from the commanders down to the privates, had lost all confidence in their fighting abilities. All those retreats without putting up any resistance had taught them to fear the Union troops. If I ordered them to assault an entrenched line, hell, they wouldn't even move. When they did attack, they only made a half-hearted effort. It was as if they had already resigned themselves to the fact the assault was gonna fail."

Harris was nodding again. He regretted he had said anything to make Hood think he doubted him. Hood cleared his throat and nodded toward the men digging behind him. "It's taken a lot of work, but those men understand now that safety lies in the attack."

He exhaled heavily. He'd let it all out. It was almost as if he had been holding this in for a long while and felt better now that it was all off his chest.

Harris smirked and said, "Johnston says he was waiting to get Sherman far from his base of supplies and then destroy him."

Hood laughed, but it was a forced laugh. He began to shake his head. "So he said, Governor. So he said. He retreated over a hundred miles through the mountains in just sixty days." Hood paused as if he had just remembered something. He looked back at Harris and asked, "You ever been through North Georgia, Governor?"

Harris nodded. "Yes, by train a few times."

4

"Then I'm sure you noticed the terrain there." Hood was shaking his head in disbelief that a commander could be as incompetent as Joseph Johnston. "Hell, those mountains make the entire country there one vast fortress. Only a fool couldn't hold out in those mountains." He looked at the staff officers and continued. "You put General Lee in those mountains with his army, and Sherman would grow old and die before seeing Atlanta."

The staff officers began to laugh at the thought. One man said, "You're right about that, sir."

Hood continued with his rant. "You see, Governor, when you're facing an army superior in numbers, you want to keep your enemy in a tight spot if possible. You give him room to maneuver, and he'll turn your flank. As much as Pete Longstreet loves fighting on the defensive, he'd warned Johnston to take the initiative or Sherman would flank him. Once Sherman got beyond those mountains, Atlanta was as good as lost. I was able to hold it for forty-five days by going on the offensive. I took the fight to him just like Lee and Jackson used to do back in Virginia. If I would have been served well by my commanders, I still may have beaten him."

Quintard thought about General William Hardee. Hood had blamed him for ruining his chance to destroy Sherman on July twenty-second. He accused Hardee of intentionally delaying his march around Sherman's flank. Now Hardee was gone, shipped off to the east coast to some minor post. For two long years this poor army had been ill-served because of infighting among the commanders. Quintard prayed that would stop also.

"I learned from the two best commanders in the Confederacy," Hood was saying. "General Lee drove McClellan's army back from the gates of Richmond in the Seven Days Battles by attacking his flank. We whipped Pope's army at Second Manassas by attacking his flank. It works, I'm telling you. I've seen it work time and again. We just have to get the men to understand that it works. I learned from Lee and Jackson that a smaller army can defeat a larger army by taking the initiative and keeping the larger army on the defensive. You give the larger army the initiative the way Joe Johnston did, and he'll just wear you down."

Hood thought about the condition of the army in Georgia when he'd first joined it. The men's spirits were high. The men had cheered him when he rode through camp back then, but not as much as they had Johnston. They didn't understand that while Johnston was saving their lives by only fighting behind breastworks, he was also losing the war.

Hood turned back to his aides and continued, "You men remember that safety in combat doesn't come from fighting behind breastworks, but in getting into close combat with your enemy. The only thing that signifies a victory is the number of cannons and flags you capture."

The men were nodding, listening patiently. They were eager to learn from one of Lee's best division commanders. Hood said, "I learned a lot at Gaines' Mill. Lee had attempted to flank the Federal army there but failed. As a last resort, he'd made a massive frontal attack. Every command that charged

5

across that creek and into that open field had been repulsed with heavy losses. General Lee came to me personally and asked if I could take that hill. I told him I believed I could, and there was a reason I thought I could. I'd been watching the other commands and learning from their mistakes. They were all stopping in the open field and returning the enemy fire. I told my men to keep moving up the hill until they were among the Federals where we would drive them out with the bayonet. It worked too. We overran the first line and went into the second line with them. The second line couldn't fire for fear of hitting their own men. It was a beautiful charge. I'll never forget it."

Hood smiled to himself as he remembered that day over two years ago. He'd earned the nickname "The Gallant Hood of Texas" that day. He'd saved the day for General Lee on that hill just outside Richmond. What most people didn't know was that he'd sat on a cracker box that night and cried his eyes out. He'd felt extremely guilty that he'd lost so many men and yet he was untouched. Those men were irreplaceable. He'd trained those men, and they were some of the finest the Confederacy had to offer.

He remembered finding a friend from the old army there. Federal Captain William Chambliss had been shot six times. The surgeons said there was no way the man would live. Hood had the man sent to a hospital in Richmond where he eventually recovered.

He had tears running down his face and into his beard the next morning at roll call because so many of his men were gone. He'd tried to hide the tears but found it impossible.

He turned to the staff officers and added, "That was when I first learned that the tide of battle can be turned regardless of how strong your enemy is. A determined assault will carry the day every time."

The men were nodding in agreement. Hood asked, "What is the most important branch of service in an offensive?"

A young, sandy-haired lieutenant spoke up. "Artillery, sir."

Hood shook his head. "Artillery is pretty much useless on the offensive. I've seen artillery fire for hours without doing any damage. No, sir, infantry is the queen of battle."

Quintard spurred his horse forward and looked downstream toward the pontoon bridge. Just beyond it stood the pilings of the railroad bridge that connected the Memphis and Charleston Railroad to Florence. The bridge was long gone, destroyed by the Federals. He watched the Confederate troops moving slowly across the span. He could see the pontoon boats sinking low in the water from the weight. From this distance, the men looked like a line of ants making their way to a picnic. He could see a horseman feebly making his way south against the traffic of infantry. Quintard turned to Hood. "General, I think there's a courier coming back across the river."

Hood looked up and said, "Let's go meet him, then get back to headquarters and rest a spell."

They rode west toward the pontoon bridge, past more men digging breastworks along the edge of the hill. None of the men stopped working to cheer him like they would have Johnston. Most didn't even bother to look up from their work. A lieutenant watching his men dig turned, and seeing Hood, he saluted. Hood ignored the man and kept riding. He'd never felt a connection with this army quite like he had with his men back in Virginia. These men loved General Johnston. To them, Hood was the man who had replaced their beloved general. They just couldn't seem to understand that the man was slowly losing the war by not allowing them to fight.

One of the staff officers asked, "General, how did you end up in Longstreet's corps? You seem better fitted for Jackson's style of warfare. I mean, everyone knows Longstreet comes from the Joe Johnston school of defensive warfare."

"I truly felt out of place in Longstreet's corps," Hood was shaking his head. "The man played favorites also. He loves George Pickett, one of his other division commanders. In his eyes, Pickett can do no wrong. George isn't an extremely intelligent fellow, but he and Longstreet were old friends from the Mexican War. McLaws used to be one of his favorites, but they've had a falling out since. Longstreet brought his friend up on court martial charges. Micah Jenkins was another of his favorites. There was a big controversy in Longstreet's corps after I was wounded at Gettysburg. Law was my senior brigade commander, yet Longstreet wanted to promote Jenkins around him. Poor Jenkins was killed at the Wilderness last May."

Hood was rambling and realized it. He said, "But, back to your question, Longstreet wasn't quite as bad as Joe Johnston. Longstreet would attack if it was called for. Joe Johnston had too much of the old army way of doing things. He'd spent his entire life trying to win promotions and had done so by not making mistakes."

Chaplain Quintard thought to himself, not Johnston again.

Hood continued. "He understands that if you don't fight a battle, you can't make a mistake. He had seventy thousand men before the Atlanta Campaign began, and if he'd attacked Sherman's rear the way Lee and Jackson would have, he would have forced the Federals back."

Governor Harris was nodding in agreement. Hood was making a valid point. Johnston had retreated everywhere he had commanded. He said, "He's a strange man. Definitely not cut out for army command."

"I tried every way I could to get Johnston to go on the offensive, but to no avail. When I first came to the army as a corps commander, he assured me he would take the fight to the enemy, but it's just not in the man. There's not an aggressive bone in his body. He hasn't the stomach for warfare. Only General Stewart was in agreement with me. He felt that if we stayed on the defensive, Sherman would be free to build his army and then drive us back at his leisure."

They rode on west until they came to the top of the trail that snaked its way down to the pontoon bridge. The path was full of men. Some of the men recognized Hood and raised their hats. Below them, a rider pushed his horse up the steep slope through the crowds of men moving down. Hood recognized the man as one of Stephen Lee's staff officers. He tried to remember his name but couldn't.

The man reined up, saluted Hood, smiled a toothy grin, and said, "Negotiating my way back across that pontoon bridge was a nightmare, General. I thought a couple of times that me and Nelly here were going into the creek."

Hood nodded, leaning on the crutch. "You have a report for me?"

The man had sense enough to know Hood was in no mood for small talk. He rose in the saddle and jerked a thumb back toward the river. "Sir, General Lee begs to report, sir. He's had a sharp little skirmish over there. Your reports were correct, General. It was one brigade; that's all. We've taken the town, pushed 'em back out toward the north. The townsfolk are all out in the streets cheering us. They seem damned glad we're here, sir."

"Very well," Hood said. He thought a moment and then asked, "Casualties?"

The man raised his eyebrows in thought. "Yeah, we got a few. General Lee didn't say how many. There weren't that many though. General Gibson's Louisiana brigade did all the fightin'."

Hood nodded. "Give my compliments to General Lee. Tell him to form a good defensive line just outside town in case they come back. Once he has the place secure, I'll move my headquarters over. Then we can get the rest of the army over and begin preparations for the coming campaign."

"Very good, sir," the man saluted and turned his horse back down toward the crowded pontoon bridge below.

November 3, 1864

CSA

He sat at the table leaning heavily on his left side. The wooden leg lay propped against the wall nearby. John Bell Hood reached down and rubbed at the four inch stump of his right leg. When he wasn't riding, the artificial leg was more cumbersome than anything. He'd thought he would be walking on it without using the crutch by now, but it was growing painfully obvious that would never happen.

General Pierre Gustave Toutant Beauregard had just been shown into the room. He took a seat at the table across from Hood. Neither man was happy about having this war council.

Since the newspapers had all called for Hood's head following the debacle at Atlanta, Davis had been forced to place Beauregard in overall command to pacify the public. Davis had made it clear that though Beauregard was in overall command, he wasn't being given field command. He was not to give direct orders to Hood, but only to make suggestions.

Hood wondered what it was about this small man of French lineage that so fascinated everyone. President Davis hated the man. The war hadn't been kind to Beauregard. He'd wanted to be like his hero Napoleon Bonaparte, but he'd spent the entire war fighting with President Davis. Davis took things personally, held grudges, and because of that, Beauregard hadn't held an important field command since the spring of 1862.

Beauregard ran his hand through his graying hair. Hood thought about the rumor he'd heard back in Richmond about Beauregard's hair. He claimed the pressures of command had caused his hair to begin graying, but rumor had it the Federal blockade had cut him off from his supply of foreign hair dye.

Virginia Irvine, the mistress of Irvine Place, was hovering just inside the dining room door. She had been fawning over Beauregard since his arrival. She could hardly believe she had all these prestigious officers in her home. She looked at Beauregard and asked, "Is there anything I can get you gentlemen before you begin your meeting?"

"No thank you, ma'am," Beauregard bowed slightly. His voice betrayed a thick French accent. The man was born in Louisiana to French parents who spoke French as their first language. "We do appreciate you allowing us the use of your home for army business."

"The honor is all mine, sir," Virginia Irvine was practically beaming. She watched him for a long moment and then left the room. Beauregard was used to this type of attention. It tended to feed his enormous ego. Since the death of his wife, he had enjoyed the company of women, but this Misses Irvine's husband was also in the house.

Hood had already been through all these formalities with Virginia Irvine when he'd moved his headquarters here yesterday. The home wasn't nearly as nice as the Foster Home at the north end of Court Street, but it had few steps and that was more important to a one-legged General.

Governor Harris and Chaplain Quintard were also seated at the table to each side of Hood. There were a few of Hood's staff officers also seated at the long table. Sitting next to Beauregard was his adjutant general, Colonel George Brent, looking prim as usual. The man had taken the place of Beauregard's trusted companion, Thomas Jordan, when that officer was called elsewhere. Brent was the only staff officer Beauregard had brought along.

Colonel Brent was staring at Hood through his piercing green eyes. Unlike most men in the room, he was clean shaven. His hair ended in a mullet just below his collar. He held a very low opinion of General Hood. He'd been writing the correspondence from Beauregard to Hood and understood Beauregard's anger with the man.

Beauregard was tired of dealing with Hood already. The man had given him little notice of where he intended to go or when. That made things extremely difficult for Beauregard to keep Hood's army supplied. For some reason, Hood just refused to cooperate.

9

Chaplain Quintard noted the cool greeting between Beauregard and Hood. They'd barely acknowledged each other when he'd entered the room. Quintard could almost feel the tension in the air. *This army doesn't need more fighting among its commanders, he thought.*

It was amazing how much alike Beauregard and Brent were. Both acted so proper, giving off an air of superiority. They both acted as though it bothered them to have to be in the room with all these inferior men. Beauregard crossed his arms, sat back in his chair and stared hard across the table at General Hood. "What are your plans?"

Hood said nothing for a long moment. Beauregard sat patiently waiting. There was a faint trace of a sneer on his face. Quintard began to regret he'd come to this meeting.

After a long, awkward pause, Hood reached over and patted Governor Harris on the shoulder. "I plan on installing the governor back in his capital."

Beauregard wasn't impressed at Hood's attempt at humor. He hadn't come all the way from Montgomery to be entertained. That idiot Davis had already notified Beauregard that Hood was invading Tennessee. He'd ordered Beauregard to see to it that Hood's army was properly supplied and equipped for the move. "And how do you plan on accomplishing that task? Do you know the state of your supply line?"

Hood didn't reply. He looked down and began to rub at a dirt stain on his frock coat with his good hand. He'd known this meeting was meaningless when Beauregard had wired him that he was coming. *Hood wondered, why does he think I care about the supply situation? It's his job to keep me supplied.*

Hood thought he understood why Beauregard disliked him so much. It was the friendship with Davis. It was widely known throughout the Confederacy about Davis and Hood's friendship. It probably galled Beauregard to know Hood was a confidant of the Confederate President.

"I'll only need enough supplies to get me there." Hood tried to sound cheerful. He loved strategy and tactics, but logistics just didn't interest him at all. "After I retake Tennessee and invade Kentucky, I'll forage my army among the civilians."

Beauregard frowned and began shaking his head. "Getting enough supplies here just to get you started is going to be a challenge in itself…" Beauregard looked at Colonel Brent. Brent nodded in agreement.

Beauregard continued, "After I get the supplies sent up through Mississippi on the Mobile and Ohio Railroad, I have to transfer them to the Memphis and Charleston Line at Corinth. The track from Corinth to Cherokee is in horrible shape. From Cherokee to Tuscumbia, the railroad is gone, destroyed. We're forced to have everything loaded onto wagons and pulled here. That's about fifteen miles of the muddiest roads I've ever seen. The horses and mules are half starved. From Tuscumbia to Cherokee, the roads are littered with the bodies of these poor beasts, not to mention the broken down wagons. It's almost more than we can do just to keep you supplied daily. I don't see how we can get you a surplus of supplies before you leave."

Hood looked at his fingernails and calmly said, "I'll just have to put the men on half rations I guess."

Beauregard let out a long hard breath. The man just wouldn't see. *How can Davis put such a man in command? Here I am the greatest general in the Confederacy and not allowed to command an army in the field, while fools like Hood get commands.* Beauregard looked at Brent and rolled his eyes up in his head. He was growing agitated with Hood. He said, "I don't think you understand the challenges you face, General Hood. I've repeatedly asked for your plans. You act as though you've given little thought to this campaign. You keep saying you're going to retake Tennessee and invade Kentucky as though both places will just fall into your hands without much effort at all."

Hood's face looked as though someone had just slapped him. The sad expression had vanished. He glared at Beauregard. "General Beauregard, I have spies in Nashville at this very moment. My reports indicate that Thomas has only eight thousand garrison troops defending the city. You know as well as I that those troops are practically worthless…" Hood was growing angry at having to defend himself to Beauregard. *The President has endorsed my plans, Hood thought. Why do I have to defend myself to this elitist snob?* He raised his fist in the air and brought it down hard on the table with a crash. "Thomas has more troops, but they're scattered to hell and back. He'll never get them concentrated in time to stop me from taking Nashville. So, as you can see, I'm not going off half-prepared as you say."

There was a light tap on the door. The knob turned and the door slowly opened. Virginia Irvine stuck her head just inside and asked, "Is everything all right?"

Hood looked down again, trying to compose himself. Beauregard turned toward her and said, "Everything's fine ma'am. Sorry for the disturbance."

"You're not disturbing me, General," she gave a weak smile. "From the sound, I thought someone may have fallen."

Beauregard watched her ease the door back closed. *She's just letting us know this is still her house, he thought.* Hood glanced up at Beauregard then quickly looked away. Beauregard tried to sound soothing. "There should be plenty of supplies in Nashville."

Hood nodded. "Once I'm in Nashville, I won't have a supply problem. My reports indicate that Nashville is the second largest Union supply depot in the country next to Washington."

Hood thought about "Stonewall" Jackson's daring move during the Second Manassas Campaign. He had flanked Pope, got in his rear and captured his supply depot. What his men couldn't carry, he had destroyed.

Beauregard started to say something, but Hood interrupted. He wasn't quite through with his argument yet. "As I move through Kentucky, I'll recruit more troops there…" He gave Beauregard a sly wink. Beauregard knew what he was insinuating. He would conscript men into the Confederate army whether they were willing or not. "After I move north and threaten Ohio, Sherman will be compelled to give up Georgia and come back north. Grant will probably have to send men from his command as well. While this is occurring, I will move my army through the mountain passes and link up with Lee's army in Virginia. As Lee fights Grant from in front, I'll move around and attack him in his rear. After General Lee and I finish up Grant, we can both turn back and deal with Sherman together."

Beauregard watched Hood's staff officers nodding their heads in agreement. Brent looked at Beauregard, trying to gauge his reaction to this. Beauregard lowered his head and began to rub his eyes in thought. It all sounded a bit grandiose, but these were the types of plans Beauregard loved. He wondered why Hood had been so secretive about this. It was ironic once Beauregard thought about it. He'd been drawing up grand campaigns just like this one since the war began. He'd begged Davis for permission to make just such a move, a move that could turn the war in the South's favor. Davis, the self-proclaimed military genius, would never allow Beauregard to implement his plans. He claimed they were just too risky. Now, here was Hood about to set out on a campaign that sounded as though Beauregard himself had drawn it up.

The question that worried Beauregard was manpower. Earlier in the war while the armies were still strong, a plan like this may have been feasible. This late in the war, however, the army was a mere shadow of its former self. He said, "The plan is sound, General Hood, but I'm not sure it can be accomplished with just forty thousand men. That's a lot of marching and fighting."

"If my reports are correct…" Hood drummed the fingers of his right hand on the table. His useless left arm remained in his lap. "Thomas has about twenty thousand men in Pulaski. That's all that stands between us and Nashville. I'll bypass 'em or capture them. Either way, once I'm in Nashville, I'll replenish my supplies and move into Kentucky."

"Time is your enemy then." Beauregard added.

"I'll need help from you once Nashville falls." Hood decided things may go more smoothly if he played to Beauregard's ego. Let him think he is playing a larger part in this campaign than he actually will be. "The entire North will be stirred to action against me. I'll need you to send me any troops you can spare."

"I'll do what I can." Beauregard uncrossed his arms and leaned on the table. "I can't promise it'll be a lot, if anything. The important thing here is speed. For this to work, you need to get to Nashville before they get up reinforcements. You should leave immediately. I'll try and send you supplies while you're marching, but you need to leave now."

"Forrest hasn't arrived yet." Hood wasn't about to leave without a cavalry screen. Davis had forced him to leave Joe Wheeler's cavalry back in Georgia to slow Sherman's march. "If I leave now, Thomas will know my every move. Jackson was such a great commander because he kept the enemy from knowing his movements. There's a brigade of Union cavalry watching us here. They're waiting for us to move so they can report it to Thomas. I'd prefer to wait for Forrest to clear that cavalry out so I can keep Thomas guessing until its too late."

Beauregard rubbed his temple. He was beginning to get a headache. "He should be here anytime. Will you be ready to move upon his arrival?"

"I've still got to get Cheatham and Stewart's corps across the river." Hood sighed. He was growing tired of Beauregard badgering him to move. "We've had trouble with the pontoon bridge. As soon as Forrest arrives and they cross, I'll be ready to move."

Beauregard slowly rose from the table. Brent stood with him. Beauregard said, "I feel better about things since we've talked."

All this could have been avoided if he would have just been up front with me from the beginning, Beauregard thought. He added, "I'll return to Montgomery and continue supporting you all I possibly can. God go with you, General." He bowed slightly.

Hood bowed his head in reply and said, "And with you, General."

Beauregard and Brent turned and walked to the door. Brent opened the door for Beauregard, but the General turned around. He asked Hood, "Where's Rene's command? I'd like to see him before leaving for Montgomery."

Hood had almost forgotten about Lieutenant Rene Beauregard, commander of Ferguson's South Carolina Battery and the son of the man standing here before him. Hood said, "He's in Cobb's Battalion, Cheatham's Corps. They're camped near Tuscumbia. You can ask Cheatham exactly where he has them camped."

"Thank you," Beauregard said and turned to leave. As he stepped into the foyer, Virginia Irvine stood there waiting with a pencil and sheet of paper in her hand. She said, "Now, General Beauregard, don't you think you're leaving here without giving me an autograph."

Beauregard smiled, took the paper and pencil and signed it. He thanked her again for the use of her home before stepping out the front door. On the portico, Beauregard leaned against a huge white column. He gazed up into the dark sky and felt the first drops of rain.

By the time he and Brent mounted their horses, the sky had opened up. Rain was the one thing he didn't want to see just now. Rain would mess the roads up and slow things even more. The supply line between Tuscumbia and Cherokee was almost at a standstill already.

They turned their horses south toward the river. It was taking awhile for all the information Beauregard had just learned to soak in. He asked Brent, "Well, what do you think?"

Brent thought a moment. His eyes were almost glowing out here in the light. He replied, "The man is an ass, sir."

Beauregard had a dry sense of humor, but smiled at the remark. Brent was right, of course. Hood was an ass. Anyone who could be friends with Jefferson Davis had to be an ass. He nodded over his shoulder toward Irvine Place. "I'm afraid the last hope of our country rests on the shoulders of that ass back there. If he's not successful, we may find ourselves in the regrettable position of surrendering soon."

November 4, 1864

CSA

The general was exhausted. He slowly climbed from the saddle and squatted down. His knees popped. Standing back up, he rubbed his lower back and tried to stretch. The three men accompanying him dismounted and waited. General Nathan Bedford Forrest continued rubbing his lower back. "Gettin' to old for this shit, Morton," he said. "What I'd give to be your age again."

The squeaky voice made Morton smile. That was one thing he found odd about Forrest. His voice was so high-pitched that it didn't seem to fit his body. Brigadier General Lawrence Sullivan Ross pointed through the trees toward a large building that looked like a castle. He said, "That's Wesleyan University; I attended college there."

"Is that right, Sul?" Forrest asked. Everyone called the man "Sul." "It's not much of a University at the moment," he added. "I hear they're using it to put up some of our troops."

"Wasn't that long ago I was here." Ross stroked his thick bushy mustache. The man was only twenty-six years old, but his hair was already beginning to recede. "I always thought this was a nice little ole town."

Morton asked, "How the hell did you find this place from way out in Texas?"

"Long story," Ross replied.

Forrest slapped Morton on the back. "Stop asking so many damned questions, boy."

Morton smiled. He and Forrest hadn't always been so close. The first time Forrest had met him, he thought he was just a kid of about fifteen and didn't want any part of him. He had said that he wanted a man to command his artillery, and they had sent him a snot-nosed schoolboy. Morton had proven himself to Forrest quickly. He had proven that he was just as brave and daring as Forrest. Now Forrest wouldn't trade him for anyone.

Forrest's assistant adjutant general, Major J.P. Strange, seemed in awe at the sight of the building. "Looks just like a castle with those towers on top."

Forrest pointed across the road toward a large plantation home standing at the north end of Court Street. "Morton, I want you to go over there and see if we can use that house for my headquarters while I step in here and talk to Hood."

"Sure thing," Morton climbed back onto his horse. "You know those folks, General?"

14

"George Foster is his name," Forrest replied. "I had some dealings with 'im back before the war."

He watched Morton turn his horse and start down the road. He turned to Sul Ross and J.P. Strange and said, "Let's go in here and see what this idiot Hood wants."

Forrest stepped onto the portico at Irvine Place and knocked on the door. He wondered why Hood chose to stay in this house with the Foster Home just across the way. From what he'd heard, the man wasn't very bright. *Another one of those damned West Point trained officers, he thought.*

A staff officer opened the door, saw the stars on Forrest's collar, and quickly saluted. Forrest half returned the salute. He was in no mood to fool around at the moment. He'd been in the saddle for almost a month straight. Hood had made him call off his present raid in Tennessee, ride all the way back to Alabama, and now turn around and escort him back into Tennessee. Forrest didn't see West Point officers as having much common sense. He had to wonder why Hood didn't just meet him in Tennessee. It seemed a better idea to him to save wear and tear on men and horses.

The officer identified himself as Captain Hamilton of Hood's staff and led Forrest into the parlor. There on a sofa lay General Hood, a blanket covering him from the waist down. His left arm lay at his side.

Hood looked at Forrest a moment. Though they had fought together at Chickamauga, they had never met until this moment. Hood extended his hand and said, "General Forrest, I'm glad to have your services for this coming glorious campaign."

Forrest grunted and moved over and shook Hood's hand. The proper thing for him to say as a subordinate officer is how much of an honor it was to serve under Hood. Instead, Forrest said, "I don't know how much help we'll be. We've been a campaigning hard in Tennessee, and my men and horses are exhausted."

"They'll be fine," Hood insisted. He motioned for Forrest to take a seat. Forrest motioned for Sul and Strange to have a seat also. Hood added, "I hate I had to recall you from Tennessee. I heard you were having a good time up there."

I would still be up there having a good time if not for you, Forrest thought, but he didn't say it. He had only gotten the message to report here two weeks ago. Forrest said to Hood, "This is Major J.P. Strange of my staff..." Strange shook Hood's hand, "and this is General Sul Ross; I'm not sure if ya'll have met before."

"Actually, I think we met during the Atlanta Campaign," Hood said as he shook Ross's hand. "You were with Joe Wheeler awhile down in Georgia weren't you?"

The lanky cavalryman nodded, his black curls bouncing. He knew Hood had adopted Texas as his home state since the war began. "I was there a short time. I command the Texas Cavalry Brigade."

"That's right," Hood said. "I remember now."

15

Lieutenant General Nathan Bedford Forrest. "The Wizard of the Saddle."

Forrest looked at Hood's artificial leg propped against the wall. It was a grotesque sort of thing carved from wood. It even had the toes carved into it. *What in the hell for, he wondered.*

Hood tried to get a reading on Forrest. He looked like a leader. He also acted as though he would put up with very little nonsense. The man was about six feet tall, but slim built, probably not over one seventy-five, he estimated. Hood was well aware of Forrest's reputation. He said, "We fought on the same field at Chickamauga. I don't recall if we met or not."

"We didn't," Forrest said plainly. It was obvious he wasn't going to try and get to know Hood, but Hood didn't want any trouble with his new cavalryman. He decided to try and become friendly with Forrest.

"I heard you once threatened to kill General Bragg when he was in command of this army." Hood smiled.

"That wasn't a threat," Forrest relaxed a little and began to recall what he'd said to Bragg. He smiled and said, "I told him if he was any part of a man, I would slap his face and force him to resent it. If he ever interferes with me again, it will be at the peril of his life. It wasn't a threat. I meant every word of it."

Hood laughed. "I hope you and I don't have any problems of that nature."

Forrest said nothing. He stared at Hood, waiting. Hood figured the man was probably just tired. He'd been in the saddle for a while now. The man looked like he needed about a month's rest. Hood wished he could give it to him, but there was just no time.

"General," Hood decided to skip the small talk. It didn't seem to be getting either of them anywhere anyway. "I want you to take command of all my cavalry. General Roddey came by yesterday and offered the services of his cavalry as well. He calls it a division, but I don't think the numbers warrant it. He has several Alabama cavalry regiments with him near Cherokee. You're familiar with General Roddey?"

"Yeah," Forrest replied. "We've worked together before."

16

"I know your men are exhausted and need rest," Hood tried to sound like he was genuinely concerned for Forrest and his men, "but the campaign can't be delayed much longer. We need to strike before the Federal army brings up reinforcements."

"When do you need us to move?" Forrest asked.

"You may have a few days of rest," Hood struggled to raise himself up on his good arm. "Cheatham has finally gotten his corps over the river, but Stewart hasn't. We've had problems with the pontoon bridge. Besides, we can't move with the roads in such bad shape. If it would just stop raining a few days, we could get under way. Try to get your men in the best shape possible with what little time you have."

"I'm making my headquarters at the Foster Home across the way," Forrest said as he stood up. "Will there be anything else?"

"When you get your men all up, I want you to move out north of town and push that Federal cavalry back toward Tennessee." Hood scratched at his long tawny beard. "I don't want Thomas to know where we're going or what I have in mind."

Forrest nodded at Hood and walked toward the door. He didn't bother to salute or say goodbye. Major Strange and Sul Ross shook Hood's hand politely before following their commander out the door.

Forrest stepped onto the portico and placed his hat back on his head. *I came all the way here so I could turn and go right back where I was, he thought. Damn these West Point idiots.*

He and Major Strange rode across the field to the Foster Home. Ross was forced to find other lodgings as his headquarters. He'd arrived and just settled in, when there was a knock on the door. It was a courier from Hood's quartermaster.

Major Strange read the order to himself and frowned. He dreaded reading this to Forrest. The man wouldn't be pleased. He continued staring at the piece of paper.

Forrest realized that Strange was stalling. He said, "Well, read the damned thing."

"Sir," Strange shook his head. "It's an order from Major Landis, Hood's quartermaster. It seems General Hood has issued orders to reduce the number of mules per wagon to just two. He wants the extra animals to be turned over to the quartermaster department."

Strange waited for Forrest to go into his usual tirade, but Forrest said nothing. Maybe the man was just too exhausted, because he remained calm. Strange continued waiting.

Forrest said, "Thank you, Major."

Major Strange, Captain Morton, and Forrest were eating breakfast at the Foster Home early the next morning. Misses Foster had her servants fix the officers breakfast, and then she disappeared upstairs.

A guard was posted at the front door and allowed one of Hood's staff to enter the house. Forrest didn't bother to look up from his meal when the officer entered the room.

The man cleared his throat and waited. Forrest continued eating. Major Strange looked back and forth from Forrest to the officer. He was beginning to feel uncomfortable. He asked, "Can I help you, sir?"

"Yes, you can," the man looked a little peeved. He held his head high like a man with some authority and proud to have it. "I'm Major Landis, Quartermaster of the Army of Tennessee. An order was sent here yesterday about the extra mules of your command. I'm here to find out why that order hasn't been obeyed."

Strange turned to Forrest and watched his face grow red. This was what he had missed out on yesterday, but here it was, the full fury of Nathan Bedford Forrest about to be unleashed.

Forrest stood up from the table and glared at the man. He'd dealt with people like this his entire life. Men who felt they were better than him, just because they spoke proper and had a good education. Now he was about to give him some more educating.

"Let me tell you something, you pecker-necked son-of-a-bitch," Forrest's voice was shrill. He practically screamed at the young officer. Major Landis was caught off guard by the display. His face betrayed his shock. The man actually took a step back. Forrest continued, "Go back to your damned quarters and don't ever let me catch you here again, and don't you send nobody else here about no damned mules. I will not obey the order. It's a damned fool's order anyhow, and you can go tell that idiot Hood that I said that. Have any of you shitheads been on the road from here to Pulaski? Hell no, you ain't. If you had, you wouldn't be issuing orders like that. I kicked the Yankee's asses and captured every mule, wagon, and ambulance in my command. I ain't made no requisition from the Confederate government for one thing in two years, and my teams will go as they are or they won't go at all."

The major was in a state of shock. He began to turn and start for the door. Forrest screamed, "I'm not done with you yet! I'll dismiss you when I'm through. Now, if you bother me anymore about this matter, I'll come down there to your damned office and I'll tie them damned long legs of yours in a double knot around your neck and choke you to death with your own shins. *Now* you're dismissed."

The major spun and headed for the door. Nothing from the commander of the Army of Tennessee would ever be said to Major General Nathan Bedford Forrest about his mules again.

November 6, 1864

USA

George Thomas peered out the window of his modest hotel room. He could see men throwing up fieldworks for as far as his eyes could see. *Garrison troops may not be worth much in a fight, he thought, but they're doing a fine job strengthening the defenses.* A lot of these men were nothing more than government clerks. He'd been out inspecting their work yesterday and noticed the condition of their hands. Some of those men had never performed manual labor in their entire lives. He'd noticed how their hands were covered with blisters. Some had broken open and began to bleed, but few were complaining, at least not to him. That was the best part about being a general—he didn't have to listen to men complain.

Thomas walked across the room and sat at the table. He began to study the map again. He wondered what Hood had in mind. Thomas began to worry again, realized what was happening, and put it out of his mind. It wasn't like he didn't have enough troops. There were plenty of men, but he needed time to get them all concentrated. If Hood decided to cross the river and march hard for Nashville now, there would be little he could do to stop him. Those government clerks won't put up much resistance against veteran rebel infantry.

Major General George Henry Thomas. "The Rock of Chickamauga."

Thomas looked up at his Adjutant General, Brigadier General William Whipple. The heavyset man with the thick scraggly beard was leaning his chair back against the wall reading a newspaper. Thomas looked at the front legs of the chair. They were about three inches off the floor. Thomas asked, "Will, how many times have I told you to keep all four chair legs on the floor? You're gonna end up busting your ass."

Whipple lowered the chair back onto the floor. He kept reading the paper, never bothering to look up. Thomas shook his head and asked, "Now, how many men did Hatch's report say Hood had in Tuscumbia?"

"He's trying to get forty-five thousand troops plus about sixty cannons over the river now." Whipple lowered the paper a little and peered over the top at Thomas. "Would you like to see the report again, sir?"
Thomas shook his head.

"There's no need. Finish reading your journal. I was just thinking out loud."

Whipple continued watching Thomas over the top of his paper. He knew Thomas was worrying himself sick over the coming campaign. He only wished he could say something to get the General to relax a little. All this anxiety couldn't be good for the man. He watched Thomas begin to stroke his gray-streaked mustache as he went on studying the map again. He'd been looking at that map for over a week now as if he expected it to tell him something important.

Thomas tried to hide the worried look on his face but found it impossible. He could feel Whipple watching him. He placed his palms on the table and slowly stood over the map.

Whipple lowered the paper into his lap and watched Thomas. If there were only something he could say to ease the man's mind. Suddenly, Thomas said, "Twenty-three thousand troops under Schofield at Pulaski are all that stand between Hood and Nashville."

"Don't rule out the garrison troops." Whipple added. He realized the garrison troops wouldn't be much help, but thought he would remind Thomas that he had them. Whipple tried to sound cheerful. "I know they're not much, but it's another eight thousand men behind the fortifications. You have to admit, those boys sure are working hard."

"I'll give them that." Thomas sighed and began to rub his eyes. "Those men will never hold against veteran infantry, regardless of how strong the fortifications are. Most of them have done nothing but push pencils their entire lives. Schofield must delay Hood until A.J. Smith gets here from Missouri with his twelve thousand men."

Whipple had been with Thomas for a long time and could never remember seeing him this worried. The man had been called the "Rock of Chickamauga" because of his steadiness there when the world seemed to be coming to an end. He could remember him being the only officer not rattled after Bragg made his surprise attack at the Battle of Stones River. It bothered him seeing Thomas upset like he was. During the course of this entire war, he had never seen Thomas this worried, even under the heaviest fire.

George Thomas had come a long way since West Point, where he'd earned the nickname "Old Slow Trot." Everything the man did in life was slow and methodical. There was absolutely no rush in Thomas. He would have already been the lieutenant general in overall command instead of Grant had he not been born in Virginia. When the war began, Lincoln hadn't trusted him. Grant had a congressman backing him while Thomas had no one.

Thomas began to pace back and forth. He pulled a cigar from his pocket and lit it. His huge head disappeared in a cloud of gray smoke as he puffed.

"I wouldn't worry too much, George." Whipple raised the paper back up. "The weather will slow Hood's march. The roads are gonna be a mess with all this rain."

"Perhaps," Thomas said with the cigar clenched in his teeth. He walked back to the window. "I only hope he moves toward Pulaski and attempts to destroy Schofield before coming to Nashville. Surely he wouldn't leave an entire corps in his rear. If he attempts to bypass Schofield, Schofield will be in a race for his life..." He paused a moment and then added, "and our life also."

Whipple watched Thomas stop and begin to stare out the window. *He's the best general in the army, he thought. He just doesn't have the reputation of Grant or Sherman.* It truly was a shame. There were generals that had been fired for incompetence that were household names, but not George Thomas. It had to be his Virginia birth.

There was a knock at the door. Whipple stood up, placed the newspaper on the table, and went to the door. Standing there was a skinny young man he recognized as James Wilson. Wilson's uniform had the shoulder straps of a major general. Whipple hadn't seen him in over a year. He had ranked Wilson back then. Wilson had gone from lieutenant colonel to major general in only a year's time. He owed his rank to Grant. Grant loved the man. *That could have been me, Whipple thought. If only General Thomas had won the respect and awards he was due.* Out of respect for the uniform, Whipple saluted.

The skinny young man with the spade-shaped goatee returned the salute. Wilson cleared his throat and said, "Major General Wilson reporting to General Thomas."

It may have been Whipple's imagination, but it sounded as though Wilson had emphasized the major general part. He said nothing, stepped aside, and motioned Wilson inside.

Wilson was also a little worried about the meeting. The last time he had seen Thomas was in Chattanooga. Grant had arrived there wet, cold, and filthy from a fall he had taken on his horse. He'd gone to Thomas's headquarters and was sitting by the fire, water dripping from his uniform. Wilson had been the one to call it to Thomas's attention that he should feed Grant and provide him with dry clothing. He knew that Grant hated Thomas and figured the feeling was probably mutual. He wondered if Thomas would treat him any differently because of his and Grant's friendship.

Thomas turned from the window and saw Wilson. He said bluntly, "Come in, Wilson."

Wilson saluted and walked forward. Thomas looked at the twenty-seven-year-old major general standing before him. He wore the high riding boots of a cavalryman. His uniform looked as though it was made for a man twice his size. *Probably don't make uniforms that small, Thomas thought.* He guessed Wilson didn't weigh much over one fifteen.

Thomas nodded toward the table. "Have a seat, young man."

Wilson insisted on shaking Thomas's hand before sitting. He mumbled something about it being an honor to serve under Thomas.

Thomas grunted. He wasn't sure if Wilson was here to serve him or if he was here to serve as Grant's watchdog.

Whipple watched the two men standing there shaking hands. They were quite a contrast. Thomas, over six feet tall and weighing around two fifty. Wilson, built like a rail, probably five feet ten and not weighing over one fifteen. Thomas was forty-eight but looked older, his leathery face full of wrinkles. If not for Wilson's mustache and goatee, he would have looked like a school boy. Thomas slowly eased into a chair at the table. Wilson plopped down in his and fidgeted with his kepi. *The two men are as opposite as they can possibly be, Whipple thought.*

"I've been expecting you," Thomas said.

"Got caught up on the railroad," Wilson pointed back over his shoulder. "It was a mess trying to get here."

"Speaking of a mess," Thomas offered Wilson a cigar. Wilson shook his head. "The job you've got before you is gonna take a lot of work to sort out."

Wilson smiled. He doubted he would have much trouble. "What seems to be the problem?"

"We've got cavalry," Thomas said between puffs on the cigar. He eyed Wilson through the acrid smoke. The last time he'd seen Wilson, he was just a snot-nosed staff officer. The one thing that hadn't changed about Wilson was his gigantic ego. "The problem is the condition it's in. It's scattered from here to Alabama, and most of the troopers are without mounts."

"I'll just have to requisition horses from the citizens then," Wilson smirked.

The expression on his face told Thomas the man was underestimating the task before him. Thomas began to worry again. *If this man gets in trouble, Grant will blame me.* He could already see this wild young man getting himself into a mess with the ego he's got. Thomas said, "That brings me to the second problem. Your opponent is a bit tougher than what we faced back in Georgia. We're not dealing with Joe Wheeler anymore."

Wilson knew immediately who Thomas was talking about. The man Sherman referred to as "That Devil Forrest." Forrest was fast becoming known as the greatest cavalryman this war has produced. He had hardly any education to speak of. Even Grant feared Forrest when he was trying to take Vicksburg. *We'll just see how good the man is, Wilson thought. He hasn't met me yet.*

Thomas studied Wilson's reaction to this news. If he was worried at all, he didn't show it. Thomas continued, "General Forrest has just been on a raid up here destroying everything in sight. I'm sure he's already acquired all the horses the citizens had for his own men."

22

"I read in the paper that he made quite a mess at Johnsonville," said Wilson.

Tennessee State Capital building in Nashville. Next to Washington, it was the most fortified city in America.

"The latest word I have..." Thomas picked up a piece of paper from the table and began reading from a list, "over six million dollars worth of mess there. He's destroyed four gunboats, fourteen steamboats, seventeen barges, and at least thirty-three cannons. He also stole about five thousand dollars worth of supplies. It sure is hard to defeat the Confederacy when we keep supplying their armies."

Wilson looked shocked. "How in the hell does a cavalryman destroy gunboats?"

"The man's not normal." Thomas decided this would be a good time to educate the young cavalryman. "That's the reason I'm worried about our cavalry, Wilson. He doesn't do normal things. I don't want you to underestimate your opponent."

"Sounds as though I have my work cut out for me," Wilson shook his head. He hadn't known Forrest had done that much damage. He asked, "So where do you want me?"

Thomas pointed at the map. "Schofield has a little cavalry operating with him down at Pulaski. There's also a brigade near Florence watching Hood.

23

All told, you'll have about three thousand mounted men. The rest are without horses and pretty much useless to you. I guess you better get down to Columbia and establish yourself a headquarters there. Keep in contact with Schofield. When the Confederate army leaves Florence, make sure he knows where they're headed. I don't want Hood getting between Schofield and Nashville."

Wilson nodded as he watched Thomas's finger moving across the map. Thomas turned to Whipple and said, "Write an order saying that Major General James Wilson is in command of all the cavalry in this district. Make sure it says that all cavalry commands are to report to him for orders."

Whipple nodded and sat at his desk. Wilson was practically beaming now. Thomas turned to Wilson and continued. "Hood is as unpredictable as Forrest. He's just as liable to turn and go after Sherman in Georgia as to come up here. There's no way of predicting what the man will do, but one thing is certain with him."

"What's that?" Wilson asked instinctively.

"Hard fighting," Thomas replied. "Keep me informed often. The most important thing I need you and Schofield to do is delay Hood's advance long enough for General Smith to get here with his men; they're coming by boat from Missouri. If Hood gets here before Smith, I'm not sure we can hold the city. If Nashville falls, then Sherman is left hanging out to dry in Georgia."

Wilson nodded. "I'll go to Columbia first and play it by ear. Once I figure out where I'm needed the most, I'll let you know. I'll leave today."

Thomas nodded. He watched Wilson spring from his chair and turn to leave. Suddenly, he spun back around and asked, "This Forrest is supposed to be a fighter, right?"

Thomas nodded. "He is a fighter." He wondered where Wilson was going with this.

Wilson smiled. "I can't wait to meet him." He saluted and turned toward the door again.

"Just one more thing before you go," Thomas was beginning to worry again. "I know you're young and eager, Wilson, but don't do anything rash down there. The Union cause is depending on you." After he finished, he felt foolish. *Stop being such a mother hen, he thought.*

"You can count on me, General Thomas," Wilson smiled again. He turned, took the orders from Whipple, and left the room.

When the door closed, Whipple asked Thomas, "So, what do you think?"

Thomas shook his head. "I think General Wilson is about to get his belly full of Bedford Forrest. We'll be lucky if he's not back here in a week with his tail tucked between his legs."

Whipple was nodding his head in agreement. "I've heard a lot about that young man. I hear he claims responsibility for some of Grant's victories."

"I've heard that also." Thomas thought about the Battle of Missionary Ridge in Chattanooga a year ago. The great charge was an accident. Grant's plans had failed. He'd ordered Sherman to flank the Confederates off

24

Missionary Ridge, but he'd run into Cleburne's division and stalled. Grant had ordered Thomas to make a demonstration in the Confederate center to relieve the pressure on Sherman. The men had done more than demonstrate. Without orders, they charged the Rebel center, broke their battle line, and put their army into flight. After it was all over, Wilson had told anyone who would listen that the entire plan was his.

Thomas said, "Wilson is a Grant man. You know what that means, Will?"

"I'm not sure," Whipple looked confused.

"It means he can do no wrong." Thomas grimaced at the thought. "If he gets whipped, it'll be my fault."

Whipple nodded. He couldn't believe he hadn't thought about that before. "George, let's just hope he's as good as he thinks he is."

November 20, 1864

CSA

His men were camped in a field south of Florence on the north bank of the river. There was a large Indian mound just east of them. He, Mangum, and Govan had ridden over there this morning and climbed to the top. It was an imposing mound. He wondered how long it had taken the Indians to build it and why they had built it to begin with.

Pat Cleburne was sitting in his tent writing another letter to Susan. He had lived thirty-six years of his life without meeting someone he loved. That had changed in Mobile earlier this year. He had been serving as best man at Hardee's wedding there. Susan had been the maid of honor. During that trip, they had just hit it off. Now, Cleburne wrote her every night, despite the fact that she's not much of a writer herself.

He was thinking about Mobile. Here they were, in the same state yet a world away. They were on extreme opposite ends of the state. Cleburne had asked Hood for a furlough to go see her once more, but Hood had denied it. Hood told him that they were going on a very important campaign. He said it was a move that may actually win the war for the Confederacy. Cleburne remained doubtful about Hood winning anything after Atlanta. Now he had received orders that the army was to march at first light tomorrow.

As he wrote the letter, he heard footsteps outside and the sound of hushed voices. It sounded like a lot of voices. Cleburne stood up from the table and opened the tent flap. There, surrounding his tent, was what appeared to be his entire division. He wondered what was going on.

Suddenly a man shouted, "Let's give it to 'em boys!"

The entire division burst forth singing "The girl I left behind me." As

25

soon as they finished, they started another song. They loved Cleburne, and this was their way of showing it. They sang for about an hour. Pat Cleburne was moved. He had ordered these men into battle. He'd sent these men's friends and family to their deaths. Yet, here they were serenading him. He tried to make sense of it all. He could feel the warm tears running down his face and into his goatee. He lowered his head as they finished singing.

The men waited for their beloved General to say something. They had come to sing to him, just to show him how much they loved him. Cleburne thought about what he should say. He raised his head. The tears were glistening in the firelight. His voice was shaky as he began. "This campaign we are on is very important, and I want every man in this division to do his whole duty. Back in Ireland, everyone suffers from oppression. If the North wins this war, it will be much worse for us."

He turned his face up toward the heavens and wiped the tears off his cheeks. His voice became firm. "This cause is very dear to me. I came to this country without any friends, and you all treated me as an equal. If our cause is to fail, I pray to God that I may fall also with my face to the enemy and my arm battling for what I know is right."

A man yelled, "We love you, General!"

There were a few more yells, but most just lowered their heads and began to move away. It was an emotional moment for them all. They understood their General loved them, but they also knew that wherever Cleburne went there would be hard fighting. They hadn't gotten the reputation as the hardest-hitting division in this army by not fighting. There stood a good chance that a good many men in this division wouldn't live through the coming campaign, but they would go anywhere that Pat Cleburne led them.

Cleburne stepped back into his tent and picked up the letter he had from Susan. The letter was disturbing. She said she was suffering from neuralgia because of her nerves and wouldn't be able to write again until she recovered. She said she had cried when she received his letter about not getting the furlough. He'd almost done the same thing. She told him that she didn't know if her nerves could stand another campaign.

He heard a man clear his throat. He turned and saw his aide-de-camp Lieutenant Learned Mangum raise the tent flap. Mangum asked, "Everything all right, sir?"

"Everything is fine," Cleburne tried to smile. "You can turn in for the night if you'd like. We'll be busy after tomorrow."

Mangum nodded but paused in the doorway of the tent. He had been worried about Cleburne lately. The General had been acting depressed for no reason. Cleburne could see past Mangum; the campfires were reflecting on the smooth water of the river. It reminded him of home. Back in Helena, he had often stood on the banks of the Mississippi River and watched the moon reflecting off the water. It had amazed him how a river that muddy could look so clear and clean under the moonlight.

Cleburne felt Mangum watching him and asked, "What's wrong, Mangum?"

"Nothing," Mangum replied, but he continued standing there watching. After a long, awkward moment, he said, "Sure was nice what the men did for you tonight."

Cleburne lowered his head, and with a voice full of emotion said, "I'd give my life for those men out there. I'm not sure I have done enough to warrant their love. I mean, I've always tried to do my best for them."

"You've done more than any other officer in this army, General." Mangum raised his chin high in the air. "I wouldn't still be here serving under you now if you weren't a good man. I can go to my grave and proudly say I served under the great Patrick Cleburne."

"Thank you," Cleburne said. Mangum quickly spun and left the tent. The comment would have sounded fake if Cleburne didn't know Mangum so well. He had been a law partner with Cleburne back in Helena.

He turned back to the table and tried to finish the letter to Susan. For some reason he just couldn't keep his mind on it now. He began to think back on his life. It was just fourteen years ago that he had arrived in this country. He had first landed in New Orleans and made his way to Cincinnati, Ohio. He'd been a clerk in a drugstore there. The place was full of drugstores, and he stood very little chance of moving up. That's when his big break came. He was given the opportunity to run a drugstore in Helena, Arkansas, for a Doctor Nash. Through hard work, he had made a success in that rough and tumble Mississippi River town.

Everyone he had talked to in Ohio had warned him not to accept the job. You'll never become anything in the south, they had said. You have to be manor-born to ever have anything in the south. They said there were only two classes of people in the south, the rich and the dirt poor. They claimed it would be impossible to work your way up from the bottom. People in the south don't like outsiders, they'd said, especially foreign-born outsiders. Cleburne smiled when he thought about it now. He had proved them wrong. He had worked his way up, and through hard work, he had become a lawyer and one of the most influential citizens of Helena.

Doctor Nash had been impressed with his work ethic and had taken the clumsy Irishman under his wing. Cleburne would never forget Doctor Nash. He felt like he owed the doctor everything. Several times, Nash wondered if there was any hope in turning Cleburne into a gentleman, but he kept working on him. Anytime he introduced Cleburne to a lady, Pat would become red-faced and almost stutter. There were even times Cleburne had thought it useless himself. He was sure he would never marry because he just couldn't talk to women.

He had thought he would die a bachelor, but all that was before he met Susan. She changed the way he viewed life. He began to think about the wedding trip again. *I would gladly give five years of my life to have those two weeks back, he thought.*

27

The candle-lit wedding between General Hardee and Mary Lewis was very romantic. Hardee was Cleburne's best friend in the army. Hood had blamed Hardee for his failure at Atlanta. Now Hardee was gone, shipped off to some unimportant command. Cleburne had been contemplating asking for a transfer to the Trans-Mississippi department where he would be closer to home and out of all this internal squabbling that's haunted this army since the war began.

All the women were wearing their nicest dresses, and the officers were all in their finest dress uniforms for the occasion. Hardee looked distinguished with the young woman on his arm. Cleburne was wearing his best dress uniform, Richmond gray shell jacket and maroon sash. Mary was thin with long, dark hair. She was only twenty-six. But, it was the maid of honor that had caught Pat's eye. He had attended to her every need throughout the occasion. She was twenty-four with dark hair. She was just as shy as he was, which made conversations difficult at first. It had been a bit of a shock for her, being courted by one of the most famous generals in the Confederacy. She'd awed him with beauty and refinement.

It was the next day, however, that Cleburne would never forget. The entire wedding party boarded a steamboat and traveled downriver to stay at the Battle House Hotel in Mobile. After he broke through her shyness, he found her charming and quite educated. There had been romantic walks and singing and music. It had been almost like paradise. Then he begged her to marry him. She wasn't sure; everything had happened so suddenly. Before he left, she had finally agreed to marry him. Now he was an engaged general waiting for the war to end so he could marry and get on with his life and start a family.

Cleburne stood up from the table and wiped more tears from his eyes. He took out his pocket watch and looked at the time. It was nearing ten, but he wasn't tired yet. He decided that what he needed just now was some company. So he stepped from his tent and headed toward the fire where his staff were all laughing and joking around.

Cleburne walked over and stood by the fire. Lieutenant James Brandon, one of his staff officers jumped to his feet. He had been in the middle of a war story when Cleburne walked over. He asked, "Can I get you anything, General?"

It had caught them all by surprise. Here lately, Cleburne had been in a dark mood and hardly ever left his tent after dark.

"Can't sleep," Cleburne replied. He noticed how everyone looked so shocked. "Relax, gentlemen. I'm just taking a walk. Go on with your story, Lieutenant, but try not to stretch the truth so much."

All the other officers laughed. Lieutenant Brandon's face turned red. Finally, he shrugged his shoulders and sat back down. He asked, "Now where was I?"

Cleburne turned and walked toward the river. He watched his men sitting around their campfires. They seemed like a happy army. Men were laughing and talking; they didn't realize they were being watched by the division commander. He saw a group of men near the river sitting around their fire laughing. That's just the kind of company he needed at the moment.

He came out of the darkness and sat on a bare log next to a boy who didn't look old enough to shave yet. The boy looked at Cleburne, his eyes growing as big as saucers. One of the men on the other side of the fire said, "My God, it's the general."

Cleburne smiled. He asked, "How are you, men?"

"Fine," the man stammered. He wondered what brought Cleburne out here. "You want me to go get the lieutenant?"

"No, I don't," Cleburne said quickly. He didn't want any officers here ruining this moment. He just wanted to sit and talk to the men. He asked, "What regiment do you men belong to?"

"16th Alabama," said the man across the fire. Cleburne noticed for the first time that the man had sergeant's stripes on his sleeves. "We're in Lowrey's brigade."

"And where is the fighting preacher?" Cleburne hadn't seen Lowrey all day. Brigadier General Mark Perrin Lowrey had been a Baptist preacher before the war. Most men referred to him as the fighting preacher. Cleburne didn't mean any disrespect when he called him that. Lowrey was one of Cleburne's best brigade commanders.

"He's around," said the sergeant, glancing over his shoulder. "He's probably holding a tent meeting somewhere. We have to listen to him enough as it is. If we go, he'll just pass us the collection plate."

Cleburne laughed. The other men saw him laugh and joined in. They were still a little nervous. The sergeant asked, "What brings you out tonight, General?"

"After that fine job of singing you fellows did earlier, I couldn't sleep." Cleburne rubbed his hands together and then placed them near the fire. "Don't let me interrupt anything. I just want to sit here a spell."

"Oh, we were just having a little laugh at these two arguing," said the scruffy-faced sergeant. "I'm John Hurst, and these two women are George Askew and John Morgan. You'll have to look over 'em if you plan on hanging around here long cause all's they do is fight."

The two men nodded when they were introduced. Several others around the fire introduced themselves. The sergeant continued, "We don't miss women with these two here. George argues 'bout like a woman, and John there knows ever thang."

Cleburne smiled. The other men were laughing and nodding in agreement. There was a young man curled up in a blanket near the fire asleep. He looked as though he wasn't old enough to shave. His face was smooth.

Sergeant Hurst said, "Reckon I ought to wake Jimmy up? He won't believe the General came by if we don't."

Cleburne shook his head. "Nah, let 'im rest. He'll need it tomorrow." He looked toward George and John and asked, "What were you two arguing about?"

29

George jerked his thumb toward John Morgan. "John don't believe I caught a fifteen pound catfish out of this here river. He don't believe they's catfish gets that big."

"That ain't true," John spoke up. "I knows they's catfish in that river bigger'n fifteen pounds. I just don't thank you catched one."

Cleburne regretted he had gotten them started again. The other men seemed to be enjoying it immensely. He noticed a heavyset man sitting off to the side who wasn't laughing. He had a long, scraggly beard and red, bloodshot eyes. He held something in his right hand, which he kept hidden behind his leg. Cleburne asked him, "What's your name?"

"Name's Gabriel, sir, Gabriel Warhurst," the man's voice was deep and hollow. "We all from Cherokee, General, and we do appreciate that three-day furlough you give us to see the folks."

Cleburne smiled and pointed toward the man's hidden hand. "You better get that flask out from behind your leg and drink up. There won't be much time for drinking come morning."

Gabriel slowly raised the flask as he eyed Cleburne warily. He knew Cleburne didn't drink and still wasn't sure if he should drink in front of the general. The other men were smiling. Someone patted Gabriel on the back. Gabriel smiled weakly, held the flask out, and asked, "Want a shot, General?"

"No thank you," Cleburne held a hand up as if to ward off the offer, "but I could go get Frank Cheatham. He'd probably empty that flask for you."

The men all laughed. It was well known throughout the army about Cheatham's drinking. It was said he had been so drunk at the Battle of Murfreesboro he couldn't even mount his horse. Miraculously, he had avoided being court-martialed.

Cleburne stared into the fire. He realized this was what he had needed for a while. Just to relax around the fire and talk about nothing important. He actually felt good for a change. It was obvious to everyone that the Confederacy was losing this war. Lately, he had spent a lot of time worrying about it. He had not only been worrying about the war, but he was also worrying about Susan.

He reached out and began to warm his hands over the fire. George and John were now arguing again. Cleburne didn't know what they were arguing about this time. He heard John saying, "You tell the tallest tales, George. I still remember you telling us your grand pappy grows the biggest watermelons in the whole state."

Cleburne grew serious and asked, "Have any of you fellows ever boiled a watermelon?"

Everyone stopped laughing and looked at him. John Morgan's mouth hung open. He asked, "Boil a watermelon? Well, what in the hell for?"

"As most of you probably already know, I came to this country almost fifteen years ago," Cleburne said. He noticed the men nodding, hanging on his every word. *He thought, I could be talking about the price of eggs in China and they'd still be listening.* He continued, "Back in Ireland, we didn't have

30

watermelons. Not long after I moved to Arkansas, an old man brought a wagon full of watermelons to town one day. He was selling them pretty cheap; I forget the price now. Well, I'd never seen a watermelon before, so I wanted to try one. I bought the biggest one he had and carried it back to the drug store I was running. My apprentice was a carefree boy about fifteen years old named Joe Maxey. I asked him how to cook a watermelon. Without a pause, he told me that watermelons had to be boiled. He stood right there watching me build a fire without ever cracking a smile. When I got the water boiling, I dropped the watermelon in. Soon, the store got busy, and people were giggling and pointing. Then Doctor Nash came in. He owned the drug store. Anyway, he just burst out laughing when he saw me boiling that watermelon. When I looked at Joe, he could hold it no longer and burst out laughing and turned and ran out the door. I was right behind him, but he was too fast for me."

The men were all in an uproar at his story. Some were slapping their knees. Cleburne smiled; he was proud of the success of his story. He added, "He didn't come back to the drug store for about a week, which was a good thing for him."

"That's a damned good story," said Sergeant Hurst, wiping tears from his eyes. "Sounds like something half of these idiots would try and pull on someone."

"What was that boy's name we carried out in the woods that night a snipe huntin'?" John Morgan asked. "Damn, I can't remember that boy's name. He stayed out there all night. He was a damned sight mad the next morning when he come back to camp with all us a laughing."

Some of the guys were in deep thought, trying to remember the boy's name. Someone asked, "What happened to that boy?"

"He got shot in the chest at Chickamauga," John replied. "He said before the battle that he wouldn't make it through. Amazing how some men know when their time is up."

"Hell, if that was true," George Askew grumbled, "you'd a been dead a long time ago. You say ever battle is your last."

Cleburne saw they were off arguing again. He rose and stood over the fire. "You men try and get some sleep; we move at first light."

He turned and disappeared into the night. Behind him he heard someone say, "Now, how many other generals you hear of coming out and just sittin' with his men telling yarns?"

Part 2

Race to Columbia

"Sweat saves blood."

Erwin Rommel

November 21, 1864

CSA

They'd gotten up before daylight and cooked breakfast. The entire corps was standing in column on Court Street waiting for the order to march. All the townsfolk were on the street corners cheering and wishing the army good luck.

Mack Keenum turned and looked over his shoulder toward the bluffs on the south bank of the river. He lived just east of Tuscumbia, probably not five miles from this spot. He wondered if he would ever see Margaret and the girls again. He tried to push the thought out of his mind.

After a long moment, he turned back and looked at what was left of Company B, 35th Alabama Infantry. They were a pitiful-looking group. Dick Bernard was almost barefoot. His shoes were separating from the soles. 'Rip' Baker was hatless, and his coat was full of holes, but everyone's coat was full of holes. Poor Captain Sam Stewart was without a horse and forced to walk in riding boots.

The blonde-haired Stewart was only nineteen when he'd joined, one of the youngest men in the company. He was fearless in combat, and all the men loved him. It had seemed strange to the thirty-three-year-old Mack Keenum at first, being ordered around by a boy.

Despite all their shortages of food and supplies, Mack noticed the morale had improved. Part of that was also because of Captain Stewart. The boy refused to allow the men's morale to go down. He constantly encouraged his men. He worried over them as if they were his children, and that's the reason they loved him so. Stewart was mature beyond his twenty-one years.

Mack saw their brigade commander, General Thomas Moore Scott, riding down the road. The man looked nothing like a soldier but reminded him of a college professor he had met once. Scott stopped his horse not twenty feet from Company B and waited facing south. He appeared to be waiting for someone.

Behind him, Mack heard horse hooves on the road. He turned and saw Major General William Loring, the division commander, coming up the road followed by Brigadier General Winfield Featherston and their staff officers. Both officers reined up beside Scott and exchanged salutes. Mack tried to overhear their conversation, but the crowd was still cheering, and men were talking. It was impossible to hear the officers in this din.

Loring was in a new gray frock coat, the gold braid and stars shining in the morning sun, his armless sleeve pinned to his chest. He wore a pair of blue Union trousers with a red stripe down the side. His head was balding, and the short general looked comical sitting next to the six-foot-two-inch Featherston. He heard Loring tell Scott to read the speech to his brigade.

34

Scott took the sheet of paper from Loring and rode forward toward the column of men. He stopped his horse so close to Mack that he could have reached out and touched it. The general cleared his throat and called for the men's attention. The crowd grew quiet, the men turning their attention to their commander. Up close, Mack realized just how odd-looking Thomas Scott was. When he spoke, his oversized Adam's apple bobbed up and down. His head looked too big for his long, lanky body. His face was freckled from the sun, even covering his large hawk-billed nose.

"Gentlemen," Scott's voice was shrill; he was a planter before the war and not used to speaking in front of people. "General Hood says we are going into Tennessee. We will be moving into territory occupied by the enemy. We'll be leaving our supplies behind…" Scott glanced down at the paper, having lost his place. He soon found it and started reading again. "He says we'll have hard marching and some fighting, but he's not gonna risk a defeat. We'll only fight on ground of our choosing and against equal odds. We may be on short rations at times, but he will do his best for us."

Most of the men cheered, and all the citizens were cheering. *Mack thought, I bet they would cheer at anything he said at this point.* They probably weren't even listening. Private Dick Beaumont yelled, "We've never been whipped by the Yankees when we was fightin' on our ground, especially with anything close to equal numbers."

General Scott smiled and turned his horse back over to where Loring and Featherston were patiently waiting. Mack hadn't bothered to cheer. *When was the last time we weren't on short rations, he thought. It's been three years since I've had a decent meal.*

He listened to General Loring telling Scott and Featherston the details of the day's plan of march. He never said how far they intended to move today, only stating that the army's three corps were all taking different roads once they got out of town, to make better time.

Tom Barrett was watching the three generals also. He asked Mack, "Reckon where 'Old Blizzards' Loring got his damned nickname?"

Mack shook his head. Nobody seemed to know the answer to that question. "They say he joined the army when he was thirteen, got to be an officer at eighteen. He said the proudest moment of his life was when he lost his arm in the Mexican War. You ever hear about his amputation?"

"I didn't even know he lost it in the Mexican War," Tom looked surprised.

"Yeah, they cut his arm off without anesthetic. He smoked a cigar during the entire operation. He's a tough old goat." Mack had heard Joe Thompson reading about Loring in a newspaper once.

"Damned right," Tom said. "They try that with me and they'll hear me for miles."

"He's one of the most cantankerous generals in the entire Confederacy. Don't nobody want him. You hear 'bout him arguing with Lee and Jackson in Virginia?" Mack Keenum leaned on the barrel of his musket.

Tom was shaking his head. "No? Well, he thought he knew more than 'Stonewall' and Lee both. They shipped him out of Virginia. He's been in about every army in the Confederacy."

"So we get all the misfits," Tom said, still staring at the generals.

"You're right 'bout that," Mack said. "Even 'Old Swet' there is a misfit…" He was referring to General Featherston. His men had nicknamed him 'Old Swet.' "He was in Virginia too, but got Longstreet pissed off at 'im. So they sent him to us cause he ain't worth a shit either."

Tom was shaking his head. He hadn't heard any of that about Featherston before. Of course, Featherston commanded a Mississippi brigade, so it didn't really matter anyway, but Loring could get them killed. He commanded the entire division.

It started at the north end of Court Street and moved southward, increasing in volume as it came nearer. They instantly recognized the rebel yell and joined in. It meant the army was moving out. Mack yelled at the top of his lungs with the rest of the army. The sound echoed off the buildings. The civilians were even joining in. The sound roared on down through Cheatham's corps near the river. Moments like this still gave him goose bumps. They could be heard for miles. He looked over at the three generals. Scott was smiling. Loring and Featherston were just sitting there as if in a daze.

After what seemed like an eternity, the line slowly lunged into motion. It reminded Mack of a great long train stretching the slack out. He stole one last glance back south across the river. As they marched north past the cheering crowd, Tom said, "If soldiering was like this every day, it wouldn't be half bad."

Mack leaned in close to Tom and whispered, "Can't help but worry about Joe."

Tom nodded and spun around looking south toward the Tennessee River. The entire company had gotten a furlough when they'd arrived in Tuscumbia. They'd been told to rejoin the army when it moved across the river. Everyone had returned except for Joe Thompson.

Tom walked backwards as he looked southward. He whispered, "You kind of know the ones that are subject to desert, but Joe ain't the type. I'd a called anyone a liar if they told me Joe would desert us."

Mack liked Joe. The man was educated. When a letter arrived from home, Joe was the man who read it to him. He wrote letters home for Mack also. If they happened to get hold of a newspaper, it was Joe who read it for those of the Company like Mack, Tom, and countless others who couldn't read.

They made their way past the mansion at the north end of town swinging slightly to the right past Wesleyan University into the countryside dotted with modest farms. Tom and Mack marched side by side. They had been best friends since Mack's brother Willis had been killed at Chickamauga.

The country lanes were a mess from all the rain. Wagons had cut great furrows in the roads, making each step difficult. Tom stepped on the side of a rut, slipped, and almost regained his balance before falling headlong into the mud.

Dick Beaumont and Mack Keenum both reached down and helped him up. Tom wiped at the mud covering his clothes. "Damn, I just got this uniform."

The other men were laughing at the remark. No one in this regiment had seen a new uniform since the war began. Mack thought back to when the war had first begun. Every time a man would fall, the entire regiment would erupt in laughter. Those days were long gone. After two long years of campaigning, it just wasn't funny anymore.

He remembered when the 35th Alabama had been formed in March of Sixty-two at Lagrange Military Institute just a few miles from his farm. Of the four hundred men in the regiment, most were schoolboys from fifteen to eighteen years old. Most of the cadets were made officers and drill instructors. It had felt strange at the time to Mack, his brother Willis, and Tom Barrett. They were in their thirties and being ordered around by mere boys. Those boys were some of the South's most educated young men, and here was Mack Keenum who couldn't even write his own name.

Mack smiled as he thought about the first march they'd taken. It was just after the Battle of Shiloh. The 35th Alabama had been ordered to march to Tupelo, Mississippi, and join Beauregard's army. The first day out, those boys were worn out. Their feet were blistered, and most hadn't done a day's work in their lives. Mack and the other farmers were in shape. They'd ended up walking twelve miles that day, and Mack could have gone twelve more. Those young schoolboys were in high spirits, but they couldn't hide the fact that they were hurting.

Soon, the sky began to cloud up, and a cold wind began to blow out of the north. He remembered something his pa had said about wind that blows out of the north. He said to no one in particular, "That wind picking up out of the north ain't gonna be a good thing, I'm afraid."

They struggled on a half mile before the first flakes began to fall. By noon, it appeared they were marching into a blizzard. Snow was falling so thick; they could barely see the regiment marching in front of them. The cold wind blew into their faces for the rest of the afternoon. The march became pure misery.

Tom said, "Well, at least the rain is gone."

"It's too damned cold to rain," Mack laughed.

By dark, their faces had become chapped from the cold wind. The temperature had plummeted into the teens. They had struggled through the weather to make twelve miles today. There had been places along the road where they were forced to help the horses pull the wagons and guns up the hills.

At one point, as they struggled up a hill, Waddy Mosely said, "We're off to one hell of a start with this campaign. It's a damned good thing I'm not superstitious."

37

They camped that night in an old cornfield. Word soon spread through camp that Forrest had driven the Union cavalry almost to Nashville, but Mack had learned to take camp rumors with a grain of salt. After supper, Mack and Tom put their blankets together and settled in for the long cold night.

They awoke the next morning to a winter wonderland. The ground was frozen. Icicles hung from the trees. Not only was the ground covered with snow, but it had sleeted on top of the snow forming a thick crust. Men were up shaking the snow off their blankets and building fires.

Mack thought about how, as soldiers, they were almost no longer human. They went weeks without taking a bath, ate whatever they could find, and he'd forgotten how it would feel to sleep indoors again.

"It's gonna be another miserable day," Mack told Tom as they stood shivering by their fire.

Tom asked, "What happened to the good ole days when we'd go into winter quarters this time of year?"

"There were good ole days?" Mack laughed as his teeth began to chatter. "I remember Bragg making us fight at Murfreesboro in December."

They were soon on the road trudging north through the sludge. They hadn't gone far when they came to a group of mounted men beside the road. Mack Keenum recognized General Hood and his staff. There was a man dressed in civilian clothes and a top hat sitting on his horse near Hood. A staff officer asked, "Is this a Tennessee regiment?"

"35th Alabama," Captain Stewart replied. The snow made his blonde hair appear almost white. "Why?"

The staff officer said, "That's Tennessee Governor Isham Harris. He's speaking to all the Tennessee men."

Stewart shrugged and kept walking. Tom mumbled, "He's trying to get some votes come next election."

Mack Keenum poked Lieutenant Bluford Harris on the back and pointed toward a crude sign posted beside the road. He asked, "Blue, what's it say?"

Blue read out loud, "It says 'Tennessee, a free home or a grave.' It means we're not in Alabama anymore, boys."

November 23, 1864

USA

There was a knock on the door. General Whipple opened the door, and to his surprise, Lieutenant Colonel James Russell was standing there. Russell started to salute, but Whipple extended his hand. As they shook hands warmly, Whipple asked, "What brings you here, James?"

Russell reached in his pocket and pulled out a piece of paper. "I was down at the telegraph office, and they said they had an important message for General Thomas. I hadn't seen you fellows in a week, so I volunteered to bring it over."

Whipple motioned for Russell to come inside. Russell said, "If I'm disturbing the General, I can just leave it with you."

"Not at all," Whipple motioned him in again. "He needs a diversion anyway."

Russell walked in, noticing that the room was filled with cigar smoke. You could always find headquarters by following the smell of expensive cigar smoke. General Thomas was sitting at his table reading dispatches. He had the cigar clenched in his teeth as he read. As he looked up, Russell saluted. Thomas motioned Russell toward a chair at the table. He asked, "Colonel, how are things over in supply?"

"Same old story, sir," Russell replied as he sat down. "We have everything we need except horses."

"Seems to be a shortage of horses and troops around here," Thomas puffed on the cigar, nodding at the paper in Russell's hand. "What you got there?"

"I was over at the telegraph office," Russell handed the message to Thomas, "and I overheard them saying they had an important message for you…" He reached in his coat pocket and pulled out a small box of cigars. "These arrived by transport this morning, and I was planning on bringing 'em by to you later, so I volunteered to bring the telegram over." Russell laid the box of cigars on the table.

Thomas thanked him, took the paper, and opened it. He'd been getting preliminary messages from Wilson saying he thought Hood was on the road north. He couldn't verify anything because it was impossible to penetrate Forrest's cavalry screen.

As Thomas read the message, Russell watched his face change into a scowl. Deep furrows appeared on his forehead. Thomas finished the message but continued staring at the paper for a couple minutes.

Whipple was at his desk writing something. Thomas said, "Will, prepare a dispatch for Schofield immediately."

Whipple spun around in his chair. "Is something the matter, General?"

"Hood is definitely on the move," Thomas placed the cigar on the edge of the table and began to stroke his gray mustache. "Wilson says Hood is well into Tennessee. He is closer to Columbia than Schofield. He says he can't buy any time for Schofield either. Forrest has pushed his cavalry almost to Columbia. The man is relentless."

Whipple grabbed a clean sheet of paper. "What shall I write?"

"Tell Schofield that Hood is closer to Columbia than he is." Thomas stood from the table and began to pace. "Advise him to move back to Columbia as fast as possible. Tell him he must not allow Hood to get between him and

39

Nashville. Tell him if it's possible, I want him to hold Hood at Columbia until A.J. Smith arrives here with his men."

Whipple was busy jotting down the message. "Is that it, sir?"

"Have a telegram sent to Washington also." Thomas watched Whipple pull out another piece of paper. "Tell General Halleck that Hood is in Tennessee marching hard for this place. Tell him General Schofield is in a race for his life."

Colonel Russell could see the worry on Thomas's face. The stakes in Tennessee just got higher. It was obvious Thomas had a lot on his mind just now. He stood up from the table and asked, "General, is there anything else I can do for you before getting back?"

Thomas shook his head and motioned back toward the chair. "You just got here. Sit back down. I could use the company."

Russell nodded as he sat back down. Whipple finished the messages and left the room to find a courier. Thomas asked, "Russell, you were at Bull Run also, McDowell's staff?"

Russell remembered that Thomas had been there also. He was only a colonel at the time. Russell said, "Yes sir. Most men didn't care for McDowell, but I never had any problem with him. He was just a little difficult to get to know."

"I remember how melancholy he looked when we lost that battle," Thomas sat back down at the table and began to rub his eyes. "Everyone was afraid they might miss that battle. We all believed it would be the only battle of the war. My, what fools we were. Here we are, over three years later, and still the fighting goes on."

Russell nodded and asked, "What made you think of Bull Run?"

"To be honest with you," said Thomas, reaching for the cigar and striking a match to relight it, "I was thinking about what would happen if Hood takes Nashville."

Russell was taken aback. He'd never heard Thomas talk this way. Thomas saw the look of shock on his face, cleared his throat, and said, "If I lose Nashville, they'll cashier me just like they did McDowell. You know, McDowell's plans at Bull Run were excellent. He just had a green army. Sometimes, you just can't win; it's nobody's fault, yet the politicians don't see it that way. Remember General Stone?"

"Not sure," Russell was shaking his head. "Which General Stone are you referring to? I believe there was more than one Stone."

"The General Stone of Ball's Bluff," Thomas said as he blew out a large cloud of cigar smoke. Russell was nodding that he knew the man. Thomas continued, "Anyway, they sent him to prison, saying he was a traitor for losing the battle. I knew Stone; he was no traitor. It could have happened to any of us. If we lose Nashville, the same thing may happen to me."

Russell began to worry. He had never seen General Thomas like this, not during the entire war. It just wasn't Thomas's nature to worry. He asked, "You say Schofield is in trouble?"

40

Thomas pointed at the map on the table. "Schofield has two corps at Pulaski. I don't think he's even aware that Hood has left Alabama. Not only is Hood on his flank, but he's marching hard for Columbia in his rear. If Hood gets to Columbia before Schofield, well, the game is up."

"Got any word on Smith's troops?" Russell asked. He liked General Thomas. Of all the generals he had served, he liked Thomas the best. The strange part was, he really didn't understand why. Thomas wasn't the flamboyant type; his personality was dry.

Thomas was shaking his head. "Not only is there no word from Smith, but Forrest is playing with Wilson like a cat would a half-dead mouse."

"I thought Wilson was Grant's wonder boy," Russell said sarcastically.

"Yeah, well," Thomas smiled a little, "Grant's wonder boy is getting an education from that devil Forrest. Yesterday, Forrest pushed him all the way to Mount Pleasant, just south of Columbia."

Whipple came back into the room. He had another message with him. As he handed the message to Thomas, he said, "Another important telegram from General Wilson, sir."

Thomas opened the message and began to read it. He began to frown again. After he finished reading it, he forced himself to smile. "Well, he says the weather has cleared up, as if we didn't already know that. That should help Hood make better time. Now it seems the weather is conspiring with the Rebels."

"It may help Schofield make better time," Whipple said. He tried to sound cheerful. He was growing weary of hearing Thomas being so pessimistic about everything.

"Wilson says Capron's brigade is on the verge of collapse." Thomas took a deep breath, and then let it go with a loud sigh. "He says Forrest hit him in front and on both flanks, and then the man took his escort around and hit them in the rear. One trooper shot at him at point blank range, yet he missed. I don't think the man can be killed. Maybe he's not mortal."

"His luck is gonna run out one day," Russell said, "but I have to admit, he is one lucky son-of-a-bitch."

"Capron's brigade fell back to Columbia." Thomas stood from the table and began to pace again. "Forrest captured about fifty men, twenty horses, and an ambulance. To top it off, Wilson says the road to Columbia is wide open to the Confederate army now, and there's nothing he can do about it."

Russell said, "I guess I'll get back to my post, General. I can see you have a lot to see to."

Thomas turned around and took Russell's hand in his. "Thank you, Colonel, for the cigars. Tell everyone in your department that we're gonna have a fight here pretty soon. I know I can count on every man to do his whole duty. Hood's army is gonna be a severe test for us."

"I'll pass that along, sir." Russell stepped back and saluted before turning for the door.

Thomas said, "Russell, swing back by sometime when things aren't so hectic."

Russell nodded and left. It looked as though it would be awhile before things weren't so hectic around here.

November 24, 1864

USA

Things had started to get frustrating for General Schofield. He had gotten a message from General Thomas that Hood was closer to Columbia than he was. He couldn't help but worry about the danger his army was in at the moment.

He had used his discretionary orders to move his troops halfway to Columbia, but he still wasn't sure that's where Hood was headed. Wilson wasn't giving him any information about the Confederates. *Forrest could drive Wilson to Nashville if he wants, Schofield thought.*

He caught up to Major General David Stanley. Stanley, seeing Schofield ride up, gave a half-hearted salute. Schofield said, "Well, I finally got Cox moving with the Twenty-Third Corps. Damned courier didn't reach him with the order to move out until four this morning."

"Hard to move your men out at two if the orders don't get to you before four." Stanley removed one of the huge gauntlets and searched in his pocket for a cigar. "What's the latest on Hood?"

"Thomas seems to think he's closer to Columbia than we are." Schofield tried not to appear worried. "If he's there when we arrive…"

He left the rest unsaid. Schofield ran his hand through his long beard that reached almost to his stomach. It was something he was extremely proud of.

There was one thing Schofield liked about Stanley: the man was older, but he didn't seem to mind that Schofield ranked him. Schofield removed his hat and rubbed his balding, egg-shaped head. "Seems like forever since we were back fighting at Wilson's Creek, doesn't it, David?"

Stanley looked over at Schofield and grunted. He couldn't help but notice how Schofield looked. He was short and rather plump. He looked nothing like a soldier. "That was some serious fighting there."

"Yeah," Schofield placed the hat back on his head. "I was just a staff officer back then."

"I almost forgot," Stanley placed the oversized gauntlet back on his hand. "You were on Lyon's staff. Poor soul, did you see him get hit?"

Schofield lowered his head. He could remember the man with the wild red hair and beard as if it were only yesterday. "You ever notice how you can tell a man's going to get it before you even go into battle?"

Stanley nodded, waiting for Schofield to continue. Schofield said, "He was trying to rally his men when he was hit in the head and leg, but he didn't go down right off. He walked back to me and said he thought the day was lost."

"He was right about that part, there were just too many damned Rebs," Stanley said between puffs on his cigar.

"Well, it wasn't over right then," Schofield held up a hand. "I told him the men could still be rallied. He seemed to be happy about that. So he mounted his horse and rode to the left. I can still see the blood running off his head. He was in obvious pain, but he never flinched. When we got to the left, he decided to lead an infantry charge while on horseback. No sooner had he started than a bullet hit him in the chest. I believe he was dead before he hit the ground. Then everything went to hell."

"Yeah," Stanley said, "I remember his body being left behind."

"But it was the damnedest thing," Schofield was still in deep thought, "like I was saying about the premonition earlier. It was as if he knew. As we were approaching the field, he suddenly grew quiet. Whenever someone spoke to him, he acted as though he didn't hear a word. Reckon how that could be; how a man can know ahead of time that his life is about to be over? I heard it a thousand times, and every time it seems the man dies."

Stanley grunted and began to shake his head. "You're starting to unnerve me a little, John."

"Sorry," Schofield said. "Did I ever tell you I went to West Point with John Hood?"

"Yeah," Stanley said, happy to change the subject. "Yeah, you did. What's he like?"

"He was a jolly good fellow." Schofield smiled. "I used to help the bastard with his math. He didn't give a damned about his school work. All he worried about was Benny Haven's tavern."

"I miss old Benny Haven's," Stanley began to laugh. "It was a challenge sneaking out and going there. I was almost caught several times."

"I used to go there and play cards," Schofield loved playing cards. "Maybe when we get to Columbia, we can play a few hands. I miss playing cards."

"I don't know if I want to give you my money or not." Stanley took the cigar out of his mouth and looked at the end of it. "We better get there ahead of Hood, or we may be playing cards in Libby Prison."

A dust-covered courier came charging down the road. He reined up and saluted, passing a message to Schofield.

Schofield took the message and opened it. He said to Stanley, "It's from Wilson. He says it's all he can do to avoid being captured by Forrest. He says his cavalry isn't gonna be much help to us."

43

Stanley frowned. "Like that's some kind of surprise. Why can't we get someone who can fight with Forrest?"

"I don't know," Schofield folded the message and placed it in his pocket. He was quickly growing frustrated with Wilson. The man had come to him all full of himself and his abilities, and now he's writing messages about how he can't hold off Forrest. "I'm not gonna be responsible if Hood gets between us and Nashville. I'm laying the blame where it belongs, right at Wilson's feet."

November 24, 1864

CSA

He'd had Chalmers's men on the road since one this morning. He was keeping to one of his favorite maxims. When you get the enemy scared, keep him scared.

Forrest turned to Major Strange and said, "Send a message back to Hood. Tell him we've captured about thirty-five thousand rounds of ammunition from the damned Yankee cavalry. Tell him this has been just one big race. They're so scared, we can't catch 'em. We've also captured four of their damned battle flags. Tell him the door is open all the way to Columbia if he can just push his men on up."

Strange had learned to write and ride his horse at the same time. After he had finished writing, he called for a courier. He watched the courier gallop away, and then he turned and looked at Forrest's face. He could tell when they were about to fight. Forrest's eyes would begin to flame.

Lieutenant Colonel William Dawson of the 15th Tennessee Cavalry rode up along side Major Strange. "Everything all right today, Major?"

"Going well, Colonel," Strange liked Dawson. The man was a fighter. "We got the Yanks a running and should have Columbia in our possession soon."

Forrest was riding just in front of them. Dawson nodded at Forrest and asked, "So how's the General today?"

"He smells blood," Strange rolled his eyes. "You know how he gets when he smells blood."

The stories about Forrest were legendary. During the retreat at Shiloh, he had led a charge against Sherman to buy time for the Confederate army to get back to Corinth. When his men had reined up short, Forrest had charged right on through the Union pickets. Seeing that he was all alone, he thought fast. Just as a bullet struck Forrest in the back, he reached down from the saddle and grabbed a Union soldier and pulled him onto the back of his horse and used him as a shield while he rode away. *The reason he's so good, Dawson thought, is because his men are more afraid of him than the enemy.* Forrest had killed over twenty Union soldiers with his own hands during this war. He was wild and reckless in battle. He'd been wounded numerous times.

Brigadier General James Chalmers came galloping back down the road toward Forrest. His staff and escort were having trouble keeping up with him. Chalmers reined up in front of Forrest and half saluted. "I was chasing Capron's brigade into Columbia when we ran into infantry. It's some of Schofield's troops. They're winded, but they got there just before we did. They must have run the last few miles to beat us. It's a damned shame too, because Capron's brigade had fallen apart."

"Damn," Forrest said. If there was Union infantry in Columbia, there would be nothing left to do but wait on Hood to flush them out. Still, he felt like he had to try. He turned in the saddle and said, "Strange, get up as many men as you can. I'm going to ride forward with Chalmers."

"Yes, sir," Strange turned toward Dawson. "I guess that means you. I'll go toward the rear and forward anybody else I can find."

Dawson nodded. He turned and started shouting orders to his regiment.

Forrest and Chalmers started down the road. The two men didn't like each other very well. Chalmers was a gentleman. Forrest was rough and spoke his mind. Chalmers felt he should rank Forrest.

Chalmers was saying, "I tell you something, General, there was a boy chasing the Yanks on a beautiful black charger that was all foam flecked. He had a beautiful yellow saddle blanket. He rode all the way to the edge of town. Wish I could find out his name. I never saw anything quite like it. He was riding along with the Yanks while they were running for town. He was shooting them in the back of the head with his revolver. It was just him and him alone. Someone finally shot him from the saddle. He was dead before he hit the ground; but still, it was the bravest thing I ever saw. That was one of the most gallant and brave soldiers I have ever seen, and him just a boy."

Forrest nodded but said nothing. They topped a small rise, and there was the town. On the edge of town, Forrest could see an infantry line. "You say they was winded?"

"That's right," Chalmers watched as his men were skirmishing at long range with the Union troops.

Lieutenant Colonel Dawson reined up beside Forrest. "Your orders, sir?"

"Take your regiment and charge that infantry line yonder." Forrest was watching the action in front of him. He didn't notice Dawson's eyes grow wide at the thought.

Chalmers saw Dawson with the doubtful look on his face. He said, "Don't worry, they're winded; they ran the last few miles to get here. You can sweep your horses down on them before they put up much resistance, but you need to go in there pretty damned hard."

Forrest was nodding. "Line up your men now, before they catch their breath. Hit 'em hard as hell."

Dawson turned and got his cavalry on line. Forrest and Chalmers watched them prepare to charge. Suddenly, Dawson raised his sword and stood in the saddle. He yelled, "Charge, men! Charge them!"

The line sprang forward. The charge was going well at first, but then saddles began to empty from the fire. Forrest kept his eye on the young Colonel. The man's horse crashed into the infantry line. He saw him reach out and attempt to take a Union battle flag, but the color guard shot him out of the saddle. The Colonel lay face down in the road. His regiment had broken and came galloping back toward Forrest.

Chalmers was shaking his head. Forrest said, "Chalmers, regroup your men back here. There ain't no sense in trying that again. We'll have to wait on Hood."

Forrest lowered his head and rode back to meet Major Strange. He would have to send a message to Hood to let him know the Union army had beaten them to Columbia.

Major Strange met him just over the rise. He said to Forrest, "General, I don't think it will do any good to attack the Union infantry at this point. I just got a message from Hood. He says he's still thirty miles away. He won't be here before day after tomorrow."

"Now you tell me," Forrest replied. "Find us a good house for a headquarters. I suddenly feel like taking a nap."

November 26, 1864

CSA

The clouds hung low in the sky and a heavy mist filled the air. It was a dark, dreary day that matched Cleburne's mood. The mist and fog reduced visibility to a few hundred yards. The air was cool as it blew the mist against his face.

The speed of the march had improved since the pike they were on was gravel. Cleburne felt sorry for his soldiers without shoes. They were limping along as best as they could, some with their feet bleeding.

They had just passed through Mount Pleasant; Ashwood lay just ahead. He wondered if Lucius Polk would be there. He missed Lucius dearly. Next to William Hardee, Lucius had been his best friend in the army. When Cleburne had been promoted to division command, Lucius had been given command of Cleburne's old brigade. They'd fought through the entire war together until earlier this year at Kennesaw Mountain. That's when the cannonball had mangled Lucius's leg, ending his military service. Lucius had been lucky. His uncle, Lieutenant General Leonidas Polk, had been killed at Pine Mountain just before his nephew was wounded. The cannonball had hit him in the chest and passed through his body.

The last Cleburne had heard was that Lucius was now on crutches. *It would sure be nice to see him again, Cleburne thought.*

Lieutenant Mangum eased his horse up alongside his commander. He eyed Cleburne warily and asked, "Everything all right, General?"

Cleburne nodded. "As well as can be expected, I reckon."

"Begging the General's pardon, sir…" Mangum paused a moment. He didn't quite know how to say what was on his mind. He'd been Cleburne's law partner back in Arkansas, and he'd never seen the man as despondent as he'd been since leaving Tuscumbia. "I'm just gonna be frank with you. I'm concerned about you."

Cleburne looked shocked. He started to say something but stopped.

Mangum held up a hand. "Just hear me out, sir. The rest of your staff is as worried as I am. Me and Hanley have been with you the entire war. He's noticed it also."

Cleburne looked at Mangum and then quickly looked away. What was there to say? *We're losing this war, he thought. Am I supposed to be happy? We could have won it long ago if these men would have been properly led. I'm sick of seeing men die because of poor leadership.*

Cleburne spurred his horse out into the field beside the road so no one could hear their conversation. He said, "Mangum, I'm growing tired of this war. It should have been over long ago. We're losing this war, may have already lost it. Sherman is tearing up Georgia as we speak."

Mangum was shaking his head. It surprised him hearing Cleburne talk this way. "It's not over yet, but even if it is over, we still got an obligation as soldiers."

Cleburne sighed and began to rub his chin. "I've tried to get every man in this army to understand subjugation. I've tried and failed. My being from Ireland may help me to understand it better; I'm not sure. If we lose this war, the history of it will be written by the enemy. Our children will be taught by Northern school teachers. A hundred years from now, people will believe that all these brave men who have died fighting for our freedom of self government were nothing but traitors. They will have been taught that we were fighting to preserve slavery…"

Mangum was shaking his head. He hadn't thought about what the future would look like if they lost. Cleburne continued, "You and I have never owned a slave. We care nothing for slavery. We both know that's not what this war is about. It's about one section trying to establish its superiority over another section. They want to form a centralized government that will deprive us of our individual rights. Fifteen years ago I left a country that had done that very thing. I had to come here to escape a life like that. Now I find myself fighting to prevent it from happening to my new home, a home that allows a

47

man to become something if he works hard at it. I refuse to live in a country like the old one again."

"I've never thought that far ahead," Mangum said. "I know if we lose it won't be pleasant, but it sounds as though you've thought it through."

Cleburne felt better getting it all off his chest, but he wasn't finished. "That's the point I was trying to make with my proposal to arm the slaves. These are desperate times, and desperate measures must be adopted. Now I'm castigated for it. I can't understand why someone would rather lose the war than give up that primitive system. We lose this war, and they'll lose their slaves anyway. Not just their slaves, but everything they own. And some of us will be sent to prison for treason, if they don't hang some of us."

"Surely they wouldn't do that," Mangum began to get a worried look on his face.

Cleburne shrugged. "I've tried everything in my power to win this war. You remember the Comrades of the Southern Cross?"

Mangum nodded, "That was a brilliant idea, sir, and I'm not just saying that."

"Yeah, well…" Cleburne was shaking his head, "not everyone thought it was brilliant. Only a few embraced it. My belief in God teaches me that with faith all things are possible. In Matthew 21:21, Jesus says if you have enough faith you can say to a mountain, 'Be lifted up and thrown into the sea' and it will be done. That's why I founded the Comrades of the Southern Cross. If this entire army would come together as a group and have faith in God, we could take Nashville on this campaign. We could invade the North and conquer. Everyone listened to me politely and then went on about their business. I just don't understand. If everyone wants to win this war, why don't they act like it?"

Mangum began to worry that Cleburne had taken the rejections personally. Maybe that's why he'd been so depressed lately. He may have thought they turned him down because he's not from this country. Mangum said, "I wouldn't take it personal, General. I think everyone is just so worried about their own commands. They haven't really put as much thought into all this as you have. I know I haven't."

"That doesn't bother me, Mangum," Cleburne was shaking his head. "Let me explain something to you. A good commander learns from the past. From the mistakes he's made in the past. Do you understand what I'm trying to say here?"

"I think so," Mangum answered, but he wasn't sure where Cleburne was going with this.

"I'll give you an example," Cleburne paused a moment, thinking back to his first major action of the war. "At Shiloh, I led my brigade in a direct frontal assault. Now, the Yankees weren't entrenched, but they had a good defensive position on the high ground. I had about twenty-five hundred men going into the battle. After those fierce frontal assaults, we returned to Corinth with only about a thousand men."

48

"That was some of the bloodiest fighting I've seen," Mangum said. He'd been at Cleburne's side during the entire battle. "It was bloody because the men were still green. Hell, I didn't know what I was doing then either."

"I have to disagree with you somewhat," Cleburne said politely. He wasn't a know-it-all and didn't want to sound like one. He rarely argued with anyone. He continued, "You see, I was partly to blame for the high casualties there. I ordered the charge as soon as we came up on the enemy. We just went straight in and hit them, man to man. If I would have thought a moment, I could have flanked them."

Mangum thought about it a moment and realized there was some truth in what Cleburne was saying. He could still remember the field after the Sixth Mississippi made its charge. That poor regiment had gone in with four hundred and twenty-five men. After the charge, they had only sixty men unhurt.

Cleburne said, "Now think ahead to the battle at Richmond, Kentucky. It was a lopsided victory because I took my experience at Shiloh and learned from it. I refused to hit them head-on at Richmond, but kept flanking every strong position they took. I was not about to feed my men into a meat grinder."

Mangum was nodding. He remembered it well. They just kept flanking the Union army until they finally broke and fled in wild disorder. It had been brilliant. Cleburne had been shot in the mouth, knocking two teeth out, but refused to leave the field until the battle was won. Mangum asked, "I understand what you're getting at now, but still, what does all this have to do with you being so depressed lately?"

"This army has been mismanaged from the beginning." Cleburne took his pipe out, loaded it, and began to tamp the tobacco down into the bowl. "The Battle of Shiloh was bravely fought and just as stupidly lost by Beauregard. Then, Bragg takes command, and look what we went through. We fought at Perryville and had the battle won, but he retreated back to Tennessee for no reason. When we attacked at Murfreesboro, we bent their army back like a hair pin, but he retreated again. We practically destroyed their army at Chickamauga and lost a lot of good men doing it, but he refused to believe we had won. So, he let them fall back to Chattanooga and regroup. Now we have General Hood, and we haven't had a successful operation under his command. You see, Mangum, these men never learn from their mistakes, but they're not the ones paying for their stupidity. It's the men who pay—my men."

Mangum didn't know what to say. There was truth in what Cleburne was saying. Mangum said, "Back in Tuscumbia, Hood said he wasn't gonna attack the enemy in his entrenchments. He says he will only fight on ground of our choosing."

Cleburne took a deep breath and let it go. He forced himself to continue the discussion. He added, "He also said we would march hard for Columbia, get in Schofield's rear, and capture him before moving on to Nashville. Of course, we fooled around and let Schofield get to Columbia first. As if I didn't know that was gonna happen when we left Alabama. When we get to Columbia, we'll have to attack him. What else can we do?"

49

Mangum began to shake his head. "All I know is Hood promised not to waste men like he did at Atlanta. I'm gonna go on believing the man learned his lesson."

"Mangum," Cleburne turned in the saddle and looked his aide in the eyes, "I have a bad feeling about this campaign."

Mangum didn't know what to say to this. Finally, he asked, "May I make a suggestion, General?"

"Sure," Cleburne lit the pipe and let out a puff of smoke.

"Just don't let the men see you this way," Mangum tried to sound cheerful. "I mean, I know how you feel, but the rest of your staff may not understand. Bad morale is contagious."

"I never meant to do that," Cleburne looked hurt.

"I know, Pat," Mangum reached over and patted his commander on the arm. "My morale doesn't really matter. So if you feel the need to vent a little, just call me off to the side and let 'er rip."

"Thank you, Mangum," Cleburne said. They had ridden up in front of Saint John's Episcopal Church. Leonidas Polk had built it before the war. They stopped their horses to admire it. It was beautiful in the mist and fog. Ivy grew on the walls, and magnolias and cedar trees dotted the churchyard. A three-foot-high rock wall surrounded the place. It was almost identical to St. Mary's Church back in County Cork, Ireland. He wondered what the odds were that he would happen upon a church built identical to the one he'd been baptized in years ago and half a world away.

The rest of Cleburne's staff had ridden up and were staring at the beautiful structure. Cleburne climbed from the saddle and handed the reins to Mangum. Mangum said, "That's the most beautiful thing I've seen since we've been in Tennessee."

Cleburne walked through the opening in the rock wall and began to slowly make his way beneath the magnolias. He seemed to be in awe at the place. His staff watched him moving slowly about the churchyard. It was as if he was studying the place. The men of his division were trudging past them moving on north toward Columbia.

Cleburne eventually made his way to the rear of the church. There was a small cemetery there. His staff could see him at times back there moving among the stones. He seemed to stop and read every marker, pausing in deep thought at each one. The staff officers began to eye each other warily. They'd all noticed how depressed he'd been lately.

What they didn't know, was that Pat Cleburne wasn't really studying the markers. He was in deep thought. He was thinking about Susan again. He was ready for this war to end so he could get on with life and a family.

He'd been back there for what seemed a long time to his staff, when he came slowly around the other side of the church. He had his head down as he moved back toward the gate. He walked over to his horse and gently patted the muzzle. "Red Pepper" was his favorite horse. He took the reins from Mangum and climbed back in the saddle.

Staff member, Captain Charles Hill, was on the north side of Cleburne. As Cleburne turned his horse northward, he looked at Hill and said, "It would almost be worth dying to be buried in such a beautiful place."

He spurred his horse and began moving toward Columbia with his division. Mangum noticed him turning in the saddle and taking one last look at the beautiful churchyard.

November 27, 1864

USA

He made his headquarters at the Rectory of Athenaeum School for Girls. The building was odd looking, painted pale blue with white trim and columns. Huge round shrubs dotted the yard. It was raining again.

John Schofield leaned against one of the modest white columns and puffed away at his cigar. He could finally relax a little. Both corps of his army had made it to Columbia well ahead of Hood's infantry. Forrest had made an attempt at first, but that was repulsed easily enough.

He couldn't relax as much as he would have liked. He needed to preserve the railroad and wagon bridges across the Duck River just north of town. If Hood flanked him and got in his rear north of town, saving those bridges will have been a waste of time. He realized that he will probably have to destroy the bridges anyway if Hood forces him to retreat.

As he stood puffing on the cigar, he noticed a small entourage coming down the street. He instantly recognized the erect physique of Brigadier General Jacob Cox, commander of the Twenty-Third Corps. Cox rode up to the Rectory and dismounted. Schofield watched him walk across the lawn toward him. Cox had a funny way of holding his head back, chin held high, that made him look like he thought himself superior to others. Schofield shook his head. *You can't judge a book by its cover, he thought.*

"What's the word, John?" Cox called out.

"We're to hold Hood right here," Schofield replied. "General Thomas wants us to keep him on the south side of the Duck River until Smith arrives with his men, then we can fall back to Nashville."

"Can we do it?" Cox asked as he walked up the steps and shook Schofield's hand.

"I'm not so sure," Schofield shook his head. "I've got Wilson out watching the flanks. It'd be just like Hood to try and get around us again. Before they arrive, I want to pull back across the river and hold the heights. Even Hood won't attack across that river. Our position will be too strong on that high ground."

"He may try to flank us again, but I think that'll be a waste of time." Cox pointed back toward Nashville. He looked like a drowned rat from the rain. "Hell, we got the only good road. How can he get around us with his entire army without us knowing about it?"

"With Wilson out there guarding our flank, it may be easier than you think." Schofield puffed on the cigar. Cox was taller than he was, and it forced Schofield to have to look up to him. "He has been totally incapable of dealing with Forrest thus far."

"When's the last time we had a commander that could deal with Forrest." Cox smiled. He didn't mean any offense by it. "Wilson will do all right I believe, once he gets his feet on the ground."

Schofield wasn't so sure. "If he doesn't stop him, we'll be forced to fall back. I don't like Thomas putting me on the spot like this. He acts as though it's my responsibility to hold Hood until Smith arrives. I'm not sure we can."

"Do you want me to move my men on across Duck River?" Cox asked.

"Yeah," Schofield said, "move on over now. I'll have Stanley follow you. I'm gonna send some men out on the flanks to watch the river crossings. I don't trust Wilson to keep me informed. I've learned that you must rely on yourself if you want things done right."

"I'll keep my men moving," Cox saluted quickly and walked off the porch. "If you need anything, I'll be on the heights over the river."

"Very well," Schofield replied. "Have your engineer officer form a line of works guarding those bridges. If Hood flanks us and gets across the river…"

Schofield left the rest unsaid. Cox smiled and said, "If Hood gets across the river, I'll have my men use those little candlestick holders they carry for instruments of warfare."

Schofield smiled at the thought. Because bayonets were rarely used in combat with the range of the rifle musket, men had used their bayonets as candle holders.

Cox saluted and turned back for his horse. Schofield turned and went into the school for some rest. The stress of his position was beginning to wear on him.

Part 3

Chessboard of War

"Speed is the essence of war. Take advantage of the enemy's unpreparedness; travel by unexpected routes and strike him where he has no precautions."

Sun Tzu

November 28, 1864, 7:05p.m.

CSA

Misses Warfield opened the door and saw them inside. Cheatham made a big scene fawning over Misses Warfield. As usual, Cleburne was quiet. After the formalities, they were shown into the dining area. The room was filled with officers. There were six sitting at the table; General Hood sat at the head. His chief of staff, Colonel Mason, was seated to Hood's right. Governor Harris sat to his left. Beside Harris sat General Forrest with his arms crossed. Beside Mason sat another staff officer. Cleburne didn't know this man. Lieutenant General S.D. Lee sat at the opposite end facing Hood.

Generals Cheatham and Cleburne, arriving late, were forced to take a chair against the wall. After Cleburne sat down, he noticed Lieutenant General A.P. Stewart sitting against the wall across the room with part of his staff. Some of Hood's staff officers were forced to stand. Cleburne wondered why he was the only division commander asked to attend this meeting.

Misses Warfield excused herself and went upstairs. General Hood was smiling and appeared to be in rare good humor. He chided Cheatham for arriving late, "Did you run into some belles on the way over?"

Cheatham laughed, motioned at Cleburne, and said, "Nah, it was Pat. You know how hard it is to stop him from talking when ladies are present."

Cleburne could feel his face turn red as everyone in the room burst into laughter. Even General Forrest smiled at the remark. Cleburne was famous for his shyness around women.

"Gentlemen," Hood began, "we are about to embark on one of the most beautiful moves on the chess board of war."

Cleburne sat up and listened carefully. Forrest, with his arms crossed, remained dubious. S.D. Lee, Hood's faithful servant, was waiting eagerly. Without Hood, he would still only be a Major General holding a minor command in Mississippi. A.P. Stewart was sitting erect, chin held high as he looked at Hood. Beside Cleburne, General Cheatham had taken out a pocket knife and began to clean his fingernails.

Cheatham considered himself a fighting general. All this planning and strategizing was unbecoming to him. *Just point me in the direction of the fight and get the hell out of the way, he thought.*

Hood paused a long moment. He enjoyed moments like this immensely. It was these moments that made him feel the power of his position. He had the power to send men to their deaths or cancel an attack and spare their lives. He said, "I plan on moving to the right and flanking Schofield."

No one said anything. Cleburne wasn't impressed yet. He'd seen too many plans that looked good on paper end in futility. He remembered Hood's flank attacks at Atlanta. Those beautiful moves had accomplished nothing but high casualty lists.

Hood turned to Forrest and asked, "First thing I need to know is whether or not you can push their cavalry away from their left?"

"You're damned right I can," Forrest's voice squeaked. It was almost comical hearing him talk. His voice didn't fit his body or his reputation as the fiercest cavalry leader in the world. He added, "Only thing that can stop me is infantry."

"The bulk of their infantry is across Duck River," Hood looked at S.D. Lee. "We'll keep them occupied. What can you tell me about the roads we'll be taking?"

"Country roads and farm lanes," Forrest replied. "They're muddy as hell, but they lead directly to Spring Hill. I doubt you can get the artillery over them without a time consuming struggle. You get to Spring Hill before Schofield, and he's in a heap of trouble."

Hood smiled a sly grin. "What about the terrain?"

"Rolling hills and open fields mostly," Forrest stared at the ceiling in thought. He looked at Hood. "As soon as we move over there, he's gonna run like hell."

"I'll deal with Schofield," Hood smiled again. He began to drum his fingers on the table. "You just get Wilson out of the way. Clear the way to Spring Hill, and keep Wilson out of the picture."

Forrest nodded. He didn't like the way Hood had told him to worry about himself, but he decided to let it go this time. It was something he rarely did.

Hood turned to the staff officer sitting beside Colonel Mason and said, "Gentlemen, this is my chief engineer, Lieutenant Colonel Stephen Presstman..." The man nodded his head. Hood asked him, "What is the status of the pontoon bridge?"

"With General Forrest's assistance," Presstman looked at Forrest and then back at Hood, "we've found a good crossing point due east of Schofield. My engineers are constructing the bridge now."

"When will they be completed?" Hood looked worried.

Presstman shook his head. "There's nothing to worry about, sir. We'll work all night. It should be ready long before daylight."

"Very good," Hood relaxed. He turned to Cheatham and said, "General Cheatham, your corps will lead the march."

Cheatham looked up from cleaning his fingernails. "All right, show me the way."

"A member of my staff will direct you to the crossing point after this meeting is over." Hood leaned forward and nodded to Cleburne. "I want Cleburne's division in the lead."

Now Cleburne understood why Hood had wanted him in attendance. None of the other corps commanders had brought their division commanders with them.

"Don't worry about supplies either," Hood said. He turned to Colonel Mason and asked, "You did order those wagons of corn to the ford, didn't you?"

"Yes, sir," Mason perked up. "They're either already there or on their way."

Hood nodded. He looked at Cheatham, still worrying with his fingernails, Cleburne sitting by his side patiently listening. "Gentlemen, we'll move in the morning as soon as the pontoons are ready. We're not waiting until dawn. I'm going to ride with you tomorrow, Cleburne."

Cleburne nodded. Hood said, "General Cheatham, you stay at the ford and make sure the crossing goes smooth as silk. Once Bate and Brown have their divisions across, you can join us at the front..." Cheatham was nodding his head. Hood continued, "Now, when you get to Spring Hill, I want you to throw your men across the pike and commence fighting any Federals you find there."

Cheatham grinned and patted Cleburne on the shoulder. "I'll have my best man on the job."

Hood turned to Lieutenant General A.P. Stewart. "Straight, I want you to follow Cheatham..." Stewart's nickname from West Point was 'Old Straight.' "As soon as you get your men up at Spring Hill, I want you to be prepared to crash into Schofield while he is engaged with Cheatham's corps."

"Yes, sir," Stewart nodded. Cheatham was again working on his fingernails with the knife.

"Gentlemen," Hood banged on the table with his fist for emphasis, "it is imperative that Schofield not get through to Nashville. Next to Washington, Nashville is the most heavily fortified city the North possesses. If Schofield gets through, we won't be able to take it."

Cleburne's spirits began to rise. This could actually work. It was an honor to be chosen by the commanding General to lead the advance.

Hood paused and asked, "Are there any questions thus far?"

Forrest cleared his throat. "I still don't see how you're gonna keep Schofield from beating you to Spring Hill. He's got a damned good road to march on. We'll be struggling through mud up to a horse's belly."

Hood smiled broadly. "General S.D. Lee is gonna keep him too busy to notice that we're gone."

Lee sat forward in his chair. He reminded Cleburne of a child about to receive a birthday gift. Hood said, "General Lee, I want you to take all the artillery and pound Schofield's position with it. Take your corps and make him think our entire army's about to charge across Duck River. Make him think we're dumb enough to attack him in his strong position on those heights."

General Lee's head was bobbing up and down. It made him feel good being entrusted with such an important assignment.

"You won't need your entire corps," Hood said. "You're not gonna be doing any actual fighting anyway, just marching your men back and forth. I want you to temporarily give Johnson's division to General Stewart. I do want the artillery duel to be impressive. I'm gonna leave most of the army's artillery here with you because of the condition of the roads we'll be traveling on." Hood looked at Stewart. "General Stewart, you and Cheatham are to only carry one battery of artillery with your corps. Leave the rest with Lee."

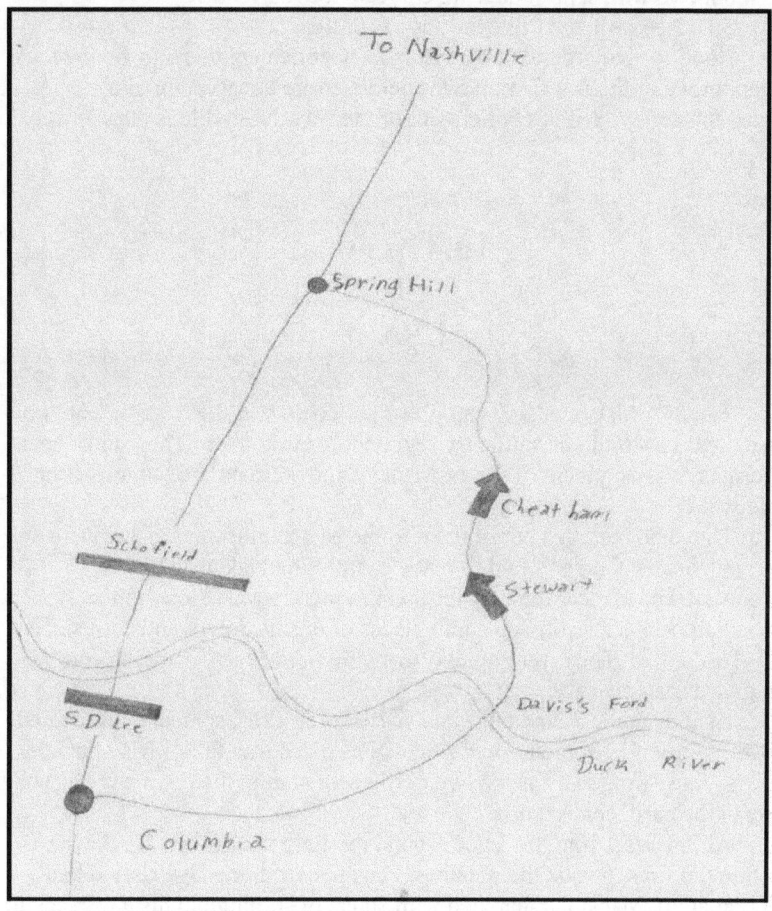

S.D. Lee holds Schofield in place at Columbia while Hood moves Cheatham and Stewart's Corps around the Federal flank attempting to cut Schofield off from Nashville.

Stewart nodded and said, "Understood, sir." Cheatham had put the knife away and sat looking at his fingernails.

Hood wondered if Cheatham was even listening. "General Cheatham, you're to take your artillerymen with you. Have them march with the infantry. When we capture Schofield, they can use his guns. It'll be hard enough making our way up those muddy roads with wagons."

Cheatham looked up. "I'll see to it."

Hood looked back at General Lee. "You may have the most important mission here. As soon as you see Schofield begin to withdraw, I want you to cross the river and attack him. Try to slow him down. Once he is caught between our two wings, he'll have no choice but to surrender."

S.D. Lee smiled. "I like the sounds of this."

Hood looked around at his officers. "Gentlemen, this may be the most important move of the war. I want Schofield's entire army captured or destroyed tomorrow. With Schofield out of the way, Nashville is ours for the taking."

10:45p.m.

CSA

The 35th Alabama had been given police duty in the town of Columbia because they'd been the first infantry regiment to enter town. They'd just been given orders relieving them of the assignment and were ordered to move out east of town.

They had marched out of town to the east a little ways. They were pointed into a dark field and told to make camp. It had taken awhile for Cheatham's corps to clear the way for them to march. Mack Keenum's regiment had been subsisting on small pieces of unsalted pork and corn since leaving Tuscumbia. They were quickly growing tired of it. Too much corn would give a man diarrhea.

As they made their camps and started their fires, someone discovered they were camping in some farmer's field. The place was full of Irish potatoes. *This is our lucky day, Mack thought.* Soon, every man in the regiment was busy digging in the hard, cold ground.

All the rails from the fence around the field were soon torn down to throw into the fires to cook the potatoes. For the past three days, they'd had little to eat at all. Mack had marched with stalks of sorghum in his haversack to chew on and help alleviate the hunger pangs.

The Confederate money had become worthless. They only received eleven dollars a month. A pound of flour was selling for nearly five dollars, so they couldn't buy much food with their pay. Despite the hunger, worthless money, and bad fortunes for their country, the men were in surprisingly good spirits.

Mack and Tom were eating their potatoes, when two men walked up to the fire and began to warm their hands. Mack instantly recognized Joe Thompson and his body servant, Jim. He said, "Well, Tom, look what the cat dragged in."

Tom looked up and shook his head. "I thought you was a deserter, Joe."

The rest of the company gathered around the new arrival. Captain Stewart looked at his corporal and shook his head. "Where you been, Joe?"

"It's a long story," Joe smiled. "I'd be willing to tell ya'll, but I'm gonna need a plate of them taters."

Bob Wheeler began to scoop potatoes into a couple of plates for Joe and his servant. Joe took his plate and sat on a log by the fire. Bob handed Jim a steaming plate. Jim nodded and said, "Thank you, suh."

Joe took a bite. The potatoes burned his tongue, but he kept chewing. He said, "I never heard when the army crossed the river. When I did hear, I packed my stuff, and me and Jim set off to catch you fellow's. We got to the pontoon bridge and the engineers was taking it up. They wouldn't gonna let us cross. They was two Missouri boys there wanting to cross also. So we finally convinced them to let us on across before they took up too much of the bridge. That was two days ago."

Newton Cameron was still limping from the wound he'd received at Decatur a few weeks ago. 'Newt' said, "I believe I'd a headed back home and not argued with them boys."

"I would have," Joe took another big bite of potatoes, "but I knew ya'll would miss me so bad. Anyway, we got out north of town before dark and had to camp where all them Tories is raisin' such a fuss. We heard they killed a Mister Wilson close by there a short while ago. It was still me, Jim, and those two Missouri boys. We found us an abandoned cabin to sleep in. There was snow on the ground by then, and I don't have to tell ya'll how cold it was."

"You sure don't," Sergeant Dan Downs was shaking his head. "I had to sleep with Tom Peebles that night. He's too damn skinny to keep a man warm."

Joe scooped another spoonful of potatoes. "'Bout two in the morning they was someone on the porch trying to get in. We thought it was the Tories. I just knew that was it for us. We loaded our rifles and aimed as Jim jerked the door open. There before us was a damned old army mule trying to get out of the cold wind. 'Bout near gave me a heart attack."

The entire company was in an uproar with laughter. Mack was glad Joe was back with them. The man kept him entertained. Mack thought he was the most fun guy in the company next to him and Tom.

Joe was still loading his mouth with potatoes. He asked, "So, what did I miss?"

"Not a damned thing," replied Lieutenant Farris.

The word was soon passed down through the ranks that they'd be moving out early in the morning. Captain Stewart told the men of Company B to try and get some sleep. It would be easy to sleep with a full belly.

November 29, 1864, 3:00 a.m.

CSA

Cleburne mounted his favorite horse, "Red Pepper" and rode forward to the Davis Ford. He could see Lieutenant Colonel Stephen Presstman, Hood's chief engineer from last night's meeting, standing near the pontoon bridge warming his hands over a fire. Cleburne spurred his horse toward him. The man looked exhausted. True to his word, the engineers had worked through the night.

Presstman turned and recognized Cleburne from the glow of the fire. He saluted.

Cleburne asked, "How are things coming?"

"Won't be long now, sir," Presstman replied. The poor man looked as though he was about to collapse.

Cleburne nodded. "I'll be forming my division. Let me know as soon as the bridge is ready."

"Yes, sir," Presstman jerked his thumb toward the bridge. "It hasn't been easy, but I'm hoping it's complete in the next hour."

Cleburne turned the horse and rode back across the dark field toward the campfires on the other side. The morning was bitterly cold. He could hear Red Pepper's hooves crunching on the frost. He slowed the horse to a slow pace. It was moments like these that he seemed to enjoy more nowadays, out here in the dark away from everyone. It felt great. *When this war is over, he thought, I may build Susan and I a cabin back in the woods away from everybody.* The thought almost made him smile.

As he drew near the camp, he saw a large group of mounted men on the edge of his encampment. He rode toward them. As he got closer, he recognized General Hood and his entire entourage. Cleburne wished his commander wasn't riding with him today. He'd rather ride without any distractions.

Cleburne reined up in front of Hood and saluted. Hood was beaming. He said, "Morning Pat, did you get any sleep?"

"I got a few hours, General," Cleburne reached down and patted his horse on the neck. "How about yourself?" he asked.

"I haven't slept a wink really," Hood didn't appear very tired. "I tossed and turned an hour or so and finally got up. This is gonna be the greatest move of my career. Everything is going according to plan thus far."

Cleburne spoke to Governor Harris and Chaplain Quintard. Hood asked, "Has anybody seen General Cheatham?"

Cleburne shook his head. He said, "General, if you'll excuse me, I'm gonna form my division."

"Very well, Pat," Hood smiled. "I'll be riding with you when you start to cross the river."

Cleburne turned his horse and rode through his men as they cooked what little they had to eat for breakfast. Pretty soon, it became apparent that things were not going according to plan. He had formed his division, thinking they would be crossing within the next hour, but that hour turned into another. The men were shivering in the cold morning air. If they were marching, they would be warm, but just standing out here in the cold air of pre-dawn was rough on the strongest of them. Cleburne began to chaff at the delay. *When do things ever go according to plan, he thought?*

The light was showing through the tree tops when a staff officer finally approached Cleburne. The man saluted and asked, "Are you General Cleburne?"

Cleburne nodded and said nothing. The man said, "Colonel Presstman sent me here to tell you the bridge is ready."

"Very well," Cleburne reached into his pocket and pulled out his watch. It was almost 6:30 a.m. He shook his head and gave the order for the division to move out.

The sun was now visible as they made their way across the pontoon bridge. Presstman and his men looked as though they were about to drop. One of the engineers stood beside the road shouting for the men to break their steps before crossing. They had crossed enough pontoon bridges to know that already. There was a heavy fog hanging low to the ground this morning, and the men disappeared into it as they crossed the river.

Cleburne and his staff crossed first, followed by Hood and his large group of officers. Brigadier General Mark Lowrey and his brigade followed behind them. Cheatham managed to get across before any of them and waited patiently on the other side. His eyes were bloodshot and he looked like he had a hangover.

Hood and Cleburne paused next to him. Hood laughed and asked, "What happened to you?"

"Long story," Cheatham held up a hand. "Let's just say it has something to do with a local woman and a flask. Hell, I'll be fine, General, let's get to work."

Hood shook his head. "You stay here and make sure the division gets across, and then you can catch up to us. We're gonna go on and lay the trap."

Cheatham nodded. He reached up and rubbed his temples.

Hood, Cleburne, and Lowrey rode together up the road in front of the division. Governor Harris and Chaplain Quintard rode just behind Hood. Hood was still beside himself with glee at the thought of the movement they were making.

The morning was cold, but the sky was clear for a change. The sun soon burned the fog away and warmed the marching troops. The frost on the ground was soon gone.

Cleburne was beginning to enjoy the march and the weather. Soon, Lieutenant Mangum came galloping to the front, saluting as he reined up. He said, "The entire division's over the river. General Brown's men have begun to cross behind us."

"Very good," Cleburne pulled out his watch. It was now 7:30 a.m.

Hood smiled broadly, turned and looked back toward Chaplain Quintard and said, "The enemy must give me battle, or I will be in Nashville before tomorrow night."

Cleburne was proud of how smoothly the crossing had gone. There's usually some unexpected congestion that occurs, but not today. Maybe their luck was beginning to change.

Hood rode up beside Cleburne. His eyes betrayed his lack of sleep, but he was in good spirits. He asked, "Mind if I ride with you a spell, Pat?"

"Not at all," Cleburne replied. He removed his kepi and ran his hand through his dark red hair. "You look tired."

Hood shook his head. "Didn't get much sleep is all. I'm fine. I remember when I first came to this army; everyone thought I would be too weak from my injuries to ride a horse. I showed 'em though. I rode up to twenty miles a day without the least bit of pain."

"I remember," Cleburne smiled. "When you lost that leg at Chickamauga, they weren't giving you much chance of surviving."

"I showed 'em there too," Hood laughed. "The papers were already reporting me as killed."

"I think that's happened to all of us at one time or another," Cleburne nodded. "Damned reporters write stories to sell their newspapers and could care less about the truth."

Hood thought about how hard that had been on Buck when she read that he'd been killed. When he'd finally gotten well enough to travel and had gone back to Richmond, he'd expected her to fawn over her wounded hero. Instead, she'd played hard to get. She was a difficult lady to court. He'd met women like her before. She would keep him at arms length, but when he was just about ready to give up on her, she would act as if she couldn't live without him.

Cleburne asked, "You're from Texas?"

"Owingsville, Kentucky," Hood replied, "but I spent several years in Texas after finishing West Point. I'd determined before the war to make Texas my adopted state. I'd even gone so far as to purchase a spot of ground to build a home on, but that fell through with the war. What part of Ireland you from, Pat?"

"County Cork," Pat waved his hand at a gnat. "My father was a physician, and that's what I was supposed to be. I failed the entrance exam to the Trinity College of Medicine. I thought I'd disgraced my family, so I up and ran away. Joined the Forty-First Regiment of Foot in the British Army, and that's where I learned to be a soldier."

62

"My father was a doctor also," Hood smiled broadly. "He always wanted me to become a doctor, but it just wasn't in me. I spent my childhood outdoors, swimming, fishing, hunting, and riding. I was a pretty rowdy boy. My grandpas are the reason I became a soldier. I never spent a great deal of time with my father, but my grandpas always had time for me. Both were old veterans. You know, Indian fighters and such. One had fought in the Revolutionary War, and the other was scalped by Indians once and left for dead. I used to sit and listen to those war stories all day. I even had a great grandpa that fought in the French and Indian War."

Cleburne noticed Hood was more talkative than normal today. The man was genuinely excited about the movement they were making. He had to admit that the plan looked good on paper. He just hoped it would turn out good. He'd seen too many of these brilliant plans fall apart at the last moment.

Hood suddenly spun and looked at Cleburne through sad eyes. "Pat, I'm terribly sorry I had to turn down your furlough. I know how much you wanted to go to Mobile and see Susan."

"It's understandable, sir," Cleburne glanced down at his gauntlets and adjusted the reins in his right hand.

"I hope it works out for you," Hood sounded genuine. "I've fallen in love several times. Women come and women go. People got the impression I would be crushed when Buck broke off the engagement. Did you know I was engaged before I left for West Point?"

Cleburne shook his head.

"I was," Hood continued. "Anne Mitchell was her name. She lived just down the road. We were childhood friends. I was what you call 'a little ruff around the edges,' I guess you could say. Of course, her father didn't approve. We tried to elope, but he caught us, and it was over. That poor girl was forced to marry a man she didn't love. She was later struck by lightning and killed. Life is funny, you know."

"I would have to agree with you on that," Cleburne nodded his head.

"You're an attorney?" Hood asked. He watched Cleburne nod his head then stared at him a long moment. "Lots of book study to learn the law, I hear."

"That's right," Cleburne wondered where Hood was going with this.

"I had a hard time at West Point, you know." Hood smiled again. He nudged the horse forward with his good leg. "Book study and John Bell Hood don't get along at all. Schooling was a necessary evil for me to become what I most wanted to be. I was carefree at the Point. I guess you could say I matured later than the other boys. I got busted once for sneaking out after curfew to visit Benny Haven's, a local tavern. Me and Lucius Rich of Missouri were both caught. I almost quit the Academy when that happened. When the war began, Lucius joined the Federal army, and I heard he was killed at Shiloh. He was a good soldier—a good friend."

"This war's killed off a lot of good men," Cleburne stroked his goatee, "and it's not over yet."

63

As the morning wore on, Hood began to get tired. He pulled out his watch and looked at it a long moment. It was only 9 a.m. A courier caught up to the group and told Hood that A.P. Stewart's corps was now over the river. They have Johnson's division bringing up the rear. He also reported that Lee had sent a message that he has Schofield's full attention in Columbia just like Hood had planned. All morning they'd been hearing Colonel Beckham's guns banging away toward the southwest.

Hood was elated. The march was slowed by the horrible condition of the roads. He smiled and turned to Governor Harris, "Schofield doesn't even know what's about to hit him."

The march continued for a while, when Hood suddenly ordered Cleburne to stop. He took out his map and began to study it with his good hand. He sat his horse in the middle of the road while studying the map.

Cleburne asked, "Is there a problem?"

"I think we're on the wrong road," Hood's hand was trembling as he tried to study the map. The artificial leg was sticking straight out from the horse. He had a puzzled look on his face. "The map differs from the road quite a bit."

Cleburne pulled his horse over to the side and began to question his own guide. He turned around and looked at Hood and said, "My guide says we're on the right road."

Hood ignored Cleburne. He turned to Colonel Mason and said, "Where's that cavalryman Forrest sent me?"

Mason turned in the saddle and motioned for the young man to be brought forward. Hood eyed the boy up and down and asked, "What's your name?"

"John Gregory," the boy beamed at the thought that he was actually helping the commanding general. "Ever body just calls me Sol."

Hood passed the map to him and asked, "The road we're on differs from the one on the map. Are we not on the wrong road?"

"I growed up here, sir," Sol said. "I know ever twist and turn on this here road. It's the right road, all right."

Hood reached over and pulled the map back. He began to shake his head. "I'm not so sure. This map shows Spring Hill to be just twelve miles from Columbia…"

"General Hood," Sol interrupted. He looked hurt that Hood didn't trust him. "Your map shows a straight line from Columbia to Spring Hill. This here road ain't got no straight line in it. It's only twelve miles from Columbia to Spring Hill, but its seventeen miles on this crooked ass road."

"My guide confirms that," Cleburne said.

Hood was getting really tired and was beginning to grow agitated. The road is in too miserable a condition to make very good time, and to top that off, it's five miles longer than the map shows. It's muddy and all washed out from the rain. *Why can't things just go smooth for once, he wondered? Everything starts out looking good, but then goes all to hell. He shrugged his shoulders.*

There's little I can do about it now. He looked at Cleburne, "You may resume the march, Pat."

Cheatham soon caught up to them and joined in the ride with the Generals. Hood asked, "How's the head?"

"It's tolerable now," Cheatham laughed. "Women are rough on a man."

They struggled on down the muddy road. Hood's horse stumbled and almost fell. *That's all I need, he thought.* He began to wonder if things could get any worse. Suddenly, he heard a yell and looked back to see a man galloping through the fields around the road filled with soldiers.

It was one of Stewart's staff officers. The man rode up, his horse foaming. The man was breathless from the hard ride. He said, "Sir, General Stewart reports…" He paused to catch his breath. "Sir, there's Union infantry been spotted way out east of Columbia on a hill."

"Infantry?" Hood looked shocked. "How many?"

"We don't know, sir," the man was still breathing hard.

Hood started to worry. *What if Schofield finds me all spread out on this pitiful road. If he attacks me here, there's no way I can concentrate the army in time to stop him from destroying a big part of it. It'll be a disaster.* Hood asked, "Well, what in hell were they doing?"

"Nothing," the man was shaking his head. "General Stewart believes they were just observing us. He thinks Schofield will now turn tail and run for Spring Hill. It's his opinion we should march hard to beat him there."

If he is indeed marching for Spring Hill, Hood thought, we'll never beat him anyway on this miserable road. It's better to be safe than sorry. Hood quickly made a decision to take the safest course. He would put someone out there on the flank to guard against an attack.

Hood turned to General Cheatham and said, "Have Brown move his division to the west of the road a few hundred yards. He's gonna have to march through the fields and woods to guard our left flank from attack. Make sure he knows that he's got to keep pace with Cleburne and Bate."

Cheatham didn't protest the order. He spun his horse and rode back down the line toward Brown's division. Cleburne looked surprised. He started to say something but stopped himself. It wasn't his place to give advice to the commanding general.

Hood turned back to Stewart's staff officer. "Tell General Stewart to throw one of his divisions out on his left to guard his flank. If it slows us down, it's just the price we have to pay. I can't take a chance on having this army crushed."

Cleburne thought about how exhausting it will be on those men marching through the woods. It's difficult enough on this road in ankle-deep mud. *Lee and Jackson are Hood's heroes, he thought, every move he makes he tries to emulate them. Why does he not have the confidence of a Lee or a Jackson? He admits this move is a desperate gamble, yet half way through it,*

65

he starts second guessing himself. Cleburne thought about how confident Hood had sounded back in Columbia last night.

"Pat," Hood was watching Cleburne. He had noticed that Cleburne was in deep thought. Cleburne jerked his head up. Hood said, "We'll just wait here until Brown gets in position on your flank. Don't you think that's best?"

Cleburne pulled his watch out and looked at it again. "We're losing a lot of precious time here, sir."

"You're right, yes," Hood was nodding, "but it's necessary."

Cleburne studied the man. He was beginning to look careworn. The lack of sleep was beginning to tell on him.

Hood turned and began talking politics with Governor Harris. If he noticed that Cleburne wasn't agreeing with him, he chose to pretend otherwise. Cleburne could still hear the roar of S.D. Lee's guns back in Columbia. *If Schofield was about to attack Hood's army, Cleburne wondered why Lee was still be firing across the river at nothing?*

Cleburne reached in his pocket and pulled out the picture of Susan. If it wasn't for his strict sense of duty, he could just resign from the army. He could resign now and start making his way to Mobile. He could probably be there in a week, but then he would never be able to live with himself. He'd begun this war with these men, and now he was gonna see them through.

Cheatham returned to the front about thirty minutes later. The order was given, and the march resumed.

Brigadier General Hiram Bronson Granbury. Commander of Cleburne's Texas Brigade.

Cleburne rode along admiring the beauty of this country. The trees were turning, and it reminded him of a different time and place. The cool weather made him think of Ireland. For some reason, he was thinking of a girl from his school days. A girl he never got the courage to talk to. *I wonder where she is now, he thought. I wonder if she remembers me. If she does, I wonder if she ever thinks about me.*

The march carried them past old plantations. The road was a mess. Men were slipping and falling all down the line. Every now and then, a horse would slip and stumble before regaining its balance. Men were cursing. It was a typical Confederate march.

As they came to the top of a hill with a scenic view, Hood said, "Pat, we'll halt the march here. Let the men eat…" Hood grimaced. "I've got to get out of the saddle a bit."

His staff spread a blanket beneath a huge oak tree for Hood to lie on. Cleburne picked himself a tree away from everyone else. General Lowrey, the "Fighting Preacher," came over and sat next to him but didn't say anything. He was a good man, Cleburne had to admit. If you were in the mood to talk, he was in the mood to listen. If you were in deep thought, he would remain quiet. He couldn't help but respect a man like that.

Cleburne pulled out a piece of paper and began to write to Susan. He'd only written a few lines, when a man rode up on horseback. A lanky figure climbed from his horse and looked at Cleburne.

It was Hiram Granbury, commander of Cleburne's brigade of Texans. Granbury looked like a warrior in his gray uniform, stars on the collar surrounded by the wreath. He wore only a mustache on his face, and his dark hair was always wild looking. It was so thick that the man never bothered to comb it. He just let it stand in every direction. Granbury stood there a moment and rubbed his lower back. He watched Cleburne a moment, trying to decipher his mood and began to walk that way.

Hood opened his eyes, raised his head, saw Granbury, and said, "General Granbury, a word please."

"Sir," Granbury looked surprised. He walked to the edge of the blanket. "How can I help you, General?"

Hood said, "It has been called to my attention that you have allowed your brigade to straggle behind General Lowrey's."

Granbury still had the confused look on his face. He reached up and ran a hand through his thick hair. "I'm not sure I know what you're implying. I've had my men directly behind General Lowrey's all morning."

"You understand, sir," Hood's voice had grown firm. "I consider my home state Texas now."

Granbury was nodding. Hood said, "I can't have the Texans straggling. The march hasn't been what I expected."

Granbury looked at all the staff officers gathered around Hood. They acted as though they weren't listening, but Granbury knew better. He saw Hood's wooden leg lying in the grass at the edge of the blanket. As Hood talked, Granbury could feel his face growing red.

If the commanding General has a problem with me, he should talk to me alone. Granbury began to wonder what Hood was upset with him about. His voice was strained as he asked Hood, "Are you implying that the speed of the march has been the fault of me and my men?"

"I'm saying that it reflects badly on me when the Texans don't perform as they should," Hood raised himself up on his good arm. "If the responsibility for that happens to be you, then you're my problem."

"I've already heard about your faulty maps, General Hood," Granbury began to unbutton his frock coat. He was growing rather warm here, being accused by the commanding general of negligence. "Now, if I've done something wrong, I will take full responsibility, but I'll be damned if me or my men will be your scapegoats."

"The maps have nothing to do with this." Hood snapped back. "I'm referring to…"

Granbury threw his coat on the ground and stepped forward on the edge of the blanket. The tall lanky man towered over the general sitting on the ground before him. He interrupted Hood. "They have everything to do with it. A real man admits his mistakes. Evidently, you haven't reached that maturity level yet."

Cleburne started to say something on Granbury's behalf, but decided the man was doing rather well on his own. He had a feeling that the Texas lawyer was about to embarrass the Texas general before this conversation was over.

Hood's face was red. He sat glaring at Granbury. He opened his mouth to say something, but Granbury began again. "Now, I've kept my brigade directly on the heels of General Lowrey's. I haven't received permission from anyone to pass him. From what I know, General Lowrey has kept his brigade on your heels. So, if anyone's to blame for this supposed slowness, it's you. You are still in command, ain't you?"

Hood lay back down on the blanket. He stared into the top of the huge oak tree. Finally, he said, "That'll be all, General. You're dismissed."

Granbury continued standing on the blanket towering over Hood. Hood closed his eyes, wishing Granbury would go away. After a long uncomfortable pause, Granbury reached down and picked up his coat. He turned toward Cleburne again. As he walked away, he said to himself in a loud voice, "Unbelievable."

He walked over and knelt next to Cleburne and Lowrey. Cleburne extended his hand. "You handled that rather well."

Granbury shook the hand and asked, "Why didn't you say something?"

"How could I?" Cleburne smiled. "General Hood couldn't even say anything; you were so riled up."

Granbury managed a weak smile, but it was obvious he was still upset. He asked, "What's his problem anyway?"

Cleburne shook his head. "He wants to make these grand moves, but once he does, he grows afraid he's walking into a trap. You hear what he's done with Brown's division?"

"Yeah," Granbury was looking back at Hood still lying on the blanket. "Those men will be too exhausted to fight after walking through the woods."

"Exactly," Cleburne said.

11:55 a.m.

CSA

Forrest turned to Major Strange and said, "Send a report back to Hood. Tell him I'm within five miles of Spring Hill. I'm driving Wilson back without much resistance at all."

Major Strange saluted and turned toward one of the couriers. Forrest watched the last of the blue troopers disappearing over a rise to the east. *I ought to turn around and take Spring Hill, he thought. I can hold the town until Hood comes up.* Those weren't part of his orders, but it seemed the safe thing to do at the moment. The Union cavalry had been whipped, and nothing should stand in the way at Spring Hill.

He rode his horse over to General Lawrence Ross's position. He said, "Sul, take your brigade..." He paused in thought and asked, "How many men you got?"

"Close to six hundred," Ross replied.

"That should be plenty," Forrest said. "We got the scare on him now. Take your brigade and stay after Wilson. Keep the scare on him."

"Yes, sir," Ross turned in the saddle and started giving the necessary orders.

Forrest made a quick calculation in his mind. *That'll leave me with about forty-five hundred men. That should be more than enough to hold Spring Hill until Hood arrives.*

He soon had his troopers turned and riding hard for Spring Hill. General Chalmers rode along with him. As they approached the edge of town, they could see Union defenders behind rail barricades, waiting. Forrest rode his horse up on a small knoll and dismounted. Chalmers followed behind him. Forrest pulled his field glasses out of his saddlebag and began to patiently survey the position. Chalmers quickly dismounted and did the same.

Forrest gave the barricade a quick looking over, and then trained his glasses on the road leading into town from Columbia. Federal wagons lined the road as far as he could see. *The Union army must be on the verge of retreating from Columbia, he thought. Schofield has probably sent the supply wagons back first.* As he studied the situation, he realized that a great opportunity lay before him.

That's probably a small force of dismounted cavalry behind that barricade, he thought. I bet we can attack, sweep that small enemy force guarding town out of the way, and take their entire supply train.

He turned to Chalmers and noticed him studying the works in his front intently. Forrest said, "Take your brigade and attack that position yonder."

"I don't think that's a very good idea, General," Chalmers lowered the glasses and began to shake his head. "That's infantry behind those works."

"I think you're mistaken, Chalmers," Forrest put the glasses back to his eyes and quickly scanned the position again. "Their infantry's still in Columbia. That's got to be dismounted cavalry, and a small force at that. Throw in everything you have. You'll sweep 'em."

Chalmers shrugged. He knew the one thing you didn't do was argue with Forrest. He said, "I'll try."

Forrest watched from the knoll as Chalmers rode back to his brigade to prepare for the attack. After a few minutes, he watched the line move out. They rode ahead slowly at first, but then began to build speed like an irresistible wave. It was beautiful. The field to the works was open, and the men kept their horses in perfect order. As they reached the halfway point, the line sped into a gallop. It couldn't last very long at that rate.

Suddenly, the enemy behind the barricade opened fire. Not only was there infantry behind the works instead of cavalry, but there was artillery as well. Forrest watched horses plunging wildly, saddles emptied of men. Some of the horses were racing back across the field without their riders. He saw one horse dragging a man back across the field. The man's foot hung in the stirrup. The way his arms flailed along behind, it appeared the man was already dead. It became painfully clear to Forrest that the charge couldn't possibly succeed. The entire affair was over in seconds. The survivors were now racing back to the safety of the Confederate lines.

Chalmers rode back up the knoll to Forrest's position. His face was red, and he appeared to be angry. The expression on his face said, 'I told you so.'

Forrest smiled a sheepish grin and said, "They were in there, sure enough, weren't they Chalmers?"

Chalmers said nothing. He simply shook his head and looked back across the field at the bodies of his unlucky men.

Forrest raised his glasses and studied the position again. He could see more Union troops racing out of town to strengthen the position he had just attacked. To the south, he could see Union infantry moving up the road from Columbia.

He began to think about his situation here. The men were running low on ammunition as a result of all the skirmishing with Wilson. Most of his men looked as if they were about to drop from the saddle with exhaustion. *It's been one running fight since we left Alabama, he thought. There's no way these men will be able to push infantry out of Spring Hill.*

He watched the infantry racing into town and began to calculate the numbers in his head. There's probably a full division in town already. Forrest turned to Chalmers and said, "There's nothing more we can do here. We'll have to wait on Hood and the infantry."

2:15 p.m.

CSA

They could almost see Spring Hill when they topped the hills. Hood was growing excited about the prospect of what he was about to pull off. Several times he had reminded his staff that this was the greatest move of his career.

Back to the southwest, he could still hear the roar of S.D. Lee's artillery holding Schofield in place at Columbia. He could also hear firing from the direction of Spring Hill, and that worried him. If Forrest had indeed pushed Wilson away, and Lee was holding Schofield at Columbia, who was doing the firing at Spring Hill? Hood began to grow concerned.

He rode on until they came to a small creek. His guide told him it was called Rutherford Creek. The man said they were within a mile of Spring Hill. Hood's heart began to race as he spurred his horse across the shallow water and on up the road. This is the moment of truth.

He rode up a small rise just southeast of Spring Hill and studied the situation. General Cheatham had ridden with him and was now waiting at Hood's side. Hood pulled out his watch. It was almost two-thirty.

This could be the greatest day of his career. He asked an aide for field glasses and waited for the man to pass them to him. He trained the glasses on the town itself but could see very little movement. He looked to the road leading in from Columbia and saw that it was also empty.

Hood lowered the glasses and looked at Cheatham. "We've done it. Schofield is still at Columbia watching Lee's artillery show. We'll soon have him trapped between us and Lee, and then it'll be over. If he doesn't surrender, we'll crush him like a pecan."

Cheatham nodded his head; his long dark curls bounced as he did.

"Let's ride back and hurry your corps forward," Hood passed the field glasses back to the aide. "I don't want this beautiful move to fail like all the others at Atlanta."

They turned their horses and rode back to Rutherford Creek. Cleburne's division was there preparing to cross. Men were removing their socks and shoes and rolling up their pant legs. Cleburne saw the two generals approaching and rode across the creek to meet them.

Hood said, "Pat, the road's wide open. There's no enemy in sight. The place is there for the taking."

Cleburne nodded and said, "I should have my division across in fifteen minutes. How much farther is it?"

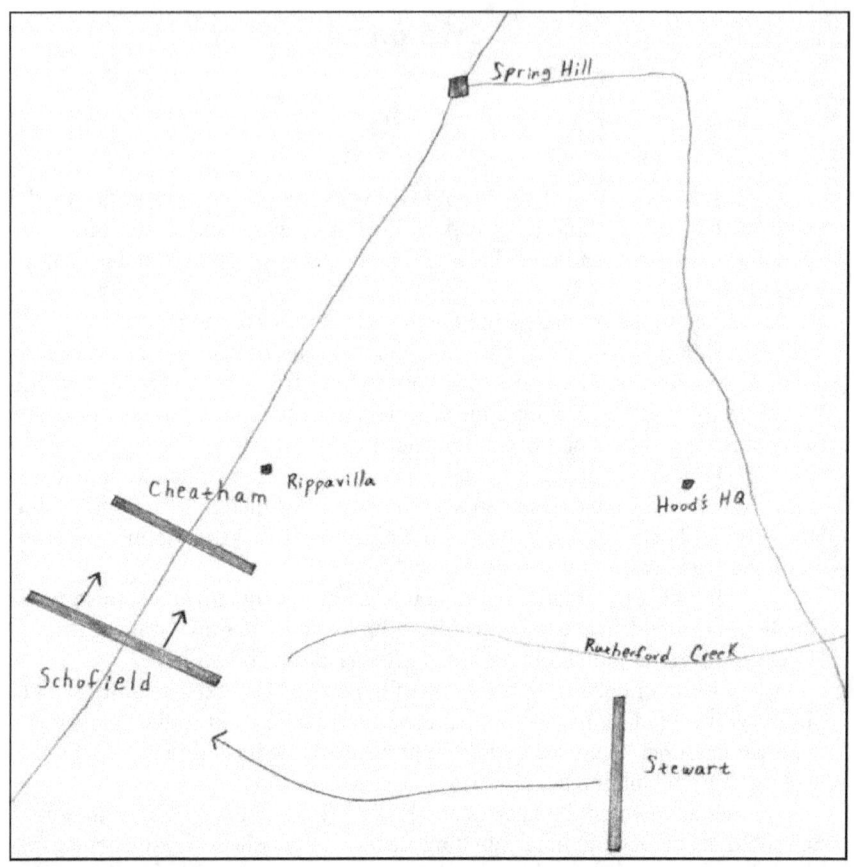

Hood plans to send Cheatham's corps to the Columbia Pike blocking Schofield's retreat route. Stewart's corps is held south of Rutherford Creek. When Schofield engages Cheatham, Hood will have Stewart slam into Schofield's flank and rear. Schofield will be forced to surrender or have his army destroyed.

Cleburne was nodding, listening carefully. Cheatham sat on his horse, head lowered. His mind seemed to be someplace else.

Hood continued, "Hold Granbury back a few hundred yards. When you reach the turnpike, wheel your division south to face the Federal army. Engage anyone that comes up that road from Columbia."

"Right," Cleburne nodded. He spun his horse back across the stream to hurry his men.

Hood turned to Cheatham and said, "Frank, you go with him. Make sure this thing is done right. I'll remain here and forward you troops."

Cheatham snapped out of his reverie and saluted. He moved his horse across the stream to join Cleburne. *So Hood wants Spring Hill taken, Cheatham thought. That shouldn't be a problem at all.*

72

Cheatham watched as Cleburne's division crossed the creek and made their way up the road. He followed along with Cleburne. Cheatham seemed to have his mind elsewhere. He asked Cleburne, "Have you heard of Jesse Peters?"

"I don't think so," Cleburne replied. He wondered if he should have heard of the man. He asked, "Who is he?"

"She's not a he," Cheatham laughed. He waited for Cleburne's reaction. He asked, "You remember General Van Dorn, don't you?"

Cleburne raised his eyebrows. He said, "Of course. His corps joined ours after Shiloh in Corinth. He was killed around here somewhere, wasn't he?"

"Yeah," Cheatham smiled. "Her husband is Doctor Peters. He shot Van Dorn in a house in Spring Hill. They were supposedly enjoying each other's company a little too much."

"Oh yes," Cleburne nodded his head. He remembered reading in the journals about the entire ugly affair.

"She's still here, you know," Cheatham said. He had a sly smile on his face.

Cleburne wondered why Cheatham was bringing this up to him, especially at this moment. He simply nodded and continued staring straight down the road, waiting for Cheatham to finish.

Cheatham continued, "I'm thinking about going over and seeing the young lass tonight. She's in her early twenties and simply worships Confederate generals."

Cleburne didn't have time for this conversation. He had a far more important mission ahead of him. He asked, "General Cheatham, how much farther before I need to deploy my men?"

Cheatham grunted. They'd come to the top of another small rise. He pointed toward the valley between this rise and the next. "Form your men down there. Hood and I rode up the other hill over there and scouted the area. Just move your men forward over that hill; you can't miss it. I'll ride back and bring up Brown and Bate's divisions."

"Very well," Cleburne nodded and turned to give the orders to his men.

Cheatham turned his horse and began riding back toward Rutherford Creek past Cleburne's steady stream of troops. Along the way, he ran into General Forrest on horseback riding in the same direction.

Forrest saw Cheatham and spurred his horse that way. He asked, "Where's General Hood?"

"Back over the creek somewhere. He's placed me in charge of the battlefield at the moment while he rushes reinforcements to me." Cheatham jerked his thumb over his shoulder. "We should have Spring Hill in less than an hour."

"I have a message for you," Forrest eyed Cheatham carefully.

Cheatham was taken aback, as he asked, "From whom?"

"A beautiful young woman by the name of Peters," Forrest said. "Do you know her?"

Cheatham broke into a big smile. "Yeah, I know her. She's a big fan of race horses, same as I. What'd she say?"

Forrest thought about what she'd said first. He had been riding down the road and saw her standing in the front yard of a nice home. She had called to one of Forrest's staff officers and asked if Forrest was a general officer. When the staff officer told her who he was, she had run into the road in front of his horse and stopped him. She'd invited him to come in and have supper with her and use her home for the night, but Forrest had turned her down. "Gonna be a little busy tonight, young lady" was what he'd told her. Besides, he was devoted to his wife back home. Still, the thought was extremely tempting. The lady was beautiful, and it'd been awhile since Forrest had seen his wife.

Forrest said, "She asked if I'd seen you. When I told her you were on your way to this very place, she said to tell you where she was staying."

Cheatham's expression changed to a sly grin. He asked, "And where exactly was she staying?"

"Back up this road about a half mile on the right in a large white house. You can't miss it. She's probably still standing out there. I just left her." Forrest was growing annoyed at the conversation. He had business to attend to, and he sure as hell wasn't Cheatham's messenger boy.

Cheatham pondered the situation a moment. Finally, he said more to himself than to Forrest, "I think I'll ride back up there and see her. It's not polite to keep a young lady waiting. I'll have time to get up there and back before the rest of my corps reaches the field."

Forrest shook his head and continued on down the road to find Hood. He looked over his shoulder at Cheatham riding up the road in the direction of the beautiful young lady with the long brown hair. He could see Cleburne down in the hollow forming his division. *Why is Cheatham not overseeing Cleburne's movement, he wondered? One of his divisions is moving into position in one of the most important moves of the entire war, and he's riding up the road to see a lady.* Forrest turned and spurred his horse down the hill toward Cleburne's division. He had seen Spring Hill and its defenses. He could at least tell General Cleburne what lay ahead of him.

4:15 p.m.

CSA

Stephen Lee studied the Union position across the river through his field glasses. Compared to the Tennessee River, the Duck River was really just a large creek. He could see Union troops on the Pike leaving the heights across the way marching hard toward Spring Hill.

His orders were to attack the rear of Schofield's columns if he withdrew. Stephen Lee was walking a fine line here. He couldn't attack Schofield's entire force. Johnson's division had been sent north with Stewart, leaving him with only two divisions. Schofield outnumbered him by at least two to one.

He stood there looking at the Union position and pondered what he should do next. He quickly decided to test the Federal position before sending in his entire force. Lee lowered the field glasses and looked around. The nearest troops were General Holtzclaw's Alabama Infantry Brigade. He mounted his horse and rode to their position behind the flaming cannons.

He saw Holtzclaw standing beneath a tree talking with his aides. Lee rode up and dismounted. Holtzclaw and the aides saluted. Lee nodded back and said, "How are you, James?"

"Never better, sir," Holtzclaw replied. "What can I do for you?"

Lee looked at the man with the large round head. Holtzclaw's face was fat; his chin was clean shaven, betraying a double chin. Lee said, "I think Schofield is withdrawing now. I'm not sure though. I need you to send over a couple of your regiments and test the heights across the way."

"I'll get them started right away," Holtzclaw turned to an aide and began to give orders.

Lee interrupted him. He said, "I need you to be very cautious over there. Don't rush to the point that you get engaged with Schofield's entire corps."

Holtzclaw nodded, turned, and continued giving the necessary orders. There was nothing further Lee needed to do here, so he remounted and rode back to his observation post.

On the way back, he rode past Colonel Robert Beckham, his chief of artillery. Beckham was busy supervising the artillery bombardment of Schofield's position. Besides, the noise here was too great for communication. Lee raised his hat to Beckham as he rode by. Beckham nodded and smiled.

Lee, trailed by his aides, rode back to the position he occupied before and dismounted. They didn't have long to wait before Holtzclaw's regiments came over the hill behind them. They moved forward, quickly passing the cannons and making their way to the river. When they got to the river, he lost sight of them as they moved through the trees lining the bank. After a fifteen minute pause, he saw them moving up the other bank toward the position Schofield was supposed to be occupying. It was the moment of truth.

He could see Union skirmishers firing and falling back before Holtzclaw's infantry. The Confederate troops pushed on a few hundred yards and stopped short of the main Union line. Lee wondered what they saw. He could distinctly hear the rifle fire across the way but couldn't tell anything more. The Union artillery was still firing from the trees on beyond them.

A rider came back across the river and rode hard for Lee's position. The man reined up his horse and asked, "General Lee, should we push on up the hill? There's artillery up there firing; there's got to still be infantry there supporting it."

Lee shook his head. "Tell them to hold their position where they are if they can safely do so."

"Right, sir," the man was nodding, sweat dripping off his forehead. "We pushed their skirmishers back, but we're not sure we can take that hill while it's covered with artillery."

"I don't need that hill," Lee said, "I just needed to know if they were covering a withdrawal or holding on here."

"There's Union infantry moving back up that road toward Spring Hill by the thousands," the man said. "I don't know how many are still here."

"Just hold your positions until I figure out what to do next," Lee said.

The man saluted and rode back toward Duck River.

Lee watched as the Union artillery fire began to pick up. Several rounds were landing nearby. He heard a loud crack and looked to his right. Between two cannons, he could see a man lying on his back. He raised his glasses and looked to see if he recognized the man. The Uniform told him it was his artillery chief. Lee said to no one in particular, "Beckham is down."

He walked back and mounted his horse and rode that way. As he got nearer, he noticed several men gathered around the fallen officer. Lee dismounted and walked into the group. There was another officer sitting on the ground holding Beckham's head in his lap. He had Beckham's blood all over his arms and hands.

"Is he alive?" Lee asked.

"Just barely," the officer answered. "Somebody help me load him in a wagon. Find a nice home nearby to carry him to."

Lee nodded. Several men began moving to carry out the order. Lee squatted down beside the officer and looked at Beckham's head. There was a gash just above his forehead. The skull was split open, and he could see inside his head. Blood and brain matter were oozing from the wound. Lee looked at the officer and asked, "Did you see it happen?"

The man nodded and swallowed hard. "He was looking through his field glasses at the Union position…" The man paused and swallowed hard again. "I was looking right at him when it happened. It was a freak accident actually. Just as he lowered his glasses, a Union shell hit that rock yonder…"

The man nodded out in front of the cannons. Several men stepped aside and looked behind them. There was a large rock there, shining as if it had just been broken open. The man continued, "A piece of that rock hit him square in the head. It wasn't the cannonball, sir. Killed by a damned rock—what a shame."

"He's not dead yet," Lee corrected the man, but the man wasn't listening. He looked down at Beckham's blood-covered face and began to shake his head.

76

Lee reached over and patted the officer on the shoulder, then stood back up. Someone shouted that they'd found a wagon, and several men helped raise Beckham up and began carrying him that way. Lee was impressed at how tenderly the men carried him to the wagon and placed him inside. The cannons were still firing around them. Lee fought back the urge to cry. He loved Beckham. He looked down at his hands and noticed they were trembling. Lee kept standing there, distraught over his loss, until the wagon began to slowly move south.

He thought about what the young officer had said. Beckham had been killed by a freak accident, a flying rock. Lee was standing there shaking his head. He decided to wait until dark before moving against Schofield. *It's better to be safe than sorry, he thought.* After seeing Beckham wounded, he was in no condition to supervise a movement at the moment anyway.

4:20 p.m.

CSA

Cleburne was busy getting his division ready to move forward over the rolling hills and to the Columbia Pike. General Forrest rode up and nodded at Cleburne and asked, "Care if I ride into battle with you, Pat?"

"Not at all," Cleburne replied. "I need a good man that knows the ground."

"I've got a brigade of dismounted cavalry in that tree line to your right. I've ordered them to move when you move. I just didn't want your men to get excited and open fire on 'em." Forrest pointed to the trees to their right. "Cheatham tells me you're gonna take Spring Hill."

"Hood said for me to take the Columbia Pike and sweep south toward Schofield," Cleburne stopped and stared at Forrest.

"Whatever," Forrest said. "Town's to your right a mile or so; the pike's directly in front of you."

Cleburne nodded and looked over his division one last time. He could see the anxious look on his men's faces as they began to realize something was about to be done. The blue battle flags were hanging limp in the evening light. Cleburne nodded to one of his staff officers and said, "Give the order."

The line surged into motion, climbing the hill out of the small valley. It was a magnificent sight, the men moving all together, even if his once-proud division now only numbered three thousand. Forrest looked down and turned to Cleburne. He had a puzzled look on his face and asked, "Is this all your division?"

"Three brigades of it," Cleburne began to slowly draw his sword from its scabbard. "Hood left James Smith's brigade back in Florence to escort supplies."

Forrest drew his sword also. *Hood is an idiot, he thought.* Forrest asked, "You mean to tell me that General Hood left a brigade behind from his best division to guard supplies?"

Cleburne said nothing, only nodded. Forrest was shaking his head. Both men held their swords at their sides as the line approached the top of the hill.

The division marched on over the hill, past the Thompson house on their left, and down into another valley. The Thompson home was called "Oaklawn" and was a magnificent structure. There were women on the front portico watching the sight of three thousand men marching into battle. Cleburne could now see the small brigade of dismounted cavalry for the first time. They were moving up to join his division. It was obvious they belonged to Forrest, because they marched like veteran infantry.

Govan noticed the two generals riding side by side and moved over to join them. He had a funny thought as he watched the two of them riding behind his brigade. For the first time in the entire war, the two best generals in this army were riding together into battle. He almost smiled at the thought.

As the line started up another hill, Govan was impressed how the division looked today. They looked unstoppable as they moved forward. It made him think of a giant wave about to crash against a sand castle.

Soon, they were over the hill and could see the pike ahead just a few hundred yards. There was nothing there to stop them. Forrest's brigade was hanging back a little. Suddenly, there was a ripple of rifle fire and then a cannon shot from the far right. Everyone instinctively looked that way.

There was a small line of timber on the right flank and the fire had come from there. The fire had crashed into the right flank of Lowrey's brigade. Cleburne did a few quick calculations in his head. Hood had directed him to form his brigades in echelon to sweep down the pike to his left. This flank fire coming from his right created an entirely new problem. It would take a good deal of work to shift to the right now and face this enemy that wasn't even supposed to be here. There was gonna be no easy way to shift Granbury over there, so he turned to Govan and yelled, "Start moving your brigade over there to help Lowrey."

Govan saluted and rode forward to his men. Cleburne turned his horse and began to move toward his right flank. Forrest turned and moved to his brigade of dismounted cavalry.

When Cleburne got to the right, he could see Lowrey was already doing all he could to meet this new threat. He could sympathize with a man like Lowrey. The man had married at twenty-four totally illiterate, but his wife had taught him to read and write, and then he had become a Baptist preacher. Cleburne respected the man.

Lowrey was in the process of wheeling his brigade to meet the threat, when Cleburne rode up. Men were falling from the fire every second now. They could hear the Union men cheering and taunting from the tree line ahead. Lowrey saw Cleburne and said, "I think they mean to charge us."

Cleburne's normally dull eyes were flashing now. He quickly scanned the Union position. He raised his sword in the air and brought it down quickly in a striking motion and said, "I'll charge them!"

Lowrey nodded, eyeing Cleburne through his piercing eyes. Cleburne said, "I'll bring Govan up in support before we do."

Cleburne jerked the reins on his horse so hard, the animal reared a little and galloped back toward Govan's brigade. Lowrey turned back and continued realigning his men. He had just got his men in position, when Govan's brigade came marching up. Cleburne was with them and rode over to Lowrey.

"It's our turn now," Cleburne said and nodded for Lowrey to move out. The Federal troops had stopped cheering now. They knew what was coming. Cleburne's divisions carried the distinctive blue battle flags and were known to be the hardest hitting division in this army.

Cleburne could almost feel them steeling themselves for the blow across the way. He loved the feeling of being feared by his enemy. Now it was time to make them run. The two brigades surged forward. It was obvious that Lowrey's brigade was gonna flank the Federals on their right. As they closed with the Union line, Cleburne watched Lowrey's men pour around the exposed right flank and begin to unravel the line. It was moments like these that Cleburne loved the most. He hadn't even had to give an order for the men to know to attack the flank of the enemy position. That was the kind of men he commanded.

He could feel the Union brigade beginning to buckle under the pressure. He saw their line unraveling, coming apart at the seams. It wouldn't last much longer. It all happened very quickly. The Union line was there one moment and running the next. Cleburne smiled, but there was no time to stop and enjoy his little victory. He wanted to finish it. He wouldn't stop until he had destroyed their will to fight. If he had anything to do with it, Hood would capture Schofield's army here.

The Federal troops were panicked and growing confused. Cleburne could see Lowrey ahead cheering his men on as they fired into the confused mass of Federals. The men that could were running hard to get back to Spring Hill behind them. Cleburne spurred forward among his charging and firing men. He could see the enemy troops racing across a farm lane toward a high rail fence. It was perfect. He yelled again, "Charge 'em!"

There was a gap in the fence, and all the Union troops were racing for this one gap. Cleburne's men concentrated their fire toward this one large mass of men. He could hear the yells of men being trampled to death in the panicked flight. *What a sad way to die, he thought. You're fighting in a battle and a bullet doesn't even get you, but you get trampled to death by your own men in a retreat*. He could see the smarter men crossing through the fence away from this panicked mob and avoiding this death trap.

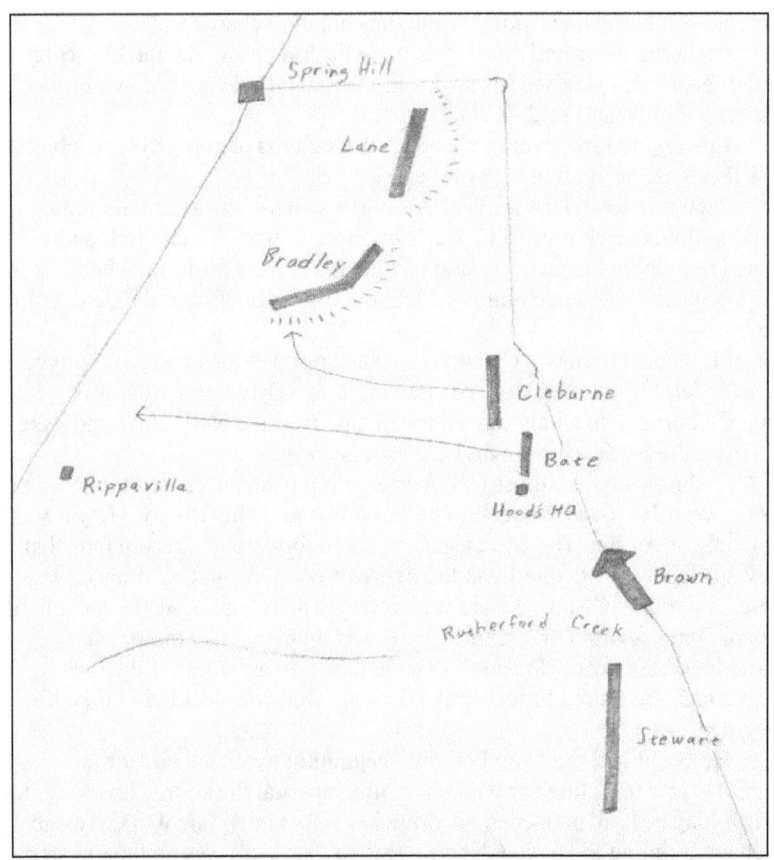

Hood has sent Cleburne and Bate to secure the Columbia Pike. Cleburne finds Federal infantry on his flank and is forced to turn and deal with this unexpected threat.

He saw an officer trying to force his men to stand firm. He grabbed an unarmed man by the belt and tried to spin him into line. Cleburne could hear the man yell above the roar of the guns. The man yelled, "Let me go! For God's sake, I'm just a chaplain!" The officer turned him loose, and Cleburne watched the poor man race for the rear.

The Confederate line quickly changed direction on its own. He couldn't help but be amazed at moments like these. His division seemed to act like one giant animal with a mind of its own. There was no controlling an animal like this. You just pointed it in the right direction and watched it work.

80

Once the flank had collapsed, the entire battle was over. He could hear his soldiers cursing the fleeing enemy troops and calling on them to surrender. They called them cowards and yellow dogs.

Men were too panicked to listen. The Confederates out beyond their flank were shooting them as they raced past. Some were so close; the Confederate rifles almost touched them as they ran by. The fire left powder burns on their bodies when they fell.

Cleburne heard a man cry out. He looked and saw a Union soldier drop his gun and begin to stagger toward Spring Hill. The man had a hole through his shoulder and blood was pouring down his arm. He could see light all the way through the man's shoulder. There was no time to feel bad about what was happening. He had to press his advantage and finish this thing.

He saw a Union soldier covered in blood holding a Union battle flag over his head. The man was surrounded by Confederate soldiers, some with rifles raised. They were calling on the man to surrender, but he refused. The man staggered and fell to the ground, and several of the Southern soldiers moved forward and tried to pull the flag from his hands. The man refused to give it up. Cleburne spurred his horse that way. He saw the man stagger to his feet and wave the flag above his head. He yelled, "You may shoot me if you want, but I'll not part with this flag as long as I draw a breath."

Several Confederate soldiers raised their rifles and prepared to fire. At that moment, Cleburne rode into the crowd of men and said, "Lower your rifles. This man is too brave to be killed this way. Now move aside and let him take his flag from the field."

The men parted slowly and watched the wounded man limp past toward Spring Hill.

The Federals were running, and he intended to keep it that way. He quickly decided to keep Lowrey and Govan after the retreating enemy. While they were doing that, he would shift Granbury's brigade over to cover the pike as Hood had ordered.

Cleburne noticed Lieutenant Mangum at his side. He said, "Mangum, go to the left and find Granbury. Tell him to form his brigade on that fence to his left facing the Columbia Pike. Tell him to prepare to move forward and take the pike when I give the order. In the meantime, I'm going to see Govan about finishing this business in our front."

Mangum saluted and was about to spur his horse, when a shell exploded overhead. The sound was deafening. When his head cleared, he could see Cleburne's horse rearing wildly. When the animal settled down, he noticed Cleburne slumping in the saddle. The horse had begun to squat a little. He saw blood pouring down the horse's flanks. Mangum's ears were ringing. He yelled, "Are you hurt, Pat?"

"No!" Cleburne yelled back. His blood was up, and he was always intense in battle. "Now go on, Mangum, and tell Granbury what I told you."

As Mangum spurred away, Cleburne didn't have time to check on his favorite horse. He spurred the wounded animal toward Govan's position.

81

Across the way, he could see the Union troops trying to reform across the field. It was obvious to Cleburne that they were through fighting and just wanted the Confederates to leave them alone. He wasn't about to allow that to happen.

As soon as he had Govan and Lowrey moving again, a new line of artillery opened up from the north. There were too many of them for Cleburne's two brigades. He had no choice now, but to bring Granbury up and help eliminate this new threat. He rode back over to Granbury and had him bring his brigade up beside Govan and Lowrey.

Cleburne rode forward with Granbury. He liked the tall lanky Texan. Like Cleburne, the man was a lawyer. His beloved wife, Fannie, had died of ovarian cancer two years before the war began. Cleburne watched Granbury's wild hair waving as he rode from one end of his line to the other.

Granbury's left flank was just a few hundred yards from the pike. Cleburne looked to the west and watched the sun growing low in the sky. It would soon be dark, but what could he do? He could call off his attack and take the pike as Hood had ordered, or he could press his advantage here and take Spring Hill. If he turned and took the pike, he would leave an enemy force in his rear. That would be a dangerous proposition. They could reform and strike about the same time Schofield's army arrives from Columbia. That would mean he would be the one caught in the trap. He spun around and looked to the rear. He wondered where Bate and Brown's divisions were. He quickly decided that he must finish off this threat in his front and rode to Lowrey's position.

He ordered Lowrey and Govan to move forward through a cornfield in their front and take Spring Hill. As soon as they moved, more Federal artillery opened fire from his front. Through the fading light, he could make out a long line of artillery just on the edge of town. Men were beginning to fall in Lowrey and Govan's brigades. As he rode along with his men, he noticed blood on the brown leaves that covered the ground. Still the men pressed forward. Cleburne was on the verge of victory here. He could feel it. He could sense the defeat in the Union ranks. His division swept on across the field like an irresistible wave.

It was growing dark and difficult to see now. A horseman came galloping up and asked, "Where can I find General Cleburne?"

Several of Cleburne's aides said, "Over here."

The man rode up and looked at the mounted group. Cleburne said, "I'm Cleburne."

The man saluted quickly and said, "General Cheatham sent me here to tell you to hold up your attack until further notice."

"What do you mean?" Cleburne was dumbfounded.

"Not sure, sir," the man replied. "I think the plans have changed."

"Changed," Cleburne said, more to himself than anyone else. He couldn't see the man in the growing darkness. It felt as if he were talking to a shadow. "Where is General Cheatham?"

"I'm not sure where he is, sir," the man replied. "I think he's bringing Brown's division up now."

Cleburne shook his head. He just couldn't believe what he was hearing. He couldn't very well leave his division here in the open under that vicious artillery fire. He had no choice but to order his men to fall back behind the last rise they had come over. He gave the orders and watched his men fall back.

As he got his men back in position below the rise, he dismounted, took a lantern, and began to inspect his wounded horse. The poor beast had three gashes in his back just behind Cleburne's saddle. He turned to tell Lieutenant Mangum to take the horse to the rear and bring up another, when he saw General Chalmers approaching.

Cleburne extended his hand. Chalmers took his hand and shook it. Chalmers asked, "What does it look like out there?"

Cleburne had always liked Chalmers, though the man was the aristocratic type. He thought he was a little better than most men in this army. That's one of the reasons he and Forrest disagreed so much. Chalmers resented having to serve under a lowly slave trader. Cleburne said, "This beats all I've ever seen, Chalmers. The enemy is badly paralyzed. My men are following right on their heels. They were running for their lives. I rode to within fifty yards of their position without encountering much danger, and now I've been ordered to stop the attack."

Chalmers was shaking his head. He asked, "By whose order?"

"One of Cheatham's staff officers," Cleburne set the lantern on the ground. "He says Cheatham wants to get Brown up first. I'm sick of seeing us allow a defeated enemy to regroup when all we need to do is hit them one more time to finish it. It's the same old story since Shiloh."

"I know exactly what you're saying," Chalmers replied. His brigade was making the last push at Shiloh when Beauregard had called off the attack. They had lost that battle the next day. Chalmers still blamed Beauregard for that failure.

"I've still got my men in line of battle in case he changes his mind," Cleburne nodded over his shoulder.

Chalmers reached in his coat pocket and pulled out a flask. He offered it to Cleburne. Cleburne shook his head; he didn't drink. Chalmers took a long hard drink from the flask and said, "Good Tennessee bourbon. The people are so glad to see us back here in Tennessee, they've been handing us flasks all up the road. I could open up a tavern with all I've been given."

A horse appeared out of the darkness, and Cleburne watched General Govan dismount. Govan spoke to Chalmers and then turned to Cleburne and said, "What's happening? I could be across the pike in twenty minutes if given the order. We could have already destroyed the enemy and taken Spring Hill if they hadn't stopped us."

Cleburne nodded. "I know it, but what can we do?"

Govan noticed that Cleburne was as frustrated as he was. Chalmers said, "I think I'll ride over and see where Cheatham and Brown are. I'll tell them you're ready to move, Pat."

Cleburne nodded. He began to pace. Govan said, "If left alone, we could have taken the Union wagon train and planted our entire division across the pike."

Cleburne said nothing; he was in deep thought. Suddenly, he turned to Mangum and said, "Let me borrow your horse. I'm gonna ride to the right and find out what's happening myself."

6:30 p.m.

CSA

He sat on his horse in the darkness beside General Brown. They were surrounded by staff officers. Men were moving on line, officers were giving orders in hushed tones. They knew the least noise could cause the Federals to open fire. No one was quite sure how close they were to the enemy line.

Cheatham tried to gauge Brown's state of mind in the darkness. Something was obviously wrong with the man. He just wasn't acting right. The two, both Tennesseans, had been friends a long time.

Cheatham saw a lone horseman appear out of the dark to his left. The man was working his way through the deploying men of Brown's division. When he got to where all the mounted men were, he asked, "Anybody here know where I can find General Cheatham?"

Cheatham instantly recognized the voice of Patrick Cleburne. He replied, "You've found him, Pat."

"My men are reformed and ready to go back in," Cleburne said dryly. It was obvious he was aggravated for being halted. He added, "I'm awaiting orders."

Cheatham said, "As soon as Brown gets his division on line, he will go in first. When you hear him firing, you go in on his left. If Bate gets over here in time, he'll go in on your left. I realize I've delayed your attack, Pat, but it'll be worth the wait. We'll have more hitting power if we all go in together."

"Where's Brown?" Cleburne asked.

"He's right here," Cheatham motioned toward the man next to him, but Cleburne couldn't see him in the darkness. Brown said nothing.

"Very well," Cleburne said. "I'll return to my division and wait for the signal."

"All right, Pat," Cheatham smiled. He could always count on Patrick Cleburne to have his men in position and ready. He added, "It won't be long now."

Cleburne turned his horse and moved away. Cheatham turned to Brown and said, "When your men are formed, move straight ahead. The enemy may not be a hundred yards in front of you. Hit the bastards hard. General

Hood wants Spring Hill before we bivouac tonight."

Brown said nothing. Cheatham noticed the dark shadow rocking forward in the saddle. He asked, "Are you alright, John?"

"Yeah, hit 'em hard." Brown shook his head, coughed and then asked, "You were saying?"

"Forrest's cavalry is protecting your right flank. Cleburne's on your left." Cheatham squinted into the darkness trying to see what Brown's problem was. "The responsibility for the attack is yours. Everybody else will move when they hear your attack. I'm hoping the bastards will shift to meet you, and then Cleburne can rip into their damned flank."

Brown gave a little chuckle. He said, "Sounds good."

Cheatham said, "I'm gonna go find Bate and try to get his division into position to go in on Cleburne's left. Don't wait for him though. Go on and attack as soon as your men are ready."

"I will, Frank," Brown said.

Cheatham turned his horse toward the left. His staff followed behind. Major Jo Vaulx rode beside Cheatham.

Cheatham said, "Jo, we've got to get this show on the road. I've got something important to attend to."

"What's that, sir?" Vaulx asked.

"Do you know Jesse Peters?" Cheatham asked.

"No, sir," Vaulx replied, but he knew of Cheatham's reputation with women. Everyone in the army knew of Cheatham's reputation of being a heavy curser, hard drinker, and notorious womanizer.

"She's very young and very beautiful," Cheatham said. He was talking more to himself than to Vaulx. His voice betrayed his excitement. The more he talked about her, the more he wanted to go and see her. "I do enjoy the company of young beautiful women. It makes me feel young again. It's good to be back in Tennessee among friends, Jo. There are women and celebrations everywhere, not to mention good old Tennessee whiskey."

Vaulx couldn't help but wonder what a beautiful young lady would want with such a rough-looking man as Cheatham. Besides the lines in his face from hard drinking, he was short and heavyset. He looked nothing like the striking Bedford Forrest or the stalwart Pat Cleburne. Besides his looks, he was a profane man, subject to say anything, regardless of who's present. Vaulx asked, "Is she the one…" he paused a moment not sure how to word the question.

Cheatham knew what Vaulx was asking. He said, "Yeah, her husband shot General Van Dorn last year."

"Right," Vaulx said. He was a little nervous about the direction this conversation seemed to be heading. It was a bit embarrassing to think about his commander fornicating with a married woman. In this day, in the south, this type of thing was unheard of. Vaulx asked, "Are you not worried about Mister Peters?"

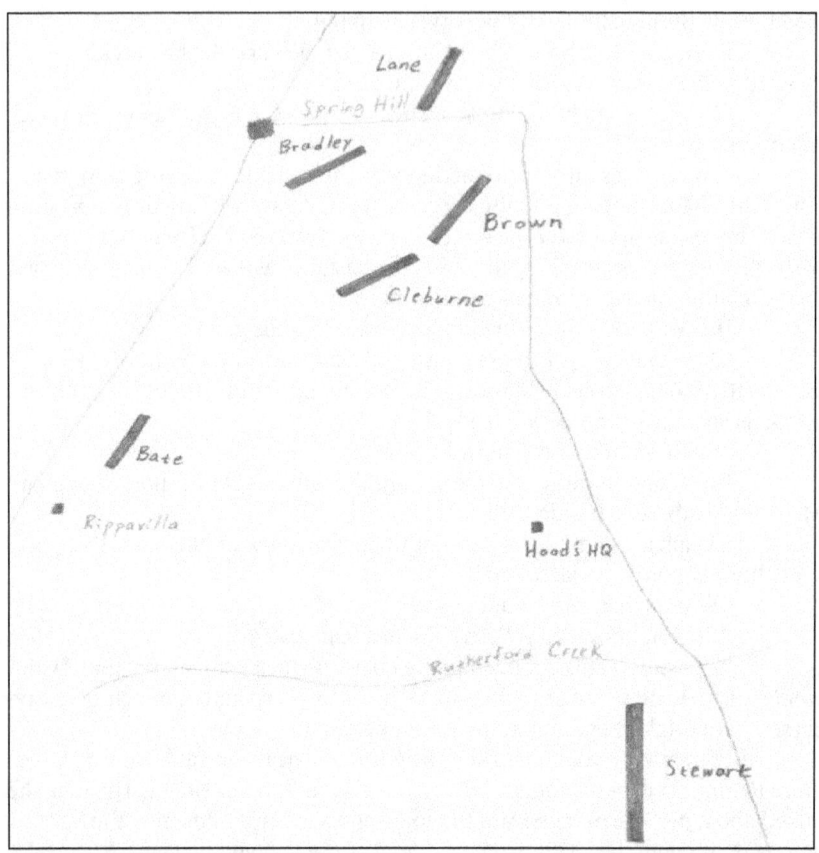

The situation at sunset. Cleburne and Brown's divisions face Federal troops at Spring Hill. Bate is within a hundred yards of securing the pike. Stewart continues to await Hood's order to strike Schofield's flank.

Cheatham laughed out loud and said, "It's Doctor Peters, and no, I'm not worried about him. The man's a coward. The most yellow coward there is. He ran off to Nashville to hide behind the Union lines when he heard we were coming. Did you know that he slipped around behind Van Dorn and shot him in the back of the head while he was working at his desk?"

"They're still married?" Vaulx sounded amazed.

"Yeah," Cheatham replied, "but don't think badly of her because of what we'll do tonight, Jo. The poor woman is married to a coward. I'm sure she just wants to know how it feels to be held by a real man every now and then."

Vaulx decided to change the subject. He said, "We should be getting near Bate's position. Don't want to ride into some nervous pickets."

"Why don't we hear firing?" Cheatham asked.

"Sir?" Vaulx asked. He didn't know what Cheatham was talking about.

Cheatham said, "We should have heard Brown's guns by now."

They rode on a little farther without talking. Cheatham was listening for Brown's attack to begin. Finally, he stopped. He turned to the staff officer riding directly behind him. It was too dark to see who the man was, so Cheatham asked, "Who are you?"

"Lieutenant Abraham Schell, sir," the man replied.

"Schell, I want you to ride on and find General Bate," Cheatham cleared his throat and spat. "Tell him to halt wherever he is and move to the right. I want him to link up with Cleburne's left and prepare to attack."

"Yes, sir," Schell replied and rode on past.

Cheatham turned back to Vaulx and said, "Let's go see what the problem is with Brown."

As they began riding back, Cheatham called Vaulx up near him and spoke in a low whisper. "I think Brown's got a problem."

Vaulx was surprised. He leaned closer so he could hear Cheatham whispering. He asked, "What kind of a problem?"

"Well," Cheatham made sure he whispered so none of the other staff officers could hear him. "All those flasks being passed up today, I'm afraid he may have imbibed too freely. I'm almost afraid to send him into battle in that state. You remember Murfreesboro don't you?"

"Yes, sir," Vaulx replied. He remembered Murfreesboro alright. How could he forget? Cheatham had been so intoxicated; he could barely climb into the saddle. He'd been embarrassed publicly by Bragg after the battle. He had narrowly avoided a court-martial.

Cheatham said, "Brown is too good a friend for me to allow what happened to me at Murfreesboro to happen to him. Hell, it's too damned dark to attack now anyway. That's how accidents happen. Fighting at night, you don't know who in hell you're shooting at half the time."

Cheatham thought to himself. He'd told Jesse he would be there by seven, now everything was going amiss here.

Up ahead, they met a horseman moving in their direction. The man said, "I'm looking for General Cheatham."

"Damn, ain't ever body," Cheatham said. "What can I do for you?"

"I'm Major Joseph Cummings of General Hood's staff," the man said. "Hood sent me to instruct you to attack at once."

Cheatham knew Major Cummings. He asked, "Where's Hood?"

"He's made his headquarters at the Thompson House," Cummings replied.

"Very well," Cheatham said. He rode on past Cummings toward Brown's position. He rode on a few hundred yards, and then suddenly spun his horse toward the rear. *He thought, Brown's drunk, Bate's out of place, and we don't know what in hell we're facing in Spring Hill. Besides that, it's gotten so dark; I can't see my hand in front of my face.* Cheatham said, "Jo, lets ride back to see General Hood. See if we can't get this movement called off until tomorrow when we can see what the hell we're shooting at."

As they rode along, Cheatham thought about Jesse Peters. If he was gonna get to see her tonight, he needed to get a move on. There wasn't time enough for a battle and a little private party with her.

6:45 p.m.

CSA

Ever since he'd gotten his division across Rutherford Creek, the movement had been nothing but confusion. He was growing more frustrated at each passing moment. He didn't like this maneuvering around in the dark. It was dangerous. Not only was he liable to run into hidden enemy troops, but just as liable to run into friendly troops with itchy trigger fingers.

The war hadn't been kind to William Bate. He was severely wounded at Shiloh. During the same charge, his brother was killed at his side. He'd spent a long year recovering, almost losing his leg in the process. That had been over two years ago, and he still walked with a limp. After he recovered, he'd been wounded twice more. He'd just gotten back a couple months ago. If not for all the wounds, he may have been a lieutenant general by now.

His division was depleted badly. He'd moved toward the pike the way Hood had told him. Henry Jackson and Thomas Smith's brigades were in front, while the tiny brigade of Robert Bullock's Florida troops was behind in reserve. He hated trudging around in the dark with the smallest division in the army.

The confusion had started when he'd moved forward a mile from where Hood had him form his division. He had fully expected to come up on Cleburne's left flank there. Instead of finding the left flank of Cleburne's division, he'd found himself far south of what sounded like a battle raging. The farther he marched, the more it sounded as though it was occurring in his right rear. It soon became painfully clear that Cleburne was engaged north of him with a heavy force. As the battle became a roar, he decided to find a guide to help him locate the pike and Cleburne's flank.

In the process of getting into position, the battle to the north had soon died away as the sun set in his face. Bate was unsure what was happening, but Hood had made it clear that he should occupy that pike, so he pressed forward. It was getting dark fast. After securing the pike, he would worry about linking up with Cleburne. He was already having difficulty just seeing a hundred yards in front of him.

As they moved forward, the pike came into view. There were a few enemy pickets standing there, but nothing strong enough to stop him. His line opened fire on these few men and watched them scatter. He only saw three of them get hit and crumple onto the road. Just as he was about to give the order to move forward and take the pike, more enemy troops appeared from the direction of Columbia moving his way.

According to Hood's orders, these were the troops he was supposed to attack. The problem was the fact that he was supposed to attack in conjunction with Cleburne's division. Cleburne was somewhere to the north fighting with God knows who. Bate wasn't sure what he should do.

He rode to the left of his line to see if he could tell how many Union troops were moving up. Several of his staff officers trailed behind. Through the growing darkness, he could make out 'Rippavilla,' the home of Nathaniel Cheairs. Just in front of his home was the Columbia Pike. He could see lights illuminating the windows in the giant house. It appeared someone was still home there. He wondered if they knew what was playing out just outside their house.

Some of his pickets were beginning to open fire at long range against the Federals down south on the pike. For the first time in a while, Bate could feel success. Deep down, he knew Hood had been right this time. He could feel it in his bones. The war had appeared to be lost when they marched away from Sherman in Georgia. He began to think that Hood may be smarter than everyone in this army had given him credit for.

I may not have but twenty-one hundred men, he thought, but I'm about to get my division across that pike. The Union army will be trapped, and they'll be forced to surrender in the morning.

Bate swung his horse back toward the center of his line. With one word, one nod of his head, he would block that pike and seal the fate of an entire army. The thought made him feel powerful. When he had gotten back to the center of his division, he prepared to give that order. Instead, he found a staff officer searching for him. The man identified himself in the darkness.

"General Bate," he said, "I'm Lieutenant Abraham Schell."

Bate knew who Schell was. The man served on the staff of General Cheatham. Bate asked, "What can I do for you?"

The Union infantry from the south began to return fire. Bullets whistled by overhead. Bate watched Schell's silhouette flinch in the darkness.

Schell said, "Sir, I have a message from General Cheatham. He wants you to halt your movement and find General Cleburne's left flank."

Bate couldn't believe what he was hearing. He asked, "General Hood gave me direct orders to take the pike. Does General Cheatham mean to countermand those orders?"

"All I know is what I've just told you, sir," Schell replied.

Bate shook his head. This was simply incomprehensible. How could he just pass up this beautiful opportunity to cut off the escape route of Schofield's entire army? Bate turned and spoke into the darkness behind him, "Major Pirtle."

"Sir," a staff officer spoke up.

89

"Go find General Cheatham at once," Bate scratched at his thick black beard. "I want confirmation of this order. Tell him if he will allow me to occupy the pike, I will be able to hold off all of Schofield's army in the darkness with only my division. Tell him I have the Federal army stalled on the pike to the south."

The man turned his horse and started for the rear. Bate sat still for a long moment trying to figure what he should do. The night had grown as dark as pitch and it was a good mile to Cleburne's left flank.

Finally, he decided there was nothing left for him to do, but to obey Cheatham's order. He slowly began to move his men to the right and away from the pike.

7:00 p.m.

CSA

After Cheatham had left, he had finished forming his troops for the attack. His staff officers had done most of the work. Brown was having trouble just staying in the saddle. He hadn't realized he'd had that much to drink today. It was rare for him to drink anyway.

Brown had already sent out his skirmishers and sharpshooters. He could hear the occasional pop of a rifle in his front. He rode forward and was just about to give the order to advance, when a man on horseback rode up at high speed. The man pulled so hard on the reins that his horse squatted low to the ground. One of Brown's staff officers said, "Don't ride in here like that, you could hurt someone."

"I have important information for General Brown," the man said.

Brown immediately recognized the voice. It was General Otho Strahl, one of his best fighters. His brigade was on the extreme right of Brown's line. He asked, "What's the problem, Strahl?"

"If I advance, I'll be outflanked. There are Union troops on a wooded knoll to my right. If I advance, I'll get fired on in front and rear," Strahl said excitedly.

"Nonsense," Brown replied. He felt light-headed from the whiskey. He fought off a sudden urge to burst out laughing. He said, "Forrest's cavalry is protecting our flank."

"That's what I thought," Strahl said. He was almost breathless from the excitement. "They're gone now, General. It's the damnedest thing I've ever seen. They just up and left the field. What do you want me to do?"

"Let's go look again," Brown said as he nudged his horse forward. "I need to see these Yankees before I call off the attack I've been ordered to make."

90

Brigadier General Otho French Strahl.
Born in Ohio, he commanded a brigade of
Tennessee infantry.

They rode toward the right flank. Brown was growing uneasy about this night attack. It had still been light enough to see when Cheatham had ordered it, but it was growing so dark, he was having trouble seeing his hand in front of his face. The entire division wasn't all on line yet. General Gist was still somewhere in the rear with his South Carolinians.

Once they had ridden out beyond the right flank, Strahl dismounted and pulled out a pair of field glasses. He studied the wooded knoll the best he could in the darkness. He pointed toward the trees ahead.

"There are men in there, all right," Strahl said.

Brown strained to see in the trees, but it was too dark. He asked, "Who are they?"

"No idea," Strahl replied raising the field glasses to his eyes again. "They're not ours, that's for sure."

Brown thought about getting off his horse to see for himself, but thought better of it. As intoxicated as he was, he was afraid he may not be able to climb back on. That would be embarrassing.

He looked down at Strahl and asked, "How many?"

"I haven't seen many," Strahl lowered the glasses and turned toward Brown, "but the thing is, where you find a few, there are always more close behind."

Brown shook his head. He asked no one in particular, "Where in the hell is Forrest?"

"His cavalry was just to our right a few moments ago." Strahl took his kepi off and rubbed his head. "They just up and marched for the rear. They didn't say a word, just left."

Brown rubbed his eyes. He wished he could think clearly just now. He said, "Doesn't make sense."

91

He thought about Cheatham's orders. "The responsibility for the attack rests with you," he had said. Things had changed drastically since Cheatham had left. The cavalry support had just up and abandoned the field just as he was about to give the order.

After a long pause, Brown said, "If we go in now, we will meet with inevitable disaster. I must suspend the attack until I can confer with Cheatham. Hold your men in line of battle until I get back."

Strahl nodded. Brown turned his horse and started back to the center of his division. He would have to send a staff officer to find Cheatham.

As he got back near the center of his line, he met General Gist bringing his brigade onto the field.

Gist asked, "Where do you want me, Sir?"

"We've got a problem," Brown said. His words were slurred a little. "My cavalry support left the field. Take your brigade to the extreme right and extend my line. There are Federal troops beyond our right."

"I should have my men on line and ready to move in half an hour," Gist said.

Brown watched Gist and his men begin moving toward the right. He decided to dismount before he fell off the damned horse and broke his neck.

He was standing beside the horse, leaning heavily against the saddle, when he noticed how quiet his men were. They were all straining their ears trying to hear what was in their front. Despite the fact the Confederates had almost seven thousand men on the field; there was no way of knowing what they were up against. General Brown wasn't taking responsibility of possibly walking into a trap without confirmation from higher authority.

Brown heard the sound of horse's hooves behind him. He turned unsteadily and strained his eyes to see into the darkness. The outline of a man leading a horse was moving toward him.

"Brown, is that you?" the man leading the horse asked.

"Yeah," Brown replied. He could see there were two men with horses there now. "Who the hell are you?"

"General Chalmers," the man replied. He held something out toward Brown in his hand. "Care for a drink, General?"

Brown knew he'd already had too much to drink. "No thank you. Do you know where the cavalry on my right went?"

"Forrest had them all pulled back for the night," Chalmers replied.

"Why?" Brown asked. "I've been ordered to attack, and you were supposed to protect my flank."

"Couldn't be helped," Chalmers sounded awfully calm. *Of course he's calm, Brown thought, he doesn't have the responsibility to attack without support like I do.*

Chalmers said, "We were out of ammunition. We wouldn't have been much help to you."

"Damn," Brown said.

"Why haven't you attacked yet?" Chalmers asked.

"The situation has changed now," Brown replied. "I'm waiting for Cheatham to issue new orders."

Chalmers couldn't believe what he was hearing. His voice had a hint of frustration in it. He said, "General, when I was at Shiloh in the position you're now in, I attacked without orders."

"I have no orders," Brown said again, more to himself than to Chalmers.

Chalmers let out a loud sigh. He climbed on his horse and turned in the saddle. "Come on, James. Let's go turn in for the night. This fiasco is none of our business."

Brown tugged on the reins of his horse and slowly began to lead him toward the rear. He told one of his staff officers to start a fire a safe distance from the enemy lines. Once the fire was lit, he had them remove his saddle and lay it on the ground. He lay next to the fire using the saddle as a pillow. The whiskey was making him feel sick now.

Captain H.M. Neely and Major John Ingram of General Carter's staff soon appeared out of the darkness. Neely said, "General Brown, are you all right?"

"I'm not feeling well at the moment, gentlemen," Brown replied. "What can I do for ya'll?"

"We've just left General Carter," Neely said. Carter was still back with the brigade sitting under a tree awaiting orders like everyone else in Brown's division. Neely said, "He's wondering what the delay is."

Brown was growing tired of everyone pressing him to do something. The whiskey had made him over-cautious. He'd lost his nerve. All the man wanted to do was find a quiet spot to rest. His voice betrayed his agitation. He said, "I don't know, I have no orders."

Ingram staggered forward and for the first time, Brown noticed the flask in his hand. *Is everybody in the army drunk tonight? he wondered.*

Neely didn't appear to have been drinking. He was speaking politely, as he always did. He said, "General Brown, I mean no offense, but if you would start the attack without orders, you can count on getting a feather in your hat. It'll be short easy work to destroy Schofield's army. He's all strung out between here and Columbia."

Brown began to grow more aggravated. It was one thing to be pushed to do something you didn't want to do by your fellow generals. It was another thing entirely to be pushed by one of your own brigadier's staff officers. Brown snapped, "No, I'll wait for orders."

At that, Major Ingram staggered forward to the edge of the fire. His eyes were glazed over. There was no doubt in Brown's mind that the man was drunk. Ingram yelled, "General, if you'll loan me your escort company, I'll drive that little regiment of Yankees off by myself!"

Brown wasn't in the mood for this. He snapped back, "Major Ingram, you can consider yourself under arrest for insubordination."

Ingram started to say something else, but before he could, Captain Neely grabbed his arm and pulled him back into the darkness.

A few minutes after they had left, Generals Strahl and Gist, along with one of Gist's regimental commanders, Colonel Capers, arrived. Gist was wearing a new dark gray uniform. He had a small goatee below his chin; otherwise, he was clean shaven. Strahl looked like a small man beside the heavyset Gist.

Gist said, "General Brown, my brigade is ready. All we need are orders."

"I'm awaiting word from Cheatham," Brown said. He let out a long sigh. The conversation about advancing was beginning to get old.

"All three of us have been over on the right listening," Strahl said. "The Union troops are tearing down houses and barns and building breastworks. If we don't attack tonight, we'll face an entrenched foe in the morning."

"Besides that, they're getting away," Gist added. "We can hear wagons and horses moving up the pike toward Nashville."

Brown lay on the ground and acted as though he was sleeping.

Strahl said, "Colonel Capers here was so aggravated at not being allowed to attack that he emptied his revolver toward the enemy lines."

Brown opened his eyes and raised his head and asked, "Did he kill any?"

Capers's face was already red. He turned to Strahl and said, "This is extremely disappointing. Everyone in this division is ready to attack, except the commander. I don't think I've ever seen anything like it."

Brown closed his eyes and lay back on the saddle. He hoped if he kept his eyes closed long enough the three men would leave.

Gist said, "Sir, if we don't move now, I'm afraid we're losing the greatest chance of the entire war."

Brown said nothing. He lay still a few more minutes. His mind was made up. There was no way they were going to force this responsibility on him. *Hell, if things go bad, it'll be my ass. One of those assholes will then be given command of my division.* After a few moments, he opened his eyes and discovered, to his relief, they were indeed gone.

As Gist, Strahl, and Capers made their way back toward their commands, Capers shook his head. He said, "Let me get this straight. He wouldn't attack because Forrest left his flank. Then he put Gist over there where Forrest had been. Now what reason is he giving exactly for not attacking?"

"I'm not sure. I've never quite seen him act this way," Strahl said.

Gist kept walking and said nothing. This wasn't the first time this army had been mismanaged when the victory was practically won. That's the reason he had sent a letter to President Davis for a transfer. It was too disheartening to be a part of an army that can never win because of poor commanders. He'd built a solid reputation as a commander. He'd temporarily commanded a division at Chickamauga and Chattanooga and fought well. When a vacancy finally occurred for a division commander, William Bate of Tennessee had been chosen. He was passed over for the command position because he was from South Carolina, not Tennessee.

7:15 p.m.

CSA

They had helped him dismount near the pond just north of Oaklawn. The Thompsons had been extremely happy to give Hood the use of their home. Hood sat on a log Mister Thompson had placed by the pond to sit on while he fished. Several orderlies had built him a fire. The evening was growing chilly and a light drizzle had begun to fall.

It had been a long, hard day, but it wasn't quite over yet. The roads were in terrible shape, and just before getting to Oaklawn, Hood's horse had stumbled. If he hadn't been strapped into the saddle, he would have taken a nasty spill. He had hung from the horse at an awkward angle until a staff officer had helped him back up. It was an embarrassing moment for the general.

Before it had grown dark, he had been able to survey the area. The home Thompson owned had been built in 1835. Like the other homes in the south, it was beautiful. Hood could see cattle on the rolling hills, and small tracts of forest dotted the land.

Hood had been sending one staff officer after another to Cheatham reminding him to be sure to place his corps across the Columbia Pike. The staff officers had all returned with word that Cheatham would have the pike soon.

Then it had gotten dark. Hood was growing uneasy. He still didn't have word from Cheatham regarding the pike. He'd sent couriers to scour the field to find Cheatham and learn what he had accomplished. They'd all returned with the same story—Cheatham was nowhere to be found.

Hood had finally asked Governor Harris to go find Cheatham. Harris hadn't gone far, when he met Cheatham coming to see Hood. When they returned, they could see Hood was sitting on the log staring into the fire. His expression betrayed the fact that he was upset. Governor Harris, General Cheatham, and Major Vault, of Cheatham's staff, all dismounted.

Hood looked up and saw Cheatham. He suddenly felt helpless. If he was his old self, he could have ridden forward and delivered the orders without having to go through Cheatham. He was also exhausted. He needed rest.

Cheatham walked up, saluted, and said, "General Hood."

Hood's eyes flashed. He asked, "General Cheatham, why in God's name have you not moved forward and occupied the pike?"

95

Cheatham looked a little surprised. He said, "Have you not heard about my flank?"

Hood said nothing. He continued staring at Cheatham out of angry eyes, waiting.

Cheatham could feel a small rage building inside of him. He wasn't about to take the blame for this mess. "Forrest was protecting my right flank, but he just up and left the field. If Brown goes in, his line will be raked by those damned Yankees on his right."

"I ordered Bate to take the pike," Hood said. "Is he in possession of it?"

"No, sir," Cheatham shook his head. "I moved him up to cover Cleburne's left flank. There are just too many damned Yankees here for me to handle with my corps alone."

Hood shook his head. He brought his fist down hard on the log. "How exactly is your division aligned in relation to the pike?"

Cheatham removed a glove, slapped it against his thigh, reached up and rubbed his forehead. "Best as I can tell in the dark, we're out east of town, running sort of perpendicular with the pike. Brown is up north with his right flank exposed, Cleburne is in the middle, Bate down south covering his left."

"So I take it, by what you're telling me," Hood paused a moment, thinking. "If I bring Stewart's Corps across Rutherford Creek and place him on Brown's right, his line will extend across the pike just north of town?"

Cheatham nodded and said, "I think so, yes."

"I've got reports they are escaping now," Hood hadn't given up on the idea of stopping them with Cheatham's Corps while Stewart came up. "I still think it would be best if you hit them now with what you've got."

Cheatham had already started shaking his head before Hood could finish the sentence. "It's awfully dangerous to attack at night, General. The last time I was involved in a night assault, it was a fiasco, with men firing into their fellow troops. We killed more of our men than we did those of the enemy. It's just not a smart move."

Hood shook his head. "If you would have thrown a division across the pike, we wouldn't even be having this conversation."

"General Hood," Cheatham was tiring of the argument. He didn't see any point in arguing. At the moment, Bate was out of place and Brown was drunk; it would be better to wait. Brown was a good man, a good friend, and Cheatham planned on going to his grave without telling anyone of his drunkenness this afternoon. He continued, "The Union line was just too long for my corps. I did all I could. If you will just place Stewart on my right, we can capture their entire army in the morning without a fight."

Hood turned to Captain James Hamilton of his staff and said, "Ride to General Stewart and tell him to march on up here and get on Cheatham's right. Tell him it's imperative that he take possession of the Columbia Pike north of town."

96

Cheatham was standing there nodding as Hamilton repeated the orders, mounted his horse, and rode away.

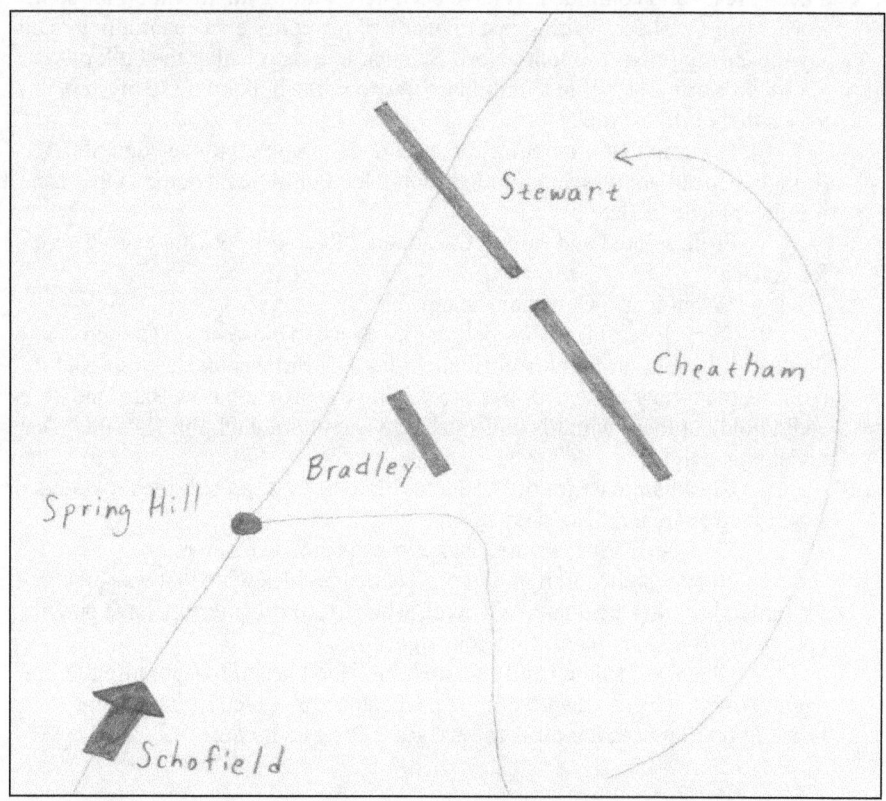

Cheatham reports to Hood that he has failed to reach the pike because of troops on his right flank. Hood asks if he sends Stewart to Cheatham's right will this place the Confederate line across the pike. Cheatham answers that it will. This map shows how things look in Hood's mind.

Hood wasn't through with Cheatham just yet. He said, "It pains me to know that after marching all this way, my army, from privates to generals, are still afraid to attack the enemy."

Cheatham's face was turning red. He asked, "General, are you referring to my command?"

It was an absurd question. Of course Hood was referring to his command. It was the only command on the field at the moment. Hood suddenly unleashed himself on Cheatham. "General Cheatham, you have repeatedly ignored orders from me all afternoon. I've sent everyone on my staff to you telling you how important it is to get possession of that damned road, and yet after a good four hours, you still haven't taken it."

Hood had been operating on very little sleep. He'd been in the saddle all day, and he couldn't seem to get his subordinates to do as ordered. He took a deep breath and continued, "I have been here waiting all afternoon for some word. Hell, I've been waiting just to hear firing, yet there's been nothing. You say the enemy line is too long. Now, Stephen Lee reports that the bulk of Schofield's army is still in Columbia. So who in the hell are these mystery troops that outflank you?"

It was at that moment a horse came galloping up to the edge of the firelight. Cheatham was about to light into Hood until he recognized the man. It was John Pirtle of Bate's staff.

Pirtle saluted and said to Cheatham, "I've been looking everywhere for you, sir."

"What is it?" Cheatham snapped.

"Sir, General Bate has delayed his move to close up on Cleburne's flank until I could discuss his position with you," Pirtle said. He was about to tell Cheatham how close they were to seizing the pike and how Bate said he could hold out there with his undersized division until daylight. He said, "Our division is only..."

Cheatham cut him off. "You tell Bate that he can either obey orders or report here to General Hood under arrest!"

"Yes, sir," Pirtle saluted and climbed back on his horse.

Hood watched him gallop off. He had no idea what that was all about. He turned back to Cheatham. "General, when Stewart comes up, have one of your staff officers help him find your right flank."

Cheatham saluted and said nothing. Hood began to stare into the fire again. After a long, awkward moment, Cheatham mounted his horse and headed north into the darkness toward Jesse Peters's home.

7:30 p.m.

CSA

Old Straight's corps had been ready to cross Rutherford Creek since five, but for some reason, he had been ordered to remain there waiting. Hood hadn't bothered to explain the plan to him. Now his men were crossing the creek behind him in the dark as he rode ahead to see Hood.

Stewart was a little agitated that Hood had waited so long to order his men across. It had been a warm day, but now they were crossing a creek in chilly air and a light drizzle.

As he approached Oaklawn with a few members of his staff, Stewart noticed Hood sitting on a log by a fire. He turned his horse and rode that way.

98

Stewart thought it strange that Colonel Brent was the only other person with Hood.

Stewart climbed from the saddle, looked around, and then asked, "Where is ever body?"

"I've got 'em all at the front trying to get something done, Straight," Hood replied. "That damned Cheatham has repeatedly ignored my orders to attack all afternoon."

Stewart felt like asking Hood why he hadn't rode forward and pressed the attack himself. He was no fool though. Stewart hadn't made Lieutenant General by being insubordinate with his superiors. He had always been a likable man. He had even gotten along with Braxton Bragg. No one else in the army had been able to accomplish that. He didn't know that several of his fellow officers called him a "kiss-ass" behind his back. If Cheatham wasn't doing his job, it was Hood's responsibility to relieve him. Besides that, Hood is on the field, and the attack was his responsibility anyway.

Stewart asked, "Where do you want me, sir?"

Hood turned to Brent and said, "Go up to the house and get the guide."

Brent nodded and moved off. Hood turned back to Stewart and said, "John Gregory is a local boy. He knows the ground here. He's gonna take you to Cheatham's right. Cheatham says that once your corps is on his right, you'll be astride the Columbia Pike, cutting off Schofield's retreat route. He'll be forced to surrender come morning."

Hood took a small twig and began to draw a map in the mud. Stewart walked over and knelt beside him and watched carefully. When he had finished, Stewart asked, "I still have Johnson's division with me. Do you want me to take them along also?"

Hood shook his head. If Johnson goes, there'll be nothing between Oaklawn and the enemy. He said, "Leave Johnson here. Have him bivouac his men across the road there."

Stewart nodded and stood up. Colonel Brent was approaching with the guide. The boy looked like he was about fifteen. *Stewart thought, of course he's young; if he was any older, he'd be in the army.* He asked the boy, "Do you know where we're going, young man?"

"Yes, sir," the boy replied.

"Then let's go," Stewart said as he climbed back into the saddle.

Hood told Brent to help him into the house. He looked even more exhausted than Stewart's men. *The poor man is hardly able to command in the field, Stewart thought. It must be hard to have been such a strong man and now having to deal with all his handicaps.*

Stewart and the guide turned their horses south to meet the lead elements of his corps. He didn't have to go far before meeting his weary men trudging up the road. They were exhausted, and it showed as they stumbled along. They'd been up since before dawn, and most of that time had been spent either marching or standing around in battle formation.

Stewart met Loring at the head of these troops and turned and began to ride north. Before getting back to Oaklawn, Major Blanton of Hood's staff rode up. The poor man looked like he was about to drop from the saddle. It was obvious the man had been running errands all afternoon.

"General Stewart," Blanton said as he turned his horse and fell in beside Stewart and Loring. "General Hood wanted me to tell you it is imperative for you to get your corps across the pike above Spring Hill and cut off Schofield's escape route. He says that's more important than extending Cheatham's right flank."

"I understand," Stewart replied.

Blanton saluted and rode back toward Oaklawn.

Stewart's men made their way to the north on the small country lane. With the light rain, the road became even messier than before. The darkness didn't help matters any. Men were slipping and sliding as they made the miserable night march.

After a good mile of marching, the guide turned to Stewart and said, "This here is about where Cheatham's right is. It's just west of us a couple hundred yards."

Stewart took out his watch, struck a match, and looked at the time. It was almost nine. He turned to Loring and said, "Hood said it's imperative that we occupy the Columbia Pike. We'll worry about Cheatham's right flank once we are across the pike. Keep your men moving up this road while I scout ahead to ensure we're going the right way."

Loring nodded. Stewart took his staff and the guide and rode on out the road. As they moved around a long curvy section of the road, they came up on an old gate. It was standing on the right side of the road.

Stewart turned to the guide and asked, "What's that gate for?"

"There used to be a road running through that gate, sir," the boy replied.

"Does it lead to the pike beyond Spring Hill?" Stewart asked.

The boy nodded. "It'll take you about a mile beyond Spring Hill to a toll gate on the Columbia Pike."

"That's the road we want to take then," Stewart said as he nudged his horse through the gate.

It wasn't much of a road, but it would have to do. They soon came to a house with cavalrymen camped in the yard. Men were sitting around fires trying to keep warm.

This has to be someone's headquarters, Stewart thought. Only a general would get to use such a nice home for the night. He turned his horse and rode onto the lawn to the nearest group of men. The men looked up, saw the three stars surrounded by a wreath on Stewart's collar, and jumped to attention.

Stewart asked, "Who's in the house?"

"General Forrest's inside, sir," a long-haired boy replied.

Stewart nodded and then rode on past them to the front portico.

Forrest would know the ground. He would know the position of the Federal army. Stewart knocked on the door. A beautiful young girl opened the door, saw that he was a general, and welcomed him inside.

"I need to see General Forrest, little lady," Stewart said.

"He's in the parlor," she replied, "this way, sir. Excuse me, but are you General Cleburne?"

"I'm General Peter Stewart," he said smiling. It didn't hurt his feelings that she wanted to see the red-haired general from Arkansas.

They walked into the parlor. Forrest was telling the family a story about the time he got shot in the big toe. He turned, saw Stewart, and motioned him over to a chair.

"What can I do for you, Stewart?" he asked.

Stewart walked over and sat down. He said, "General Hood wants me to get my corps across the Columbia Pike north of Spring Hill. I was just wondering if you had any information that would help me out."

"Won't do no good to get across the pike now," Forrest replied. He leaned back and crossed his arms. "I'm pretty sure the Yankees are moving up the Carter's Creek Pike to the west."

Stewart began to rub his eyes. He was beginning to get a headache. It seemed as if Hood's left hand didn't know what his right was doing. Stewart thought for a long moment. Finally, he said," Since your information is different than what Hood has, I'll have to confer with him about where he wants me."

"Wish I could be of more help, but my men are exhausted," Forrest said. Stewart noticed that the family hung on Forrest's every word. They practically worshipped him like a god. "Most are waiting to get their ammunition re-supplied. I'm pretty much down for the night."

"I understand," Stewart said as he stood up. He excused himself and left. After they rode back down the road and past the old gate, he met Major Hamilton of Hood's staff.

Hamilton said, "General Hood says you're on the wrong road. He sent me here to guide you into the position he wants you to occupy."

Stewart shook his head. He couldn't believe what he was hearing. *How the hell does Hood know I'm taking the wrong road, he wondered. The man is over a mile away and has never even been up here to view the position.*

"When did he send you?" Stewart asked.

"I just came from him," Hamilton replied.

Stewart started to explain to Hamilton what he had just learned from General Forrest but decided not to. The man was just a staff officer; he couldn't change the instructions he was carrying anyhow. The entire movement was becoming one big fiasco.

Stewart said, "The last time I talked to Hood, he said it was imperative I get here on Cheatham's right and get across the Columbia Pike."

"He may have received new information since then, sir," Hamilton said politely. "All I know is he wants me to get you into position."

101

There was nothing Stewart could do but obey orders. He said, "Well, Hamilton, which way do we go?"

"We've got to turn around and link up with Brown," Hamilton said.

Stewart shook his head. He hated double marching. His men were already exhausted, but he had no choice; orders were orders. When they got back to the right flank of Brown's division, Hamilton told Stewart to extend Brown's line to the right.

As the men began moving into position, Stewart turned to his staff. "Gentlemen, I'm certain a mistake is being made here. As soon as the men are on line, have them bivouac for the night. They look like they're about to pass out now. I'm gonna ride back and see General Hood and find out what he really wants us to do."

Stewart took his watch out again and struck a match. It was almost ten now. His men had been in formation for six hours straight, not to mention the long hard march up from Columbia. He wasn't sure they were capable of doing anything more tonight. The temperature had plummeted, and his men hadn't eaten anything for almost twelve hours.

10:00 p.m.

CSA

He had finally stumbled around in the darkness and found Cleburne's flank. Bate had been wondering why Cleburne and Brown hadn't attacked yet. It had taken three hours to find Cleburne's left flank less than a mile away. After his men came on line, he kept hearing enemy troops on the road out beyond his left. He sent a staff officer to find Cheatham and ask him for support for his exposed flank. He told another staff officer to go have Colonel Bullock refuse his line in case they were attacked.

Bate told a staff officer to hold his horse and made his way to the right of his line. Beyond his lines, he could see the men of Cleburne's division mostly lying around campfires. They didn't look as though they expected to see action tonight. He made his way among the fires until he came across a fire with several officers seated around it. He walked toward them. Bate soon recognized them as members of Cleburne's staff. As he approached the group, he noticed a man at the edge of the darkness pacing back and forth. He instantly recognized Pat Cleburne.

Bate called out, "Pat, what in hell is going on?"

Cleburne paused and looked up. He stared at the thick man with the spade-like beard for a moment. Bate had been a colonel commanding one of Cleburne's regiments at Shiloh. As long as he lived, Cleburne would never forget the badly-wounded man being carried from the field, crying because his brother had just been killed at his side.

Cleburne said, "I don't think General Hood could answer that question, much less me. Are you on my left now?"

"Yeah," Bate replied. "I was less than a hundred yards from occupying the Columbia Pike before Cheatham pulled me back to join you and Brown for an attack."

"Sounds about right," Cleburne was clearly frustrated. "I was within twenty yards of the Union lines and had them whipped. There was no fight left in 'em when Cheatham made me pull back and wait for Brown, and that's what I'm still doing."

"Has Brown not come up yet?" Bate asked as he stroked his long, brown beard.

"Oh, he was on line about seven." Cleburne started to pace again, realized what he was doing, and forced himself to stop. "My last orders were to wait until I hear Brown's guns before going in."

Bate began to shake his head. Cleburne said, "In the meantime, I'm sitting here listening to Union troops passing right by on the pike, and there's nothing I can do about it. General Granbury sent Captain English of his staff to find out whose troops are moving up the pike. We thought they may have been yours. When he didn't come back, we knew he'd been captured, and we knew whose troops were moving right past us."

Bate said, "Yeah, I exchanged shots with 'em earlier before I was pulled back. Cheatham threatened to arrest me for wanting to take possession of the pike instead of joining you and Brown."

"You don't think he's..." Cleburne stopped in mid-sentence. He was about to ask if Bate thought Cheatham was drunk but thought better of it.

Bate knew exactly what Cleburne was insinuating. He said, "Probably..." He paused in thought and then added, "Most likely."

"I sent a message to Hood that the enemy's getting away. Marching right by us on the pike," Cleburne said.

"What did he say?" Brown asked.

"I haven't heard a word back from him," Cleburne started to pace again. He stopped and turned to Bate. "If we do go in, it may not be as easy this time. They've been up there building breastworks for the past three hours. I just don't understand what a man must be thinking when he has the enemy whipped and then calls off the attack. It sounds like something Bragg would have done. If anything, he should have let me press the thing while Brown caught up to me."

Cleburne let it all go with a sigh. There was no use in discussing it further. He couldn't redo the past.

Bate said, "General Hood sent me in personally and told me to not stop until I had possession of the pike. Cheatham pulled me back. I think I'll ride to Hood's headquarters and let him know what's going on up here. Have you seen Cheatham lately?"

103

"Not since about seven," Cleburne was shaking his head. "Rumor has it that he's off seeing a local belle."

"'Bout right," Bate nodded. "Take care, Pat."

"You too," Cleburne called as Bate turned and disappeared into the darkness.

Bate made his way back to his division. His staff was all gathered around waiting for orders. Major Pirtle seemed irritated now. When Bate walked up, he pretty much exploded.

He said, "It is a criminal mistake for not allowing us to take that pike. General, I want you to just listen to the bastards walking right past us. Someone should be held accountable for this damned blunder."

"What about my request for support on the left?" Bate asked.

"We finally found Cheatham," Pirtle said. He was angry now. The man was almost yelling. "He was way the hell up at the Peters's House. That's almost a mile away behind Stewart's position. He didn't tell anyone he was going there. Someone suggested we look there for him because Miss Peters's husband is out of town. Ain't that something?"

"So, what did he say?" Bate asked. He didn't care where Cheatham was, he just wanted some support. It was like pulling teeth getting information out of Pirtle when he was upset. It seemed like the man's thoughts had become all jumbled.

"Oh," Pirtle gave Bate a sheepish grin. "Sorry, sir, he's sending Johnson's division to our left. I don't know how the hell he managed that. The last I heard was that Johnson was attached to Stewart's Corps."

Bate turned to one of the couriers standing nearby. "Ride over and make sure that Colonel Bullock refused his line. I don't like the idea of having my flank in the air, and besides that, there's no telling how long it will take Johnson to get here. If they hit our exposed flank in the dark, they could roll up the entire division."

The man climbed into his saddle and trotted off into the darkness. Bate turned back to Pirtle. "Major, let's ride back to Hood's headquarters and see if he's aware of the mess up here."

"That's the most sensible thing I've heard all night," Pirtle said as they climbed into the saddle and rode back to the east.

11:00 p.m.

CSA

Hood had eaten dinner with the Thompson family. They had done everything in their power to ensure he was as comfortable as possible. They had offered him the use of their best rooms at the top of the stairs, but he had declined. A one-legged general with a paralyzed arm avoided stairs at all costs, he had told them. He, Governor Harris, and Lieutenant Colonel Mason retired to a modest room downstairs to the left of the front door for easy access, if needed.

They had turned in at nine. His leg wasn't hurting at all tonight, but the rest of his body was aching. He was exhausted. John Darby, his personal surgeon, had come into the room while they were getting him into bed and offered to give him something to help him sleep.

Hood had been up since three this morning and had slept very little before that. He didn't need anything to help him sleep. He was unconscious almost as soon as his head hit the pillow. The last thought that passed through his mind before falling asleep was how sweet it would be in the morning to arise and accept the surrender of one of his old West Point buddies, General John Schofield.

He hadn't even awakened at eleven, when there was a hard knock on the front door. A staff officer let the two gentlemen in and woke Hood. There in front of him stood Stewart and Forrest. They had given him a few moments to compose himself and watched him wash his face in a basin of cold water.

When he had finished, he looked up and asked, "What can I do for you gentlemen?"

Stewart couldn't help but notice how groggy he sounded. The man was barely conscious. Stewart asked, "Did you change your mind and send Major Hamilton to move me into position beside Cheatham?"

"Yes I did," Hood replied, rubbing at his eyes.

Stewart stepped closer to the bed. Governor Harris and Colonel Mason were sleeping through the conversation. It seemed everybody at headquarters was exhausted tonight. Stewart asked, "So you've changed your mind about cutting the pike north of Spring Hill?"

"No," Hood said slowly. It was obvious the man was trying to get awake enough to comprehend what he was hearing. "The plan is the same as before. Cheatham has been asking for support on Brown's right."

Governor Harris heard Hood talking and sat up. Hood sounded a little grumpy now. Stewart seemed to be a little upset himself. Harris wondered what they were arguing about.

"I've ordered my men to bed; they're exhausted," Stewart said as he began to rub his forehead. "They've been marching since daylight and haven't had a bite to eat since this afternoon. I came here because I'm confused about the plan."

"It's not material," Hood said. "Just have your men ready to move toward Franklin in the morning. You are across the pike at the moment, right?"

"No, sir," Stewart said more forcefully this time. He hoped he could get Hood awake enough to understand what he was telling him. "Major Hamilton came and formed my corps to the right of Cheatham. We ain't even close to the pike now."

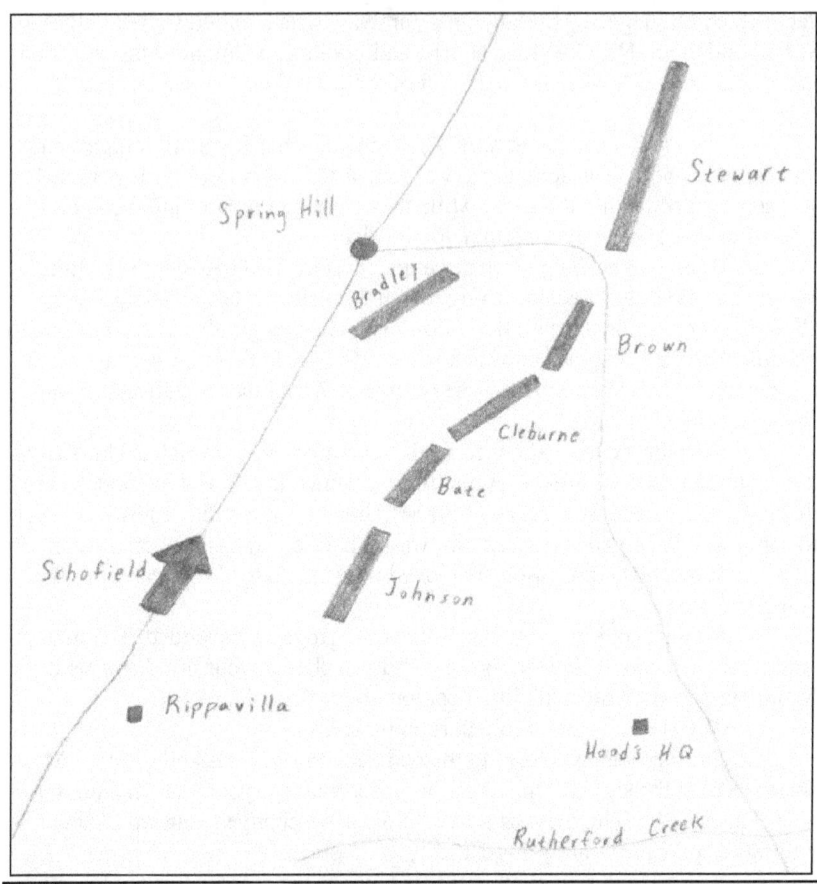

This is the true situation once Stewart has moved onto Cheatham's right. Bate has moved onto Cleburne's flank and Hood has sent Johnson's division to join Bate. Hood believes that Schofield's army is cut off and must surrender or be destroyed at daylight.

"What?" Hood asked. He was finally coming awake. He simply couldn't believe what he was hearing. Cheatham had told him that Stewart would be across the pike if he formed on his right. Now Stewart was here telling him that he wasn't even near the pike. Things just weren't making sense in his fog-clouded mind. He asked, "Well, Straight, can't you just throw a brigade across the pike till morning?"

"My men are exhausted. They've been on the move all day, sir," Stewart replied. "From where I'm at, I don't even know where the pike is. I was well on my way there when Hamilton forced me to turn and march all the way back to Cheatham's position. I just don't think I can move my men tonight in the condition they're in, General. If I could just…"

"General Forrest," Hood interrupted Stewart. The look on Stewart's face showed that he didn't appreciate it any. Forrest stepped forward beside Stewart but said nothing. Hood continued, "Can you not send some of your cavalry to hold the pike until morning?"

"I don't think I can," Forrest frowned. "Chalmers and Buford's divisions are all out of ammunition. The only troops I have available are in Jackson's division."

"Stewart," Hood looked back to General Stewart. "Give some of your ammunition to Forrest. It's the least you can do if you can't move your men tonight."

Stewart nodded. He didn't like Hood's tone. It almost sounded as though Hood was calling him a coward.

Hood turned back to Forrest and said, "Problem solved."

"I can't promise anything, Hood," Forrest's voice was high and shrill. He was shaking his head. "My men have been a ridin' and a fightin' since we left Alabama. I don't know what they can do. They're more exhausted than the infantry."

"Just do what you can," Hood said as he lay back on the pillow. Hood hadn't received word from Stephen Lee that Schofield had left Columbia yet. There was no reason to panic. In the morning, Schofield would be forced to surrender his army right here. All this was much ado about nothing.

Stewart spun and walked out the door. He saw the two members of his staff he had brought with him waiting with the three horses. As they mounted their horses, Lieutenant Binford asked, "Is there gonna be a battle tonight?"

"I don't think so," Stewart's mood was beginning to grow sour.

Back inside, Forrest was trying to explain the condition of his cavalry to Hood, when General Bate arrived. Bate patiently waited in the foyer. He could overhear some of their conversation. Forrest's high voice seemed to echo off the walls. The man wasn't happy about something Hood was ordering him to do. Hood's voice was low. Bate couldn't understand anything he was saying. He heard Forrest say, "That's fine then. I'll send Jackson's division up there, but they ain't gonna be able to hold against no damned infantry all night. Just want you to be aware of that. If you want 'em trapped, you better send infantry—and plenty of it."

A couple of moments later, Forrest came stomping out of Hood's room. He almost ran into Bate, spun to his right, and headed for the front door. Bate started to say something, but realized that Forrest wasn't in the mood for small talk. The man's eyes showed anger. Forrest slammed the door as he left.

An aide told Bate to go on in. Hood was ready for him now. Bate walked to the bedside and saluted. Hood nodded and asked, "What can I do for you, General Bate?"

"You sent me to take the pike this afternoon, sir," Bate sounded a little nervous. He wasn't sure how Hood was gonna take the information he was about to give him. "I was within a hundred yards of taking it. There wasn't nothing in front of me but some skirmishers. Just as I was giving the order to move, General Cheatham ordered me to pull back. I'm not in possession of the pike, sir."

Hood acted as though he was listening, but Bate wondered if he was. The man looked like he was about to fall asleep sitting straight up. Hood didn't reply, so Bate continued, "Sir, I tried to go on and take the pike like you wanted, but Cheatham threatened to arrest me if I didn't pull back."

Hood opened his eyes. "It makes no difference now anyhow. General Forrest just left here. He is gonna take his cavalry up north of town and hold the pike until morning. In the morning, they'll surrender without a fight."

Bate relaxed a little. At least now he knew he wasn't gonna be blamed for the Federal army escaping if that's what ended up happening. Hood had taken the news a lot better than Bate thought he would.

"Congratulations, General Bate," Hood managed a weak smile. He realized Bate was nervous. "You've done your job. We can sleep well tonight."

"I'm glad to hear it, sir," Bate said. "I've been extremely worried about it."

Hood nodded and lay back on the pillow. Before Bate reached the front door, Hood was asleep again. He slept like a rock until just after midnight, when there was yet another knock on the door.

Hood sat up in bed again and rubbed at his eyes. Before him stood a private dressed in ragged clothes. He scratched at his unshaven face. Hood rubbed his eyes again and asked, "What can I do for you?"

"I have important information, sir," the man removed his hat and waited.

"Go on," Hood said a little impatiently.

"Sir, I was exhausted today," the man stammered. "I'm a little shamed to admit it, but I couldn't keep up with my regiment. My shoes are 'bout gone, and I was just too weak. I was way back behind and just got up here awhile ago."

Hood watched the man shift from one foot to another uncomfortably. He wondered if the man would ever get to the point. He said, "That's quite all right, soldier. It happens to all of us from time to time."

"Sir," the man nodded, "thing is, when I came up here, I stumbled out on the Columbia Pike by accident. The whole damned Yankee army is retreating up the road like a bat out of hell and I thought you might want to know 'bout it, so's you can do somethin'."

"What time is it?" Hood asked the aide standing beside the man.

"It's 'bout quarter to one, sir," the private replied.

Hood nodded and asked, "You sure they were Union troops?"

"Yes, sir," the man laughed. "They was Yankees, all right. They was a runnin' like hell, all confused. They's got cannons and guns and troops racing up through there like stink after shit. Excuse my language, sir."

Hood looked at the staff officer sleeping on the floor. "Colonel Mason, I need you to write an order for me."

The Colonel stirred on the floor, trying to come awake. Hood turned back to the soldier standing before him. "Private, you've done a great thing coming here. I want you to know I'm proud of you. You're excused."

The man put his ragged hat back on his head, saluted, and turned for the door. Hood had to yell at Mason a couple more times to get him up.

Mason slowly got off the floor and fumbled around finding a pencil and paper. When he was ready, he nodded to Hood.

Hood said, "Send an order to General Cheatham. Tell him to attack the enemy troops that are retreating along the Columbia Pike in his front. Also, send that private along to him, so he can tell him what he saw. You got it?"

Mason nodded as he scribbled the last sentence. He then turned and went out the door, giving the note and private to a courier to be sent to Cheatham. He then came back in and collapsed in the blankets on the floor.

Cheatham hadn't been in his tent very long when the courier arrived. All of Cheatham's staff officers were asleep, and that's what Cheatham was preparing to do. He had been thinking about Jesse Peters when the horses arrived. She had begged him to stay the night, but he had refused. He had pushed his luck already by being away from his command this long.

Major General Frank Cheatham heard horses outside. He stepped out of the tent and made his way over to the fire. It had gotten a lot colder since dark. The courier climbed off the horse, followed by a private. The man handed the note to Cheatham, motioned toward the ragged private, and said, "I'm supposed to leave him with you also."

Cheatham looked at the man for a moment. "What in the hell am I gonna do with him?"

"He has important information about the Union army," the courier replied. "May I go now, sir? I'm about to freeze to death."

Cheatham nodded and motioned with his arm as if he were shooing a fly away. The private started in with his story before Cheatham finished reading the note from Hood.

When the man had finished, Cheatham walked over and nudged Major Bostick with his boot. Bostick grunted and sat up shivering. "What is it, General?"

"I need you to go find Edward Johnson," Cheatham said. "Tell him to take a brigade or his entire division if necessary and move over and take the Columbia Pike. Tell him to stop anybody from retreating up that road."

"Yes, sir," Bostick said. He arose from his bed roll and climbed on his horse. A good staff officer had to be able to spring straight out of bed and deliver orders regardless of the situation.

It took him about thirty minutes to find Johnson's headquarters. A guard directed him to the general's tent. Bostick made his way through the tent flap and saw the bald-headed Johnson sleeping on his cot. He had a pile of blankets thrown over him. It made him look like a giant man, but Bostick knew better.

Bostick gently nudged the general. Johnson opened his eyes and squinted. "What is it?"

"Sir," Bostick said, "General Cheatham wants you to advance your division to the Columbia Pike and stop the Union army from retreating past us."

Johnson became angry. He hated to come out of the warm blankets, but he finally sat up. He said, "This is what happens when you're loaned out from one corps to another. You get all the shit work. Why didn't Cheatham send one of his own divisions, damn it?"

"I'm not sure, sir," Bostick replied. Johnson was comical to watch, but Bostick knew better than to laugh at him. He had spent the entire war in Lee's army before being sent west.

"I know why," Johnson said as he began to pull on his boots. "We came up here after dark. Hell, I don't even know the ground, son. I don't know which way to go to get to the damned pike to start with."

"Sir," Bostick said, "If you would like, I'll go with you."

"Yeah, yeah," Johnson said. He reached for his kepi and gloves. "You know how dangerous it is to start moving men around in the dark? That's how accidents happen. Hell, Stonewall lost his life that way, you know."

Bostick wanted to laugh at the man. Johnson had served under Richard Ewell, who was one of the most eccentric men in the entire Confederacy. Johnson was pretty eccentric himself.

Johnson stepped out into the cool night air and looked for his horse. Luckily, no one had bothered to remove the saddle tonight. Everyone was expecting a fight at any moment. He said, "Damned if I don't get the short end of the stick on everything nowadays. Back in Lee's army I was appreciated, but out here…"

He left the rest unsaid. It was obvious Johnson resented being sent from Lee's winning army to the always-losing army of Tennessee.

Bostick said, "Sir, I'm sorry 'bout this. You understand I'm only following orders?"

Johnson climbed on his horse as Bostick climbed on his. Johnson eyed Bostick a long moment. "Tell you what, son. Let's me and you ride up to that pike alone and see what's up there before we turn out an entire division for nothin'."

"Sounds good to me," Bostick replied.

Before Johnson spurred the horse, he called to one of his aides lying near the fire half asleep. He told him to get up and at least have all the officers get their men ready to move if it's necessary. Then he and Bostick spurred their horses toward the west.

As they rode through the cold night, Johnson was still grumbling about the way he and his men were being treated. He said, "Those poor men have been marching all day, standing in line of battle, and now I've got to get 'em up and move 'em again. Hell, they didn't get to sleep till ten. What time is it now?"

110

"It's after midnight, sir," Bostick replied, "Maybe later than that."

As they approached the pike, they slowed their horses and listened for sounds of movement in front of them. All they heard was the cool wind blowing in their faces. Soon, Johnson and Bostick were both mounted on their horses in the middle of the Columbia Pike. There was no one moving up the road. Johnson looked at Bostick and said, "Let's wait here about fifteen minutes just to make sure no one's coming."

Bostick agreed. They sat there in silence straining their ears, but there was nothing to hear. Johnson began to shake his head. He looked at Bostick after they'd sat there awhile and said, "See there, young man. If I would have moved my entire division up here, it would have been a complete waste of my time and their energy."

Bostick could do nothing but agree with him. There were obviously no troops passing along this road. Johnson struck a match and looked at his watch. "It's nearly two in the morning. What do you say we ride back and try to get some sleep before the sun comes up?"

"I'm with you on that, sir," Bostick replied, and they rode back to the east.

When Johnson got back, he found his division had all gotten up and formed line of battle. They had loaded their guns and were prepared to move. Johnson shook his head. He saw an officer in front of the lines sitting on horseback, waiting. Johnson called into the darkness, "Who the hell are you?"

"Brigadier General Deas," the man replied. "Just who the hell are you?"

"Major General Edward Johnson," the general laughed. "Turn your men back in, it was a false alarm."

"Damn," Deas said and passed the order along.

Part 4

Pursuit

"The man of knowledge must be able not only to love his enemies but also to hate his friends."

Friedrich Nietzsche

November 30, 1864, 7:00 a.m.

CSA

He rode out into the cool morning air. The sun was rising, and it promised to be a clear day. Hood was on his way to the Cheairs home for breakfast. He'd received the news just after dawn. Schofield's entire army had escaped in the night. They had passed by the Confederate army so close that they could see soldiers sitting around the campfires. The more Hood thought about it the angrier he became. He had laid the perfect trap, and his subordinates had failed him.

Hood turned to Major Cumming and said, "Joe, I have a number of officers I want brought to the Cheairs house."

Cumming nudged his horse up alongside of Hood and asked, "Who do you want, sir?"

Deep down inside Hood was beginning to fume. The rage began to build with each passing moment he thought about what had happened. Hood said, "First, I want General Cheatham. I also need to see Generals Brown and Forrest."

"Will that be all, sir?" Cumming asked. He'd never seen Hood this upset before.

"Yeah," Hood glared, "for now anyway."

Governor Harris volunteered to go with Cumming and help round up the generals.

As Hood and the rest of his staff crossed the field near the Cheairs home, known locally as Rippavilla, Hood could see Johnson's division to the north cooking breakfast. He wondered if the men were aware of what had happened.

Hood and his staff rode toward the beautiful home on the Columbia Pike. He rode his horse on to the yard and toward the door on the north side of the house. His staff helped him dismount near the young magnolia tree there.

Hood took his crutch and hobbled onto the porch. As one of his aides was about to knock on the door, they heard horses coming down the pike at high speed. Hood turned, saw that it was General Forrest, and waited as he turned onto the lawn.

Just the man I need to see, Hood thought. I gave him orders to move north and secure the road, and he failed me.

Forrest rode directly towards Hood, past the beautiful magnolia and the aides holding the horses. He never took his eyes off of Hood the entire way. As he reined up, Hood could tell he was angry but couldn't understand why.

"You pecker-necked son-of-a-bitch," Forrest nearly screamed. His voice was more shrill than normal this morning. "You've gone and let the bastards escape!"

Hood started to say something but thought better of it. He noticed that Forrest's face was pale, and his lips were quivering. Several of Hood's staff officers thought they may have to restrain the wild man on the horse. Most just stood there in shock, not quite believing what they were seeing. Forrest's staff had seen him talk to superiors in this way before, but that didn't make these moments any less tense. It wasn't something a man got used to.

Hood asked, "Were Jackson's men not able to block the Union retreat?"

After he asked, he realized how dumb the question sounded. He knew they hadn't or Forrest wouldn't be here cursing at the moment.

"You're one of them damned West-Point-trained sons-of-bitches, ain't you?" Forrest fairly exploded. "Maybe they couldn't teach you a damned thing there. How in the hell are fifteen hundred men gonna stop an army of thirty thousand?"

Hood opened his mouth and started to say something, but Forrest continued.

"Somebody ought to take your ass out behind the woodshed for lettin' them bastards get away. Just think, I was saying Braxton Bragg was the worst son-of-a-bitch to shit behind a pair of boots. Well, I think I just found a son-of-a-bitch worse than him." Forrest's eyes were flashing. Hood had often heard that Forrest's eyes did that in battle, and now he knew what people meant. "Ain't you got a damned thing to say?"

"General Forrest," Hood's face was red, but he decided it best to try and smooth things over with this man. "I in no way accused you of allowing the Federal army to escape."

"Me?" Forrest jerked back in the saddle. "You think that's why I'm here? I'll tell you why I'm here. My men have been a ridin' and a fightin' since we left Alabama. We had to abandon the best raid I ever been a part of to go down there and hold your damned hand all the way back up here. Now, you trap the bastards and up and let 'em get away. I'll be damned if I ain't glad I didn't go to no West Point."

Hood stood there and listened to Forrest's rant as if he was the subordinate and Forrest was his superior. He had suspected that Forrest hadn't liked him the moment they'd met in Florence. Now he was sure of it. It began to dawn on Hood that perhaps Forrest was the type of man that never got along with superiors.

"If I weren't sure people would call me a coward," Forrest wasn't showing any signs of tiring out, "I'd get off this horse and stomp your ass, you miserable bastard. As it is, I don't beat on no cripples."

Hood stared at Forrest's saber and pistols stuck in his belt. He thought some of his staff would have intervened for him by now, but they all seemed to be in shock.

"I'm assuming you plan on following the damned Yankee army," Forrest wasn't about to ask Hood for orders. Hood was afraid of him now. Forrest could see that in his eyes. He planned on keeping it that way.

115

Hood said nothing but nodded.

Forrest leaned forward in the saddle and stared hard at Hood. "I'm gonna follow them with my cavalry, unless you have other plans."

Again Hood simply nodded.

Forrest jerked the reins and galloped away. Colonel Mason, who was standing behind Hood, said, "General, you should place that man under arrest."

Hood turned to Mason. His face was still red, but a funny thought crossed his mind. "If I did that, Mason, he may get pissed off. Now, you don't want to see that man get mad, do you?"

Mason glanced at Hood, and then looked at him again. At first he managed a weak smile, until he was sure Hood was kidding. Mason began to chuckle. "No, General, I don't suppose I do."

Mrs. Cheairs had heard the commotion and opened the door. She welcomed General Hood into her home and thanked him for having breakfast with her family.

Hood thanked her for having him. She saw his face and knew something wasn't right. She asked, "Is something the matter, General?"

"Nothing to trouble yourself about, ma'am," Hood tried to sound cheerful. He reached over and patted her on the shoulder. "It's just army business."

She showed Hood and his staff through the house to the dining area on the south side. There was very little furniture in the house, and the table he was seated at barely had room enough for four.

Mrs. Cheairs could almost read Hood's mind. She said, "My apologies, General Hood. When Bull Nelson made this place his headquarters back in sixty-two, he stole all my furniture and carried it up north. He even made my parlor into a tavern, complete with a bar. I'm almost ashamed of some of the things that have gone on in my home. Of course, he moved me and the children out into the slave quarters."

"No apologies, ma'am," Hood waved his hand at her. "Just be thankful you still have your family. Besides, I should be the one apologizing to you. My job is to prevent that sort of thing from happening to the citizens of my country. We were supposed to protect you."

While Hood sat talking to Mrs. Cheairs, there was a knock at the door. A staff officer went to see who was there. He came back, followed by General Cheatham and Major Vaulx of his staff.

Cheatham knew the Federal army was gone, but he wasn't sure why Hood wanted to see him. Mrs. Cheairs saw Cheatham and extended her hand. Cheatham took her hand, turned it over, bowed in a courtly manor, and kissed the back of it. As he began to fawn over her, her face turned red, and she began to slowly back away.

"Sit down," Hood said forcefully.

Cheatham nodded at Hood and took a seat. Major Vaulx stood against the wall with Hood's staff. Cheatham didn't bother to ask Hood what was wrong. He knew Hood was about to tell him anyhow.

116

Hood leaned forward, his elbow resting on the table and his bad arm lying in his lap. "As you've no doubt learned by now, the Federal army has escaped."

Cheatham shrugged, placed his hands on the table, and said, "Couldn't be helped."

"How do you figure?" Hood asked. "All that had to be done was for someone to get a brigade across the pike."

Cheatham looked down at his hands. He considered Hood a friend. The man had recommended to Richmond that Cheatham be promoted to Lieutenant General. He still hadn't grasped that Hood was laying the blame for Schofield's escape on him.

"We tried," Cheatham shrugged again. "There were just too many of the enemy, and we ran out of daylight before the rest of the army got on line."

Hood turned, as he saw Mrs. Cheairs bring a ham in and set it on the table to his right. Hood asked, "Ma'am, would you mind stepping from the room a moment?"

"Not at all," she replied and bowed. "I'm afraid your breakfast is gonna get cold though."

"That's quite all right. We're soldiers; we've eaten the stuff raw before," Hood said. He watched her leave the room and then turned back to Cheatham.

"Every time I think about yesterday, I just want to pistol-whip somebody," Hood's voice began to get louder. "The greatest move of my career was brought to nothing because you were out chasing skirts all evening!"

Hood slammed his fist onto the table. The ham seemed to jump into the air.

Cheatham glanced around at the staff officers. He didn't appreciate Hood talking to him in front of everyone this way. Cheatham said, "Sir, begging your pardon, but this wasn't my fault."

"It wasn't?" Hood raised his eyebrows. "Then tell me who's at fault."

"Sir, I left General Brown with instructions to attack as soon as he was on line," Cheatham mumbled. He wouldn't tell Hood that Brown had been intoxicated yesterday, but he wasn't about to take the blame for his failures either. "You can ask Major Vaulx. He was with me the entire afternoon. We were riding to the left to locate Bate and wondering why we weren't hearing the attack begin."

Vaulx was standing against the wall. He cleared his throat and began nodding. What Cheatham was telling Hood wasn't the entire truth. Vaulx had been with Cheatham until he went to see Jesse about seven. Cheatham was sensing now that he was in enough trouble. He didn't need to bring Jesse up anymore.

"Before we found Bate, we turned back to see why Brown hadn't attacked as ordered." Vaulx was standing behind Cheatham nodding in agreement again. Cheatham continued, "Brown had called off his attack because of the Federal line extending beyond his right flank. That's when I came to you and got permission to wait for Stewart."

"That mystery line on Brown's right turned out to be about twenty-five or thirty skirmishers," Hood said as he began to shake his head. He slapped the table with his open hand. "It is incomprehensible to me that an entire corps was held back from attacking because of a handful of men beyond their flank."

Cheatham was growing agitated having to defend himself. He was beginning to get the feeling that Hood was trying to make him the scapegoat for his own failure here.

"How the hell was I supposed to know that in the damned dark?" Cheatham's voice was growing louder now.

Hood slammed his fist on the table, again making the ham platter bounce. "You mean in the damned bed sheets over at the Peters House. It's hard to tell what's on your flank when you're rolling around with some young gal."

"Sir," Cheatham said, "I did the job you asked of me. I gave the orders, although I was against a night assault. You told me to wait on Stewart. Now I feel you're trying to place the blame on me."

"There's plenty of blame to go around," Hood began to rub his temples. The argument was beginning to give him a headache. "At the moment, I'm discussing what part you played in this mess. I repeatedly gave you orders to take the pike. You repeatedly ignored those orders. If you had been on the field where you were supposed to be, Schofield would be surrendering at this very moment. Instead, you threw it all away for one night with another man's wife."

"That's a damned lie!" Cheatham roared and slammed his fist on the table. He'd had enough of Hood's innuendos. "I was with my command until after seven last night. After that, I went and had dinner with Mrs. Peters. There is no wrong in that. I will not sit here and allow you to disrespect a lady like that, especially a Tennessee lady."

Hood began to rub his forehead. "Maybe you can enlighten me on what went wrong last evening. No one else has been able to."

"When we sent Cleburne in yesterday," Cheatham decided that his best option was to pass the blame on to his subordinates, "he was going in the right direction…" Cheatham decided it best not to mention his little trip to see Mrs. Peters while Cleburne was advancing. "Somewhere along the way, he found a line of Federal infantry on his right. Without asking for permission, he just changed front and attacked them instead of moving on to his objective."

"So you're saying Cleburne disobeyed his orders also?" Hood asked.

"The man becomes so aggressive at times. He forgets what his primary mission is." Cheatham spoke low as if he were afraid Cleburne would walk in and hear him. "That was the first blunder. The second happened when Brown became concerned about the men beyond his right and called off the attack I'd ordered him to make. After that, it took Bate until ten to get in position on Cleburne's left to support the attack. I thought I was gonna have to place him under arrest to get him to comply."

"I personally sent him to occupy the pike right here in front of Rippavilla," Hood began to shake his head again. "This is in no way his fault. You were giving him orders that conflicted with mine."

"Sounds like we had a case of too many chiefs and not enough Indians," Cheatham tried to lighten the mood. *This entire situation is like a big pot of shit, he thought. The more you stir in it, the worse it smells.*

Hood didn't quite feel that way about it. He said, "I'm gonna have to withdraw my recommendation that President Davis promote you to permanent corps command."

Cheatham felt his face redden. *I'm being punished now, he thought.* He started to argue, but he restrained himself. He said, "You do what you feel you have to do."

Hood turned to Major Hamilton and said, "Please ask Mrs. Cheairs to come back in."

Cheatham asked Hood to be excused to go see that his men were up and about. Hood granted him permission and then waited for Mrs. Cheairs to finish placing breakfast on the table.

Cheatham and Vaulx were riding back, when they met Brown riding toward Rippavilla. Brown saluted and said, "Frank, everything all right?"

"Not exactly," Cheatham replied. He noticed that Brown's eyes were bloodshot. The man looked like he was about to fall from the saddle. "Schofield's army escaped last night."

"I heard," Brown said. He watched Cheatham closely. He wondered if he had said anything to the General Hood about his drinking last night. He asked, "Any idea what Hood wants to see me about?"

"He's looking for someone to pin Schofield's escape on," Cheatham said. "At the moment, that someone is me."

Frank Cheatham is a good man, Brown thought. He could have easily saved himself by telling what I did last night. Brown looked at Cheatham and said, "I'm sorry, sir."

Cheatham held up his hand. He knew what Brown was apologizing for, even if he didn't say it out loud. "No apologies, John."

Brown nodded and began to ride on. Vaulx turned in the saddle and called out, "I'm warning you; Hood's as wrathy as a rattlesnake this morning."

Back at Rippavilla, General Hood finished his breakfast and thanked Mrs. Cheairs for her hospitality. She asked him if there was anything else she could do for him, but there wasn't anything. He continued to sit at the table and stew over what had happened. Hood could hardly believe it himself.

Major Hamilton had stepped outside for a moment. He walked back into the room and said, "Sir, General Brown has just arrived."

"Show the general in," Hood said dryly. He began to grow irritated again. He placed his good hand on the table and began to slowly drum the surface with his fingertips.

119

Hamilton walked back outside and then returned with General Brown. Brown saluted. He looked awful. Hood watched him stand far across the room from him. The man was nervous.

Hood didn't invite Brown to sit. He decided to make this meeting short and sweet for the man. Brown had the look of concern on his face already. Hood said, "General Brown, there's one thing I want you to remember today. It is an important military principle. When a pursuing army catches a retreating foe, he must attack at once. Now, if you only have a brigade on the field when you catch him, don't wait for the rest of your troops. I want you to attack him with what you have. If you've got but a regiment up, attack him. If it's only a company against the entire Federal army, still I want you to attack 'im. While we're marching today, if you find the road blocked, march through fields and forests to get around it. Do not stop for even a minute. Are we clear, Brown?"

Brown nodded and said, "Yes, sir."

"You're dismissed then," Hood waved his arm as if driving away a pesky fly. "Go form your men."

Brown saluted and left the room. He had just been dressed down by Hood, yet inside he felt lucky. He could have been arrested for his actions last night.

After Brown had left, another general arrived. It was Edward Johnson commanding the "loaned out" division of S.D. Lee's Corps.

Johnson walked in and saluted. Hood asked, "What can I do for you, Ed?"

The two were acquainted from their service in Virginia, though they didn't know each other very well. Johnson had served under Jackson and Ewell, while Hood had spent his time there under Longstreet.

"Sir," Johnson cleared his throat, "my men are formed and ready to move out. I took the liberty of marching them past Rippavilla to the pike. I thought you might want to say a few words to them before we start."

Hood thought a long moment. He wondered what he could possibly say to them that would be encouraging under these circumstances. After a long moment, he said, "Gather your men on the lawn outside, and I'll go onto the upstairs landing and address them."

"Thank you," Johnson said and turned to leave.

"General Johnson," Hood called out. Johnson stopped and turned around. "I don't want you marching with the rest of the army. Your men will wait here until Lee's corps comes up and you will rejoin him."

"Right," Johnson said. He bowed and left the room. That was good news for him. He hated being loaned out to other commands and getting all the shit jobs.

Half an hour later, Major William Clare came in and told Hood that Johnson's division was waiting outside. Several of Hood's staff helped him up the stairs to the second floor. They followed him out onto the landing and

120

looked down at the sea of faces. Hood guessed there were around three thousand men standing on the lawn below.

He hobbled over to the rail and propped the crutch under his arm. He cleared his throat and began. "Men, as you've no doubt learned, the Federal army escaped our trap last night. I don't want you men to lose hope. The failure is not your fault. The blame rests on a few commanders from another corps. It would have been easy to cut the enemy in two as they passed last night. The blunder must be corrected at once. No time must be lost in catching Schofield's army and destroying it."

As he turned to go back inside, the crowd of men burst into cheering. His staff carried him back down the stairs and sat him back at the table.

Hood took out his watch. It was almost nine. He asked his staff to help him get saddled up so he could join his army for the pursuit. They helped him out of the house and strapped him to the horse. They followed as he turned his horse away from Rippavilla and to the edge of the Columbia Pike. A few hundred yards south, they could see a handful of horsemen approaching. Hood waited to see who they were. As they got closer, he recognized S.D. Lee, followed by most of his staff and escort.

Lee rode up, saluted, and said, "Tell me it's not true."

"It's true," Hood replied shaking his head. "The greatest move of my career has been pissed away by lazy subordinates. It was a once-in-a-lifetime opportunity, gone."

"Damn," Lee said. Hood was the man he had to thank for his promotion to Lieutenant General. He said, "I'm sorry, Sam."

Hood held up his hand. "We were within a hundred yards of taking their only route of escape. A hundred yards, and Cheatham messed the entire thing up. All he wanted was to roll in the hay with some woman. We were that close, Stephen. Nashville would have been ours for the taking."

Lee looked up the road toward Nashville. He looked as if he were trying to see what lay down that road for the army. He asked, "What now?"

"We'll pursue," Hood said softly, "but they ain't gonna stop before they reach Nashville. Schofield made a mistake once, but he's no fool. We scared him last night. He won't stop running until he gets to those fortifications. All we can do is follow and hope he makes another blunder."

"My men are 'bout a mile back," Lee said. "I'll ride back and try to rush 'em on up."

"Never mind that," Hood held up his hand. "There's gonna be no more action, except maybe with their rearguard. When they get here, let 'em fall out and eat breakfast. There's no rush now."

"All right," Lee nodded. He looked past Hood at the field north of Rippavilla. It was full of soldiers. "Whose troops are those?"

Hood turned and looked. "They're yours again. That's Johnson's division. I can't seem to get Cheatham or Stewart to use them. I may as well give 'em back to you. I wish I would have had you in the lead yesterday."

121

"Thank you, sir," Lee smiled. He really respected General Hood. "When they started pulling out yesterday evening, I was sure you would capture every one of 'em. I thought we would get up this morning and march up here to see their entire army as prisoners."

"You saw them pulling out yesterday?" Hood looked shocked. "What time?"

"Around four or so," Lee replied. He wondered where Hood was going with this.

"Damn," said Hood. He couldn't believe what he was hearing. S.D. Lee, his best corps commander was sitting here telling him that he had allowed the enemy to pull out without hitting him. Hood started to say something to Lee about his orders to attack. He wondered why Lee had waited until this morning to march north if the enemy had pulled out last evening. After a long moment, he decided to just let it pass. It no longer mattered.

"Sir, is something wrong?" Lee asked.

"Never mind," Hood said. "Just let your men eat and then get them on the road north."

Hood turned his horse and started toward Nashville. After coming all this way and pulling off the perfect plan, his army and his commanders were still afraid to attack. It seemed as if they would only fight if they were protected by breastworks. He wondered if he would ever be able to eradicate this evil. Hood dug around in his mind, trying to find the perfect solution. What could he do to turn this thing around?

9:30 a.m.

USA

He'd arrived with his troops at three this morning. A courier met them on the road just north of Winstead Hill. Cox could only see the man's outline in the darkness.

"General Cox?" The man seemed a bit anxious.

"Yes," Cox replied. He heard the man exhale as if he'd been out searching for him all night.

"Sir," the man paused, "General Schofield says for you to form your men on the southern edge of town. He wants you to give them a couple hours sleep, their morning coffee, and then to have them entrench."

"Entrench?" Cox interrupted. He couldn't believe what he was hearing. "He doesn't expect us to hold here, does he?"

"Yes, sir," the man stirred nervously. "General Thomas didn't send the pontoon bridges that General Schofield asked for. It seems the man is willing to sacrifice our army to hold Hood out of Nashville until General Smith

122

arrives from Missouri. The bridges over the Harpeth River are wrecked, and it's gonna take some time to get them repaired."

"I see," Cox frowned. Just when he thought things couldn't get any worse. He said, "Continue."

The man jerked a thumb over his shoulder pointing back toward town. "General Schofield wants you to let the artillery pass on into town with the wagons so they can be prepared to cross as soon as possible. He says we'll pull the troops out tonight. The general doesn't think Hood will attack us here across two miles of open terrain, but he's extremely concerned that we'll be flanked before we can get the bridges completed."

Cox grunted. He could barely make out the man's salute in the darkness. The man spun his horse and moved away. Cox began to think to himself as he rode on north. *This thing could get ugly in a hurry if Hood gets behind us while we wait on those damned bridges to get repaired.* He wondered if Thomas truly intended to sacrifice them to buy time.

His staff had found him a modest brick home right on the Columbia Pike. He rode into the yard and dismounted. Captain Levi Scofield, his engineer, was just climbing from the saddle.

Cox said, "Captain Scofield, I need you to mark the lines and place the troops. We've got to hold here until the bridges are repaired across the Harpeth River."

Scofield slumped back into the saddle. He was exhausted, but he wasn't about to complain. He gave a small salute and spun the horse back onto the road.

Cox waited in the yard a few moments. Everything was as still as a grave. He couldn't help but wonder what the day would bring. They'd been in a race for their lives for the past few days, and it wasn't over yet. He stepped over to the road and peered south into the darkness, but he couldn't see anything. A bird in a tree across the road was alarmed by his movement and began to protest. Cox stood there until he could hear the head of his column arriving from the south. Out in the darkness, he could hear footsteps falling on the road. The clank of tin cups and canteens echoed out of the night. He couldn't see his men yet, but he could feel their exhaustion. The stress of the hard marches, protecting the wagon train, and worrying about Forrest's roving cavalry had taken its toll on his men. He wondered if they would be worth much if they were required to fight now.

He turned and followed his staff into the little brick cottage. The people who lived there were named Carter. When they'd knocked on the door and informed the old man they were taking his house for Cox's headquarters, the old man had protested. Soon, everyone in the house was in an uproar.

Cox had tried to reason with the old man. He'd learned the man's name was Fountain. His son's name was Moscow, a captain in the Confederate Army who had been wounded, captured, and sent home until exchanged. Both men were soon protesting to Cox. The poor old man with gray hair and long, gray beard had a sad countenance that made it look as if life had dealt him a

123

few hard blows. The captain looked to be in his twenties, with dark hair and a short, trimmed beard. He walked with a noticeable limp. It was pretty obvious to Cox that this man's war service was pretty much over.

The protesting had done no good. Cox and his staff were so exhausted they had collapsed on the hardwood floor in the foyer and fallen asleep.

He had awoken there, the sun shining through the windows in front of the house. The home was facing east. Several of his staff were trying to round up some breakfast. The Carter girls weren't pleased when it was suggested they fix breakfast. Even the offer of money hadn't interested them in cooking for the Yankee officers that had intruded into their lives.

Fountain and his son had both been asking when they were leaving. General Cox was growing tired of them already.

Cox stood and stretched in the foyer. One of the girls came walking down the stairs. Cox glanced up and noticed one of the posts in the banister on the landing had been installed upside down. There was a pair of baby shoes on each side of the post. The girl acted nervous around Cox and his officers. He thought it would help if he tried to talk about something other than war with her.

"Why's that post upside down?" Cox asked with a smile. "Was someone drinking when they put it in?"

"No, sir," the girl looked sad as she stopped about three steps from the ground floor. "My father and brothers were moving furniture up the stairs when they knocked it loose. My younger brother was three at the time. Mother told him to come down at once. He wasn't allowed on the stairs. He wouldn't come down, just stood up there laughing. Anyway, he was trying to get her to try and catch him. You know, wanting to play. He leaned on that rail, fell through it, and landed headfirst on the floor. The fall broke his neck. He died instantly. Those are his shoes. Father put the rail back in upside down so we'll never forget."

"I'm sorry," Cox said. The story was so sad; he wished he hadn't asked about it. "I'm also sorry we had to use your home today. There's a lot in life that's sad. Just like this war. I've seen a lot of death since this thing began."

"Yes, I'm sure you have," the girl walked on down the steps. "The lists of local boys who've been killed are so long; it's almost unbelievable."

"I hope it doesn't last much longer," Cox said. He wanted to ease her mind. "I want you to know that you're in no danger here. Our army's falling back to Nashville as soon as the bridge over the Harpeth River is repaired. If anyone in this army gives you any trouble, just let me know, and it'll be taken care of."

"Thank you," she said as she turned and walked into the parlor, looking out the front window at the wagons passing up the road.

Cox turned and stepped outside the front door and yawned again. It had been pitch dark when he had arrived. This was the first time he'd gotten a chance to survey the area.

124

He nodded to a teamster passing by on a wagon and then descended the steps into the yard. The house was a beautiful red brick home built in the Federal style. It was a modest home, meaning that Fountain Carter wasn't a planter, but a farmer. That meant the man worked instead of watching others work.

South of the house were open fields, and the arriving troops were forming a line of battle there. Just a few yards farther south of the house were two buildings. One was a deep-red painted farm office and the other a smokehouse made of the same red bricks that were on the main house. There was a garden just beyond those two buildings.

Carter House. Scene of some of the most fierce fighting of the war.

Cox was almost jealous of Fountain Carter. The small farm was beautiful. The area sat on a slight rise of ground that looked down upon the town and river to the north.

Cox turned and walked around to the back of the house. There was a red brick kitchen directly behind the house with the door standing wide open. Fountain Carter and a black man were beside the kitchen putting a wheel on a wagon. He walked toward the two men. Once he rounded the corner, he noticed the house was bigger than he had thought. Fountain had built an extension onto the back.

125

He walked over to the wagon and asked, "How big a farm do you own, Mister Carter?"

Fountain stood up, leaned on the wagon, and said, "I got two hundred and eighty-eight acres."

"All you do is farm then?" Cox asked.

"I own that cotton gin there," Fountain pointed to the south.

Cox turned and saw the gin about a quarter mile away. Federal troops were digging breastworks just in front of it.

The old man turned his head and spat a stream of tobacco juice. He said, "Look, Colonel..."

"General," Cox interrupted. "My name's Jacob Cox."

"Whatever," Fountain looked at Cox. The look on his face told Cox that he didn't give a damn what his name was. To Fountain Carter, this man was the enemy. Both of his sons had fought for the Confederacy, and the youngest was with the army pursuing them at this very moment. "Look, General, I've worked hard all my life for what little I've got."

Cox began to nod. He thought he knew where this was going. Fountain held out his hands and continued, "What I've got, I got with these hands and the sweat of my brow. I'm not one of those rich planters you're used to dealing with."

Cox looked down at the black man still working on the wagon wheel. He wondered if this man was Carter's slave. By the way Carter was talking; he didn't think he owned any slaves.

"What I'm trying to say," the old man continued, "is that I don't want your army destroying what it took me my whole life to obtain."

Cox began to shake his head. "I was just inside talking to your daughter. I'll tell you the same thing I told her. If anyone gives you any problem, please don't hesitate to tell me. We don't make it a practice of making war on civilians."

He regretted saying the last sentence almost as soon as it was out of his mouth.

Fountain Carter eyed him a long moment out of disbelieving eyes and said, "I've heard stories."

"Mister Carter," Cox said, "I give you my word as a gentleman."

Carter nodded and bent back down to help the black man with the wagon wheel. Cox wondered if Fountain Carter believed him. It didn't really matter. The bridges would be finished soon, and the Federal army would be leaving.

He turned and walked back around to the front of the house. When he rounded the corner, he saw a bald man with a long scraggly beard that reached almost to his belly. General Schofield sat on his horse surrounded by his staff. He looked as though he might collapse at any moment.

Cox walked out to the road. "Are you alright, John?"

"I'm fine," Schofield said, but he didn't look fine. "Just tired is all."

"Begging your pardon, sir," Cox reached up and patted the muzzle of Schofield's horse. "You look like shit."

Schofield stared north, down the hill toward town. "The lack of sleep and the mental strain's about been more than I can bear."

"This house here is quite comfortable," Cox motioned toward the Carter house. "You're more than welcome to rest here."

Schofield started shaking his head. "Jacob, I'm gonna go on across the river to Fort Granger. I've got to make sure the bridges are completed, and I need to get in contact with General Thomas. You're familiar with the ground here. I'm placing you in charge of positioning the men as they come up. Have them dig in. I'm not sure how close Hood is behind us."

"I'll take care of it, John," Cox reached over and patted Schofield on the leg. He really wasn't familiar with the ground. It was dark when he'd arrived early this morning, but he was confident he could handle placing the men. "Go try and get some rest."

Schofield lowered his head and nudged the horse toward town. Cox watched him go, then turned and called for his own horse. They quickly had it saddled. Cox mounted and rode south toward the cotton gin.

His men had dug a salient around the gin. Men were busy tearing down the old building and throwing the boards into the breastworks. Fountain Carter wouldn't be happy about that. Men were busy with shovels, digging like a bunch of gophers. Cox turned and rode his horse east along the line and instructed all the men to dig in, just in case. He really didn't think there would be a fight here today.

He looked south across the open fields toward the long ridge. The Columbia Pike went through a gap there about two miles away. It would be suicide for anyone to attack across such an open space. He felt like telling the exhausted men to get some rest, but orders were orders. They'd marched all night and now were forced to dig in. Cox felt sorry for them. At least they were being given a whiskey ration as a stimulant. That should at least help. He noticed how formidable the position appeared. It would be the same story as before. Hood would come up and throw a few artillery shells while his main army swung around the flank.

He rode on down the line toward the east. Men here were cutting down an Osage orange hedge and weaving the limbs together facing south. There was no way anyone would be able to successfully break through those thorny trees.

The line of works stretched from the river east of town to the river west of town. Cox felt sure the army was secure here. He wondered why Schofield was so nervous. He turned his horse and rode back toward the Carter House.

By the time he got back, more troops were forming a second line there. The line ran just south of Fountain Carter's office and smokehouse; the Carter's garden was between this line and the advanced line. This wasn't really a line but more like a retrenchment. It only ran a few hundred yards each side

127

of the pike. The only gap was where the road passed through. The works were almost complete everywhere. Cox felt sorry for these men wasting their time and energy building entrenchments that would never be used. As the men finished with the breastworks, he watched them drop on the ground exhausted.

Fountain Carter walked out of his office and started toward Cox. The old man didn't look very happy. His fields and yard were being dug up. Cox could almost read the old man's mind. *I'll try and calm him down, Cox thought, and then I've got to find some breakfast.*

10:30 a.m.

CSA

The army was in amazingly good spirits as they hurried up the pike. Although the Federal army had escaped, there were signs everywhere that they were in disarray. There were dead horses and mules blocking the road. Most had been sabered to prevent the Confederates from using them.

Broken-down wagons had been burned to prevent their capture also. All types of equipment littered the roadside. Anything a soldier could possibly need lay scattered along the route. There were blankets, coats, canteens, and even rifles thrown away by the Union troops in their haste to escape.

Cleburne had sent Mangum ahead to locate General Brown. He wanted Brown to wait for him so they could talk. Mangum had talked to Major Vaulx this morning and learned that Hood blamed Cleburne for last night's failure. The war will be lost; he had no doubt about the final outcome now. He was frustrated with bad generalship. Above all things, Pat Cleburne believed in duty. He had never failed in that regard, and he wasn't about to allow his reputation be tarnished by a bungling commander that needed a scapegoat.

As he topped a small rise, he could see Mangum and Brown on the roadside ahead, waiting. Cleburne nudged his horse out into the field and rode past the men marching on the road. That was another reason his men loved him. Most generals made the troops clear off the road when they passed, but Cleburne thought of his men before himself.

He'd been thinking about what Vaulx had said. He had been stewing over it all morning. Now he was in a bad mood.

He rode up and shook Brown's hand. Brown looked like hell this morning. Cleburne asked, "You all right, John?"

"I've been better," Brown managed a weak smile. "What's going on, Pat?"

Mangum knew Cleburne wouldn't mind him listening in on the conversation, but he politely moved away. Cleburne didn't seem to notice. He

128

and Brown rode their horses away from the troops marching on the pike. They moved out into the middle of the field and began to ride north as they talked.

"I've received word that Hood is blaming me for Schofield's escape last night." Cleburne held his chin up high. He wasn't about to let Hood damage his reputation or his pride. He knew he'd done his job regardless of who Hood blamed.

Brown began to shake his head. He could clearly see Cleburne was upset. "I think you're mistaken, Pat. I haven't heard anything about it, if he's accused you."

"I'm afraid it's true," Cleburne's expression was grim. "It came from a very reliable source."

"You'll probably hear no more about it, Pat," Brown tried to sound cheerful.

"I can't just let this go," Cleburne shook his head. "I can't let this man imply that I didn't do my job."

Brown knew Cleburne wasn't a bad-tempered man. It took quite a bit to upset the man. Pat Cleburne was one of those rare people who had no gray areas. To Pat Cleburne, there was only right and wrong. That was what helped him become known as the 'Stonewall of the West.'

Brown looked at Cleburne and asked, "What do you intend to do?"

"As soon as this campaign is over," Pat's voice was now strained with emotion, "I'm gonna call for a full investigation into what happened."

Brown began to worry a little. What he didn't need was an investigation. He had dodged the bullet once. So far, there were only a limited number of people that had seen him drunk last night. He wondered if Cleburne was here now because he knew also.

Brown decided to feel him out. He asked, "Pat, who do you think is to blame for Schofield's escape?"

"The responsibility rests with the commander of the army." Cleburne felt Hood was seeking a scapegoat for his own failure. "He was on the field all evening. Everyone in the army sent messages to him telling him the enemy was escaping."

A courier rode across the field toward them. He reined up, saluted, and said, "General Cheatham wants to see you both. Something about what we'll do if we catch the Yanks."

Cleburne turned to Brown and said, "We'll finish this conversation later."

They both galloped off to find General Cheatham.

11:00 a.m.

USA

He'd been fighting a rearguard action all morning without relief. Forrest's cavalry was pursuing the Union army unrelentingly. Opdycke's red-haired temper was being strained to the extreme. On top of that, General Wagner had ordered him to bring all the stragglers north with him. All of this, coupled with the lack of sleep, was making him grumpier by the minute.

Opdycke kept looking north for Wagner to send another brigade to relieve him. He stared that way in vain. Like the rest of the army, Opdycke was exhausted. Most of his men looked as though they were about to collapse any moment.

Worse still, was the fact that he had to force the stragglers to march. Many of those men were raw draftees and not used to the rigors of the field. At one point, the road was full of stragglers. Those new men tended to carry everything they owned. Opdycke realized it was gonna take a lot of work to get them all moving again.

Some of those men were sitting along the roadside crying because they believed they would be captured and sent to Andersonville Prison. Opdycke wasn't about to quit. He had never been a quitter. He had given the order for his men to cut all the gear off the stragglers and force them to march at the point of the bayonet.

He had just topped Winstead and Breezy Hills, overlooking the town of Franklin about two miles away. Opdycke took out his watch and noted the time. An hour until noon, and he had gotten the stragglers back to the army. He could breathe a sigh of relief. He hoped Wagner would relieve him now.

Opdycke was looking down toward the fields before him and could see the Union army digging entrenchments. A courier was making his way up the road from the direction of town. The courier rode to the top of the hill and saluted.

He said, "Sir, General Wagner wants you to hold these two hills as long as possible. He wants Lane and Conrad's brigades to file off to your left and cook their breakfasts."

Opdycke was about to explode. His men had been the rearguard all morning long, and now they were to hold this hill while the rest of the division ate breakfast. He started to say something to the courier but decided not to. The man was just a messenger. He had absolutely no control over the orders he delivered.

Opdycke turned and looked back toward the rolling hills to the south. He could see Confederate troops moving up the road in heavy force. They were moving fast too. His brigade would be forced from the hill soon enough. He sat with his staff and watched the Rebels steadily approaching.

Suddenly, a bullet ripped into the side of his horse only inches from his leg. The report of the rifle reached just about the time the bullet hit. There was a sharpshooter close by. His horse began to stagger. Opdycke was forced to dismount. He turned to his staff and called for a new horse. Once he was back on horseback, he decided to move on up the hill to a safer position.

As the Confederate army continued moving up the road, Opdycke realized there was no way Wagner's three brigades were gonna be able to slow them much. The entire enemy army seemed to be converging on his position here. He turned his horse and rode over to the only pair of cannons he had.

A young officer was standing behind the first gun he came to. As the man saluted, Opdycke said, "Open fire on those damned Rebels and see if you can slow down their advance any."

The man nodded and turned back to his guns. Opdycke rode back up the hill away from the guns to observe the effect. The cannons opened fire but did very little to slow the advancing enemy before him. Opdycke took out his field glasses and scanned the Confederate position from west to east. There was infantry and cavalry moving together. They were moving toward the Lewisburg Pike on his far left. He was about to be outflanked. *If the Confederate army gets behind me, he thought, Wagner's entire division will be cut off and captured.*

Opdycke asked for a courier. A short blonde boy rode up on horseback and saluted. Opdycke said, "Go tell General Wagner that the Confederates are flanking my position. If I stay here, I'll be cut off. Ask him if we can withdraw."

"Yes, sir," the boy replied. He spun his horse and galloped away.

Opdycke turned and watched the Confederate army steadily moving up the road. He was getting anxious to pull back. It seemed like an eternity waiting for the courier to get back. He pulled out his watch. It was after one o'clock.

Finally, the young boy came galloping back up the hill. His horse was winded, and the boy was out of breath from the ride. He said, "Sir, General Wagner says to withdraw the division. He says for you to keep your brigade here until Conrad and Lane get off the hill."

"'Bout right," Opdycke was shaking his head. *Am I the only damned man that can fight a rearguard in this division, he thought.*

He watched as Lane and Conrad marched off the hills. Then he put his brigade in motion. The men were exhausted and stumbled down the road toward town. Opdycke was beginning to feel sorry for them. He wasn't gonna stop this time until he got his brigade behind the Union lines below.

As Opdycke and his men topped the small rise just short of the Union main line, he was shocked to see Conrad and Lane digging their brigades in on each side of the road. They were using anything they could get their hands on to dig with. Some of the men were loosening the earth with their bayonets, while others used tin cups to move it.

Colonel Joseph Conrad was near the road watching his men dig. He walked over to Opdycke and asked, "You falling in with us, Emerson?"

Opdycke looked at the thin man with the large head. "My men deserve a rest. I'm going to the rear and let 'em relax."

Up ahead, General Wagner was sitting on his horse in the middle of the pike. As Opdycke got closer, he could tell that Wagner was covered in a layer of dust.

Wagner saw Opdycke approaching and nodded.

Opdycke asked, "What the hell do you think you're doing?"

Wagner looked a little shocked at the way Opdycke was addressing him. He said, "General Schofield ordered me to hold the hills to the south as long as possible, and that's what I'm gonna do."

Opdycke knew that Wagner was a brave man. He'd proven himself in several battles, but the man didn't seem to be thinking clearly today. To leave his division out in front of the rest of the army like this was to risk disaster.

Opdycke never stopped his horse. He rode right on past Wagner while they were talking. He was taking his brigade to the main line of works about half a mile ahead.

Wagner turned his horse and rode up beside Opdycke. He pointed toward the troops digging and said, "I want you to deploy your brigade to the west of Conrad's men and extend the line out that way."

Opdycke was tired and irritable. His face was almost as red as his hair. His temper was getting shorter by the second. He turned to Wagner and yelled, "I object to such a foolish order."

Wagner looked shocked again. He asked, "What's so foolish about it?"

"Putting your men out in an open field is beyond foolish; it's ridiculous," Opdycke stopped yelling, but his voice was still loud. Leaving a division in front of the army seemed absurd. They would be flanked on both sides and destroyed. He could see it in his mind as if it were already happening. He looked Wagner in the eye and said, "This position will aide the enemy and no one else. Besides, my men are exhausted. You've had us on rearguard duty all morning without relief. We haven't even had time to eat. We've been keeping Forrest's cavalry off the army's rear all morning long. Now, they're tired and hungry and deserve a break."

Wagner looked up and saw the main line getting closer. He was growing frustrated. He couldn't get Opdycke to halt his brigade. "Emerson, I'm gonna need your tigers. Conrad and Lane can't hold without 'em."

"There's no way they'll hold with or without my brigade," Opdycke began to yell again. He was tired of the conversation. He wasn't about to turn his men around and go back out there to a position that was nothing but a death trap. His brigade didn't earn the nickname 'Opdycke's Tigers' by holding untenable positions. They'd earned that name back on Snodgrass Hill at the Battle of Chickamauga. They held there and helped George Thomas save the Union Army.

"Colonel Opdycke," Wagner shouted back. "I'm giving you a direct order to go back and form your brigade on Conrad's right."

"Yeah, well," Opdycke sounded a little calmer now. "I'm ignoring that order, damn you."

Wagner shook his head. He knew Opdycke had a bad temper, but he never thought the man would disobey a direct order. He said, "You do understand that what you're doing is insubordination?"

"Yeah, I understand," Opdycke said through clenched teeth.

"And you do understand that I can have you court-martialed for it?" Wagner was still angry, but trying to reason with the hot-tempered redhead.

Opdycke was growing furious now. He felt like Wagner was threatening him. He yelled, "Do you understand that I don't give a damn?"

They were just entering the main works. Men stopped digging and looked at the two officers arguing while they rode toward town, an entire brigade following behind. It was definitely something a man didn't see everyday.

Opdycke looked back and saw that his entire brigade was now past Wagner's forward position. There was no way he was going to turn around now. His men had earned a rest this morning, and he was gonna see to it that they got it.

Wagner was still insisting that Opdycke return to the forward line. Opdycke wasn't listening. He was looking for a place his brigade could rest. The fields were all occupied by troops from other commands, so Opdycke kept moving.

Wagner asked, "How can you justify disobeying a direct order?"

Opdycke was through arguing. He rode on, ignoring Wagner. Ahead on the left he could see a red brick house. Men had dug another line of breastworks there.

Wagner was thoroughly flustered now. He'd never seen a man as immovable as Emerson Opdycke. He'd tried to reason with him and then tried to force him to obey, but to no avail. Now he was acting as if Wagner didn't even exist. The two men's eyes met, and they glared at each other a long moment.

Finally, Wagner said, "Go on Opdycke, fight when and where you damned well please. We all know you'll fight."

They were now directly in front of the red brick house. Opdycke saw General Cox standing near the front door. Cox called out to the two men and walked to the edge of the road. He pointed toward town and said, "Colonel Opdycke, place your men in that field just north of this house. You'll be the reserve if they hit us. Your men deserve a rest."

"Yes, sir," Opdycke turned and glowered at Wagner.

Cox turned to Wagner and said, "When your rearguard work is done, have the rest of your division move back there with Opdycke's brigade and form a reserve. Whatever you do, Wagner, I don't want those men to become enveloped by the enemy."

Wagner nodded and spun his horse around. He didn't appreciate being sent to the rear. There was no glory in being the reserve. His division had stopped Hood yesterday at Spring Hill. The Federals had whipped the Confederate army and taken Atlanta. It didn't make any sense to Wagner why his superiors were becoming cautious now.

Opdycke saluted Cox and rode on past the house and into the open field beyond. As his men arrived, they began collapsing on the ground.

Wagner rode on back south, past the main works toward Conrad's position. He reached in his pocket and pulled out a flask. He took a drink. He'd been sipping from it all morning. When he arrived behind Conrad's brigade, he stopped his horse and stared toward the hills to the south. The Confederate army was already taking position on those hills he had just vacated.

Colonel Conrad saw Wagner and walked over and saluted.

"How are you, Joe?" Wagner asked.

"Tolerable, sir," Conrad looked nervous. He'd been in command for less than a day. "If they advance, you do want us to fall back to the main line, don't you?"

Wagner pulled out his watch and noted the time. It was almost three. He looked at Conrad and said, "Hell no, Joe. We can't win this war by running from the enemy. We're gonna hold 'em right here as long as we can."

Lane, who was across the road with his brigade, saw the two men talking and rode over. He asked, "We're not staying out here if they attack, are we, General?"

"I want you men to give them hell." Wagner couldn't figure out why all his subordinates were begging to retreat. "If it's possible, I want you to drive the bastards back over those damned hills. If you can't hold them, stall 'em as long as you can. We're not retreating until we just have to."

Both men nodded, but neither looked very confident. They both looked like men who had just been given the death sentence.

Wagner said, "Have your sergeants fix bayonets and force these men to stand here and fight."

Conrad was shocked. He'd never heard an order so severe before. He looked around and noticed that several of his men were listening. His brigade had a lot of conscripts in it. He hoped Wagner was just saying that to scare them, but he sounded serious.

Wagner reached in his pocket and pulled out the flask again. He turned it up and took a couple swallows.

Conrad watched as his men were still struggling to build earthworks without shovels. They weren't having much success. He looked at the Confederate army forming in lines of battle to the south. Conrad had thought he'd smelled alcohol on Wagner earlier today.

Conrad began to worry. He'd only taken command yesterday when Bradley was wounded at Spring Hill. There were quite a large number of men in the brigade who had never seen combat. He was positioned out in front of the army with no support and both flanks in the air. That meant they were facing forty thousand Rebel troops with only three thousand men.

He began to feel sick at his stomach. If the Confederates attacked here, most of his men would die.

"Give 'em hell, boys," Wagner said. He took another sip from the flask, then turned his horse and rode back toward the main line.

Lane looked at Conrad and said, "He keeps saying 'we are gonna hold out here,' and then he rides back to the main line to watch us get wiped out."

Conrad shook his head. He didn't really know what to say.

Lane said, "Let's ride down our lines and see if there's anything else missing that we can fix before the storm hits."

Both of the men had refused their flanks. The two brigades together looked like an arrow with the tip pointed toward the enemy to the south.

Conrad said, "With our flanks refused like this, it should buy us a little time if they do attack."

"A very little," Lane said. "Leaving us stuck out here in the open like this is just daring them to attack."

11:30 a.m.

CSA

Civilians had gathered along the roadside to cheer on the advancing army. It made the men feel good. A beautiful girl standing beside the road shouted, "Keep moving. You'll capture every one of the Yanks; they're running for their lives."

The regiment raised a cheer to her. Joe Thompson shouted back at her. "We'll catch those rascals and skin 'em, ma'am. Will you cook 'em up for us?"

Everyone broke into laughter. The girl blushed and then managed a smile.

They had already passed at least thirty broken-down wagons that had been abandoned by the Union army. Their spirits were beginning to soar. The weather had turned off warm. It was a beautiful Indian summer day. They were actually working up a sweat as they marched.

They marched on up the road, their pace beginning to pick up. Mack Keenum knew they were getting close to the Union army. He could feel the tension building. Soon, they arrived at a beautiful brick home on the left side of the road.

Joe Thompson pointed toward the house and asked, "You boys know whose house that is?"

"Before this war, I ain't never been outside Tuscumbia," Tom Barrett gave a toothy grin. "How you think I'm a gonna know who lives way up here?"

"It's William Harrison's home," Joe said. He looked at Tom's blank face, and then asked, "You do know William Henry Harrison, don't you?"

"Never heard of him," Tom shook his head. "Should I know 'im?"

"He was just the president of the United States once," Joe chuckled.

Mack looked amazed. He asked, "Is he home now?"

Joe laughed. "No, he's been dead for years. That's where he used to live."

Mack shrugged and looked at Tom. They both smiled at each other. They loved the way they got on Joe's nerves with their ignorance. Not everyone had the opportunity to go to school and get an education like Joe had. Most of them had to stay home and work on the farm. Mack still remembered what his dad had told the teacher who had tried to get him to send his children to school. "Those boys don't need no schooling. They gettin' all the schooling they need from me on this here farm," he'd said.

Up ahead, they could see the Union rearguard on the hills. Before they got within range of their guns, the line made a sharp turn to the right. They were moving east.

Joe said, "Boys, looks like we're flanking 'em again."

They marched east a ways and hit another road running north. Someone said it was the Lewisburg Pike. They turned north there and started toward the hill just north of them. There were no Union soldiers on the hill over here. *It's a good thing someone's using their head today, Mack thought.*

When they reached the top of the hill, they could see the valley below with the town nestled against the river. Mack noticed the entrenchments before them. The Union army had just gotten here this morning, and already, they had thrown up some formidable-looking works.

The town beyond was a nice-looking little village. It looked like a place where refined people would live. It was one of the most beautiful places Mack had ever seen. The town in the valley was surrounded on all sides by high hills. The fields below were enclosed by stone walls, some with hedges growing around them.

Mack looked at Tom. Tom was staring at the Union army below with his mouth gaped open. Mack asked, "What is it?"

Tom said, "Look at the bastards digging. They look like a bunch of damned ground hogs. Surely, we ain't gonna attack that position."

He began to study the position. It was out in the open. If they attacked here, the Yanks would be in a well-protected place. He said to Tom, "I don't think we'll hit 'em here."

Joe added, "We'd need scaling ladders just to get across those ditches."

Dick Bernard shook his head. "They's a lot of cannons and rifles massed behind them works. I don't care to try taking that."

"They even got head logs to protect their heads," Joe was sounding a little worried now. "We won't have a thing to shoot at until we cross those works."

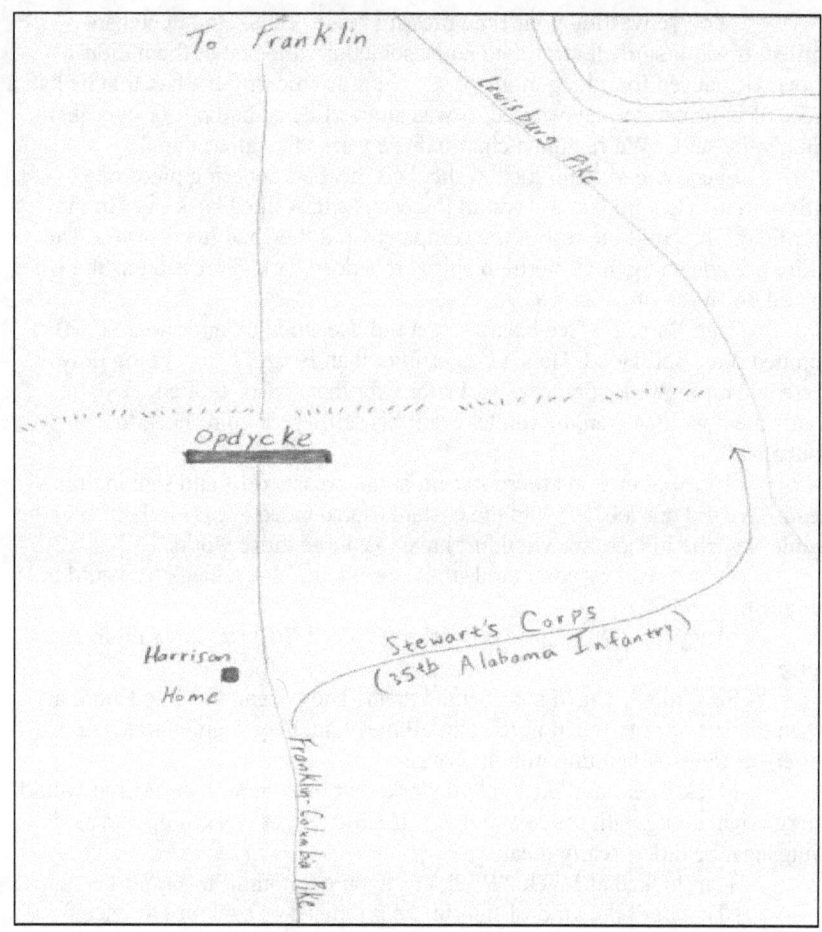

Stewart's corps flanks Opdycke off of Winstead Hill just south of Franklin.

An order was shouted, and they began to move to the left of the road. General Scott had his brigade placed in a cornfield. The corn had all been picked. The men hadn't eaten since before daylight. Someone found an old garden spot just beyond the cornfield that still had some small beans growing there. Joe shouted to his buddies, "We can cook those beans in our pork."

They all raced out and began gathering beans and shoving them into their haversacks. A young lieutenant rode by. He was in a clean, neat uniform. It was relatively easy to tell the man was a staff officer. The lieutenant laughed at them as they picked the beans.

"What's so funny?" Joe asked.

137

"You're wasting your time picking those beans," the lieutenant smiled. It was a smile that said he knew something the rest of them didn't know. He paused for a long moment as if he was enjoying the fact that he had a piece of information they wanted. It was almost like he had power over them. Finally, he said, "We're gonna charge those works this afternoon."

Every one of them looked shocked. It was a sobering piece of information. They all lost interest in the beans and walked back over to the cornfield. They told the rest of the company what they had just learned. The entire brigade had gone from high spirits to a deep dark depression as the word spread down the line.

Tom Barrett's face began to get red. He stood up and shouted, "That damned John Bell Hood. He's a bigger idiot than Bragg. I ain't going down there and hitting those damned works. Not for that son-of-a-bitch. Hell, he wants them works taken, he can take 'em his self. I'm a goin' back to Alabama."

'Rip' Baker stood there staring at the breastworks and shaking his head. "We did our job. We had the bastards surrounded at Spring Hill. If Hood would've done his job, we wouldn't have to charge those works."

"Their artillery commands the entire field," Joe added. "It would be suicide to attack here."

"They have three lines of works already," Will Bradley said in a low voice.

Several other men soon joined them. They began to curse Hood, and when they had pretty much given him all they had, they decided to curse Jefferson Davis for putting him in charge.

Mack Keenum didn't get all worked up. He knew Tom Barrett would charge right along with the rest of them. He always got worked up and said things that he didn't really mean.

Tom looked at Mack. "Well, ain't you got nothin' to say?"

"This ain't the kind of fightin' he promised us back in Florence," Mack said. "If we attack those works, we'll probably all be killed here."

"I ain't goin' down there, damn it," Tom was still shaking his head, but Mack noticed he wasn't headed back toward Alabama either.

1:00 p.m.

CSA

Hood rode north from Spring Hill with Major General Samuel French at the head of his division. He was still upset about the escape of Schofield's army. He rode most of the way without saying a word.

They were getting closer to Franklin and the Federal army. Hood could hear the skirmish firing growing louder. He shook his head, turned to French, and said, "Well, General French, we have missed the greatest opportunity of the war."

"I'm afraid you're right," French replied.

"It's days like this I wish I was back in Virginia serving in Lee's army," Hood remembered that French had served in Virginia as well. He asked, "Do you ever miss Virginia, French?"

"Not at all, sir," French was shaking his head. He couldn't help but notice Hood's sad face. "I miss home. Wish I was back in Mississippi now."

"I thought you were from up north someplace," Hood raised his eyebrows.

French began to laugh. "I'm from New Jersey, but I don't call that place home. After West Point and the Mexican War, I thought I had seen all the war I'd ever see. I married me a Mississippi gal and settled down. Let's just say I'm a Mississippian now."

"We have more in common than I thought," Hood nodded.

French looked surprised. He asked, "How so?"

"Kentucky is my native state," Hood nodded his head to the north. "When she failed to secede, I chose Texas as my adopted state."

"Why Texas?" French chuckled.

"Well, actually, I guess you could say Texas chose me," Hood managed a smile despite his bad mood. "When the war began, my good friend President Davis placed me in command of a brigade of Texans, and well, they adopted me."

French nodded. All he'd ever heard about Texas was Indians, cowboys, and a few Mexicans. Hood didn't seem like he would fit into any of those groups.

"Actually," Hood began to correct himself, "I was stationed in Texas before the war. I served with the Second United States Cavalry there."

"That's a famed unit," French looked impressed.

"Had a lot of good men in it also," Hood rubbed his temple as he thought. "Sidney Johnston, the second highest ranking Confederate general, commanded the regiment. Poor man was killed at Shiloh. He was almost a perfect commander, a real laid back type of person. Robert E. Lee was second in command. Confederate generals William Hardee, Earl Van Dorn, and Kirby Smith were all in the regiment, including myself. Federal General George Thomas was also with us."

"I hadn't realized it was quite that many." French looked amazed. "I mean, I knew about Lee and Johnston."

"You've heard that Lee is my hero, right?" Hood looked at French.

"Yes, I have," French waited.

"Most people don't realize that he was my hero before the war began," Hood began to reminisce. "He was superintendent of West Point when I was a student there."

139

"I had no idea," French looked surprised again.

"I would go riding with him often while stationed in Texas." Hood smiled at the thought. "We were out riding once and happened upon this beautiful young country girl. Lee noticed I was admiring her. In a fatherly way, he told me not to marry unless it was into a family that would make my children proud of both sides. He treated me as if I was one of his sons. I remember all the advice he gave me."

Hood remembered how hurt he'd been when Lee gave command of the Third Corps to A.P. Hill. He'd written Lee asking for the position and promotion and felt sure he would receive it. Lee had come and explained to Hood that he gave the job to Hill because he was a better administrator. Hood couldn't argue with that. Lee had a way of making one feel better about himself. He'd bragged on Hood and said that he was showing improvement and would some day make corps command. Paper was just not his thing. College had been a necessary evil for him. He had to do the schoolwork to become a soldier.

Hood looked up from his reverie. "Did you know George Thomas was my instructor at West Point?"

French shook his head.

"Yep," Hood smiled. "He taught me artillery and cavalry. I never made very good grades in his classes though. He was slow and meticulous, and I was high strung and ready to go."

"We get to Nashville, maybe you can give him a little instruction on warfare," French laughed.

"Do you know Gustavus Smith?" Hood propped his arm on the crutch strapped to the saddle.

"I know of him," French replied. "Didn't he have a nervous breakdown when given command of the army in Virginia?"

"I wouldn't call it a nervous breakdown," Hood frowned. "I don't think he was quite ready for all that responsibility at the time. Anyway, he's my cousin. He's a general in the Georgia militia now."

"Sorry," French cleared his throat. "I didn't mean to offend…"

Hood waved his hand, cutting him off. "No offense taken. You hear everything in this army."

They rode on up the pike in silence. Hood began to think about those days back in Texas. He began to think about the fight he had at Devil's River against Comanche Indians. It was his first action, and he was in command. Hood had lost seven men, two men killed and five wounded. He'd taken an arrow through the hand and was forced to pull it out himself and continue fighting. They'd been outnumbered three to one. His men had killed nine Indians and wounded about a dozen. He'd learned a valuable lesson there. It is possible to beat a larger force if you take the initiative. You must be aggressive. A good commander can't be passive like Joe Johnston and just wait for the army to come to you. Lee and Jackson had never given their enemies the initiative. They took the fight to them.

140

French looked up and saw a rider galloping down the hill just ahead. It was a courier from General Forrest.

The ragged-looking courier saluted and said, "Sir, General Forrest wants you to ride ahead and meet him at the Harrison House."

Hood nodded and asked, "How much farther is it?"

"Less than a mile, sir," the man replied. "I'll take you back there if you want."

Hood and his staff spurred ahead with the courier. They rode over rolling hills. The land around here was beautiful. The day had turned off warm and bright, despite the fact that it was so cold last night.

The Harrison House was nestled in a small valley between two hills. It looked like the place where a president would live. As they turned onto the lawn, he could see Forrest standing on the porch talking to some of his staff officers.

It was the first time Hood had seen Forrest since his outburst that morning. He wondered what kind of mood Forrest was in now. Hood reined up near the porch and waited.

Forrest continued what he was saying and then turned toward Hood. *If one didn't know any better, Hood thought, they would think that Forrest was the commander here.*

Forrest nodded at Hood. He said, "The Union army's having trouble getting across the Harpeth River."

"Are they now?" Hood asked. His face lit up and he was forced to fight back a smile.

"Yeah," Forrest replied plainly. He didn't sound very excited about the good information he was giving Hood. He said, "They're trapped in Franklin with their backs against the damned river."

Hood couldn't believe what he was hearing. It had appeared earlier the Federal army had escaped. Now, Hood had just learned, they were trapped.

Forrest could almost read Hood's mind. He said, "Their line looks damned strong. I wouldn't recommend hitting them here. You'll lose a lot of good men."

"Well, they haven't been here long." Hood began to shake his head. "How strong can they be?"

Forrest smiled grimly. "You haven't seen the position yet. It'll be a damned costly attack."

"They're bluffing," Hood said. "They can't stand a frontal assault. They want us to think they're strong, so they can buy enough time to escape again."

"I don't know 'bout that," Forrest said.

Hood wasn't listening. He said, "I'm gonna ride forward and see for myself."

Forrest watched Hood and his staff ride across the lawn and start up the pike. He turned to Major Strange and said, "That shore is a hard-headed bastard."

141

Hood rode to the top of Winstead Hill. He decided to move down the slope so he could see a little better. There was no need in taking his entire staff. All those officers together might attract sharpshooters. He turned to Mason and said, "Have Hamilton and Cooper come with us. Leave the rest here."

The four of them rode down the hill. Hood reined up under a large linden tree. It was amazing how much the temperature differed between the shade and the sunlight. Hood asked Mason for his field glasses. Mason handed them to him and watched him begin scanning the Federal position.

Hood looked over the advanced line first. Wagner's men were out in the open trying desperately to throw up some kind of protection. The position looked extremely weak. Both flanks were in the air.

He moved the glasses past the first line to the main line a quarter mile beyond. The position did indeed appear to be strong. Hood noticed the dirt looked fresh. That told him they had just been thrown up. The Federal army hadn't been here but a few hours. This position couldn't possibly be as strong as what they would face at Nashville.

Looking across the Harpeth River, Hood could see Fort Granger on a hill. He could see the ugly black muzzles of heavy artillery sticking out of the earthen walls there. He lowered the glasses and looked over the ground they would have to cross to get to the Union position. It was mostly open, except for an occasional house or small patch of trees.

He looked over his shoulder back toward the hills to the south. The Federals had fallen back from a strong position when they abandoned Winstead Hill. They had retreated without the least bit of pressure from Hood's army. From the trained eye, it appeared the Federal army was afraid to fight here.

Hood put the glasses back to his eyes. He could see the Federal wagon train parked in town waiting to get across the river.

They're trapped, he thought. They're trapped, and I'm gonna hit 'em. We've got to drive 'em into the Harpeth River before they get to Nashville. If they get there, the entire campaign will be a failure.

He began to study the Federal position again. The main line didn't appear to be more than a half mile wide. That told him that Cheatham and Stewart's men would converge on a small area. Twenty thousand men attacking on such a small front would be overwhelming. If the Federal army breaks here, Nashville will be as good as captured.

Hood handed the glasses back to Mason and tugged at his horse's reins. As he rode back to the top of Winstead Hill, he saw Peter Stewart waiting there on his horse.

Stewart nodded as Hood approached and asked, "What do you think, General?"

"We'll make the fight," Hood replied. "Go form your men."

"It's gonna be a desperate battle across those fields." Stewart shifted uncomfortably in the saddle.

"General Stewart, do you think you can get across the Harpeth River here without being seen?" Hood asked. Hood knew the answer before he asked

142

the question. It would be nearly impossible to pull the same trick over on Schofield again. The Federal army would have to be attacked here now or at Nashville where they had been entrenching for two years.

Stewart shifted in the saddle again. He turned and looked eastward. He wanted to say he could, but he didn't want to take responsibility if things didn't work out according to plan. He'd been promoted up to lieutenant general by not drawing attention to himself or taking desperate chances. After a long pause, he said, "I believe I can get across and into their rear. Wilson's cavalry is over there watching for such a move, but if we can push them back, I believe I can cut Schofield off from Nashville."

"Get Forrest to push those troopers back," Hood turned and looked over his shoulder toward the Federal lines in the valley below. "See if there's any fords there you can use. I'll get back to you directly."

Stewart saluted and spun his horse to the east.

Hood turned to Mason and said, "Find Generals Cheatham and Cleburne. Have them report to me at the Harrison House at once."

He watched Mason gallop off toward the south and then nudged his horse forward. He met Stewart's men coming up the road and moving off into the trees to his left so they wouldn't be detected. He'd almost reached the Harrison House when a courier rode up. The man held a piece of paper in his hand.

"Sir," the man coughed. He rubbed his mouth on his sleeve and continued, "General Forrest has captured a message sent from Thomas to Schofield."

Hood reached out and took the message from the courier's dirty hand. He began to read, and his eyes lit up. On the paper, General Thomas had given Schofield permission to withdraw to Nashville if he doesn't think he can hold Franklin. *Schofield is in trouble, Hood thought. Thomas wouldn't have given him permission to retire from the field if Schofield wasn't begging him to allow it. Maybe Schofield isn't as strong as he appears to be. This may be our only chance.*

1:15 p.m.

CSA

Isaac Shannon sat atop Privet Knob with the rest of the sharpshooters. He'd found a large tree stump on which to place his rifle for support. Now, it was only a waiting game. When the infantry advances, Shannon and his comrades will support them from here.

He heard horses coming up the hill behind him. He turned around and was surprised to see Pat Cleburne and a staff officer ride up.

143

Everyone jumped to their feet and saluted. Cleburne nodded and asked, "Can I borrow a scope from someone? I've left my field glasses behind."

Lieutenant John Ozanne quickly began to remove the scope from his Whitworth sniper rifle. He passed the scope to Cleburne when he had finished. Cleburne walked over and squatted behind the stump Shannon had been using. He laid the scope across the stump for steadiness and began to study the Union lines before him.

As Cleburne studied the lines, he said to Mangum, "They are very formidable."

"Yes, sir," Mangum said, "very formidable."

Cleburne stood up and passed the scope back to Ozanne. He said, "They have three lines of works…" He paused and looked toward the Union lines again and said, "and they're all complete."

Cleburne thanked Ozanne for the use of his scope and then began to fish into his inner jacket pocket. He pulled out the small memorandum book he always carried. He used the book as a sort of personal diary. He placed the book on the stump and began making some notes. After a few moments, he stood up, nodded at Shannon and Ozanne, and then moved back to his horse.

He and Mangum rode back off Privet Knob toward Winstead Hill. Once back, there was nothing to do but wait for his division to arrive. He and Mangum took sticks and scratched out a checkerboard in the soft dirt. They gathered different colored leaves to use as checkers and started a game. Cleburne wished he had brought along his chess set. He preferred chess to checkers, but this would have to do.

Cleburne and Mangum had started their third game, when a courier arrived. Mangum was still looking for his first win. The courier dismounted and saluted. Cleburne looked up from the game and gave a sloppy salute.

The man said, "General Hood wants you to return to the Harrison House for a council of war, sir."

Cleburne looked at Mangum with a resigned expression and said, "Come on Mangum, let's go."

Cleburne and Mangum mounted their horses and followed the courier back south on the Columbia Pike. When they arrived, there was a large crowd of staff officers on the front lawn. Cleburne didn't have to tell Mangum to wait outside.

A guard beside the front door saluted and told Cleburne to go on inside. The others were already inside waiting for him.

Once inside, Cleburne found the commanders sitting in the dining area around a large table. Generals Cheatham and Hood were discussing something about Schofield's intentions. General Forrest sat opposite Cheatham. When he saw Cleburne, he turned and nodded toward the seat beside him.

Cleburne walked over and sat down beside Forrest and asked, "Where are the others?"

"We're it," Forrest replied. "Stewart's over on the right getting his corps on line."

Cleburne couldn't help but wonder why he had been asked to come. Forrest commanded the cavalry and Cheatham commanded a corps, but Cleburne was only a division commander. He wondered why the other division commanders hadn't been invited.

Hood cleared his throat and said, "The Union army is trapped with their backs to the river. This is the last opportunity to fight them outside the strong works at Nashville. So, I've decided to hit them here at Franklin."

Hood waited for his subordinates to agree with his decision, but no one said a word. Cleburne knew it was a suicide mission, but he wasn't about to complain after Hood had blamed him for yesterday's disaster at Spring Hill.

"Are you out of your damned mind?" Forrest almost screamed. He wasn't about to let this go with saying something. He didn't care what Hood or anyone else thought about him.

Hood said nothing to Forrest. He had hoped Forrest would have been gone when he returned from his reconnaissance. The man was quickly becoming a thorn in Hood's side.

Forrest wasn't finished. He said, "There is absolutely no way in hell we can take those works down there without losing half the army."

"The Yankees are only acting like they are making a stand down there." Hood began to shake his head and said, "They're trapped. You said that yourself, General Forrest, and now they're bluffing. Much like what you're famous for. You more than anyone else here should recognize their bluff for what it is."

Forrest didn't like the way Hood had said the last part, but he held his temper. He wanted to tell Hood to ask those men at Fort Pillow if Forrest was all bluff. He'd warned those men that he would take no prisoners, and they'd learned the hard way that he wasn't merely bluffing.

Forrest decided it would be best to calm down and try to reason with his stubborn commander. He said, "General Hood, if you give me one division of infantry, I'll take my cavalry and have them flanked out of those breastworks in two hours' time."

Hood had begun shaking his head before Forrest finished the sentence. He didn't want the Union army flanked from their works. He wanted to hit them. *Why can't I get these men to understand that we can't win without fighting, he wondered.* Hood said, "General Forrest, I want you to divide your cavalry. Place half on the right and half on the left of the army. Be ready to help scoop up the prisoners when they break."

"I can use Holly Tree Gap," Forrest was as close to begging as he would ever get. "Give me a division, and I'll cut off their retreat route. Schofield will be forced to surrender to you."

"The time for flanking has passed," Hood said. He was growing tired of arguing with Forrest. "Look, General, we tried that yesterday, and I couldn't get any of my commanders to fight. If I gave you a division, there would be

145

some reason they couldn't fight when they got in rear of the Union army. We've got our enemy trapped here, and we're gonna finish them here."

Forrest could see that Hood's mind was made up. There was no use in further arguing with the man. He crossed his arms and sat back in his chair.

Hood nodded at Cleburne and asked, "What do you think, Pat?"

Cleburne raised his head and pondered a long moment. His face looked unusually sad. He finally decided to say something for his men. Those poor men had fought for three long years, and Hood was about to sacrifice them. He believed Hood thought him a coward, but he wanted to say something for his men. "General Hood, I've scouted the Federal position. We'll have to march across two miles of open fields just to reach their entrenchments. Those works are strong. I believe an attack here will be a terrible and useless waste of life."

Just the sort of thing I'd expect from him, Hood thought. Something about Cleburne had changed recently. Hood couldn't quite put his finger on it, but something about the man wasn't quite right. Hood looked at Cheatham and asked, "What about you, Frank?"

Cheatham was shaking his head. After Hood's tirade this morning, Cheatham didn't want to go against his commander. He was afraid Hood would call him a coward also. He wondered how he could word it that he didn't come across as being afraid. Finally, he said, "I don't like the looks of this fight, Sam. They have an excellent position and they're well fortified. I believe they're down there at this very moment hoping you'll hit 'em. An attack here will be a desperate act."

Hood reached up with his good arm and began to rub his neck. He couldn't believe every one of his commanders was afraid to attack. It appeared that Johnston had ruined this army. This army was in worse shape than McClellan's army had been two years ago. They had advanced over two-hundred miles into enemy territory and were still afraid to give battle. He was beginning to believe he would never eradicate this evil from his army. He wondered what was left for him to do. He'd tried everything he could think of.

"Gentlemen," Hood said. He was suddenly feeling weary. "Darkness is coming soon. We must act before the enemy retreats to Nashville. I would much rather fight them here where they've only had a few hours to fortify, than to fight them at Nashville where they've been fortifying for three years."

No one said a word. Hood's council of war was over. Cleburne wondered why Hood had ordered them here and asked their opinions, when he'd already made up his mind to attack anyway.

Hood said, "Let's ride to Winstead Hill, and I'll give you the final orders."

The four of them walked to the front porch. Hood hobbled along behind them with his crutch. As the staff officers strapped Hood into his saddle, Forrest moved his horse over and stared at his commander.

Forrest asked, "Can you give me my orders now? I need to get my men into position."

146

Both men seemed to want the same thing. Forrest wanted to be away from Hood and Hood was sick of his insubordinate cavalryman. Hood said, "Place Jackson and Buford's divisions on the right and Chalmers's division on the left. Exploit any breakthrough that's made."

"I believe what you're about to do is pure murder." Forrest stared into Hood's eyes. "I hope the blood about to be spilled here will haunt you for the rest of your miserable life."

Hood said nothing. He thought about placing the man under arrest, but he realized that wouldn't work. He began to understand why Forrest and Bragg had so much trouble. Forrest wasn't a gentleman. He had no military training and didn't understand how to be a good subordinate.

Hood pulled on his horse's reins and moved up the road leading to Franklin. Cheatham rode with Hood, but Cleburne rode behind all the staff officers with Mangum. He noticed how pitiful Hood looked riding his horse. His bad arm lay across his lap, while he wrestled with the reins in his other hand. On any other occasion, Cleburne would have felt sorry for the man.

As Hood rode north toward Winstead Hill, he began to think about Robert E. Lee. The man had tried to flank McClellan's army two years ago during the Seven Days battles. When his subordinates had failed him the same way Hood's had failed him yesterday, Lee had ordered a massive frontal assault. It had been costly, but it also won a major victory. *That's what this army needs just now, he thought. After being pushed all the way to Atlanta and beyond, these men need to taste a victory.*

They rode up the road to the top of Winstead Hill. Hood turned his horse to the left and rode out a few yards. He had his staff help him dismount. Cleburne and Cheatham dismounted and moved over beside Hood. Below them, Cleburne could see generals Brown and Bate standing together talking. When they saw Hood, they came up the hill together.

Hood had just gotten on the ground when they arrived. Before he could say anything, General Stewart rode up from the far right. Cleburne watched the sun growing low in the western sky. The Federal lines were plainly visible to the north. Hood nodded at the newcomers. He realized everyone was against the attack, except maybe Stewart. He pointed toward the Union lines across the way and said, "As you all can see here, the country is open. We can't flank them again without being seen. If we try it, Schofield will simply fall back to Nashville."

No one said a word. Hood looked at Cheatham and said, "We'll wait until Bate gets into position before going in."

Cheatham nodded. Hood added, "Lee's men will go in as they arrive, but we're not gonna wait for them."

"Right," Cheatham said.

Hood turned to General Bate and said, "Go get your division into position at once. You'll be the left flank. You'll form up over near the Bostick House."

Bate saluted and moved away. Hood looked toward the west. The sun

147

Major General Patrick Ronayne Cleburne.
"The Stonewall Jackson of the West."

was quickly moving low in the sky. He was in a race against darkness here. He thought about the battle at Gaines Mill again. He'd broken a strong position there right at sunset.

Stewart said, "My men are in position, sir."

"Very well," Hood said. "I'll give the signal from here when Bate is in position. When you see Cheatham's troops move out, send your corps in. I want you gentlemen to remember one thing. When you go in, withhold your fire until it can be used with deadly effect. Then you should charge and break their lines. In a long-range fight, the Yankees are our equals, but up close and personal, we are far superior. The history of this war proves that. I've never seen the Federal army stand against a determined charge. Remember, it is important to break their lines."

"Right," Stewart saluted and climbed back onto his horse.

Hood held up a hand for Stewart to wait. He said, "I want Schofield driven into the Harpeth River at all costs."

"Right," Stewart said again and then rode away.

Hood turned back to Cleburne and said, "Form your division to the right of the pike. Have your left overlap Brown's right..." He looked toward Brown. "You form on this side and have your right overlap his left."

Brown nodded. Hood looked back at Cleburne. "Tell your men not to fire until they leave their first line of works. When they run, I want you to press them. Shoot 'em in the backs while they're running. Then, charge their main line with the bayonet."

Hood paused to see if there were any questions. There were none. He said, "Franklin is the key to Nashville and Nashville is the key to our independence."

No one said a word. Hood could see they were all against his decision. General Brown was standing with his hands behind his back staring at the ground. Cleburne was staring off toward the Union lines below them. Cheatham alone was looking at Hood. Hood said, "Allow me, gentlemen, to tell you something I learned from General Lee back in Virginia. To be a good general, you must love your men; but to be a great commander, you must be willing to see those men die."

Cleburne thought, to die is one thing, but to be slaughtered for no reason is something totally different.

He looked at Hood and asked, "Will it be all right if I form my division into columns to present a smaller front to the enemy?"

"That'll be fine," Hood sighed. Cleburne was still concerned about losing his men. He said, "But when you go in, you hit 'em with everything you've got. Don't stop your attack until the last man is dead or they're driven

into the Harpeth River at the point of the bayonet."

Cleburne climbed onto his horse and looked back at Hood. He said, "We'll take those works, or I'll fall in the attempt."

Hood watched Cleburne ride back east toward Breezy Hill. He turned to Cheatham and Brown and said, "Gentlemen, now go down to the work that has to be done and go at it."

Cleburne saw his brigade commanders standing together halfway up the north slope of Breezy Hill. The rest of the division was in line of battle just below them. He rode over to the group of generals and dismounted.

Govan could tell by the expression on Cleburne's face that things weren't going well. The man looked distraught. He'd never seen the general quite this depressed. There was a sense of eternal sadness emanating from him.

"The enemy's works must be carried at all hazards," Cleburne said. He jerked his thumb back toward Winstead Hill behind him. "Hood has given direct orders that we must take those works with the bayonet. Pass the word along to your officers."

Lowrey turned and looked toward the Union lines. He slowly began to shake his head in disbelief. Granbury simply lowered his head and walked down the slope toward his brigade of Texans.

General Govan stood there looking at Cleburne a long moment. They had grown close over the years. Cleburne had selected Govan to lead his original brigade of Arkansans. He couldn't help but worry about Cleburne. Over the past few weeks, he seemed to be growing more and more despondent.

Cleburne thought about his kid brother Christopher, though everyone called him 'Kit.' He'd become a captain in John Hunt Morgan's cavalry, although he was only twenty-three. Cleburne had been more proud of Kit when he'd been promoted to captain than when he'd been promoted to Major General. The letter he'd received back in May stated that his kid brother had been killed leading a gallant charge. At least Cleburne could find solace in that. Surely, a man who died for his country would go to heaven.

After a long, awkward pause, Cleburne asked, "Govan, I ever tell you about that kid I killed on the Mississippi River?"

"Killed?" Govan repeated. The look of shock was plainly visible on his face.

149

"It was five years before the war began. James Crary, a friend of mine, invited me to go pick dewberries with him on Island Number Sixty. There were two men and a fifteen-year-old boy wanting a ride across the river to Arkansas." Cleburne paused a long moment, his eyes staring at his feet. "I was steering the boat. The wind was up, and as we approached the Arkansas shore, a steamboat suddenly got loose from the wharf. I saw it and was about to stop, but James told me to go on and pass it. I tried, but the steamboat was moving too fast. When it hit our boat, we all went overboard. James, one of the men, and the boy were all swept away by the current and drowned. I was so weak when I got to shore, I couldn't even stand."

Govan was shaking his head. "Wasn't your fault, Pat. It could have been any of us. How can you blame yourself?"

"I also killed a young lieutenant when the war began," Cleburne continued staring at the ground. "I'd made my headquarters in the courthouse at Pittman's Ferry, Arkansas. This young officer had brought in some Federal prisoners earlier that evening and locked them in the garret of the courthouse. I was asleep and heard a loud thud. Someone in the corridor yelled that the prisoners were escaping. I grabbed my pistol and ran out the door. I could see a shadowy figure coming down the corridor, so I raised my weapon and fired. When someone finally got a lantern lit, I found I had mortally wounded the young lieutenant. Before he died, he told me he had been sleep walking, a problem he'd had since he was a kid. It's haunted me ever since."

Govan couldn't believe Cleburne had kept all these stories to himself. It explained a lot about his mood. Govan tried to think of something soothing to say, but he realized it wouldn't help. *If Pat's been blaming himself for these incidents all these years, nothing I'm gonna say will help.*

Cleburne looked up, his eyes welling with tears. "Maybe its time for me to pay for my sins."

Govan stood there looking at Cleburne a few moments. He wanted to say something, but nothing came to mind. He was already having a bad feeling about this battle. He turned and stared at the Federal lines across the way. Finally, he said, "Well, General, there won't be many of us that'll make it back to Arkansas."

Cleburne's expression began to change. It was as if he was changing into his famous battle face right before Govan's eyes. He raised his chin, and his eyes flashed. With a firm voice, he said, "Well, Govan, if we're to die, let's die like men."

3:45 p.m.

CSA

Otho Strahl waited patiently behind his line of troops for the signal for the advance to be given. It amazed him how quiet his men had become when they'd been told they were gonna attack the entrenched Union army almost two miles away.

He could see some of the men's mouths moving as they quietly whispered a prayer. Every one of them had a somber expression on their face.

Lieutenant John Marsh, Strahl's inspector general, was fidgeting with his sword. He looked at Strahl and said, "I'm afraid we're all gonna be annihilated, sir."

Strahl said nothing. Marsh watched his commander standing there staring toward the Union lines. He was proud to say he'd served under the man. He'd never heard General Strahl use a word of profanity. The man was a true Christian. Strahl had come to be known as a fighter, despite the fact that he was only a lawyer before the war began. Some people referred to him as a military genius because of his ability to maneuver his brigade with such ease in battle. *If I survive the war, Marsh thought, at least I'll have some good tales for my grandchildren.*

He began to notice a look he had never seen on his commander's face before. It was a look of extreme sadness. Marsh had heard that sometimes you could look at a man before the battle and tell if he was gonna survive a fight or not. He concentrated hard on Strahl's expression trying to obtain a premonition, but he only saw sadness.

Strahl noticed Marsh staring at him. He began to stroke his long spade-like beard and said, to no one in particular, "This fight is gonna be short and desperate."

Marsh simply nodded his head. He was beginning to have a bad feeling about this fight.

Strahl said, "I think I'll walk down my lines again."

He started down the hill toward the troops in his first line. He was thinking back on his life. He was a long way from Morgan County, Ohio, his birthplace. Upon finishing college, he'd moved to Dyersburg, Tennessee, and become an attorney. He'd only been practicing law for three years when the war began. People had wondered which way he would go when Tennessee seceded, but Strahl had never doubted what he would do. He would go with his adopted state; besides, both of his grandmothers were southerners, and Strahl had always considered himself a southerner at heart.

He'd been lieutenant colonel of the 4th Tennessee Infantry at the battle of Shiloh. His regiment had captured a battery of artillery on the first day of action, but they'd also suffered fifty percent casualties. Colonel Neely had died after Shiloh, and Strahl had become colonel. At Perryville, Kentucky, his regiment had again taken fifty percent casualties. He'd been praised in the official reports for his conduct at the battle of Murfreesboro. In July of 1863, he'd been promoted to brigade command. They'd been in reserve at Chickamauga and saw very little action. He'd fought in the Atlanta Campaign but had been wounded at the battle of Atlanta on July 22 of this year. He'd just rejoined his troops last month. If he'd been slower to recover from his wounds, he wouldn't be staring across two miles of open fields toward those Union breastworks at the moment.

Strahl walked down the line of his old 4th Tennessee Infantry Regiment. He offered an encouraging word here and there for the men. The troops of his old regiment were ragged and dirty; some were without shoes. He said, "I want you men to make a valiant fight here today."

Suddenly, he saw a face he recognized. He stopped and eyed the man for a long moment. He'd talked to this man this morning, as a matter of fact, but couldn't recall his name. He asked, "What's your name, private?"

"Puckett, sir," the boy smiled, revealing large white teeth.

Strahl remembered now. This boy had family that lived just south of town. He wondered what in the world this boy was doing here standing in line of battle when he had permission to be home with his family. He asked, "Didn't I give you a furlough to go visit your family this morning?"

The boy reached into his jacket pocket and pulled out the furlough. "Yes, sir; I still got it too, sir. But this is my family now. The furlough will have to wait until after the battle. I'm not about to abandon my friends at a time like this."

Strahl placed his hand on the boy's shoulder. He lowered his head and began moving on down the line. Upon reaching the end of his line, he turned and made his way back up the hill where his staff waited. Just as he reached his original position, he saw a cluster of horsemen ride over the hill and stop just behind his brigade. He instantly recognized General Hood and his staff.

Chaplain Charles Quintard was riding with Hood. He was sitting on the horse Strahl had given him this morning. Quintard's horse had become sick and was no longer able to carry him. Strahl had given his own horse, "Lady Polk," to Quintard. The chaplain had tried to refuse the offer, but Strahl had his mind set. A good officer didn't ride while his men walked anyhow.

Quintard saw Strahl and rode down the hill. As he came near the group of officers, he called out, "Are you sure you won't take the horse back, General?"

Strahl shook his head. Chaplain Quintard climbed from the horse and took Strahl's hand. Strahl asked, "Will you pray for us, Charles?"

"Of course," Quintard nodded. "Trust in God, General."

"I do," Strahl was looking down toward his feet. "I do."

He let go of Quintard's hand and looked away. Quintard looked at the handsome face and the thick black hair. He'd never seen General Strahl this melancholy.

He turned to Lieutenant Marsh and asked, "And how are you, John?"

"I'd rather not be here. I can tell you that," Marsh managed a weak smile.

Quintard extended his hand, but Marsh didn't take it. He moved forward, grabbed the chaplain, and held him tight. Quintard was shocked momentarily. Marsh quickly kissed Quintard on the cheek and said, "Sir, if I'm killed…" He paused searching for the words. "Because of you, I know I'll go to heaven; therefore, I can go into this battle without fear or worry."

Quintard was suddenly feeling depressed. Listening to Hood, he had thought this was gonna be an easy victory, but the men who were actually gonna do the fighting didn't seem to have the same opinion. He turned and shook Captain Johnston's hand. Afterwards, he stood there a long, awkward moment. No one was saying a word. He slowly climbed back on the horse and said, "God go with you, gentlemen."

He turned the horse and rode back up the hill toward General Hood.

Strahl could remember being baptized by Charles Quintard back in April as if it was yesterday. The chaplain had baptized Generals Hardee, Shoup, and Govan that day.

Strahl shook his head and looked down at the brigade in front of his. General Gordon's Tennessee Brigade was in the lead. They would have it far worse. With any luck, Gordon's brigade would break them, and his brigade would just do the mopping up. He stared across the fields toward the Union position and realized that wasn't likely to happen.

To his left, he could see twenty-six-year-old Brigadier General John Carter on horseback behind his Tennessee troops. The man was making last minute adjustments to his line. Like Strahl, he too was in support. Brigadier General States Rights Gist's South Carolinian brigade was positioned in front of Carter.

Strahl looked to his right. His flank rested upon the Columbia Pike. Beyond the road was Cleburne's division. He stood there and admired the beautiful blue battle flags with the huge white circles in the middle that were distinctive of the Irishman's regiments. Some had a crossed cannon inside the circles, indicating that regiment had captured a Union battery at some point during the war. A band had just struck up the Bonnie Blue Flag over there.

He stood there listening to the lively tune, thought about home, and waited for the signal to be given.

3:55 p.m.

South Carolina

Nathaniel Gist was dying. The brother of Confederate Brigadier General States Rights Gist had wanted to fight in the war, but was found unfit due to the fact that he was nearly deaf. He'd been forced to retrieve the body of a dead relative who'd recently been killed in battle. It had been a somber trip; the war had gone on far too long. Upon his return from the front, he'd come down with typhoid fever.

He didn't need a doctor to tell him he was dying. He was a doctor, though he'd never practiced medicine. He'd become a physician as a profession back in college, but had bought eleven hundred acres and become a planter once he'd graduated.

The entire family was gathered around his bed waiting for the inevitable. His sister Sarah was gently wiping his forehead with a wet rag. His fever was high again, and he was beginning to show signs of delirium. He began to mumble incoherently.

Sarah leaned over and whispered into his ear, trying to calm him. "We're here, brother; everything's all right. You try and rest now."

Nathaniel seemed to understand. His body relaxed, and he stared toward the ceiling. Suddenly, his eyes grew wide as if he were seeing an apparition. His voice betrayed the agony of what he seemed to be seeing. He said, "Sarah, States was killed this afternoon leading his men in battle."

Everyone in the room grew silent. Most were leaning forward in their seats trying to understand what he was saying. It was as if he'd seen something the rest of them couldn't see. They understood that Gist's brigade was part of the army invading Tennessee, but there'd been no word of a battle.

Sarah reached out and gently patted Nathaniel on the arm. "No, brother, States is fine. You were just dreaming. It's the fever."

He shook his head as he continued to stare at the ceiling. He wouldn't be comforted by her words. He'd seen something. Something that was playing out over four hundred miles away at that very moment. Several of his family told him everything was fine, and he should rest. He ignored them.

Nathaniel lay still for a few moments saying nothing. Finally, he said, "I know States is dead."

Everyone in the room was unnerved by the scene. They were sure it was the fever, but Nathaniel had seemed so sure of what he'd seen. They wondered if being that close to death had allowed him to see something happening at this very moment in another part of the world. Nathaniel closed his eyes and waited for death to take him to that peaceful place where his brother would be waiting for him.

4:00 p.m.

CSA

He watched the long lines of men standing in formation as they shifted about trying to get a good look at the enemy position they were about to assault. The line officers were all looking towards him, patiently waiting for his headquarters flag to drop. That was the signal he was using for the advance to begin.

The long battle line was a beautiful thing to Hood. A full twenty thousand men stretching for two miles—it was something he'd never forget. He shifted in the saddle and peered past the small cedars to his left. Bate's men were still racing to get into position. He looked to the west. The sun was growing low in the sky. It was getting late. There's no more time to wait. Bate will just have to catch up.

He thought about what he was about to do. His brain spat something out at him that he'd almost forgotten. A lesson he'd learned back at West Point. It was how, at a time of great responsibility, a commander tends to hesitate. He wants to ask someone else if what he's about to do is the right thing. The professor had said that if you waver at a time like this, your decision is more likely to be in error.

He thought about Lee and Jackson. They were true warriors. They never hesitated. Those two men would make their decisions and never doubt them for a second. He thought about commanders like McClellan and Joe Johnston. They were men of caution. They were the type of men who would build a bridge and then hesitate to cross it. Men like Lee and Jackson would seize the bridge, cross it, and capture their enemy.

Their moves were often bold and reckless, but those moves usually resulted in victories. Both were now admired by everyone, even their enemies. Both men understood that fifty thousand men on the offensive were far better than one hundred thousand kept on the defensive. That was something Joe Johnston could never understand.

Lee and Jackson refused to retreat. They refused to demoralize their men by giving the initiative to the enemy and idly waiting on the defensive. Sure, they lost men in combat, but Joe Johnston lost far more through desertion and straggling. Men who retreat and hide behind breastworks have a much lower morale than men who attack.

Hood looked at the man holding his headquarters flag. The man hadn't been attached to him very long. Hood didn't even know his name. The man was patiently waiting, staring at Hood with both hands on the flag. Hood nodded his head at the man. The man knelt to the ground on one knee lowering the flag, but not quite letting it touch the ground.

Hood heard officers shouting below him. He heard "Attention" being shouted everywhere. It was amazing to watch twenty thousand men snapping to attention at almost the same instant. It made chill bumps rise on Hood's back.

He heard the command given to shoulder arms. He loved the sound the rifles made when they were passed from hand to hand to shoulder. Moments like these reminded him why he loved commanding so much.

Officers were yelling, "Brigade forward, quick time march!"

The scene was one of beauty as he watched twenty thousand men surge forward almost as one. Hood could see over a hundred battle flags floating over the men. He was sure there was no way the Federal army could withstand the coming assault. Tomorrow, Nashville would fall.

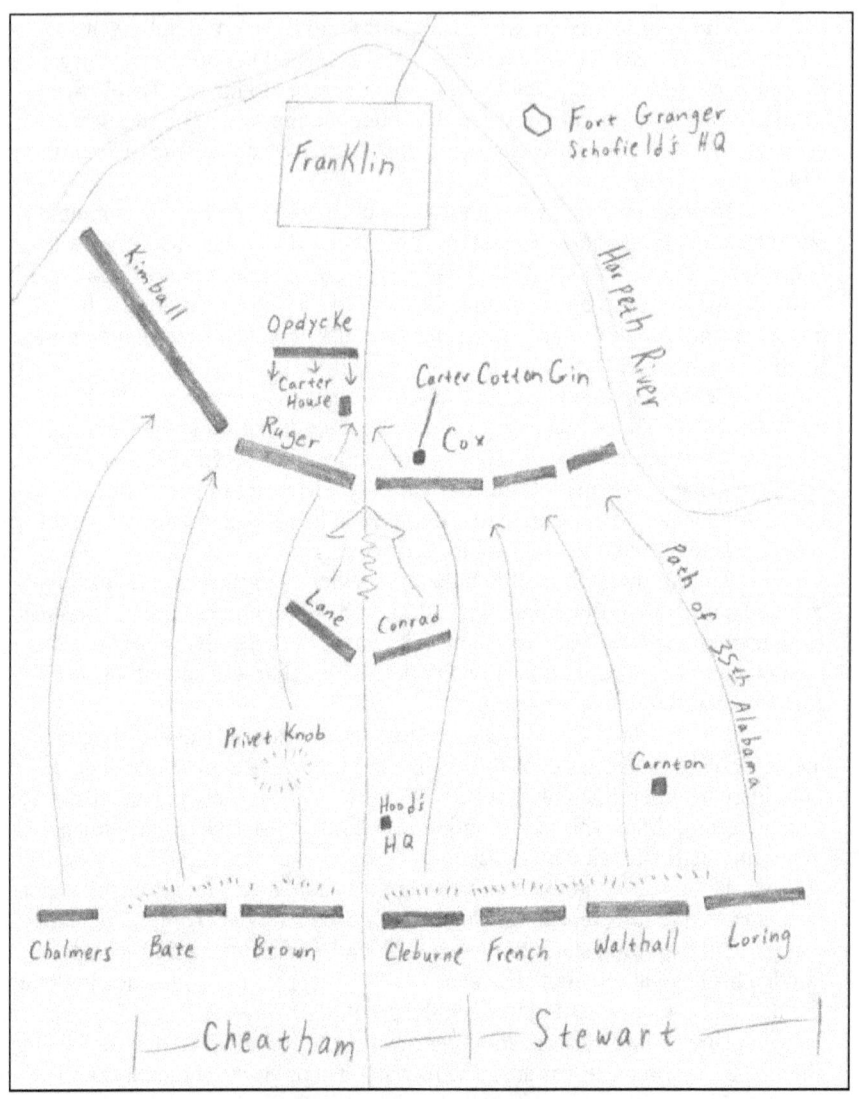

The attack at Franklin.

Hood turned his horse and spurred it onto the Columbia Pike. His staff and escort were trailing behind. Up ahead, General Cheatham was following behind his corps. He soon turned his mount and galloped across the field toward Privet Knob where he planned to watch the battle. The man was pretty much useless here. There was nothing for him to coordinate. The orders were given. General Hood had eliminated the mistake-prone corps commanders.

As his men pressed on toward the first enemy line, he saw Cleburne and Brown meeting in the middle of the pike. They were trying to keep their troops together for the big push. Hood smiled to himself. *Cleburne's a good man; he just needed a little push is all. He'll go in there now and fight like hell and probably come out of this fight a lieutenant general.*

Hood stopped his horse in front of a small farm. He remembered it from the map, the Neeley home. He rode just past the small farmhouse and had his staff help him dismount. They removed the saddle from his horse and spread a blanket on the ground. Hood lay on the blanket and used the saddle as a pillow. He then relaxed for a change and watched the battle develop just as some people would watch a play for entertainment.

He thought back to the day he had been baptized by General Leonidas Polk back in Georgia. He'd changed that day for the better. Before, he had never been very religious. Since that day, he'd neither used profanity nor drank alcohol. He thought about one of his heroes back east. Stonewall Jackson had been a Christian soldier. Poor Jackson lay in a grave in Lexington, Virginia. Polk had been blown to pieces by a cannonball at Pine Mountain. Hood bowed his head and prayed that he was doing the right thing here today.

Part 5

Valley of Death

"Never did troops fight more gallantly."

John Bell Hood

4:05p.m.

CSA

Wiley Howard rode up on "Joe Johnston" and dismounted. "Joe", as Wiley called him, was Gist's favorite horse. He pulled the saddle from Joe and turned back for the forage he had left hanging around the horse's neck. General Gist turned and saw his body servant pulling the turkey and two chickens from the horse. Wiley had been gone for two days foraging for the general and his staff.

Gist walked over and shook Wiley's hand. He was proud of Wiley. The man always made sure the general had something to eat and kept his clothes clean. Gist said, "Wiley, I don't even want to know where you got those birds."

"Why, Marse States, you know I didn't steal 'em," Wiley looked hurt. He dug around in his haversack and pulled out a couple of pieces of ham. "I knew I didn't have time to cook for you, so's I paid a lady down the road for somethin' for us to eat."

States took a piece and sat down against a small sapling. Wiley lay on the ground across from the general. He said, "Marse States, I had to go 'bout to South Carolina to find dem birds. The whole country done been picked over."

"I thought you'd taken my favorite horse and gone back home," Gist managed a smile. "I was about to ask the Union army for an exchange. I thought they had captured you."

"Oh, no suh," Wiley shook his head and took another bite of ham. "Don't talk dat way, General. You knows I'm scared of dem Yankees. Is we goin' into battle today?"

"Any minute now," Gist motioned across the field toward the Union lines. "Wiley, I want you to take my money, my watch, and my ring. I may get tripped up this evening. If I do, use what money you need. Just make sure you get my watch and ring back to Miss Janie."

"Don't talk dat way," Wiley looked concerned. He didn't like the way States was sounding. It wasn't like him to sound depressed before a battle. He was usually excited. "You gone be all right, Marse States."

Gist didn't act as though he heard Wiley. He said, "You may as well put that saddle back on Joe for me. Kitty is broke down."

Wiley was shaking his head. "Marse States, you know you ain't got no business on Joe. He ain't got no sense when the bullets is a flyin'."

"I have no choice," Gist wasn't in the mood to argue with the man. "Kitty is stumbling around and can't hardly walk. Joe's just gonna have to get used to the bullets."

160

Brigadier General States Rights Gist. Being passed over for promotion after having a sterling record as a commander, Gist had applied for a transfer back to South Carolina.

Wiley slowly got to his feet. He knew there was no sense in arguing with the general once he made his mind up on something. If he said to saddle Joe, then he was gonna ride Joe into battle, and nothing could change the man's mind.

He saddled the horse and walked him back down to the general. Gist thanked him and climbed into the saddle. He reached down and held his hand out to Wiley. Wiley shook the general's hand and said, "I'm a goin' in with you, Marse States."

Gist handed him the watch and ring. "Not this time, Wiley. I want you to do as I told you. Make sure those things get back to Janie."

"You be careful out there, General," Wiley was shaking his head. "I promised Miss Janie I'd bring you back in one piece."

Gist started to say something, but Lieutenant Trenholm was standing behind him and said, "Sir, they've dropped the flag."

"Let's go," Gist replied and spurred the horse forward.

Wiley walked back over to the sapling and watched Gist advance with his troops.

They moved down to the bottom of the hill and made their way across a small stream. There was a rock wall on the other side, and Gist halted the brigade there. Once everyone was closed up again, Gist gave the order and they moved out. They were advancing toward the right flank of the advanced Union line. A couple cannons opened fire. He decided they would be far better off if they went ahead and charged across the field and got within striking distance without having to lose a lot of men walking at a slow march under fire.

As they closed with the Federals, Joe was hit in the neck and began to plunge wildly, almost throwing Gist to the ground. He managed to get the horse stopped and dismounted. He let go of the reins and moved forward on foot with his men. He pulled his sword from the scabbard and swung it violently toward

161

the Union lines. He was yelling the 'rebel yell' right along with his men. Suddenly, he saw the advanced line breaking.

"They're breaking, boys!" Gist screamed. "Don't give 'em a chance to regroup. Charge 'em!"

He ran with his men as they pursued the broken foe. From this point to the main line, the ground was mostly level. There was a large cornfield ahead, just before they reached the line of earthworks. His men charged straight on through the corn, trampling it underfoot. On the other side of the main line and to his right, he could see the Carter House. The men in the main line were breaking for the rear, heading for the retrenchment just this side of the house. If they kept advancing, they would pass right through the backyard of Fountain Carter's home.

He moved beneath a sugar maple tree and paused to look around at his brigade. They were completely disorganized, but it didn't matter at the moment. He had the enemy running, and he didn't want to give them time to regroup. He began to move forward again when a bullet struck him in the thigh. He hit the ground hard but quickly stood up. It was a flesh wound. Pain shot through his leg, but it was gonna take more than that to keep him out of the fight. He began to move forward again.

He could see a locust grove up ahead. His men were headed straight toward it. On the other side was the retrenched line. The Union troops had cut down some of the trees and made an abatis in front of their position.

His men were mixed together with the retreating Federals and had already taken a large number of prisoners. Soon, the Union troops behind the retrenchment could hold their fire no longer. When they opened up, they killed about as many of their own men as they did of Gist's.

Suddenly, he felt as though a horse had kicked him square in the chest. He found himself on his back staring toward the darkening sky. There was a warm, wet feeling spreading across his chest. He looked down and saw dark blood spreading across his shirt. He grabbed his chest and felt for the wound. There was a neat hole where the bullet had entered the right side of his chest, and then the pain hit. He coughed, and blood came out of his mouth.

Lieutenant Trenholm leaned over and looked at the wound. He said, "Relax now, sir. I'll get the litter bearers over here. Wait right here."

Trenholm felt dumb for saying the last part. Of course Gist would wait right here. It would have almost been funny under different circumstances. He found some litter bearers and returned to the general.

Gist tried to say something but coughed up more blood. They soon had him on a stretcher and headed for the rear. Trenholm walked along beside them. He reached out and held Gist's hand. "You're gonna be fine, General. I've seen a lot worse; trust me."

Gist tried to smile, but the pain was too severe. He looked back past the man carrying the stretcher and could see his men on top of the Union works fighting. He was proud of them. It was some of the most desperate fighting he'd ever seen.

He looked back at Lieutenant Trenholm and said, "Take me to my wife."

"I'm gonna do that, General, as soon as I can." Trenholm patted Gist on the arm. "You relax now."

4:10 p.m.

CSA

Ike Shannon watched the line move out. This would be a busy time for the sharpshooters. Their job would be to keep the artillery off Hood's infantry so they could close to within rifle range.

There was a commotion behind him. He turned to see General Cheatham ride past followed by his escort. They rode on to the left and began to dismount.

Ike heard the Union artillery open fire and turned in time to see the cannonball arcing through the air toward the Confederate lines. There were more flashes as more cannons opened fire. It never ceased to amaze him how you could actually see the shell traveling through the air, yet when it was coming toward you, there was no time to dodge it.

Lieutenant Ozanne began to assign each man a gun. He gave the gun on the far right to Ike Shannon. Shannon placed his Whitworth rifle across the stump and studied the cannon crew. They were in the process of loading the piece. Suddenly, he caught sight of movement near the Columbia Pike. The Federal artillerymen were rolling out a piece of heavy artillery near the gap in the road.

"I got a big gun on the pike," Shannon yelled to Lieutenant Ozanne. "Someone else will have to take my gun."

"I see it, Ike," Ozanne shouted back as several of the other sharpshooters began to open fire. Ozanne knew better than to argue with Ike Shannon. He was the best shot under his command. "See if you can drive 'em off. I'll take your gun."

Ike watched them roll the big gun out to the right in front of the cotton gin near a small rock quarry. He looked over his scope and quickly calculated the distance. It was over a thousand yards away. He would have to put a little elevation on the trajectory of his bullet to get them at that distance.

Ike loved his Whitworth. Before the war, he hadn't known they made a gun that would shoot so far. He'd heard that General Lee had a couple of Whitworth cannons that would shoot up to nine miles.

Ike studied the cannon crew again as they loaded the gun. When they were finished, one man was busy inserting the friction primers while another bent over and sighted the piece.

163

Ike steadied the rifle on the stump and exhaled ever so slightly. He practically had this down to an art now. Once he finished exhaling he would gently squeeze the trigger. The discharge of the rifle surprised him the way it always did.

As the smoke cleared away, he steadied the rifle again and peered toward the cannon. The Federal artilleryman, who moments ago had been sighting the gun, now lay writhing on the ground holding his shoulder. Several of the cannon crew were bending over him. Ike quickly began to reload his weapon. He loved the way smoke pored out the nipple of his rifle when he rammed the charge down the barrel.

When he had finished, he laid the rifle back on the stump. The Federal artillerymen had half-dragged the wounded man toward the rear as another gunner stepped in to sight the piece. The man was bent over, looking down the barrel just like the man before him. Another artilleryman stood beside him holding the lanyard, patiently waiting.

Ike aimed at the man sighting the gun. He softly exhaled and then the gun discharged again. As the smoke cleared, he peered through the scope. The second Federal artilleryman who was just now sighting the gun was on the ground, barely moving. The artilleryman beside him dropped the lanyard and went to his knees to check on the wounded man.

Ike quickly began to reload. He was actually enjoying this. He could now understand what General Lee had meant two years ago when he had said, "It is well that war is so terrible or we may grow too fond of it." Of course, deep down, Ike knew this wasn't a bit fun for those two men he had put a hole in. He could appreciate the fact that, if not for his fine shooting skills, he too would be down there in the real mess fighting at close range, instead of killing men from almost a mile away.

Once he finished reloading, he propped the gun back on the stump. The Federals had dragged the injured man back toward the main line. Another man was reluctantly walking toward the cannon. *They're so stubborn, Ike thought. Surely they know that its death to remain there any longer. Well, there's no use in letting the poor bastard stand there dreading what he knows is coming.* He exhaled and gently squeezed the trigger. This time he actually got the gun steady in time to see the man topple over.

Ike took his time now and watched the other artillerymen rush over and check on the downed man. He expected them to withdraw the cannon after losing three men.

He noticed one of the gunners talking to an officer and pointing toward his position. They had found his position. Ike smiled to himself. He couldn't believe his eyes when several men rushed forward and turned the gun toward Privet Knob and began to elevate the barrel. Ike quickly jerked the Whitworth off the stump and frantically began to reload.

He was loading as fast as he possibly could, when he heard the discharge. He glanced over the stump to see the shell arcing through the sky toward him. It looked as though it would land right there on his stump as it

164

seemed to just float through the air. He couldn't help but notice how ugly the thing was as it came directly, almost lazily, toward him. At the last second, Ike ducked behind the stump.

The shell hit a pile of rocks about twenty feet in front of his stump. Ike's ears were ringing. He wasn't sure if the shell exploded when it hit or not. Rocks and debris blew around the stump and past him. He could feel small pebbles stinging the back of his neck. For a long moment, he was enveloped in a cloud of dust.

After the dust settled, Ike looked up to see Lieutenant Ozanne standing behind the large oak tree. The man was looking at Ike, smiling. Ozanne asked, "Are you hurt, Ike?"

"I'm all right," Ike shouted back. His ears were ringing with pain. "Just scared the shit out of me is all."

He laid the rifle back on the stump and looked at his hands. They were trembling. He noticed his clothes were covered in dust. Slowly, he began to dust himself off while trying to settle his nerves.

He finished reloading his Whitworth and placed it back across the stump. His hands were still shaking. Below him, the Union artillerymen were busy reloading the big gun. He softly exhaled and gently squeezed the trigger. The rifle recoiled against his shoulder.

This time he didn't need to look to know that he had missed his mark. Gazing back through the scope, he saw men moving back toward the gun. He'd at least hit close enough to make them run away momentarily.

Again he began reloading his rifle. There wasn't much time left before it would be too dangerous to keep firing. The Confederate infantry was getting close to the Union lines. The sharpshooters would be forced to cease firing for fear of hitting their own men.

Ike finished reloading and took a few quick breaths to help calm him. He looked through the scope and sighted at the man who at this very moment was trying to kill him. It was almost as if they were looking at each other across nearly a mile of battlefield. *Forty thousand men are between us, fighting like hell, and this bastard wants to fight me, he thought.* For a moment, Ike felt glorious. The Federal cannon crew had made this a personal thing. He exhaled softly and gently squeezed the trigger. The gun erupted, another strong blow to the shoulder.

Ike waited for the smoke to clear, but already he knew. The man was down. There was no doubt whatsoever in his mind. When he could see again, the man was lying on his back, not moving at all.

He was about to reload again, when he saw the artillerymen rush forward and begin to push the gun toward the Union rear. Ike felt good. He had done his job here today. There was no telling how many of Cleburne's men he had just saved by keeping that one cannon out of action.

Lieutenant Ozanne looked at Ike and said, "Nice shooting."

Ike smiled. He would have to agree. He had fired the Whitworth five times and hit four men at over a thousand yards. Not bad at all. The infantry was now closing with the Federals. There was nothing left to do now but sit back and watch the show, the same way General Cheatham was doing just to his left.

4:11 p.m.

CSA

He'd had to borrow a horse from Tip Stanton, a young boy in his escort. It was a nice brown mare. "Red Pepper" had been too injured at Spring Hill last night for Cleburne to ride him into battle. Tip didn't look a day over seventeen, and Cleburne wanted the boy to miss this battle.

Patrick Cleburne rode down the hill with his division. He loved moments like this. He loved knowing that the enemy across the way were looking at the beautiful blue flags with the white centers and feeling fear inside. His division consisted of troops from Alabama, Arkansas, Mississippi, and Texas. They are some of the best the south has to offer. The tread of twenty thousand men reminded him of distant thunder. Other than the sound of his men walking, it was as quiet as a grave. He could see men mouthing prayers to themselves.

He thought about Susan. She's probably walking in the garden this late in the day or reading a book there. He wished he could hold her just one last time. He could just turn his horse and resign at this moment. He could resign and go to Mobile and marry her. Deep down, he knew he couldn't. He'd always done his duty, and he would do it here, even if it meant certain death.

"Tighten up, men," Cleburne shouted as he nudged the horse forward. "Prepare to use the bayonet!"

A few cannons were firing but weren't having much luck with their aim. The infantry in the advanced line were going to be flanked soon. If they didn't run, Cleburne knew his division would overrun them. The small works they had built wouldn't even slow his men down.

They were within three hundred yards of the enemy line when he yelled, "Shift from column into battle lines! If they don't retreat, run over them and shoot them in the backs!"

The entire division made the movement look easy in the face of the enemy. *That should put even more fear into them, Cleburne thought. They know now what they're up against.*

At two hundred yards, the enemy line opened fire. Their aim was terrible. Cleburne screamed again, "Charge 'em, men, charge!"

The line surged forward. He could feel the enemy line weaken before he saw it. Then his men let loose with the rebel yell. Some of the Federal troops tried to make a stand, but the rest fled. Soon, his division was over the works and bayonets and clubbed muskets were used. Cleburne wondered what kind of idiot would leave those two brigades out here against the entire Confederate army. As the remnants began to race for the rear, Cleburne saw his opportunity for the first time.

"Go into the works with them," he shouted.

Instantly, his men recognized what he was saying and the cry went all down the line. If they could race among the retreating Federal troops, they could approach the main enemy line without being fired on. The Federal troops in the main works would be afraid of shooting into their own men.

Cleburne's horse leaped across the low breastworks as he waved his sword over his head and shouted again. "Into the works with them, men!"

He rode over to the Columbia Pike on his extreme left and met General Brown. "There's no time to reform, John. Let's just push on into the works with them while we have them running. That should prevent the enemy from getting a good volley on us."

"Right," Brown said as he jerked the reins of his horse toward the Federal main line.

Cleburne turned back across the pike toward his men. He remembered he had a couple of cannons with his division. Mangum was waiting just ahead. He yelled, "Mangum, place those cannons on this ridge to fire down the road at those retreating men!"

Mangum saluted and moved away. Cleburne saw another aide beside him. It was Captain Hanley. He yelled, "Captain, you take care of the cannons for Mangum. Send him back to me. I have another job for him."

Hanley saluted and rode hard to catch Mangum. Cleburne turned his horse and began following his troops toward the main Federal line ahead. Mangum soon caught up to him. He reined his horse alongside of Cleburne's.

"What do you need, sir?" Mangum asked.

"Never mind the guns," Cleburne's eyes flashed. His battle blood was up. He was in the zone. He said, "Forget the artillery, it's too late. Go on with Granbury!"

Mangum watched him ride away. The man had on a new gray coat with gold stars surrounded by a wreath on his collar indicating a general officer. The coat was unbuttoned in the heat, and his gray vest and white muslin shirt were visible beneath it. He wore the gold braided kepi that had been a gift to him by a group of ladies.

He rode to the right and found Govan. The brigadier was on foot racing ahead with his men. Cleburne said, "Never mind reforming. Just push straight on through with them."

Govan nodded and continued onward. Cleburne spun the horse and rode back to the left. He needed to make sure that he and Brown's division went in together as one large striking force. He rode hard into the road, almost running over Brigadier General George Gordon of Brown's division.

They were coming near the main Federal line now. Cannon fire began to erupt from behind the breastworks. He saw a piece of shrapnel ricochet off the ribs of one of Granbury's lieutenants, knocking the man out cold. He lay face down in the road.

The lines had become so jumbled together, he couldn't tell where one brigade ended and another began. It didn't matter; both divisions were going into the Federal lines as one large force.

He looked to his left and saw General Granbury racing toward the enemy ahead. Cleburne would recognize the lanky Texas lawyer from anywhere, his wild black hair waving in the evening light.

His men were screaming like demons. The Texan was screaming above the din. "Forward! Never let it be said that Texans lag in a fight!"

Granbury's troops were closing on the works now. Suddenly, Cleburne saw Granbury grab his face and sink to his knees in the road. The man had been hit in the face just below the left eye and the bullet exploded out the back of his head. The man just sat there slumped forward over his knees, hands covering his face in death.

Cleburne turned his head from the grotesque sight. Suddenly, his borrowed horse was hit by several bullets and crashed to the ground. The general was quick to his feet. Jimmy Brandon, a young boy serving as one of Cleburne's couriers was at his side on an iron gray stallion. He quickly dismounted and handed the reins of his horse to Cleburne.

Cleburne had one foot in the stirrup and was just climbing into the saddle, when a cannonball struck the horse in the chest. The poor beast was dead before it hit the ground. As Cleburne stood up, Jimmy Brandon took a bullet in the leg and sank to the ground beside the dead horse.

The noise was enormous. Cleburne couldn't recall a time during this war when there was so much gunfire. It had become continuous. He shook his head and looked toward the front. Lowrey's Alabama and Mississippi troops were hitting the breastworks and breaking through at the moment. He quickly calculated that they had already lost fifty percent of their strength getting this far.

He removed his hat and then began to wave it over his head. *This is it, he thought. This is my moment.* He removed his sword from the scabbard and charged toward the cotton gin ahead, disappearing into the smoke of battle.

4:12 p.m.

USA

Levi Scofield watched Cleburne's division moving down off of Winstead Hill. It was a magnificent sight. A sight he would never forget, providing he lived through the coming assault—something that didn't look very promising at the moment. The blue flags of the Irishman's division seemed to be floating in the cool evening air. It chilled him to know that the hardest-hitting division in the Confederate army was marching directly toward this part of the Federal line.

Levi shouted for the men to redouble their efforts in strengthening the works. There was no need; the men had been watching the Confederate line also. He began to think how stupid they'd all been to think the rebels wouldn't attack here.

He looked down the line to his left. The men there had placed logs on top of the works and cut notches beneath them. There would be nothing for the Rebels to shoot, only the gun barrels would be sticking out. The position appeared impregnable.

Just to the right of him, General Wagner was sitting on top of the breastworks, reclining on an elbow. His feet were dangling off the enemy's side of the works. His ankle was still swollen from the fall with his horse earlier, and he still held onto the stick he was using as a cane.

The first shots echoed from the south. Every man paused from his work and spun to look. Soon, there were more shots, and then a volley. After the volley, the cannons began to fire. The men quickly began digging again at a furious rate.

Levi began to stroke his long, thin goatee. A rider was galloping back down the road. It was an aide from the advanced line. The man saw Wagner and pulled his horse up just in front of the works. The horse tried to shake the bit from its mouth.

The man yelled, "Sir, Colonel Lane begs to report. The enemy have heavy columns moving out of the timber. Their lines outflank us on both sides."

"Stand there and fight 'em," Wagner growled.

The man looked perplexed. He waited a moment longer before spinning his horse and galloping back toward the front.

Wagner turned to Levi and laughed. "That stubby little Dutchman Conrad will fight 'em too."

"Sir," Levi stepped closer to Wagner. He was beginning to grow nervous. "General Cox's orders are for you to fall back except against cavalry or skirmishers. He wanted your men to join the main line if the enemy threatens to attack with their infantry."

Wagner acted as though he didn't hear Levi Scofield. The man was sick and tired of these subordinate officers trying to tell him how to handle his division.

The firing was picking up to the south. It was growing painfully obvious that a major engagement was coming. Soon, another rider came tearing back down the road at breakneck speed. He too reined up in front of Wagner and saluted.

The staff officer was winded from the hard ride. He started to speak, coughed, and said, "Sir, Colonel Lane says the enemy is advancing in heavy force. They will devour us alive if we don't pull back. Their lines are way beyond our flanks."

"You tell Lane to fight 'em, damn it," Wagner shook the stick in the air.

"But, sir," the young lieutenant looked incredulous, "it's Hood's entire army. There's no way we can…"

Wagner slammed the stick into the soft dirt. A small cloud of dust rose in the air. He yelled, "Never mind! I said stand there and fight, and that's what I want. We held their entire army off yesterday. Why should today be any different?"

The lieutenant saluted and spurred the horse back toward the front. Levi watched the man riding away. Before he could get back to the advanced line, the sound of battle was roaring. For the first time today, he heard the rebel yell. It was an eerie sound and had unnerved Levi on fields of battle before. There was just something wicked about men racing to their deaths and screaming like banshees.

Some of the men stopped and looked to the front. Levi yelled, "Keep digging, boys. You can never get it too strong."

He looked up and saw a cannon being pulled back down the road. As it passed on the pike to his right, he recognized one of the boys on the limber. It was Alec Clinton, an old friend. They spun the gun around and began to unlimber behind the main line. Alec jumped to the ground and said, "Levi, all hell's turned loose out there, and it's coming this way."

Levi walked over and shook Alec's hand. "You take care of yourself today."

Alec nodded and turned back to help the others muscle the gun into position. Levi turned around and saw a commotion in the advanced line. The Confederate line was advancing beyond the flanks and enveloping Conrad and Lane's brigades. It was madness to leave them out there with both flanks in the air.

It seemed to happen all at once. The advanced line broke under the pressure and came flooding back toward the main line. The yelling and screaming foe sounded to be a lot closer than they were as they broke the line. The blue flags of Cleburne's division on the east side of the pike and the battle flags of Brown's division to the west were coming on fast. It reminded Levi of watching a gathering storm on the horizon and knowing you had nothing to do but wait for it. A man could live a thousand lifetimes and never see anything that compares to this. It was a glorious charge, even if they were the enemy. At this moment, he had nothing but respect for the southerners. Levi also knew that those brave men would be a bleeding pile of humanity once they reached rifle range.

He noticed the men around him staring at the coming battle line, most with mouths hanging open in awe. As the retreating troops grew nearer, Levi noticed rabbits racing ahead of them. Coveys of quail were springing from the grass, flying ahead, landing, and doing the same thing again as the men caught up.

A group of horsemen came galloping down the line from the east. The sun was setting, but Levi recognized General Cox and his staff. Cox shouted, "Hold your fire until our troops are back in line."

Levi watched Lieutenant Coughlan of Cox's staff ride down the line on his black horse, waving his sword over his head, his cape flying out behind him. He cheered the men, and they cheered him back. It was an inspiring sight that Levi would never forget. He heard a member of Cox's staff say, "Coughlan will never survive this battle."

Levi hoped the man was wrong. Coughlan had always been the man who volunteered for extra duty, especially if the work was dangerous. So far, he had lived a charmed life.

Levi remembered that Coughlan had told him he'd been a school teacher before the war. *You never know about men, he thought. Who would think a school teacher would be that brave?* He didn't strike you as a man; he was only twenty-two and had never shaved. He had a thin layer of peach fuzz running across his upper lip. Everyone thought of him as a carefree boy.

Cox's men had been attacking Confederate breastworks all the way from Chattanooga to Atlanta this year. He smiled to himself. It was about time the shoe got on the other foot. The Federal troops were staring across an unobstructed field of fire. It shouldn't even be a contest.

He reined up next to Levi. "This is outstanding. I'm tired of assaulting their fortified positions. It's our turn now."

"Right, sir," Levi replied. He looked back to the south as Cox rode on down the line. He realized now what a mistake it had been for Wagner to leave his troops out there alone. The Confederate troops were intermingled with the Federals. There was no way to open fire without hitting their own men.

The Confederate uniforms were difficult to see in the evening haze. They reminded him of apparitions moving toward him. He thought of them as an army of unstoppable ghosts or phantoms sweeping along through the air. They looked much larger than humans in the twilight just before darkness. They reminded him of brown seaweed undulating in the ocean waves off Cliff Road at Newport, Rhode Island. He fought the urge to turn and run.

Suddenly, he realized something he hadn't thought about before. All the shirkers and cowards had deserted the Confederate army long ago. These men sweeping at him were the best the South had to offer. He knew now that the line would break. There would be no stopping them. They'd drive Schofield's army into the Harpeth River. Nashville would be theirs for the taking. Four years of bloody war will have been fought for naught. It would be a major blow to the Federal war effort.

To his left, he saw Colonel John Casement with the men of his brigade. He climbed on top of the breastworks in defiance of the oncoming enemy troops. He turned and looked down at his troops. His voice was loud and ringing as he shouted, "Men, do you see those damned Rebel sons-of-bitches coming?"

His entire line replied with a shout.

"Well," he screamed as he looked back over his shoulder, "I want you to stand here like rocks and whip the hell out of them!"

Casement then spun around and emptied his revolver at the charging enemy. When the pistol was empty, he jumped down behind the works with his men.

The advancing lines were now a hundred yards away. Wagner's men were running with their bodies bent forward, low to the ground, hoping they wouldn't get shot in the back. It was every man for himself. The Confederate troops were mixed with them. They understood that to safely assail the breastworks ahead, they needed to go into the works with these enemy troops.

Levi had never been in such a tense situation before. He wondered how long they could hold their fire. It was like standing on the shore watching a giant tidal wave approach and doing nothing. The men behind the works had their rifles raised. Men were shifting nervously. Every now and then, he would hear someone mutter under their breath, "Run boys, run."

It took iron discipline for those men to hold their fire. He saw motion to his right. It was Wagner, now mounted on his horse. He rode out to meet his men. The first men began to reach the main line and race down the pike. Wagner was screaming for them to stop and fight, but it was a waste of time. When the mass of men hit the line, they swept his horse along with them. Wagner was cursing, screaming, and calling his men cowards. All the time, he was swinging the stick at them. They paid him no mind. Nothing could stop them.

Levi felt bad for Wagner. He was a brave man. He'd had an outstanding career, but maybe that's where he'd gone wrong. Everything he had attempted had worked out. Perhaps he thought he was unstoppable now.

Levi jumped on his horse and rode into the mass to help Wagner try and reform his frightened men. He too was swept rearward in the rush. He heard the main line open fire and turned in time to see men in blue and gray going down. They'd held their fire as long as possible, and now they were forced to shoot into their own men.

Levi was still being swept to the rear, but behind him the main line broke as the Confederate troops came flooding over. He continued trying to get the men to stop and fight, but it was no use. As they swept him past the Carter House, a bullet grazed his leg and entered his horse. The horse fell dead in the road with a crash. Levi swung clear and stood in the Carter yard looking south. He turned and began to limp toward the rear.

He saw a sergeant stop in the yard and point his rifle to the south. He yelled, "Hold on here, boys. I'm not going back another step."

In a few moments the brave man had about twenty soldiers forming a line beside him. Levi limped over and patted the sergeant on the back. "Nice job. Move them over there to those works."

172

Levi led them toward the retrenched line behind the Carter smokehouse. He turned and watched the troops from the advanced line and the main line rushing madly for town. No one wanted to be down there by the river waiting to get across the bridge with the rebels shooting them in the backs. Levi felt disgusted.

Behind the Carter house, Opdycke's men were enjoying their first break all day. They had started fires with rails from a nearby fence and were boiling pork, frying bacon, and making coffee.

A stampede of fugitives swept past on the road. Opdycke saw his men reach for their weapons without orders. He mounted his horse and rode forward to ascertain what was happening. He hadn't gone far, when he saw the battle flags of Cleburne and Brown's men charging down the road. They'd broken through two lines of works and were about to break the last.

He spun the horse and rode to the rear of his brigade. He yelled, "Form up, men!"

His men were already in the act of forming a line of battle, when some officer yelled, "Forward, to the works!"

The mass of men surged forward. There was no order to them, just a huge mass of men in motion. He heard another officer yell, "To the trenches, men!"

He could hear angry men shouting about losing their breakfasts. As they raced forward, all semblance of order vanished. Opdycke rode into the mass of men and shouted, "First Brigade, forward to the works!"

As they reached the Carter House yard, Cleburne and Brown's men were pouring down the road and over the works. There were men fleeing from the works, but when they reached Opdycke's brigade, they were forced to fan right and left to get out of the way.

He noticed how his men look determined. Their faces set in an expression of seriousness. He heard a captain yell, "Come on, boys! We have always whipped them, and we'll whip them here!"

Opdycke's men were forced to work through a cedar fence at the edge of the Carter property. Some men were kicking at the structure while others struck at the rails with their musket butts. Others tried to squeeze through. He could actually hear bullets striking the fence; men were falling now.

They finally forced their way through the fence and surged ahead.

The two opposing lines met with a crash in the front and back yards of the house. Men were fighting with clubbed muskets and bayonets, even fists. To Opdycke, it seemed as if hell had been turned loose on earth. Men were dying on the very doorsteps of the house. He saw men swinging muskets and brains actually flying from men's skulls on both sides.

In the mass of men, he saw Major MacArthur riding his horse alongside the men. The boy major was only nineteen years old and had already become a hero at Chattanooga last year. MacArthur saw a rebel battle flag and spurred the horse that way. Then horse and rider both went down. Opdycke watched the young man spring to his feet and race toward the rebel banner again. Before reaching the flag, a bullet struck him in the right shoulder and he hit the ground.

Opdycke couldn't help but be impressed with his young officer. He thought the boy was down for good, but in an instant he was on his feet again, sword in his left hand and racing forward again. A Confederate major met him before he could reach the flag and fired a bullet into MacArthur's chest with his pistol.

MacArthur was going down again, but he surged forward and drove the sword through the body of the Confederate officer. As the enemy major sank to the ground, he managed to shoot again, striking MacArthur in the left knee. Both men were out of action now.

Opdycke could hardly believe what he was seeing here—thousands of men in this small area, clubbing and shooting each other in the faces. Men had become fiends, animal-like. The fire at point-blank range caused considerable damage to men's bodies. He saw men with blood and brain matter on their faces.

He saw Lieutenant Colonel Olson shot in the chest, the bullet passing out his back. The man had been a school teacher before the war. He went to the ground spitting blood and struggling to breath. Then an aide reported that Major Motherspaw was mortally wounded. Things were bad here, worse than he'd ever seen before in this war.

Opdycke saw a private ducking from enemy fire. He saw a captain walk over and yell, "Stand up and take it like a man!"

The words had barely escaped his mouth, when a bullet hit the captain between the eyes. He crashed to the ground. The private, never missing a beat, yelled back, "Why in hell don't you stand up and take it like a man!"

Cannons fired to his right, and he caught the sight of body parts flying through the air. Men were in the Carter buildings firing from windows. He saw a soldier on the back porch kick the bottom panel from the door and crawl into the house to escape the mayhem.

At that moment, Opdycke's horse went down. He managed to swing his legs clear of the falling beast. He jumped to his feet and raced ahead behind his men. He fired his pistol over their heads until it was empty. His men were beginning to break for the rear. He turned the pistol around and began swinging it wildly. He clubbed stragglers over the head until he broke the handle. He threw the pistol away and grabbed up a musket and threatened to shoot his own men if they ran.

Just like that, and it was all over. It hadn't lasted fifteen minutes. What it lacked in time, it made up for in intensity. The rebel lines had been pushed back. They were already exhausted from the mile-long run to reach this position. He watched them fall back behind the line of works just ahead and begin to fire from there.

4:14 p.m.

CSA

It hadn't taken him long to realize that things weren't going according to plan. Because the lines converged on a central point, Cockrell's brigade had outpaced Sears's brigade on his right. Cleburne was supposed to be on his left but had been slowed by the advanced Federal line. Cockrell and his small brigade of Missouri troops were about to hit the main Federal line alone, but there was nothing he could do about that now. This was the strongest position he'd had to face in the entire war. He couldn't very well stop out here in the middle of this terrible fire and wait for the others. There was nothing left to do but press on.

They were quickly closing on the main line just right of the cotton gin. Even from this distance, he could see a Federal artilleryman loading furiously. His face was flushed, and smoke streaked his sweaty face. The man appeared calm, as if this sort of thing happened every day. Cockrell even thought he saw the man smile once.

At the start of the war, he'd earned the nickname 'the praying Captain' because of his deep religious convictions. He'd started the war under Sterling Price out west, fighting at Wilson's Creek and Pea Ridge. He'd fought at Corinth and been captured at Vicksburg. He'd been wounded at Kennesaw Mountain and fought in the battles around Atlanta, but nothing he'd seen so far in this war had prepared him for the scene here at Franklin.

Cockrell was in shock for a moment. He shook his head and pressed onward. His men were turning sideways, attempting to move through the deadly missiles.

There were Federal regiments in front of his brigade that carried the Henry repeating rifles. They could fire fifteen times without reloading. It was certain death to be in this position. Somehow, his brigade had been the unlucky ones to have to assault the strongest position on the field. For a moment, it appeared his brigade had simply disappeared.

His horse went down with legs thrashing. He rolled away from the horse and stood up. An aide was there, instantly offering him the use of his horse. Cockrell climbed on and turned for the enemy line just seventy-five yards away. This horse had just taken a few steps when four bullets struck the general at almost the same time. He tumbled out of the saddle, the horse rearing wildly and galloping away.

Cockrell tried to stand but couldn't. One bullet had punched a neat round hole in his left leg. Two bullets had struck his right arm and another had grazed his ankle. The wounds were extremely painful. He grimaced and clenched his teeth.

To the north, he watched his men racing on into the face of sure death. Cockrell needed to turn over brigade command to Colonel Hugh Garland of the First Missouri. He strained through the gun smoke until he found the First Missouri and its gallant colonel. Garland was carrying the regimental flag himself out in front of his men. Cockrell watched as a bullet slammed into Garland's leg and the poor officer crashed to the ground, becoming all tangled in the regimental flag.

Some young officer rode in front of the men as they came near the breastworks. The man was shouting, but Cockrell couldn't hear him in this din. Just as the horse approached the ditch in front of the works, he was shot off the horse. He watched the man grab his right shoulder as he rolled on the ground. Just as he was attempting to raise himself up on his left elbow, a bullet exploded through the back of his skull.

He watched his men go into the ditch with a crash. Then they were on top of the works fighting like demons. He could see muskets being swung through the air. Brains were being bashed out of skulls. Men were clawing, scratching, and even biting. It was the wildest fight he'd ever seen, and he'd seen his share in this war.

About the only way he could describe it would be to call it a blood bath. Men were falling everywhere, and he began to wonder if he would have a brigade left after this fight was finished. The cannons were still firing, and the muzzles almost touched his men. He could hear the awful sound of canister balls ripping through bones.

He saw three sets of regimental colors planted on the parapet, but all the color bearers were immediately shot down. Cockrell would never forget the sight of blood in the dirt. He'd never seen so much bloodshed on a battlefield before. The ground was literally covered with the bodies of his men. He began to understand that this would be the last fight the Missouri brigade would ever make. After today, he would have no men left to fight again.

Then he saw something that he would never forget. A drummer boy, probably no more than fifteen, was in the ditch with his drum strapped across his back. He had a rail from the cotton gin that had been thrown into the breastworks. Cockrell could almost read the boy's mind from here. The boy was in the act of shoving the rail into a Federal cannon, thinking he could spike the gun and save lives. In an instant, the cannon exploded. The eruption shook the very ground. Cockrell rubbed his eyes and refocused. The young boy had simply disappeared into thin air. There was nothing there—nothing. It was almost as if the boy never existed. He could see all the men near the position covered in a thin mist of blood.

Cockrell struggled to put weight on his right leg and began to limp toward the rear. The left leg was now useless. It was a struggle, and he expected to be shot down any second. Then there were other walking wounded passing him for the rear. One slightly-wounded young man slowed and began to help his general to the rear.

"You in much pain, sir?" the young man asked. Cockrell was in too much pain to talk. He simply grunted through clinched teeth.

They'd gone about a hundred yards, when an aide came up on horseback. Cockrell turned and noticed the young man was leading another horse with a wounded man on its back. The man was sitting straight up in the saddle, both arms hanging limp by his sides. Cockrell blinked. It was Colonel Elijah Gates of the First and Third Missouri Cavalry Dismounted.

Cockrell stopped and saw the blood dripping off the man's hand. "You all right, Colonel Gates?"

"No, sir," Gates shook his head slowly. "I took command when you and Garland went down, but for only a few moments. I got hit in both arms. Both are broken. If it wasn't for Lieutenant Cleveland here, I would still be sitting out in the middle of that killing ground on this damned horse."

Cockrell nodded and turned back toward the rear as Lieutenant Cleveland continued leading Gates's horse ahead.

4:16 p.m.

CSA

The line moved off the hill and across a green pasture. They swept up out of a ravine and past the Carnton Plantation. Someone said that Colonel McGavock lived there, but Mack Keenum had never heard of the man. *He must command a Tennessee regiment, he thought.*

Tom Barrett was on Mack's left, 'Rip' Baker to his right. Company B was in the center of the regiment. Bob Wheeler had the honor of carrying the regimental battle flag. Bob was one of the bravest men Mack had ever met.

Looking ahead, he realized things were about to get ugly. The entire advance was gonna be across open fields. Captain Stewart was beside himself. Mack wondered if the young man was serious about wanting to charge those works, or if he was just trying to keep the men's spirits up.

Captain Stewart sounded like a boy on Christmas morning. "This is beautiful—charging across two miles of open fields. I guess we'll get to see who gets farther. All I have to say is, it better be Company B."

Mack looked around and made a few quick calculations. There were only twenty-one men in Company B. He wasn't sure how much damage a company with just twenty percent strength would make on that entrenched Federal line.

As they moved into the fields north of Carnton, they came within range of the heavy artillery in the fort across the river. He couldn't believe how accurate the Federal gunners were. The first shot sailed high over the line. The second shot fell a little short, but the shots after that began to hit home. He could see men ducking all up and down the line. So far, his company had been spared. Some of the shells were exploding in the air above the Confederate lines, tearing great gaps in their formations.

Things were only gonna get worse. There was still a mile of open ground to traverse just to reach the Federal position. Their officers continued to hold them at a slow pace, pressing on toward the works ahead. He understood what they were doing. They didn't want the men to rush ahead only to be too exhausted to fight when they reached the enemy line. Time seemed to stand still. He wondered if there would be anybody left alive to reach the Federal lines.

Ahead, he could see where the railroad crossed through the Federal breastworks to his right, but it afforded them no protection.

Captain Stewart said, "I know every man in Company B will do his whole duty. We'll end this fight by retaining the high honor we've earned elsewhere in this war."

He glanced down the line just in time to see a shell strike a man in Company A. The man dropped like a rock, but his arm went flying end over end through the air behind him. The shell, having clipped the man's arm off, buried itself in the ground beyond, failing to explode.

The men tried to speed up. It seemed insane to keep such a slow pace out here in all this artillery fire. Captain Stewart stepped in front of the line and held his sword across his body. It was the signal to slow down.

He yelled, "Slow, men, slow! Our brigade is closer to the enemy than the rest. We must give them time to come up, so we all close with the enemy together."

Each passing moment brought them closer to the enemy lines. They could hear the Federal troops cheering behind their works ahead, but so far, not a man could be seen. He could hear Captain Stewart repeating over and over, "Easy men, everything's all right."

Mack couldn't believe his ears. Federal shells were exploding over their heads. Enemy soldiers waited ahead with loaded rifles. How could he say everything was all right?

Just ahead was a small ditch. The entire line surged forward without orders to reach the cover it provided. They crashed into the ditch as one. Men fell on top of each other. Some men were screaming, others were cursing. Mack was happy to be under cover for a few moments, however brief it would be. *With all these damned officers, he thought, it won't be very long at all.*

He eased his head up and peered over the top of the ditch. The Federal line was still a good three hundred yards away. There was no more cover between here and there. He could see the brush piled high in front of the breastworks of fresh earth. They had built themselves an abatis, and there was no telling how difficult it would be to negotiate that stuff. He lay back in the ditch and tried to enjoy the few moments he had in safety. He thought about how easy it would be to just pretend to be wounded and not leave the ditch, but deep down he knew he would never be able to live with himself if he did.

178

It amazed him how alive he felt at this very moment. His senses were alert and on edge. It was as if he could see, hear, and feel everything around him. A man could live a thousand years, but until he is shot at, he will never understand this feeling.

He couldn't lie still. Mack peered over the top of the ditch again and studied the situation. He noticed a farmhouse across the Lewisburg Pike. The Federal line covered the entire field. There was absolutely no cover between here and there. This fight was gonna be one of those stand up, smash mouth type of fights. To his left, he could see an old cotton gin standing behind the Federal lines. It looked as if someone had stripped all the planks off the sides— and then it dawned on him. The Federals had used the siding in their breastworks. The Confederates were already fighting over there. The entire field roared with gunfire.

Officers were yelling down the line now. He looked over and saw Captain Stewart already standing.

"This is it," Stewart yelled. "Don't nobody stop until we reach their works there."

The entire line came out of the ditch as one. Every man was yelling as loud as possible as they began to sprint the final three hundred yards to the Federal line. It seemed strange that the Yankees were holding their fire. They were holding their fire just waiting for them to get so close they couldn't miss.

The officers tried to slow them, but it was a waste of time. These men had been in enough fights to know that the quicker they closed with the enemy, the better their chances.

They raced onward. Just two hundred yards and they'd be there. That's when Mack first realized that the thin line of brush in front of the breastworks wasn't brush at all. The damned Yankees had built an abatis of Osage orange trees. The branches were intertwined in such a way, it would be almost impossible to penetrate them as a single unit. He began to realize that the Confederate line was racing ahead just to be slaughtered.

Yet, no one slowed down. Every man just wanted to hurry and do his duty and get this over with as quickly as possible. They were only a hundred yards away now. Suddenly, the Federal line came to life. Rifle fire exploded all down the line. He could see men falling to the left and right of him. To Mack's right, 'Rip' Baker went down with a leg wound. On they charged.

As they charged forward to just fifty yards of the abatis, the artillery opened fire with canister. Thousands of tiny iron balls tore through the Confederate line. He glanced to his left and saw body parts flying through the air. It was Will Bradley, blown to pieces. Still they charged onward. He felt unstoppable.

He tripped and fell hard; someone behind him stepped on his leg. He scrambled back to his feet and charged on. The entire line ahead seemed alive with rifle fire. The roar was continuous now. The discharge of the cannons had begun to make his ears bleed.

179

Am I seeing things? he thought. The air around him seemed to be black with bullets. Then a funny thought hit him. He wondered if he could remove his hat and catch a hatful of lead. It amazed him how the human brain worked in times of such strain.

There was another blast of canister, and his face was sprayed with a thin mist. He wiped his eyes and saw that it was blood. It felt strange. There was no pain. He thought he would feel intense pain to be hit in the face like that. He realized at once that the blood wasn't his. He wiped his face on his sleeve, but quickly realized he was doing nothing but smearing it. He continued on with his company toward the abatis ahead.

They hit the abatis with a crash. He hoped if they hit it as one, their combined weight would knock it down. He could tell the men who had built this obstruction knew what they were doing. It didn't seem to move at all.

The branches tore his clothes as he reeled back from the impenetrable barrier. He raised his musket and fired through the branches toward the works ahead. There was no wind, and the smoke hung heavy in the afternoon air. He couldn't tell where to shoot, but returning fire made him feel better at least.

He stood there reloading, oblivious to the chaos happening all around him. Captain Stewart was at his side, yelling like a fiend and hacking away at the Osage orange abatis with his sword. Others were using their musket butts trying to make a hole through the branches. Mack decided that would be the best approach. He dropped his ramrod and began to swing the musket overhead and down onto the abatis. Nothing seemed to work. He felt like a man pissing in the ocean trying to make the water rise.

A bullet crashed into the forearm of his rifle sending splinters into his hand. He almost dropped his weapon. He looked to his right in time to see Captain Stewart hit in the stomach. The poor man fell forward into the abatis and hung there for a long moment. Mack thought he was dead, but then he saw the captain roll out of the brush and onto the ground. Mack was about to turn back to the thick brush, when he caught the sight of movement beside him. It was Captain Stewart who had slowly stood back up. The man still held onto his sword, and as he raised it to hack at the abatis again, another bullet took his left ear off. Stewart grabbed at the side of his head and fell to the ground again.

Mack seemed to be in shock. He stood there a long moment staring at his commander lying on the ground with blood pouring from his belly. His left hand was covering the place where his ear had been. Stewart was lying on his right side, and Mack saw blood from his ear begin to trickle across his face. He then turned back to hack at the abatis with his musket again. He expected to be hit at any moment.

He grew angry being stuck out here without cover fighting an enemy too afraid to show himself. He yelled, "Come out and fight like men, you cowardly bastards!"

He looked around and saw an officer approaching on horseback. It was General Scott, his brigade commander. The man was shouting something, but in this racket, it was impossible to tell what he was saying. Scott was pointing his sword toward the enemy breastworks. The fire slackened a moment, and Mack heard him yelling something about there being no safety out here in the open. *No shit, he thought; takes a general to figure that one out.*

He watched Scott spur his horse forward and begin to hack away at the abatis with his sword. Suddenly, a shell exploded overhead. Scott was thrown from his horse and twisted violently as he sailed through the air. It reminded Mack of one of his girls throwing a rag doll across the yard. Scott's body looked almost grotesque, and he seemed to be flying in slow motion, almost hanging there in the air. His limbs were tossed in all directions. The officer then crashed hard into the ground. Keenum thought he could hear the thud above the din of battle.

He was sure that Scott was dead, but the man tried to rise from the ground before collapsing. He watched a couple of men race to the general's side and roll him over. Mack was close enough to see the look of pain on his commander's face. *That's a good sign, he thought; it means he's not dead anyway.* There was no sign of blood on the man, but he couldn't stand. One man grabbed Scott's legs and the other his arms, and they started for the rear with him.

At that moment, Mack's knee buckled. He fell forward against the abatis and then rolled back out flat on his back. The knee hurt severely. It reminded him of banging his elbow on something, but the pain was much more intense. He knew he'd been shot. He was afraid to look at the wound. It took him a long moment to figure out what he should do now. His fight was over; that much was painfully obvious. *Hell, he thought, this fight was over before we left that hill two damned miles back.* He knew there was no way he would survive lying out here in the open between two lines of men firing at each other. He thought about General Scott being carried for the rear. *He's an officer, and I'm a lowly private. I could lie here all night, and no one is gonna come for me.* He almost laughed at the thought.

Mack Keenum rolled over on his belly and looked south. Until this moment, he hadn't noticed how bad it was. Men were lying in heaps. It looked as if half the brigade was down. He made himself as flat as possible and began to inch his way toward the rear. The ditch was a good three hundred yards away. Bullets were kicking dirt up all around him as he began crawling toward the rear. There was probably no way he would get back to that ditch without being hit again.

After crawling about twenty yards, it seemed as if he might beat the odds. He crawled slowly; the leg seemed to be throbbing now. He came up on a line of men. By the way they were lying there, it looked as if they had all lay down together. He quickly realized they were all dead. He wiggled his way through them and paused, using one of the bodies as a shield while he rested. Bullets began to hit the dead man. The sound reminded him of someone thumping a watermelon to see if it was ripe yet. The thought made him gag. He vomited on the ground.

181

The fire slackened a little, so he began to move toward the rear again. He had crawled about halfway to the ditch, when a shell exploded overhead. Iron fragments rained down all around him. The cannons in that damned fort were still firing. With every discharge, he could feel the ground tremble beneath him. It seemed to lift him clear off the ground at times.

He crawled on past bodies so torn apart that their own mothers wouldn't recognize them. It was the most awful battle he had ever seen, and he'd seen his fair share. Someone was to blame for getting all these brave men killed. He crawled past a leg that had been blown off from the knee down, the foot still inside the shoe. Ahead was a hand. It seemed strange to see it lying out there in the middle of the field all alone. He had to fight off the strange urge to pick it up.

He finally made it to the ditch and crawled inside. There were several wounded men lying back here. Mack also noticed some unwounded men back here.

He rolled his pant leg up to inspect the wound. It didn't look near as bad as he had expected. The ball had struck his knee at an angle and been deflected away. There was an open gash, and he could see down into his leg. The pain was intense, and he figured the bone was probably broken. He could see blood and something white and creamy looking. *It's probably ligaments or tendons or something, he thought.*

His hand was bloody from the splinters of his gun stock. He also had dried blood all over his face. He thought about waiting here in the ditch until it was completely dark before making his way to the rear, but he was worried if he waited too long, he might lose the leg. He quickly decided to start toward the rear again.

Behind him, the battle was still raging. Scott's brigade was pretty much gone; he was sure of that. He decided to test his leg by putting weight on it. Two miles would be a long way to crawl. He took a deep breath and rose to his feet. The pain was intense, but he found he could limp on it.

He hobbled along as best he could, praying each moment that he wouldn't take a bullet in the back. He looked up and saw Major General William Loring. He couldn't believe his eyes. "Old Blizzards" as they called him was sitting on his horse just a few hundred yards from the main enemy line. He seemed indifferent to the whine of the stray bullets passing by.

Mack Keenum expected a sharpshooter to get him any moment now. Loring was in a new gray uniform, gold braid shining in the late afternoon sun.

"Great God!" Loring shouted. His face betrayed extreme disgust. "Do I command cowards?"

Mack thought about saying something, but quickly decided against it. He wanted to ask the general how he could call any man a coward who had gone up against those damned earthworks.

He limped on past Loring toward the rear. He followed the rest of the walking wounded. They went back across the open fields toward the fine plantation they had passed earlier.

It was dark by the time he arrived. Lights in the windows of the fine home looked like a beacon of hope. As he got nearer, he could tell there was a lot of activity going on around that residence. The doors were open, and wounded men were continuously making their way inside.

He was walking toward the front door, when he noticed some strange white things in the front yard. Another hit the pile with a thump. He quickly realized the pile was arms and legs. Doctors were upstairs amputating and throwing the limbs out the second floor windows. He quickly turned and limped toward the back of the house.

The back porch was longer than the house. It was strange—he had never seen anything built like that before. He wondered what would possess someone to extend their back porch some twenty feet beyond their house. He almost laughed to himself. *I bet this porch cost more than my entire cabin, he thought.*

He limped down the long porch, stumbled, and fell on his hands and knees in the doorway. Pain shot through his knee like a bolt of lightning. Mack grimaced, holding his breath for a long moment before exhaling.

"Help me get him up," a woman's voice said. He felt gentle hands under his arms. Mack was capable of getting up on his own; he just needed a moment for the pain to pass. When he got to his feet, his eyes met a dark-haired woman in a black dress. An orderly was holding his other arm.

Mack said, "Sorry, ma'am."

He felt awkward and didn't know what else to say. He felt bad for intruding into this poor lady's house and bleeding on her beautiful floors.

"Never mind that," she said.

The orderly looked around the house. He said, "Ma'am, we're gonna have to put him outside. There's just no more room. You got about three hundred wounded in here already."

The lady reached under the stairway and opened a small door. "Put him in the boot closet here."

They lay him in the boot closet. It was small, and he felt a little claustrophobic in there. His feet extended out the door. The lady smiled at him, which made him feel better. She said, "The surgeons will have a look at you as soon as they can."

He nodded but said nothing. In a few moments, the lady was back with another wounded man, and then another. There were now three of them packed into the boot closet like sardines. None of them could move without jostling the other around.

Mack Keenum soon nodded off. He awoke sometime in the night to find the man on his right side had passed away. The man on his left was still awake and in intense pain. He'd been shot in both arms and worried constantly about losing them.

4:35 P.M.

CSA

His brigade band was playing "Dixie" as they began to move out. Brigadier General John Adams nudged the flanks of his horse 'Ole Charlie.' Staff officers Collins and Henry rode on either side of the general. He thought of his family but showed no emotion as the brigade moved forward to battle. He thought back on his career. He'd been born in Nashville in 1825 just a few miles up the road ahead. A soldier was all he'd ever longed to be. He'd obtained an appointment to West Point and graduated in the class of '46. They'd appointed him to the United States 1st Dragoons.

He'd been commended for bravery in the Mexican War at the Battle of Santa Cruz de Rosales. In 1854, he met Georgiana McDougal. She was the beautiful young daughter of the post surgeon. He still remembered courting her and how in love they had been. She had gone to every post he'd been sent. They were inseparable. They'd had six children together and were just as in love as the day they married.

He'd been assigned to the cavalry when the war began. There had been that embarrassing incident at Sweeney's Cove early in the war. His command had been surprised there, and a hundred of his men had been captured. He was lucky to have remained in command after that happened, but Joe Johnston had recommended he be promoted and given command of an infantry brigade. That's how he had come about commanding this brigade of Mississippians.

Brigadier General John Adams. He refused to leave the field when wounded in the arm, saying, "I'm going to see my men through."

He'd fought Grant's army at Jackson, Mississippi, and then fought Sherman's army through Georgia to Atlanta. Things were different now. He was back home fighting on his own ground. His brigade was in reserve here, following Featherston's brigade into battle.

Up ahead, he could see Scott and Featherston's brigades engaging the enemy. They were being slaughtered at the abatis. Still his brigade moved onward. He passed a private limping toward the rear, a hole cut through the knee of his pants.

Stray bullets began to strike several of his men. He heard a few whine overhead. He turned his head down the line and was about to yell for his men to remain steady, when a bullet struck him in the arm near the shoulder. Bright red blood stained his coat.

"You better go to the rear," Major Henry yelled.

Adams ignored him and continued riding with the brigade. He hadn't seemed to lose the use of his arm, his hand still grasping the reins.

Collins leaned over and grabbed the bridle of 'Ole Charlie' and said, "Sir, you're wounded; you must leave the field."

"I'm going to see my men through," Adams said. He pulled the horse's head away from Collins's hand.

They were closing on the abatis now. He noticed bullets kicking dust into the air all around his horse. His men surged forward through the remnants of Scott and Featherston's men. The earthworks were a mere fifty feet beyond the Osage orange abatis. It was a beautiful sight watching his men surge forward amid the death and destruction. It looked as though nothing could stop his boys.

Artillery fire began to pour in from Fort Granger across the river. It cut great gaps in his lines, but the men simply closed up and pressed on.

Adams spurred his horse back and forth behind his men. He was shouting words of encouragement, but nothing he said could be understood in the noise of battle. He was considered a handsome man. He had sandy brown hair combed across his head and a thick mustache almost hiding his lips. He looked like a very god of war in the fading light of this November day.

The men charged without being given the order. The rebel yell cut through the rifle fire. These were the best the south had to offer. The cowards and shirkers had long since vanished. Adams understood this was a must-win battle. The South had no more men to fill the ranks.

Adams spun in the saddle and yelled at Collins and Henry. "Gentlemen, go to the flanks, and I'll guide the center."

He watched them each ride away. They were almost to the abatis now. The scene there shocked even Adams. It was a horrible sight. Mutilated bodies shot all to pieces were hanging in the Osage orange branches. He'd never even had nightmares this bad.

He watched his men crash into the abatis. They had no more luck than the two brigades that had attacked here before. His men stood there hacking away at the branches as they took a murderous fire from the works just beyond.

185

A private armed only with an axe began to make a small opening to his left. He watched a few of his men work their way through the gap the man had just made, only to be shot down before reaching the enemy works.

He saw the Fifteenth Mississippi's flag bearer squeeze through a gap and race toward the Federal line ahead. It was a brave thing to do, charging ahead all alone like that. The man went down well short of the works.

I must do something, Adams thought. My men are being slaughtered without the ability to return fire. Men were being knocked in all directions from the fierce fire. Adams looked to the left and noticed an old cotton gin. There wasn't much abatis in that direction. He decided the only option was to move his men around the abatis. It was the only hope they had.

He spurred 'Ole Charlie' down the line and yelled for his men to follow him west. A private yelled, "This way, boys!"

The brigade realized immediately what the general had in mind and began to race after him. He managed to ride down the line broadside to the Federal line without being hit. The Federals were watching this brave officer with awe. Most weren't even firing at him. He came to a large gap just east of the cotton gin and spurred the horse through it. He expected to be hit any moment but felt he must have lived a charmed life to have made it this far. He'd already made up his mind to die, and it felt glorious.

He could see a Federal colonel behind the line of men ahead. He could hear the man shouting for his men to hold their fire. The colonel said, "He's too brave a man to die like this!"

Adams could see a regimental flag to the right of the officer and spurred 'Ole Charlie' that way. The horse seemed to understand what he wanted and leaped across the ditch and onto the parapet. Adams reached out and grabbed the regimental flag. The entire color guard opened fire as one. Horse and rider both crashed to the ground. Adams's leg was pinned under 'Ole Charlie.' The horse's rear legs were in the outer ditch, his front legs draped grotesquely across the works.

Adams lay there staring back at his own men. Another flag bearer came racing forward and climbed onto the works, only to be shot and pulled inside. More of his men were coming through the gaps now, but most were shot down well short of the breastworks.

Colonel Farrell was charging through the gap with a handful of men. Adams wanted to cheer him, but there was no energy. The bullets had torn through his chest. He watched Farrell take bullets in both legs and crash to the ground. The man was trying to crawl back toward the Confederate lines.

Adams felt like crying. Farrell was a good man—a great man. He had nothing before the war and had risen to command a regiment through the high respect of his men.

It was over as quickly as it began. He saw that his brigade was destroyed; the survivors were racing back out of range. They had done all that mortal man could do in this situation.

186

A lull settled over the field, except for the occasional pop of a rifle. Several Federal soldiers climbed over the works and dragged Adams from beneath his horse. They carried him back behind the lines.

The Federal Colonel walked over and knelt beside him. "I'm Colonel John Casement; sorry to meet you under these circumstances."

Adams asked, "Will you please send me to the Confederate lines and allow me to die among friends?"

Casement could tell the wounds were mortal. The man had been hit nine times. He nodded his head, and he said, "As soon as it's safe, I'll make sure you're placed among friends."

Adams thanked him. He watched Casement stand and move away. A Federal private brought a handful of cotton from the old gin and made him a pillow. Another asked, "Do you need anything, General?"

"Water," Adams said. He was so weak; the sound was barely above a whisper.

The man pulled off his canteen and gave Adams a drink. While he drank, another private said, "That's the bravest thing I've ever seen."

Adams finished drinking and laid his head back, staring at the sky. A sergeant with the color guard said, "I'm sorry for shooting such a brave man."

Adams took a deep breath and said, "It is the fate of a soldier to die for his country."

In a few moments, Casement came back. He found the Confederate general dead. He instructed a private to climb over the works and remove the general's saddle so Casement could have it for a souvenir. He then bent down and removed Adams's ring and watch to send to his family later.

After dark, he had his men carry the general's body back out in front of the works to be among his men.

5:20 p.m.

CSA

They were just west of the Columbia Pike. The bottom of the ditch was filled with the dead and wounded. It was the worst position General Strahl had been in since the war began. The ditch was only three feet deep, but the mound of earth the Federal troops had piled up stood about six feet from the bottom. He thought about poor Lieutenant Marsh. The boy had been hit before they ever got close to the earthworks.

He watched as his men scaled the side of the parapet and tried to thrust their muskets between the head log and fire at the Federals. More times than not, the men were blasted back into the ditch. He quickly began to load muskets and pass them up to the men on the parapet.

Above him was a sergeant, who was using the bodies of his comrades to brace himself there. Strahl handed him a rifle and began loading another. They had been firing for quite some time now. He had expected the sergeant to get hit as quickly as the others, but he seemed to be living a charmed life.

As Strahl began to load a rifle, he shouted to the sergeant. "What's your name, soldier?"

"Sumner Cunningham," was the reply. The Sergeant turned and fired another round over the barricade. "I'm in the Forty-First Tennessee, sir."

Cunningham waited for Strahl to finish loading the gun. He looked around and saw how few were left alive. He asked, "We're running low on men, General. What should we do?"

"Keep firing," Strahl replied. He handed the rifle to Cunningham and began loading another. He saw a Union rifle come below the head log and take aim at the Sergeant. Sumner Cunningham took a hand full of the soft dirt and threw it in the direction of the man's face on the other end of the gun. The musket discharged, missing its mark and striking in the ditch behind Strahl.

Another man climbed up on the parapet beside Cunningham and fired underneath the head log at the Union troops on the other side. Just after the smoke cleared, a Union rifle barrel came through the slit and fired. The man fell heavily against Cunningham. The shot had hit the man square in the chest, and the bullet passed completely through his body. The man began to shake violently.

This ain't what I need to deal with just now, Cunningham thought. He struggled to push the man back into the ditch below. The man finally fell down against Cunningham's right leg and began to grope at the wound. Cunningham fired the musket in his hand and turned back to Strahl. At that instant, another shot came through the slit beneath the head log and struck the general.

Cunningham jerked back from the sight. Strahl raised his hands to his face and fell forward on the bodies in the ditch beneath him. It was a sad moment for Cunningham. He'd loved General Strahl ever since his regiment had been placed under his command, but there was no time to reflect on the loss just now. He was up here perched on the parapet with rifle shots erupting around him every moment, and most of those were aimed at him.

Cunningham felt the man against his leg move again. He asked, "Where are you wounded?"

The man didn't answer. He heard a voice from the ditch below him say, "In the neck. It's not mortal, but I'm out of the fight. Sergeant, I've gotta get to Colonel Stafford and inform him that he has command of the brigade."

Cunningham looked back down into the ditch below. He had thought Strahl was dead. He looked at the blood pouring out of the general's neck and onto his frock coat. He started to ask Strahl if he wanted him to carry the message, but just then, another rifle came through the gap and fired again. Cunningham leaned heavily on the wounded man beside him, but the man didn't move.

188

He quickly began loading the rifle again. After loading, he fired through the gap at the Federals on the other side. *This is a waste of time, he thought. I can't even see anyone on the other side, much less hit them.* He turned back to check on his general again, but Strahl was gone.

He spun the other way and saw Strahl about twenty feet east of him, crawling over the dead and wounded in the ditch. Cunningham turned back to his little spot of hell.

Strahl had reached Colonel Stafford but had found the man already dead. He was wedged into the bodies in the trench and couldn't even fall over. It was a grotesque sight. He decided it wouldn't matter much who was in command now. There wasn't much they could do. This had become a soldier's fight, where every man was fighting on his own and without orders.

A man in the ditch saw the general and crawled toward him. He said, "We'll get you to the rear, sir."

Strahl said nothing. He was beginning to grow weak from the loss of blood. At the moment, he wouldn't mind getting out of this death trap. He only wished he could get his men out with him.

The man turned to a couple other soldiers hunkered down in the ditch nearby and said, "Help me get General Strahl to the rear. He's hurt pretty bad."

One of the others said, "Come on, John; let's help Letsinger get the general out of here."

The three men grabbed Strahl and began to carry him toward the rear. There was nothing but open space behind them. It was gonna be a close thing if they made it at all, but their general needed them just now. If they didn't get him to a surgeon, he would bleed to death here on the field.

They had gotten out of the trench and gone about fifteen yards, when a volley was fired at their little group. All four men hit the ground at once. A bullet exploded through the back of General Strahl's head, killing him instantly. He lay there surrounded by the bodies of his would-be rescuers. For General Otho Strahl, his war was finally over.

Part 6

Home Coming

"I'll know what I've lost and all that I've won when
the road finally takes me home."

Mary Fahl

December 1, 1864, 12:05 a.m.

CSA

The firing had finally died down. There was still the occasional pop of a musket, but for the most part, the battle appeared to be over. Hood was up on his crutches near the road. He'd sent couriers to find his corps commanders and have them report here for an impromptu council of war.

It had become painfully clear to him that his plan had failed. His men had swept through the advanced line, and it appeared his army was unstoppable. He'd watched them break the second line in the center but run into reinforcements a couple hundred yards beyond. That was smart of Scofield to place a reserve directly behind the center portion of his line.

Generals Cheatham and S.D. Lee were already here patiently waiting. Cheatham remained aloof, standing with his staff. They were all whispering to each other.

They were waiting for Alexander Peter Stewart to arrive from the right flank. The Harpeth River had funneled all his men into a quarter mile section of line. Hood couldn't believe they hadn't even made a dent there.

General Stewart soon arrived and climbed from his horse. He looked exhausted or depressed, but Hood couldn't tell which. The man paused a long moment as he held the horse's reins, one arm draped across the saddle still. He seemed to come out of the fog for a moment. He shook his head and turned toward the group of officers.

Hood was pretty sure he already knew the answer, but he asked anyway. "How are things on your front, General?"

"Not good," Stewart lowered his head and stared toward the ground. "My corps is all cut to pieces. There's no organization left. None of my commanders have any idea where their men are. The losses have been severe. My entire corps is pretty much useless at the moment. I'll have to wait until daylight to assess the situation."

Hood said nothing. He looked toward Cheatham and waited. Cheatham shifted and scratched his chin. He removed his hat and ran his hand through his hair. He dreaded making the report. He was obviously depressed. Finally, he said, "It's damned bad. The casualties, I mean. We overran the first line; it was beautiful. We broke the second line, but then we ran into reinforcements at the third line."

"I saw all that, Frank," Hood didn't need to be told the obvious. He had been sitting here watching everything just like Cheatham had been. "What is your current situation?"

Cheatham took a deep breath and slowly exhaled. "General Brown is wounded. He was shot in the leg. It's pretty serious; he had to be carried from the field. Bate says his men got into the Carter garden but could go no farther.

No one's heard from Cleburne since the attack began. I'd be surprised if I don't have at least fifty percent casualties. We got a lot of officers down also. I would have to say I'm in the same shape as Stewart. We're dead in the water till morning."

Hood turned to his friend Stephen Lee. Hood's expression betrayed his agitation. "I suppose you're turning on me also."

Lee shifted, then turned and looked toward the lines almost a mile away. "Sir, two of my divisions are badly cut up. I have one division that hasn't been engaged. If you order me to, I'll send them in at first light. If you tell me, I'll send them in with nothing but the bayonet."

Hood couldn't help but notice the way Lee evaded his question. He thought for a long moment. *There's nothing we can do now. We may as well wait until morning.* Finally, he said, "Allow your men to fall back and reform. We'll mass all our artillery in the morning and pound them out of their works. After we loosen them up with the artillery, we'll hit 'em again."

Cheatham still betrayed the melancholy expression. Stewart said nothing but mounted his horse and rode away to the east.

As Stewart rode east, he wondered if he would have any troops left to assault again. He couldn't believe Hood was ordering him to hit those works again. The area he'd been forced into had been a death zone. He dreaded just hearing the casualty report.

Hood turned to Stephen Lee and asked, "How many units you got that haven't been engaged?"

Lee said simply, "Stevenson's division and Clayton's brigade."

"Have them move up to the abandoned Federal advanced line," Hood leaned on the crutch and pointed into the darkness toward town. "We'll hit them in the center again in the morning with your fresh troops."

Lee saluted and climbed on his horse. He turned back toward the west, and there in the road was Major General Johnson patiently waiting.

Johnson saluted as Lee rode over. He asked, "What are the orders, sir?"

"We're gonna hit 'em again in the morning," Lee returned the salute. "Prepare your men."

Johnson simply shook his head and turned the horse back toward his division. There was no sense in arguing the order. He turned to Major Ratchford of his staff and said, "Find the brigade commanders and pass the order along."

"Yes sir," Ratchford spurred his horse toward the front. He found Brigadier General William Brantley sitting beneath a tree, seemingly in a daze.

Ratchford climbed down from his horse and walked over to Brantley. "Sir, General Johnson sends his compliments and says the assault must be continued at first light."

Brantley said nothing. It didn't appear he had heard Ratchford at all.

"Sir," Ratchford called out in a pitched voice. "General Brantley."

Brantley continued staring at the ground just beyond his feet.

193

Ratchford stepped closer and reached down, touching Brantley on the shoulder, giving him a gentle nudge.

Brantley continued staring at the ground. After a moment, he began to mumble to himself. "I have no brigade. They're all dead."

Ratchford was shocked. He stepped back from the brigade commander. He said in a low voice, "Surely that's not the case, sir. You must have some survivors."

Brantley continued staring ahead, making no reply. Ratchford was growing disturbed by Brantley's lack of action. He said, "Sir, if you don't make some effort to reform your men, I will be forced to report it to General Lee."

Brantley blinked his eyes and shook his head. This seemed to get a reaction out of him. He rubbed his temples and slowly rose from the ground.

His reply was simple. "I'll see how many men I have left."

Ratchford watched the distraught man disappear into the night.

12:10 a.m.

USA

General Cox was behind the breastworks with his men near the cotton gin. He peered through a gap beneath the head log to see what was happening out there. The fighting had mostly ceased in this sector. The night was dark, but he could feel the enemy troops out there. He could hear the wounded begging for help. A man could hardly stand to hear the pleading of the wounded when the war began. Now it was just another event that a man became callused to after awhile.

He'd known all along they would win this battle. There was a feeling he couldn't seem to shake. The Rebel army was broken. There was little need to retreat to Nashville. If Schofield would allow him, he intended to move out tomorrow and attack Hood and destroy what little army he had left.

"Is General Cox here?" a voice called out of the darkness from behind him near the cotton gin.

Cox kept his head low and moved that way. He wasn't about to answer and have a hundred Rebel's open fire because they wanted to kill a general officer.

It was Colonel Israel Stiles of his left-most brigade. He had a young lieutenant of his staff with him. When Stiles saw Cox, he said, "I was coming here for orders and to see what you're thinking. I've found something I think you should see."

"All right, Israel, show me the way." Cox couldn't help but like Israel Stiles. The man was a fighter. He was just the type of man he liked to have command under him.

They walked a few feet past the cotton gin, and on the ground, lay Cox's staff officer, Lieutenant Coughlan. His cape was spread over his face, but this was also a dead giveaway to who lay beneath. Cox bent over and pulled the cape off the boy's face to see if he was still alive. Deep down inside, Cox knew the answer before he looked. As the cape slid away from his face, Cox saw that his eyes were wide open, staring into the starry sky above.

"I'm sorry, sir," Stiles said. He reached over and patted Cox on the shoulder. "He was a good man, one of the best."

Cox said nothing. He replaced the cape back over the young hero's face and motioned for Stiles to follow him back to the works. The young lieutenant followed close behind.

They got behind the breastworks and listened to the wounded out beyond. Several of Cox's men were patting each other on the back and bragging about how they had escaped disaster twice in two days.

Cox looked at Stiles and asked, "What do you think?"

Stiles peered through the crack beneath the head log and replied, "I think we should stay right here and whip the hell out of 'em."

Cox smiled. Those were his thoughts exactly. He asked for a courier and waited while one was found. The man came up and saluted the general squatting behind the breastworks. Cox said, "Go to General Schofield at Fort Granger. Tell him we have whipped the Rebel army, and if he will consent, I will move out in the morning and destroy what's left of it."

The man repeated the message and moved away. Cox watched the man hurrying toward the rear, his body bent as low as he could possibly get.

Another man came limping down the line from the west. He whispered, "Where's General Cox?"

Cox recognized the whisper. "I'm right here, Levi. Why are you limping?"

"Bullet grazed my leg and killed my horse," Levi continued whispering. "I got caught up in that breakthrough over in the road. I couldn't get them to stand and fight for nothing."

"You don't have to whisper, Levi." Cox began to laugh. "You're not in a library."

Stiles chuckled behind him.

"Sorry, sir," Levi said out loud. "Didn't want to attract bullets."

"It's over," Cox said. He sat down and leaned back against the works. "Do you need a surgeon?"

"I'm fine, just painful as hell, but I'm fine," Levi replied. "Have you seen the destruction out there?"

"It's bad," Cox said.

"When I was at Knoxville and watched Longstreet attack Fort Sanders last year, I thought that was bad..." Levi eased himself down on the ground, being careful with his wounded leg. "That was nothing compared to this. Not only are there a lot of bodies out there, but they've been hit so many times that

195

most of them are mangled. It's so disgusting that I actually got sick at my stomach."

"I'm afraid I have some bad news for you," Cox reached over and patted Levi on the arm. "Your old schoolmate, Colonel Mervin Clark, was killed."

"No," Levi said louder than he meant to. "He is engaged to a beautiful young lady back in Ohio. They were madly in love. I'm glad I'm not the one that has to break the news to her. I saw him this afternoon. I started to walk over and speak to him, but for some reason I didn't bother. I wish I'd have gone over now."

"He was standing behind the works at the Carter House when the line broke is what I heard." Cox reached up and wiped his sleeve across his mouth. "They tell me he grabbed his regiment's flag and refused to retreat. He stood right there and was shot down. I'm told his men rallied because of what he did there."

"Sounds just like him," Levi was shaking his head in the darkness. "I'm gonna miss old Clarkie. He was a good friend and a great man."

"Jim Coughlan is dead also," Cox pointed toward the cotton gin. "He's lying just past the gin."

"Poor Jim," Levi said. Levi thought about Jim Coughlan always volunteering for the most dangerous jobs. He'd been suffering more and more from epilepsy, which left him depressed for days. "I think he finally got his wish. He was a good friend also. He's died a hero in one of the war's greatest battles."

Cox watched Levi reach down and rub at the wounded leg.

"There's nothing else you can do here, Levi," Cox's voice was firm. "I want you to go to the rear and get that leg looked at."

Levi recognized the tone. It was the tone General Cox used when he was giving an order that must be obeyed and there would be no arguing with him. He simply said, "Yes, sir."

Cox watched him crouch low and begin limping toward the rear. There was another man approaching as Levi left. He heard the man ask Levi where he could find General Cox. Levi pointed him back to where Cox was sitting.

Stiles said, "You're getting pretty popular tonight."

"Stanley was wounded when the fighting began." Cox continued to watch the man approaching. "I'm in charge of the field now."

The man came over and squatted near Cox. He said, "Are you General Cox?"

Cox recognized the voice as being one of Schofield's young staff officers. He said, "You've found him. I suppose you got orders from General Schofield."

"That's right," the man smiled at the thought of being recognized as one of the commanding general's aides. "He says to pull back immediately."

196

"Pull back?" Stiles repeated. His voice gave away his unbelief at such an order.

Cox said, "Is General Schofield aware of the situation here?"

"I would think he is," the young officer replied. "He has orders from General Thomas to fall back to Nashville."

"Look, we have twenty-eight captured battle flags here." Cox wondered if it would do any good to argue his case with this young snot-nosed lieutenant. He decided it could do no harm. "All the captured Confederate officers have told me this is the worst they've seen it. They say it's even worse than their attack at Atlanta. We've practically destroyed Hood's army. It would be a mistake to pull back. Some of those officers think they have no men left. Go ask Schofield if he can get Thomas to rescind that order. If we can get some more ammunition up here, we can finish Hood's army off in the morning. Tell Thomas to send Smith's corps here as soon as they arrive, and they can help us."

"I'll see what he says," the lieutenant shook his head and quietly moved away.

Cox was satisfied. He called out into the darkness for his adjutant, Theodore Cox. The man was close by and half crawled over to where the general was waiting.

Cox said, "Go tell General Schofield that if he will allow me, I will take full responsibility for holding out here. Tell him the Rebel army is practically destroyed, and we can finish it up here in the morning. There's no need to retreat."

He watched his adjutant move toward the rear. Cox looked at Stiles and said, "You think he'll allow it?"

"I hope so," Stiles evaded the question. He turned and peered through the crack under the head log again. The wounded were still begging and pleading for help.

Stiles's young lieutenant said, "I think we should stay and whip the hell out of them in the morning."

Stiles turned around and eyed the young man a long moment and said, "There's no hell left in them. Don't you hear them praying?"

He then told Cox he would return to his command and await orders there. Cox shook his hand and said, "You did good today, Israel. You did real good."

After Stiles left, Cox waited in the darkness until his adjutant returned. Cox said, "What have you got for me, Theo?"

Theodore came up, squatted next to Cox, and gave a sloppy salute. He said, "Sir, General Schofield says for me to tell you that you've won a glorious victory here today. He says he has no doubt that you could accomplish the task in the morning, but General Thomas's orders must be followed."

"Damn," Cox said. "I hate to retreat when there is no need to retreat."

Theodore lowered his voice and moved closer to the general. "Sir, I'm afraid Schofield has lost his nerve. He seems a bit shaken by the events of the past few days. The man isn't acting like himself."

Cox said nothing. He knew Schofield was exhausted, but hadn't thought it would affect the man this way. He thought a long moment and said, "Theo, have Major Dow leave a strong skirmish line in the works until we can get the army north of the river. Tell him that when he retires, he should have the skirmishers take the planks up from the bridges to slow down the Confederate pursuit."

"Right, sir," Theodore turned to leave, then paused and asked, "Is that all?"

Cox was staring at the ground in deep thought. He was frustrated with retreating. He'd watched generals lose their nerve the entire war and retreat for no good reason. The war would have been over by now if they would have just advanced instead of retreating at every little setback. He said, "Theo, we just lost a great opportunity here—a great opportunity."

Cox moved back to the Carter house and mounted his horse. He rode down into town so he could supervise the withdrawal. There were a lot of Confederate prisoners here being herded across the river. Many had bloody handkerchiefs wrapped around head wounds. Some were limping; most were wounded in some way. Most of the guards were sharing their rations with the poor men. Every prisoner seemed genuinely thankful for the food.

One guard was telling them that it was the most courageous charge he had ever witnessed. He noticed that the Rebel prisoners raised their heads at the thought. Cox felt sorry for them. They'd been sent to be slaughtered here.

Another guard tried to pick at one of the prisoners he had taken a shine to. He said, "What you planning on doing now, Johnny?"

The soldier didn't even pause to think. "I'm gonna relax in a Yankee prison for a while. I'm about tired of a marchin' and a fightin' all the time anyway."

Cox sat on his horse a long moment thinking. Cleburne and Brown's divisions had broken through and almost pulled it off. We've nearly destroyed the Confederacy's second most powerful army here tonight and now we're retreating. He said aloud to himself, "What a damned shame."

6:30 a.m.

CSA

John Bell Hood sat at a table in the front yard of the Carter House. His useless arm lay in his lap as he ran his good hand through his hair. Tears streamed down his cheeks into his tawny beard. He looked to be in pure agony. It didn't take a genius to realize what a mistake had been made here yesterday.

Brigadier General Randal Gibson was standing in the road near the house. He shook his head as he surveyed the battlefield. Bodies were piled on top of each other up to five deep in places. Gibson said to no one in particular, "This entire affair is inexplicable."

Hood looked back toward the battle-scarred home. The outbuildings were full of bullet holes. The entire south side of the main house was a mess. Bricks were destroyed by bullets, and there were several holes in the walls from artillery fire.

There were over fifty bodies lying in the front yard of the Carter home. Hood looked up and saw Colonel Mason approaching. Mason stopped in front of the table and was about to salute. Hood asked, "You have a report for me?"

"Sir," Mason paused as if he dreaded telling his commander the news. "We got between eight and nine thousand casualties. The Federals pulled out sometime during the night and left about two thousand casualties on the field."

Hood said nothing but continued to stare at the table. After a long moment, he looked at Mason and asked, "Is that all?"

"No, sir," Mason lowered his head. "We've got thirteen generals down. Generals Cleburne, Granbury, Gist, Strahl, and Adams are all dead. Brigadier General Carter is wounded, most likely mortal. He's gut shot. Generals Brown, Cockrell, Deas, Manigault, Quarles, Scott, and Sharp are all wounded. General Gordon is feared captured. We have ten colonels killed, twenty-two wounded, and three captured. There are a total of fifty-five regimental commanders out of action. Hell, a captain is the highest ranking officer left in Quarles's entire brigade."

"Enough," Hood said. He waved Mason away.

Hood turned away from Mason and looked toward the front door of the Carter house. Moscow Carter was using a shovel removing something from the steps and putting it into a bushel basket. When the young Captain had finished with his task, he started around the south corner of the home. Hood called out, "What you got there?"

Moscow turned with an expression of extreme sadness. "I shoveled up a half bushel of brains off the front steps."

Hood lowered his head. He was sorry he had asked.

A horse came up the street. The rider looked exhausted. It was Frank Cheatham. The man was looking out across the fields at the bodies. In the ditch were so many bodies that some still sat straight up, wedged in to where they couldn't fall over.

Cheatham rode up in front of the Carter House, his horse dodging bodies as he moved down the road. He recognized General Hood and stopped. He dismounted and held onto the saddle for a long moment with his head lowered.

199

Frank Cheatham walked to the table and sat across from Hood. He said, "My command has been decimated. Brown has been wounded, and his division is a mess. Of his four brigade commanders, one is feared captured, two are dead, one is wounded, and it's probably mortal. There are bodies piled seven deep out there in places. I saw a dead colonel wedged between the bodies in the trench. He couldn't even fall over. His chin was resting on his chest, and he was still staring straight ahead at the Federal lines. Hell, I can't believe they didn't stay and attack us this morning. What a bunch of cowards."

"We punished him," Hood said. "We've taken a thousand prisoners, and he's hurt just as bad as we are."

"Sir," Cheatham could barely believe what he was hearing. "The army has been practically destroyed."

Hood held up a hand. "We will follow him to Nashville and await an opening."

Cheatham was shaking his head but said nothing. *How can this man think we can take Nashville? he thought. Has he not seen the battlefield? He rode down that road this morning and saw the same destruction I did.*

"If we fall back now," Hood continued, "the men will take this as a defeat."

Cheatham said nothing. He stared at the table. *How else can they take this battle? he thought. You don't lose half an army and call it a victory just because the enemy retired from the field.*

Hood wasn't through with his one-sided argument. "We could fall back and wait for the expected reinforcements I asked for in Texas, but what would the point be? We'd just have to turn around and move back up here all over again. No, sir, I won't do it. We will go to Nashville and await the enemy to attack us in our works and then we will follow him back into his works."

Cheatham said, "Sir, it'll take me a few days to reform and bury my dead."

"It's alright, Frank," Hood ran his hand through his hair again. "Take your time. I'll send Lee and Stewart on to Nashville, and you can come later."

Cheatham stood and saluted. He looked around at the bodies in the Carter yard. He lowered his head and walked back to the horse. He wasn't in the mood for another argument with the commanding general.

Hood turned and saw Colonel Mason talking to Fountain Carter near the corner of his badly-damaged house. He called out, "Colonel, a word please."

Colonel Mason shook the old man's hand and hurried back to the table where Hood was sitting.

Hood said, "Get a paper and ink. I'd like to make a proclamation to the army."

After Mason had secured the necessary items, he sat and waited for the general.

Hood began, "The commanding general would like to congratulate the army for the splendid victory over our enemy yesterday. We fought heroically and with unequaled courage. The enemy has fallen back to Nashville in great disorder and confusion. We must lament our losses in gallant officers and men, but we have proved ourselves to our fellow countrymen that we can take any position, no matter how strongly defended."

Mason reread the letter and hurriedly moved away from the table to have other members of Hood's staff make copies to forward to all the commanders.

General Hood noticed a man stripping the clothing from a dead Federal soldier across the road from the Carter House. A girl of no more than fifteen was watching him, a look of shock on her face. When the Confederate soldier had stripped the body of all but his underwear, he stood up and inspected his new clothes.

The girl scolded him. "Looks like you would leave him something decent to be buried in."

The soldier smiled a toothy grin and kicked the dead enemy soldier in the ribs. "Where he's a goin, these fine clothes just catch fire."

The girl looked at him a long moment with a look of bewilderment.

He stood there a moment longer and added, "To hell is where he's headed, ma'am."

Hood looked back toward the house and saw Brigadier General Thomas Benton Smith approaching on horseback. People had left the cellar of the home and were meandering about the yard, trying to understand what it was they were witnessing. The small area behind the house contained over eighty bodies. General Smith had to pick his route carefully to prevent his horse from stepping on a dead soldier.

Smith rode up to a young woman and asked, "Is this the home of Tod Carter?"

The girl looked up. There was hope in her eyes. She quickly answered, "Yes, it is."

"I'm afraid I have bad news," Smith lowered his head. "Is Fountain Carter home?"

"That's my father," the girl answered and turned back toward the house.

She found the old man inside, surveying the damage to his home. Surgeons were busy in the parlor amputating arms and legs and throwing them out the windows.

Carter came back outside, followed by his three daughters and a daughter-in-law. He walked over to General Smith and nodded. "I'm Fountain Branch Carter."

"Sir," General Smith nodded. He jerked a thumb over his shoulder and pointed back toward the southwest. "I tried to persuade your son not to enter this fight. As Assistant Quartermaster of the brigade, he had no business leading a charge. He told me there was no power on earth gonna keep him out of this battle. He said he was determined to go home."

Carter nodded, waiting. Smith continued, "He's back here severely wounded. I can take you there."

Carter nodded again and motioned for the girls to follow him. Smith dismounted and began to lead the little party back across the battlefield.

"What happened?" the old man asked.

"He was on his big gray horse named 'Rosencrantz' with his saber drawn." Smith looked back and noticed the worried look on the girls' faces. "He was out riding ahead of the line, sword pointing toward the enemy, and suddenly he just charged ahead alone. Horse and rider were both hit, throwing him over the horse's head. He's been hit nine times, once in the head. He was about five hundred feet from the house at the time he was hit."

"Is he conscious?" the old man asked. He betrayed no emotion.

"He was earlier," Smith lowered his head again. "He was trapped between the lines begging for help last night, but no one could reach him. No man could live between that fire."

They were approaching the locust grove. Bodies lay scattered all around. At one place, the bodies reminded Moscow of broken cane the way they had all fallen in a single line. Most of the trees here were about five to six inches in diameter. All of them were full of bullet holes. Several had actually been shot down from rifle fire. The ground had grooves cut in it from the bullets. He wondered how anyone could have survived out here.

Just at the edge of the locust grove they found him. He lay on the ground, pale soft skin, and clean shaven. He looked like a boy, too innocent to die this way. There was blood all over his uniform; the horse lay a few feet away to the south. There was a neat little hole just above his right eye. There was dried blood from the wound all over his face.

General Smith located a couple of soldiers and ordered them to take an old army overcoat and carry the young lieutenant back to the Carter Home.

The sad little group soon returned, climbing over the works with their precious load. They carried him past the battle-damaged buildings and into the first room in the ell of the house. It was the same room where young Tod had been born just twenty-four short years ago.

Tod was moaning as they laid him in the bed. He kept calling over and over for Sergeant James Cooper, his best friend.

One of his sisters kept repeating in a soft whisper, "Brother's come home at last."

Fountain Carter walked back to the door and peered across the yard. He didn't need a surgeon to tell him that his boy would die. The wounds were just too ugly.

He saw two mounted men approaching on horse back. It was General Smith again. The general and his aide rode to the ell and dismounted. They tied the horses to the banister across the back porch.

Smith nodded to the old man and said, "Sir, this is Doctor Deering Roberts, my brigade surgeon. He's gonna do what he can for your son."

Fountain thanked the general and showed the surgeon inside. Doctor Roberts looked over the badly-wounded man. His face betrayed what he was thinking. He took a small probe from his bag and began to dig for the bullet above Tod's right eye. After what seemed like an eternity, he stopped and placed the probe back in the bag.

"The bullet's too deep," he announced to no one in particular. "The wound is mortal. I'm sorry."

"What can we do?" one of the girls asked.

Doctor Roberts turned and saw tears in the girl's eyes. "You can clean the wound and pray."

He turned and exited the room. The girls quickly got water and a rag and cleaned his wounds. They each then took turns kissing the gentle face. They hadn't seen their brother since the spring of sixty-one. They took turns holding his hands and speaking words of encouragement to him. He would squeeze their hands at times. They felt certain he could hear them. They truly believed he would pull through, but he would be dead in two days.

December 1, 1864, 8:00 a.m.

USA

Major General George Thomas motioned for General James Wilson to have a seat across the table from him. Wilson looked exhausted. His uniform was covered with a thick layer of dirt. The man looked as if he were about to fall over any moment.

Wilson rubbed his eyes and shook his head as if he were trying to clear away the cobwebs from his mind. "Sir, my men are exhausted. We need new equipment, and we need a lot of horses. I tried to stop Forrest, but he has four times as many men as I do. We're gonna need a lot more cavalry to deal with him."

Thomas nodded his head and let out a puff of cigar smoke. He couldn't help but notice the contrast between this man and the Wilson who'd left here less than a month ago. The man had said that he couldn't wait to meet General Forrest. Now he wished he hadn't met the man. He thought about the message Schofield had sent him a few days ago. He'd said that Wilson was utterly unable to deal with Forrest.

"We'll refit the cavalry before moving against the enemy," Thomas said. He took another puff of the cigar. "Our records show you have about six thousand cavalry; is that correct?"

Wilson began to shake his head. "Partially correct, only two thousand are mounted."

Thomas raised his eyebrows. "General Halleck has informed me that he has sent twenty-two thousand horses to this department in the past month. He says we should have plenty of horses. He thinks we're stalling to keep from advancing against the enemy."

"I haven't seen twenty-two thousand horses," Wilson shrugged. He rubbed his eyes again. "What does he expect me to do?"

"I have a telegram here from the Secretary of War, Edwin Stanton," Thomas took the message from the table and handed it to Wilson. "He says you have the authority to impress every horse you can find. Just provide the owners with a receipt of up to a hundred and sixty dollars depending on the quality of the horse."

Wilson looked at the telegram. He appeared to be having trouble focusing on the words.

Thomas smiled to himself. "Get some rest today, and get busy on refitting your cavalry tomorrow. Move your cavalry across the river so you can refit without anymore harassment from Forrest."

"Right," Wilson stood and saluted. "I'll get right on it."

Thomas watched him leave. He thought about General Forrest, the man they call the 'Wizard of the Saddle.' It was a damned shame that he fought for the other side. He wondered why the north hadn't provided a general like him. Deep down, he'd known all along that the cocky little Wilson wasn't going to be a match for the man, even if he was Grant's handpicked man for the job.

The next visit he got this morning was from Major General John Schofield. The man looked worse than Wilson. He practically collapsed in his chair across from Thomas. His clothes were disheveled, and his eyes betrayed the strain he'd been under the past few days.

Schofield didn't volunteer any information. Thomas barely spoke to the man. The cigar had gone out, so Thomas struck a lucifer and relit it. He asked, "What kind of condition are your men in at the moment?"

"They're exhausted," Schofield shook his head. There was a hint of anger in his voice. "Men are falling out alongside the road. Some are falling asleep while they walk."

"Reports show it's all right," Thomas puffed the cigar. "Hood's army hasn't advanced from Franklin yet."

Schofield wanted to say something but refrained. Thomas had promised to send Smith's corps and Steedman's division to meet him during the retreat last night. Instead, he'd struggled into Nashville without relief. Another thing that rankled him was the fact that the army commander had sat back here in Nashville while a big part of his army was fighting for their lives.

Schofield simply said, "We expected Smith and Steedman to meet us last night."

"Smith's corps is still on the boats," Thomas knew right away what Schofield was implying. "Steedman is still en route here by train."

Schofield fought the urge to say something. His face was turning red. He was exhausted; he'd been under constant strain for the past week, and his fuse had grown considerably short. The first mistake Thomas had made was sending him to Pulaski, which didn't even block Hood's route to Nashville. Hood's army had simply marched past the place and put Schofield in a race for his life. At Columbia, he'd been begging Thomas to send him the five thousand troops under General Steedman, but Thomas hadn't seen the need for it. Yesterday, he'd been forced to fight with his back against the Duck River because Thomas hadn't sent the pontoon train he'd asked for. He actually felt as though Thomas had sent him and his men to be sacrificed to buy time for Smith and Steedman to arrive and save Nashville.

Schofield had hated Thomas ever since his days at the Academy. He'd been a victim of hazing there. Some upperclassmen forced him to draw lewd pictures on the board. He was brought up on court martial charges. The board had exonerated him, but one member had voted to dismiss him from the Academy. That man was George Thomas.

"I've received a report that Colonel Opdycke and his men saved the battle yesterday," Thomas puffed on the cigar.

"That's my understanding also," Schofield replied.

Thomas turned to his adjutant general, William Whipple and said, "Have a courier sent to find Colonel Emerson Opdycke. Have him brought here."

Whipple nodded and moved away.

Thomas had also heard that Schofield had been so exhausted at Franklin that he didn't seem fit for command. The rumor was that had it not been for Schofield's subordinates at Franklin, his army may have been destroyed.

There was a knock on the door. Whipple opened the door, and there stood Major General Andrew Smith. Whipple saluted and shook hands with the rough-looking commander. His hair was gray and receding, his beard thick and mostly gray.

Thomas saw Smith and practically leapt from his chair. "Well, if it isn't Andrew Smith, fresh off the boats from Missouri?"

Thomas rushed over to meet Smith. Smith held out his hand. Thomas brushed on past the open hand and embraced the man. It was a rare moment for the normally-reserved General Thomas. Schofield sat and steamed at the display. He'd saved Nashville and hadn't even been thanked, yet Smith has done nothing but arrive on the scene, and Thomas acts like he's a hero.

"Everything will be all right now," Thomas said as he patted Smith's arm, "You've arrived just in time to save the day."

"I've arrived, sir," Smith explained, "but the men are still on the boats."

"It's all right," Thomas motioned for Smith to take a seat next to Schofield. "Hood's army is still in Franklin burying their dead from yesterday's fight. How many men do you have with you, Andrew?"

205

"Nine thousand men," Smith said, and then he broke into a rare smile. "You know we've been in Missouri chasing bushwhackers. My men have nicknamed themselves 'Smith's Guerrillas.'"

"I'm glad to have them," Thomas said. He looked at Schofield and seemed to remember he had unfinished business with the man. "General Schofield, my staff informs me that you failed to place the Duck River between your army and the enemy at Franklin. You state your army is in pretty bad shape. It could have been destroyed. I can't believe you neglected to get your army across the river before the attack. It could have been ugly."

Schofield was still seething. He wanted to ask Thomas why he hadn't sent the pontoon bridge he'd requested to get across the river. At the moment, he was too tired to argue. He finally said, "The bridges were destroyed. I had to rebuild them before I could get my men across. I didn't have the pontoons I had requested. I have brought over seven hundred Confederate prisoners with me, not to mention a large number of captured battle flags."

Thomas nodded but didn't seem to take the hint. "When your men arrive, have them begin working on the entrenchments immediately."

Schofield nodded his head but said nothing.

Thomas added, "You've done well enough. Now get some rest. You look like hell."

Schofield thanked Thomas and rose from the chair. Thomas began to wonder if Schofield would make it out the door before falling asleep.

Thomas offered General Smith a cigar. "Schofield has about twenty-four thousand men. I have four thousand garrison troops here in the trenches. General James Steedman is on the way from Chattanooga with eighty-five hundred men, but a good many of those troops are colored. I'm not sure they will be much better than garrison troops, but I can't be picky at the moment. General Steedman is the best division commander in the army. If anyone can get the coloreds to fight, he's the man. The main fighting will have to be done with yours and Schofield's troops."

Smith nodded in agreement and did a quick calculation in his head. That made about forty-five thousand infantry counting the garrison troops. He asked, "Do you plan for us to move out and meet Hood before he reaches the city?"

"I'm afraid we're in no position to do that," Thomas said through a cloud of cigar smoke. "Wilson hasn't got enough cavalry to deal with Forrest. He also needs horses and equipment. We'll have to retire to the trenches while he refits. His cavalry is in a real mess, but it's not entirely his fault. Forrest helped put his cavalry in such disarray."

"What about Hood?" Smith began to worry. "If he flanks us..." He left the rest unsaid.

Thomas was shaking his head. "He's not going anywhere. We've got gunboats patrolling the river. There's no way for him to get his army across."

"Right," Smith nodded.

Thomas moved some papers around on his desk. He said, "I've ordered Wilson to take his cavalry north across the river to refit. I don't want to advance until my cavalry is prepared. I'm not sure if Wilson can handle Forrest if he has equal numbers, but I don't want to assault Hood without cavalry on my flanks. I don't want him getting in my rear the way he did Schofield."

"If there's nothing else, I'll go back and oversee the unloading of the boats." Smith slowly got to his feet. "I'll march them up here as soon as they're off."

"I'll have an aide show you where I want your men," Thomas took Smith's hand in his and shook it vigorously.

After Smith had left, Thomas turned to Whipple and said, "William, have a telegram sent to Washington. Inform the authorities there that we are falling back into the entrenchments around Nashville until I can reform my cavalry. Tell them if Hood is brave enough to attack us here, he will be severely punished. When the cavalry is reformed, I will move out and destroy Hood's army."

"Got it," Whipple was scribbling furiously on a piece of paper.

There was another knock on the door, and an aide opened it. There stood the red-haired Colonel Emerson Opdycke. He walked into the room and gave a crisp salute to Thomas. Thomas waved him off and pointed to the chair across the table.

"From what I've heard, Colonel..." Thomas held out his hand. Opdycke took it and nodded. "Your brigade saved the army from disaster at Franklin."

Opdycke's chin rose high in the air at the compliment. "They did that, sir, I'm proud to say. My men charged with the bayonet and crushed the enemy before us. I'm just proud to be a part of such a group of men. Did you know they've nicknamed themselves 'Opdycke's Tigers'? If not for those men, we would have faced a disaster."

Thomas gave a rare smile. "Schofield shouldn't have put the army in that position—facing a superior enemy with his back to a river."

"I'm not sure I would place the blame on his shoulders." Opdycke looked around as if he were afraid someone might hear him.

"What do you mean?" Thomas asked.

"General Wagner is responsible for most of it. Because of his arrogance, he almost cost us an army." Opdycke looked around again. He cleared his throat and went on. "If I'd obeyed orders and remained out in front of the army with Conrad and Lane, Schofield and his army wouldn't be here today."

"Wagner left two brigades in front of the army?" Thomas looked incredulous. "In front of the breastworks? What was his reasoning?"

"The man was drunk, sir," Opdycke was angry about it all over again. He didn't care who heard him now. "He should be held accountable for what happened. He got a lot of good men killed. It wouldn't have even been a close battle if not for those two brigades isolated in front of the army. When they

207

were flanked and broke, the enemy raced into our lines with our retreating men. No one could open fire for fear of hitting our own retreating troops. That's how they broke our lines. Conrad is just as upset about Wagner as I am."

Nashville Capital. If the Confederates could capture Nashville, they could prolong the war and possibly change the outcome.

Thomas turned in his chair and said to Whipple. "William, send a courier and have George Wagner report here at once."

He turned back to Opdycke and thanked him again. Opdycke was being dismissed and had sense enough to know it. He rose from the chair and again shook Thomas's hand.

Before he left the room, Thomas said, "Colonel Opdycke, please pass on my thanks to the men of your brigade."

A courier arrived with two telegrams. He handed both to Thomas. Thomas sat reading the telegrams for a long moment. He began to frown as he read them.

The first note was from Secretary of War Edwin Stanton. The man was telling Thomas how disappointed President Lincoln was that Thomas is waiting inside his fortifications for Hood to make the first move. Lincoln had said that Thomas waiting for everything to be perfect before moving sounds a lot like McClellan's strategy of doing nothing while the enemy raids the country.

Thomas finished reading the message and flung it on the table. The next one was from General Grant. The commanding general told Thomas that if he waited in his entrenchments, Hood would wreck the railroad all the way back to Chattanooga. He wanted Thomas to place his noncombatants in the trenches and move out and strike Hood with his entire force. He said that after Hood's heavy losses at Franklin, Thomas should move out and finish his army off. General Grant also feared a footrace to the Ohio River. He stated that he had telegraphed all the governors to send emergency troops to Kentucky to slow Hood down.

Thomas was taken aback. He couldn't believe what he had just read. He was without an organized army. The government had given him a bunch of scattered detachments, and now they expect him to strike veteran Confederate infantry. His troops had never fought together before, and most of his subordinates hated each other. He couldn't believe they weren't giving him time to organize his army.

He turned in the chair again. "William, send a telegram to General Grant. Tell him General Smith's troops are getting off the boats at this very moment. As soon as Steedman's infantry and General McCook's cavalry arrive, I will be prepared to advance. Tell him I hope within the next two or three days."

He watched Whipple scribble the message out and hand it to a courier. "Send a telegram to Edwin Stanton. Tell him I plan to advance in the next couple of days, although my cavalry is less than half as strong as Hood's."

A few moments later, an aide arrived with General George Wagner in tow. The general gave a sharp salute. He seemed to be aware of the fact that he was in some sort of trouble. Thomas watched him shift from one foot to another. He motioned for Wagner to take the seat across the table.

Thomas eyed him carefully as he pulled out another cigar and lit it. Wagner stared down at the table, avoiding eye contact. Thomas blew out a cloud of gray smoke and asked, "Tell me how your men got caught half a mile in front of the breastworks facing the entire Confederate army."

Wagner cleared his throat and shifted in the chair. His eyes never met Thomas's as he talked. "It was a misunderstanding, sir."

Thomas puffed on the cigar and waited.

"I was ordered by General Schofield to be the rearguard. He wanted me to hold the Confederate army back as long as possible." Wagner put his hand over his mouth and coughed. "The enemy's attack was so sudden; my men didn't have time to pull back. The men were, uh, a bit overzealous I guess you could say. They, uh, they thought they could whip Hood's entire army by themselves. Conrad and Lane waited too long to give them the order to fall back."

"I've heard rumors that you were intoxicated," Thomas let out another puff of smoke. Wagner was shaking his head in denial. "I also have a report from Joseph Conrad that says you ordered him to hold the position if he had to use the bayonet."

209

"I can't imagine…" Wagner started to say something but stopped himself.

Thomas said, "I want you to go back to the command of your old brigade. I'm going to assign Brigadier General Washington Elliott to command your division."

"Sir," Wagner's tone was low now, "I will submit my resignation and return home if you will accept it."

"Thank you," Thomas replied quickly. "I'll accept it."

For the first time, Wagner's eyes met Thomas's. He hadn't thought he'd done anything bad enough to warrant his resignation. *Hell, he thought, I've been one of the bravest and most capable officers in this war, and now I'm being punished over one mistake. I practically saved the army at Spring Hill.*

Wagner slowly rose from his chair, saluted, and left the war.

December 3, 1864, 6:00 p.m.

CSA

Brigadier General John Carpenter Carter. Only twenty-seven years old, he would suffer horribly.

Brigadier General John Carpenter Carter lay in bed at the Harrison House. He'd been hit in the stomach by a bullet, but he held onto the hope that he would survive.

Chaplain Quintard had always been impressed with Carter's gentle nature and dauntless courage under fire. Quintard walked into the bedroom and held Carter's hand. The young general opened his eyes and tried to smile through the pain.

Quintard had already talked to the doctors. They said that when the bullet exited Carter's back, it had created a horrendous wound. The doctor had told Quintard there was very little hope of the general's recovering.

"What happened, John?" Quintard asked.

"I've never seen anything like it," Carter's voice was strained. The man was in obvious pain. "Throughout the entire war, nothing like it. Whole ranks were simply swept from the field."

Quintard patted Carter on the hand and tried to change the subject. "How do you feel?"

Carter wasn't through discussing the battle yet. "General Brown ordered me to support Gist's brigade. We were behind Gist's men…" Carter coughed and continued. "The cannons were erasing his brigade from the field. Gist's left was in the air, and when we went in to support him, my left was in the air."

Quintard nodded his head, waiting. Carter continued, "I was out in front of my brigade, recklessly exposing myself. Captain Neely of my staff was with me. You know, I've always had this superstition that if I concentrated on my own personal safety, I would be safe. In the urgency and excitement of the moment, I forgot all danger."

"You must think on other things now, John," Quintard was trying to find a way to let the young man know that his life would soon be over.

"I was hit about a hundred and fifty yards from the Federal lines." Carter grimaced against the pain. "Neely caught me before I hit the ground, which probably saved me."

Quintard didn't know what to say. After a long pause, he said, "Have you thought about dying?"

Carter grimaced against the pain again. He was slowly bleeding to death on the inside. He said, "Surely I won't die. I firmly believe I am improving."

"But, General," Quintard was responsible for helping this man prepare for the possibility of dying, "if you should die, what would you want me to tell your wife?"

Carter thought a long moment. "Tell her I have always loved her faithfully, and I respect her more than I can possibly express."

Quintard nodded and asked, "What about your spiritual well-being? Have you prayed?"

Carter nodded his head in the affirmative. "And I would appreciate you praying for me also."

Quintard nodded and bowed his head in prayer. He could feel the young general's hand relax in his and then tense up with the onset of pain.

When Quintard finished praying, Carter said, "Please send a message to my father in Waynesboro, Georgia. Tell him I am wounded but still hopeful of a full recovery."

Quintard nodded his head. The man just refused to accept that he wasn't going to make it. Quintard hoped Carter would prove him wrong. The man could survive. Heaven knew there had been enough death here already.

Carter tensed up in extreme pain and begged for chloroform. The doctor came over and administered the drug in a handkerchief, and soon the young general was asleep.

He would hang on to live for the next seven days, dying just ten days short of his twenty-seventh birthday.

December 5, 1864, 4:00 p.m.

Mobile, Alabama

Susan Tarleton walked from her home and into the quiet little garden out back. The garden was still beautiful despite it being so late in the year. That was the advantage of living so far south. She stepped beneath the shade of the large elm tree. The breeze was cool here out of the sunlight. It was a lovely day. She looked at the Azaleas and thought how beautiful they look this time of year.

She always loved to read out here in the garden on days like this. She wished she'd have brought her book. She couldn't concentrate to read today anyway. She decided to just walk through the garden.

Susan was worrying again. During the Atlanta Campaign, she had lost quite a bit of weight worrying about her general. She thought about the day that Cleburne's letter had arrived saying Hood had denied his furlough because of the coming invasion of Tennessee. She had expected another campaign. Life didn't seem fair to her. She'd locked herself in her room and cried all afternoon.

Her poor father was worried sick about her. He'd thought she was going to go insane with worry during the Atlanta Campaign. He tried to explain to her that it was all in God's hands, and worrying wouldn't help anything. Lately, her health had started to fail because of the stress. She was displaying obvious signs of depression. Everyone seemed to worry about the frail young girl.

Susan wondered what Pat was doing at this very moment. The last news she'd heard was the army was invading Tennessee, and there would be some hard fighting. There was no way the Federals were going to just give up Tennessee without a fight.

She thought about the Hardee's wedding and her first introduction to General Hardee's best man, the stalwart Patrick Cleburne. Susan would have never believed in her wildest dreams that he would fall in love with her. Everything had happened so sudden. She'd been wary at first, refusing to believe that someone so famous wanted her.

She thought about the letters he'd written. Every night before bed she would get them out and reread them. One letter had been seventeen pages long. He half jokingly chastised her for the letters she sent him, saying they were too short. Writing was just something she didn't enjoy. When she did write him, she labored over the letters for hours wanting to say just the right thing. She'd manage a couple of letters a week, but Pat wrote every day. She thought about how much she enjoyed receiving his letters and decided that she must make an effort to write him more.

212

Susan walked around the elm tree and peered back toward the house. Her father was watching her intently from a second story window. She smiled at the thought of her poor father. He'd moved here from New Hampshire and was a Union man at heart. Everyone else in the family was for the Confederacy. It had surprised her that her father hadn't minded a Confederate general courting her. Not only was he a Confederate general, but an Irishman at that. *Most people think of the Irish as dumb and bungling, she thought.* Patrick Cleburne had changed that opinion a great deal. He was a self-made man, and that had really impressed her father. He'd come to realize that Cleburne was just the sort of man who would care for his daughter and provide for her the way a father wanted.

Last time Pat had visited had been the happiest time of her life. There had been three couples that seemed inseparable—her brother Robert and his girlfriend, Sallie Lightfoot, and her sister Grace and her boyfriend, Henry Goldwaite. Susan had played the piano in the parlor and everyone sang songs. Patrick had this way of making her feel special, even with the other two couples present.

She stopped walking at the very spot in the garden where Pat had proposed to her in a fine mist one afternoon. It was a moment that she would never forget. It almost seemed surreal. Even now she could hardly believe she was engaged to such a famous person.

There was a boy shouting down the street. It was a newsboy selling papers. He was still too far away for her to hear what he was saying, but he was getting closer, his voice growing louder and more distinct.

She continued standing in the spot where Pat had proposed to her. The boy yelled again, and she caught part of the words. He was shouting something about a great battle in Franklin. He shouted again, this time much closer, and a shiver ran down her spine.

The boy yelled, "Great battle at Franklin, Tennessee! General Cleburne killed! Read all about it!"

Suddenly, the world began to spin. *It couldn't be true, she thought, surely not. Life wouldn't be this cruel; it couldn't.* Then her world went black.

Susan Tarleton would retreat to her room and go into mourning for an entire year, wearing nothing but black. She would never recover from the loss, dying three years later at age twenty-seven of what doctors would call an effusion of the brain. Everyone that knew her said that Susan had really died that bitter December day in 1864.

December 9, 1864, 7:00 a.m.

CSA

Misses Overton was seated at the dining table with Confederate generals John Bell Hood and Frank Cheatham, along with members of their staff. Her niece Mary Claiborne had just sat in a chair near the other end of the table. Before them were piles of bacon, eggs, and ham. She noticed General Hood saying a silent prayer before the meal. Frank Cheatham simply reached over and began to load his plate.

Hood and Cheatham seemed to have forgotten the Spring Hill affair. Cheatham felt better because Hood wasn't blaming him, not publicly at least. Hood believed the man had learned a lesson from the disaster.

Misses Overton looked melancholy this morning. She said, "I just read that Patrick Cleburne's body was carried back to St. John's Episcopal Church for burial. It's so sad that we lost General Cleburne."

Cheatham stopped chewing for a moment and looked up. "Patrick Cleburne was one of the best soldiers that ever drew a sword."

Hood said nothing but continued to load his plate with his good arm. The Confederate high command had been eating like kings ever since their arrival here. Misses Overton had made sure General Hood had beef, mutton, pork, plenty of fresh flour, and potatoes. Someone had even provided Hood's staff with a barrel of Tennessee whiskey for the extremely cold nights.

Misses Overton looked out the window at the snow blowing past the house. The ground was still covered with sleet and snow. She watched the small cedars bending with the wind. It had to be frigid out there. She frowned at General Cheatham and said, "It makes my heart ache to think of our poor boys having to stay out in this weather with no more clothing than they have."

Cheatham grunted and said, "I wouldn't worry too much about them, ma'am. Hell, I just issued them four ears of corn apiece."

It disgusted her to watch him digging into the plate of food before him. Tiny pieces of egg stuck in his mustache. She caught herself shaking her head with disgrace and looked up to find General Hood watching her.

Hood said, "War is a horrible thing, Misses Overton. I want to thank you again for all the kindness you've extended to me and my staff."

"You're quite welcome, General," Misses Overton exhaled with a moan. "I only wish I could prepare a meal like this for all our boys. Last night, Mary and I were watching one poor boy camped across the lawn holding an ear of corn over the fire. It was so pitiful. Every time a grain would parch, he would pull it off and stick it in his mouth. Mary went down and tried to have him come here and eat with us, but the poor man refused because of his ragged condition."

"It takes a lot of courage to be an officer," Hood set his fork down in his plate. "You must love the army, but you must also ignore the misery you are creating in the process."

"I wouldn't do it," she was shaking her head again. "I don't understand how anyone could love war."

Hood lowered his head and said nothing. He picked up his fork and pretended to eat again. Suddenly, he didn't feel hungry anymore.

Cheatham was eyeballing Misses Overton carefully. After a long pause, he said, "Hell, I sleep with a clear conscious at night."

Misses Overton ignored him. She continued looking at Hood. "I can't help but think if President Davis knew the condition these poor men were in, he'd do something."

Hood looked up. "He knows, he knows. He led men in the Mexican War. He understands what men must go through. He's not an idiot. If he wasn't president, he'd be right here with us."

Mary, who hadn't said a word all morning, spoke up. Everyone turned and listened. She said, "I once heard that because men do not shed bad blood in menstruation like a woman, they must shed other men's blood."

"Mary!" Misses Overton almost screamed. "That is not proper language for a young lady, especially at the breakfast table in mixed company."

There was a long, awkward pause as Mary's face began to redden. "I'm sorry, I didn't mean to…"

Hood was tired of this conversation anyway. He decided to change the subject before there was more embarrassment. "Misses Overton, did you know I'm a close personal friend of the president's?"

Misses Overton shook her head.

"I've always had a great deal of respect for the man—long before he was president." Hood lay the fork down beside the plate and wiped his mouth with his towel. "When he was Secretary of War, and I was just a lieutenant in Texas, my father became ill. Jefferson Davis was kind enough to give me a ninety-day furlough to go back to Kentucky and help him straighten out his affairs. When my furlough was up, he gave me another ninety-day extension. That was the last time I saw my father. He died soon after I returned to Texas. You see, he didn't have to give me anything. He truly is a great man, regardless of what all the southern newspapers say."

Misses Overton smiled at the story. "I've noticed that, as long as we were winning this war, the southern papers were singing his praises. Only now that times look bleak are they trying to crucify him. I guess it's human nature to blame someone else when things aren't going the way you expect."

Hood was nodding his head in agreement. He thought about the long carriage rides he'd taken with Davis back in Richmond after losing the leg at Chickamauga. People had hailed him a hero. He'd never felt that good in his entire life.

215

"Misses Overton," Hood's eyes were distant. The man was obviously in deep thought. "I'll tell you another great man that has had a tremendous impact on my life, and that's General Robert E. Lee."

Misses Overton was nodding in agreement. "I've never met the man, but I would have to agree with you."

"He reprimanded me once," Hood had a slight smile on his face. "Most men who get reprimanded become petulant. It doesn't work that way with General Lee. He has this way of making you want to please him. He is a very positive gentleman. I'd allowed my camps to become dirty; some of my men were without shoes. I'm a combat commander, Misses Overton. I've just got little interest in administration. At this point, I would gladly give my position as full general to take a reduction in rank and take a corps to serve under him now."

"In your opinion, sir," Misses Overton had stopped eating and was studying Hood with great interest, "why do you suppose this army has been incapable of having the success that Lee's army has had in Virginia?"

Hood reached up with his good arm and pushed the plate away. He stared into the plate in deep contemplation. A change suddenly came over his face. He raised his head, and for a moment, he looked extremely proud. He said, "Let me tell you a story about my first command. At the beginning of the war, when I arrived in Richmond, President Davis gave me command of the Fourth Texas Infantry Regiment. They were young, intelligent men. Men like that don't just give you their respect; you must earn it.

One morning, I came out of my tent and found a fourteen-year-old boy named William Lessing propped against a tree. Now that was a direct violation of orders for one on guard duty. When I began to reprimand him, he began to cry. He had big old tears rolling down his boyish face. He said he'd missed supper last night and was so exhausted and hungry, that he couldn't stand his post any longer. Now, all the other boys thought I would tear him up pretty good, but I surprised them. I took that poor boy into my tent and fed him my breakfast. Those men began to realize how much I cared for them at that moment. They became one of the hardest-hitting units in Lee's army; they just refused to lose."

Misses Overton was leaning forward. She wasn't sure what all this had to do with the question she'd asked, but she was fascinated just the same.

"You see," Hood continued, "those young men had become a reflection of their commander. Lee's army is a reflection of the commanding general. If I could get this army to fight like those men did, we could whip the Federal army despite being outnumbered. The men of this army have been mismanaged from the beginning of the war. They haven't had a chance. Joe Johnston had practically ruined the fighting spirit in these men. I have done all I know to remedy the problem and feel like I have made quite a bit of progress. Johnston's philosophy was simple. If you never fight a battle, you never lose a battle. I have attempted to instill in these men that to win a battle, you must pierce the enemy's line. You can never stop within rifle range of their

216

breastworks. You must never stop. Johnston wanted to hide behind breastworks and let the enemy come to him. Sherman simply outflanked him all the way to Atlanta."

An aide stepped into the room and looked to General Hood. "Sir, Generals Bate and Forrest are here to see you."

"Very well," Hood pushed his chair away from the table a little. "Show them in."

General Bate came in first. His beard was well trimmed, his hair almost coal black. He looked like the type of man who would struggle with a weight problem when he gets older. The fearless Forrest was behind him. Bate walked in and spoke to both Cheatham and Hood. Forrest spoke to the ladies at the table.

Hood motioned for them both to sit. Bate took the chair nearest Hood across from Cheatham. Forrest took the chair between Misses Overton and her niece Mary.

Hood looked at Bate when he spoke. "Gentlemen, I have a plan to draw Thomas out of his entrenchments where he can be defeated. You see, in Murfreesboro is a Federal garrison of about eight thousand men under General Lovell Rousseau. I want you to take your division and General Forrest's cavalry. I want you to destroy the railroad between here and Murfreesboro. Keep Rousseau trapped in Murfreesboro without supplies. It doesn't have to be an all-out assault, unless you gentlemen feel you can destroy them. I just want Thomas to think the garrison there is in trouble. He will then be forced to leave the Nashville trenches and race southeast to save Rousseau's command. When he does, I will strike him in flank and rear, just as I attempted to do to Schofield."

Bate nodded his head. He wondered why Hood was entrusting him with this important assignment. He wasn't the most experienced division commander here, but then he thought about Cleburne. This would definitely be Cleburne's assignment if he were still living.

"Sir," Bate paused a moment in thought, gathering his words carefully, "my division is the weakest in the army. At least it was before Franklin."

Hood waved him off. "Not a problem, I just want you to scare Rousseau. Make him think you have more troops than you do. General Forrest is an expert at that sort of thing. He will help you. I don't want you to attack unless you can do so with an advantage. I'm just attempting to get Thomas out of Nashville where I can destroy his army. If Rousseau thinks he faces a superior army, and you get him shaken, he will beg General Thomas to come to the rescue."

General Cheatham shifted in his chair and cleared his throat. "Sir, I understand what you're doing, but I'm not sure about sending our cavalry away at a time like this. I mean, we're on the high ground here, but both our flanks are in the air. We'll need cavalry to protect them."

217

Hood was nodding his head in agreement. "Yes, I've thought of that, but I'm not sending Forrest with all his cavalry." Hood looked toward Bedford Forrest. "General, leave Chalmers's division here to protect our left flank. The right flank doesn't need to be protected, because when you threaten Murfreesboro, Thomas will have to march past my right flank. I'll be prepared to move my army around his flank as he passes by and cut him off from Nashville."

Forrest nodded but said nothing. *He thought to himself, if it'll get me out from under this ass, I'll be glad to go to Murfreesboro. Hell, I'm ready to take all my troops and go back toward Memphis. I just can't see how anything can succeed with this man in command.*

"Are there any questions?" Hood asked. There were none. Hood added, "Then gentlemen, you may return to your commands and pass on the necessary orders."

Both men stood. Bate saluted both Cheatham and Hood. Forrest simply turned and left the room. He hadn't said a word during the entire meeting. Hood was actually glad to see the man go. He'd come to understand during this campaign that Forrest was a great commander but could never be a good subordinate. He was the type who flourished in the role of independent command, but when forced to work with a superior officer, he became sullen. *What should I expect? Hood thought to himself. He didn't attend West Point; hell, he's barely got a sixth-grade education.* Still, Hood couldn't help but admire the man.

Cheatham was digging into another plateful of eggs. He stopped chewing and looked at Hood a long moment. "We still have a problem."

"What's that?" Hood asked.

"Supplies," Cheatham said. He dug into the eggs and began stuffing his mouth.

"I've been working on that," Hood said. He watched Cheatham nodding his head up and down, his mouth too full for him to speak. "I've got the railroad running between Pulaski and Franklin. If I can get the railroad running all the way back to Decatur, we can occupy Tennessee indefinitely."

Cheatham swallowed hard and raised his eyebrows at the thought. He asked, "How many trains you got running on that line?"

"We have two captured locomotives and three railcars at present," Hood watched the worried look appear on Cheatham's face. "Relax, Frank; as soon as the other cars are prepared, we'll have about twenty carrying supplies."

Cheatham was still frowning. He wondered how twenty cars and two engines could keep an army this large supplied. He decided it wasn't his responsibility to worry about it and dug back into his eggs.

Another aide entered the room, followed by Lieutenant General Stephen Lee. Lee gave Hood a sloppy salute and looked at the table. "Looks like I'm just in time."

"You're late," Hood laughed. "Frank has eaten everything up already. Come sit a spell."

One of Hood's junior staff officers rose from the table and surrendered his chair to Lee. Misses Overton insisted that General Lee eat and had her servants bring him a plate.

Hood turned to Cheatham and asked, "What do you think the morale of your corps is at present, Frank?"

Cheatham stopped chewing again and held his fork in the air as if to emphasize what he was saying. His mouth was full, and tiny bits of egg flew out of his mouth as he spoke. "We had heavy losses at Franklin, in men and officers…"

"I know about the losses, Frank," Hood interrupted. He was tired of hearing about the losses at Franklin. "I just want to know about the morale in your corps."

Cheatham chewed some more and then swallowed hard. "That's what I was getting to. Despite all those losses, my men are in high spirits and ready for a fight. I'm not the least bit concerned about the morale of my men."

Hood looked at Lee and nodded.

"My men are determined," Lee announced with pride. He held his chin high as he spoke. "Nothing will stop us in our work, and we will not be discouraged, because we have done our duty thus far. I believe God will reward our glorious cause with a great victory here."

Hood nodded his head and smiled. They were telling him what he wanted to hear.

December 9, 1864, 8:00 a.m.

CSA

Mack Keenum limped away from the Carnton mansion and toward the breastworks where he had been wounded while fighting almost two weeks ago. He'd thanked the lady of the house, a Misses McGavock, for taking him in. The knee wasn't as badly injured as he had thought. He'd expected it to be amputated by the surgeons, but thankfully he was wrong.

He made his way north and approached the Osage orange abatis where he was wounded. The place looked like a tornado had hit it. Bullets had sheared all the limbs off the trees. He wondered how he had survived in that din. The dead were already buried in the ditch just outside the breastworks. He thought about Captain Stewart, just a boy, buried here somewhere.

Mack turned west and began to make his way to the Columbia Pike. He walked past Brigadier General John Adams's horse, still sprawled grotesquely across the earthworks. He felt guilty for surviving this battle. He couldn't help but wonder why he survived.

When he got to the pike, he paused and looked south. The temptation to just turn and limp home was almost overwhelming. He looked over the breastworks again. *The name 'Franklin' will haunt me the rest of my life, he thought.* After a long, awkward pause, he turned north for Nashville and what was left of his company.

Someone had told him it was only ten miles to where Hood's army was camped, but at the speed he was traveling, it took all day. There was a bitter-cold wind blowing out of the north, and there were ominous clouds on the horizon. It was just after dark when he located his company—if it could be called that.

The six remaining men of the twenty-one who had gone in were genuinely glad to see Mack. Especially glad to see him was his good friend, Tom Barrett.

Tom jumped to his feet and grabbed him. "Mack, I thought you would be on a wooden leg by now."

"I did too, to be honest with you," Mack Keenum smiled. "So who's in charge now?"

"Sergeant Downs," Tom pointed toward the fire. Downs was bent close to the flames trying to read a letter. The cold north wind blew the flames around, making it difficult to read. Tom grew serious. "You heard about Captain Stewart?"

"I was standing next to him when he was hit," Mack lowered his head. "The first bullet struck him in the stomach. I thought he was dead, but he got back up and began hacking at the limbs again. The second bullet struck him in the side of the head. I think he was dead before he hit the ground."

"No he wasn't," Tom corrected. "He lay wounded on the field all night. Someone brought him in the next morning. Poor fellow, he died sometime that afternoon."

"I thought he was killed instantly," Mack shook his head. "Of course, I got hit a few moments later, so it's all really a blur to me. You hear about Joe?"

"Cannonball mangled his foot," Tom lowered his head in thought. "Don't know if they were able to save it or not."

"They weren't," Mack shook his head. "They amputated his leg below the knee the next morning under a tree in front of Misses McGavock's house. There were arms and legs piled up higher than the table. Joe told me that after they threw his leg on top of the pile, they laid him just a few feet away. He said he stared at his own leg all day."

"Damned shame," Tom frowned.

Mack walked over and squatted next to the fire. Tom followed. Dan Downs was shaking his head as he read.

"What is it?" Mack asked.

Sergeant Downs glanced up, saw Mack, and smiled. "I thought you was out of action."

220

"I was," he replied. "I felt guilty laying around back there while you boys was up here in the weather."

Tom started laughing. "I wouldn't feel a bit guilty."

Dan looked back at the paper. "It's a letter from Captain Stewart's sister. She says she's heard he's sick and she's concerned about his health."

"Damn," Tom said aloud.

Dan finished reading the letter and said, "I must write her back. Help me get this right, Tom."

Together they began to work on the letter to Stewart's sister. When he'd finished, Dan read the letter out loud.

"Miss Stewart," he began, "Your brother died leading the most terrific charge this war has seen. He was shot in the bowels near the enemy works but continued to fight despite the severe pain. While continuing to fight, a bullet ripped his left ear off. He knew he was going to die, but he stared death down without fear. We buried him on the field and placed a marker there. I stayed with him until he died. All he asked for was water and for me to pray for his soul. He suffered greatly, but he died in peace and felt sure he would spend eternity with his Lord. The entire company is extremely sad to have lost our dear Sammy. Your obedient servant, Sergeant Daniel Downs."

Tom was nodding his head. "It's perfect."

"I'm not sure the poor girl wants to hear all the grisly details," Mack shook his head in disagreement. "Couldn't you have left out the bowels and the ear-shot-off part?"

"She's his family," Dan stared at the fire as he made his argument. "She deserves to know."

"Well," Mack was exhausted from his long, arduous trek. He didn't feel like arguing with anyone just now. "Just so as ya'll know, if I get killed, don't put no details in my letter home. Just say I got killed, and leave it at that."

"Your request has been noted." Tom laughed as he slapped Mack on the back.

"Of course, my wife can't read no way. So I guess you can say anything you please." Mack smiled at Tom. "You could just tell her about the price of eggs in China, and she wouldn't know any difference."

Waddy Mosely came out of the darkness with an armful of tree branches. He was also walking with a slight limp. He called out, "Well, look what the cat dragged in."

"I feel like he dragged me in," Mack replied. Waddy threw the branches on the ground and shook Mack's hand.

"You look like hell," Waddy sat next to Mack. "I lost five dollars thanks to you."

"What you talking about?" Mack asked.

"Well, I bet Tom that the next time we saw you, you'd be on one of them wooden legs like General Hood." Waddy laughed at himself. "Of course, it was five dollars Confederate, and we both know that ain't worth nothing but wiping your backside with."

"I sure am glad I've been thought about while I was suffering," Mack rolled his eyes at Tom. He asked Waddy, "What are you doing limping? You got some kind of gimp?"

"You weren't the only one shot, damn it," Waddy tried to act serious. "I got it on the ankle bone. Put one hell of a bruise on it too."

"So how many men we got left out of the twenty-one that went into the battle?" Mack looked around. He wondered if it was just the four of them.

Sergeant Downs spoke up. "We got seven here now, counting you. Maybe you can help me with what happened to the rest."

"I'll see what I can remember," Mack nodded.

"We only had four men not wounded at all," Dan pulled out his journal and began to study the names. "Tom, Mark Haley, Steve Harmon, and Dick Bernard. I got hit on the head, a grazing shot, but it knocked me out at the time. Waddy Mosely got hit on the ankle. Now you're here, which makes seven of us."

"Right," Mack thought about how pitiful it was for a company to have only seven men left, when full strength was a hundred men. "Of course, Captain Stewart was killed. Bob Wheeler went down carrying the flag, and Tom Peebles got shot all to hell and back. Will Bradley was hit by canister fire at the abatis."

"Yes, but I have a few names that I don't know what became of," Dan was busy scribbling notes on the roster. "Dick Beaumont lost a leg. What have you heard about 'Rip' Baker?"

"Lost a leg also," Mack replied.

Dan continued to make notes. "What about Cooper, Jim Murphy, Spivey, Bill Woodford, Newt Cameron, and John Greene?"

"Oh," Mack suddenly remembered something important. "I almost forgot; 'Blue' Farris was hit in the left side, but he's gonna make it. He said to tell you fellas not to let him down."

"Right," Dan replied. "I knew he was hit."

Mack nodded and thought about the names Dan had mentioned. "Spivey lost an arm. Newt was hit in the thigh, but he'll recover eventually. Those other men were all wounded, but I can't remember all the details."

"Pitiful," Waddy added. "We go in with twenty-one men, and only four come out unharmed. What a slaughter. We're not gonna make much difference in the next fight with just seven damn men."

Tom said, "You hear what the truth about Franklin was?"

"What do you mean?" Mack asked.

"We've heard all kinds of rumors," Waddy added. "We thought since you were down there longer, you may know if they're true or not."

"What rumors?" Mack was at a loss as to where this conversation was headed.

"We heard that General Forrest wanted to flank the Yanks out of Franklin, but Hood wouldn't let him." Waddy picked up a stick and began poking at the fire. "They say General Hood was trying to teach us a lesson. You know, teach us to fight."

Mack Keenum shook his head. "That's a new one on me. I did hear a wounded staff officer say that Hood wanted to hit them at Franklin before they reached the breastworks at Nashville."

"Tell you what else we heard," Tom chimed in. "We heard that Cleburne and Brown were placed in the center as punishment for letting the Yanks escape at Spring Hill. You heard that one?"

"I don't know," Mack was still shaking his head. "We went in on the right. I can't imagine them having it any worse in the center than we did."

"I'll have to agree with that," Waddy said.

Tom said, "We heard that General Adams was killed on his horse on top of the breastworks. They say he was hit forty-seven times."

Mack shook his head. "They put me in a boot closet beneath the stairs at Misses McGavock's house. I couldn't stay in there. There was three of us crammed in there; one died during the night. About daylight, my leg was stiff, so I managed to crawl out onto the back porch. I was lying there when they brought Adams's body back the next morning and laid it on the north end of the back porch. The lady, that Misses McGavock, said he had nine wounds."

"We heard they brought Cleburne back there as well," Waddy picked up a branch and laid it on the fire. "We heard he was all shot up too."

Mack shook his head. "They brought Cleburne back there all right, but he was hit only once. I heard them say he was hit in the heart and died pretty much instantly. They also brought Generals Strahl and Granbury back there. They was four generals and two other officers I didn't recognize laid out there. All of them had handkerchiefs covering their faces. Cleburne had a particularly bloody one on his face. I saw one of his staff officers come and remove it and place a pretty handkerchief over him instead. He said it was a handkerchief that Cleburne's fiancée had sent him. He handed Misses McGavock all of Cleburne's personal belongings to keep for him."

"We've heard all sorts of crazy tales," Tom added. "You know how army rumors go."

"I tell you one that sounds like a crazy tale, but it's true," Mack started poking at the fire with a stick. He looked up and saw everyone hanging on his every word. "They said that General Granbury was hit in the head and fell to his knees. His body froze in that position, with his hands covering his face. They said they found him in that same position the next morning."

Tom lowered his head at the thought. Waddy was shaking his head. "Lot of good men wasted down there. Someone is responsible for that disaster."

"Yeah," Mack said, "and we all know who that someone is. He'll probably get us all killed before this war is over. I met some poor man from Cleburne's division who had both eyes shot out. He said he lay in the ditch all night. Said he got thirsty, and there was water in the ditch, so he thought he would take a drink. He found out the hard way that it was mostly blood."

Tom had been through a lot of fighting, but he still had a weak stomach. He gagged and started waving his hand for Mack to stop. Waddy and Mack both laughed.

Mack said, "They brought our brigade commander back there to Misses McGavock's house also."

"General Scott?" Waddy asked. "How is he?"

"He's been partially paralyzed since he was thrown from his horse by the concussion of an exploding artillery round." Mack paused and thought a long minute. "You know Colonel Nelson of the 12th Louisiana of our brigade?"

"I've heard of him," Waddy replied.

Mack began to shake his head. "He was there also. It was so pitiful. His body was ravaged by bullets. I don't know how many times he was hit, but he was all torn to pieces. It was sad; he kept crying, wondering what would become of his wife and child. He was in intense pain and begging the surgeons to give him something. God was merciful enough to end his suffering the next morning."

Waddy and Tom sat shaking their heads. Waddy said, "It could have easily been either one of us."

Mack nodded. "It was the same story all over the house. They told me there were three hundred wounded soldiers in there, and the fields outside were covered with men."

"I don't know how any of us survived that battle," Tom said. He sat staring in the fire as if he were reliving it all over again.

"That Misses McGavock, Carrie I think was her name, she's the real hero." Mack smiled at the thought of her. "She was caring for the men as if she saw that sort of thing every day. Her dress was soaked in blood where she walked around us. She cut up her sheets and all her clothes for bandages, and still it wasn't enough. I never want to be in a hospital again."

"Me either," Waddy added. "I was wounded at Chickamauga last year. It was terrible. They were sawing off legs without anesthetic."

"There were piles of arms and legs in the yard about fifteen feet high. Talk about the smell. They finally got around to getting some men to bury them." Mack looked and saw Tom frowning up and decided to change the subject before he started gagging again. "There was a good story I can tell. There was this one fellow from Mississippi, a captain I believe, was shot all to hell. The poor fellow had been hit in both legs by artillery fire. One leg was broken, and the other had a gash so deep you could actually look in his leg and see the bone. Sorry, Tom."

Mack held up a hand as if to apologize. "Anyway, one arm was broken, and his hand on the other arm was blown off. The doctors refused to amputate anything. They told him his wounds were mortal. He said he didn't feel like dying just yet. When I left there today, he was making a remarkable recovery. He was one of those types of men who just refuse to give up."

224

"This country is gonna have a lot of cripples when this war is over." Waddy was still poking in the fire. "I just hope I'm not one of them. I think I'd rather be killed."

It wasn't long before the rain began to fall. Mack had thought it was too cold to rain. The bitter-cold wind was blowing out of the north and across the river right into their very faces. Hood had them on the heights south of Nashville, which meant there was nowhere for them to shield themselves from the weather. Soon, they were all thoroughly soaked. The only thing they had was one ragged blanket apiece.

About midnight, the temperature plummeted, and the rain turned to sleet. The water that soaked Mack's trousers turned to ice, making his pants stiff. The wind still blew, chilling him to his very bones. He began to wonder if he would survive the night. He'd gone back out with Waddy to round up some more branches for the fire. It wasn't the first time in this war he had slept sitting straight up beside a fire. There were five men crammed around the tiny fire, which barely burned because of the rain. There were a couple of times when a man would nod off and just catch himself before falling forward into the fire.

Mack focused on one boy across the fire. He was from another company. He didn't look a day over sixteen. The poor boy looked like a corpse. His clothes were more ragged than most, and his cheeks were sunken in. He wasn't much more than a bag of bones. Mack wondered how someone that thin could survive weather like this.

He would never forget the sound of the tree limbs popping as they would break from the weight of the ice. It went on all night long. He was more miserable than he could remember in the entire war. This was even worse than being crammed in that boot closet with those dying men at the McGavock home.

By daylight, the sleet had turned to snow. Mack and the others were up moving around trying to stay warm. At least his clothes were dry now. The fire had taken care of that for them and saved their lives. He didn't doubt that he would have perished last night had it not been for the fire.

As he walked around, he noticed stains in the snow. Some of the men were barefoot, and their feet left traces of blood behind from being frozen. He stopped near a Mississippi regiment and watched a man working on a cowhide. Someone had come up with a very enterprising idea. He was taking the hides from the slaughtered cattle and making moccasins. Mack was extremely interested, so he sat down and watched the man with his meticulous work. The man would wrap the hide around another man's foot with the cow hair turned inside. Then he would tie it up with strands he'd also cut from the cowhide.

The man said, "Now, it ain't gonna feel right for a day or two, but when that hide dries, it'll be molded to your feet. It'll be more comfortable than them dang army brogans."

It amazed Mack how enterprising a man could be in desperate times. He looked around at the snow-covered landscape. These were definitely desperate times. The snow was already four inches deep, and it was still snowing.

Mack Keenum stood up and started back down the line, where he met Tom walking around trying to keep warm. Tom's teeth were chattering.

"A farmer told Sergeant Downs that it's ten degrees below zero out here," Tom said. He pulled the ragged blanket around himself even tighter.

"I can believe that." Mack shivered against the cold. His toes were numb, his fingers hurt, and he thought his ears would just fall off. "Let's get back to the fire."

They heard horse hooves crunching in the snow and turned just in time to see a horse and buggy pass by, followed by several mounted staff officers. Mack instantly recognized General Hood and another man in the buggy with several young ladies.

Tom said, "That's General Hood and Chaplain Quintard. The chaplain is just back from attending to all them funerals down in Franklin."

Chaplain Quintard was laughing at something that Hood was saying.

"Reckon what he's so happy about this morning?" Mack asked.

"What I heard was that he held a worship service for the high command this morning." Tom began to stomp his feet trying to get the feeling back in his toes. "I heard some staff officer is getting married, and he's officiating. They say he's getting paid two hundred dollars Confederate. Guess that's why he's smiling so."

"Two hundred Confederate," Mack started laughing. "That ain't nothing to get excited about. Hell, it's worthless."

Tom laughed in agreement. Mack began to think about those men going to some fancy wedding while he suffers out in this miserable weather. *They'll probably be eating all sorts of delicacies, and I'll be eating my daily ration of two ears of corn. He frowned at the thought. Was it any wonder the Confederates were losing this war?*

December 10, 1864

USA

General Thomas sat staring out the window at the snow and ice covering the ground. He'd had no choice but to delay the attack. He watched the snow swirling on the streets below from a bitter north wind. The weather matched his mood. He'd fought hard during this long war and had built quite a reputation for being a solid commander. Now he was receiving word that he was about to be fired for not advancing against Hood's army. He'd been sitting at the window for an hour, speaking to no one.

226

William Whipple had recognized his dark mood and made sure that he wasn't disturbed.

Thomas stood up and walked back to the table in the middle of the room. Messages had been coming in during the past hour. Thomas asked, "Will, what have you got for me?"

"I have a message from General Wilson," Whipple took the note from his desk and carried it to Thomas. "It says that the procuring of horses is coming along rather slow. He says there are few horses left, and when he finds some, he has to bring them back here and shod them."

Thomas shook his head. *Just what I need, he thought, more delays. Washington is already breathing down my neck.*

There was a knock on the door. Whipple walked over and answered it. He was shocked by the image before him. There waiting, was a dapper little man in a colorful suit. The man didn't look very happy. He demanded to be taken to General Thomas.

"In regard to what?" Whipple asked.

The short dumpy man didn't have time for this. He barged past Whipple and into the room. He saw Thomas sitting at the table staring at him above a piece of paper he held in his hand. He seemed to be almost out of control. He shouted, "Are you General Thomas?"

"I'm General Thomas," he replied as he blew out a cloud of cigar smoke. Thomas had always been known as a calm and collected individual, but he wasn't in the mood today. He figured if he sounded as upset as this man, it might disarm him. He asked in a firm voice, "Who the hell are you?"

"I'm Dan Castello of Castello's Traveling Circus." The man stared hard at Thomas. "You've taken every one of my horses. I can't even leave town now. Hell, you even took Misses Lake's trick horse. A bloody trick horse, if you can imagine that."

Thomas fought back the urge to smile at the comical little man. "You were given receipts for the horses, right?"

"To hell with the receipts," Dan Castello almost screamed. "I can't pull wagons with receipts. I got a business to run. How am I to run a circus without horses?"

"Sir," Thomas rose from the chair and glowered at the little man, "I'm sure you will appreciate the fact that I have a war to run here. Good day."

Dan Castello wanted to say something more but was afraid of the heavyset general towering over him. He mumbled something under his breath and quickly left the room.

Thomas sat back down and shook his head. "Will, I just don't understand people. They refuse to join the army because they are too busy trying to make money off the soldiers. Yet, when they are forced to suffer a little, they become angry. I have no use for men like that."

"Then you're not going to appreciate this letter," Whipple smiled, holding the letter up and waving it over his head.

Thomas shook his head again. "Well, let's hear it."

227

"It seems that Vice President Johnson is upset over the loss of his bay carriage horses. He is demanding their return. He says Wilson will not listen to reason, so he is forced to take the matter up with you. He also calls Wilson a...what was it?" Whipple looked back at the letter then winked at Thomas. "He calls him a 'bumptious puppy.'"

Thomas smiled at the comment. "Please write the Vice President back and tell him that we all have to give up a few things in order to win this war. Explain to him that I'm sure he would rather provide us with a couple of horses if it will expedite the ending of this war."

Whipple was busy writing the message, when a courier walked in with a telegram. He seemed confused as to whether to deliver it to Whipple or Thomas. Thomas motioned for the man to hand it to him.

The man said, "It's from Washington, sir."

"Thank you," Thomas replied. He scanned the message. Whipple had stopped writing and was watching Thomas's expression as he read.

When he'd finished reading it, he said, "Will, it's another message from Grant. He says the longer we wait, the stronger Hood gets. He wants me to go crashing into Hood's army with what we have, because that's what he would do. Please write a telegram to the general telling him I will move as soon as it's possible."

"Right," Whipple said.

Thomas reached over on his desk and picked up his map. He began to study it as if it were going to tell him something he'd missed before. He couldn't concentrate on the map. He thought about the message that Grant had sent yesterday. Grant had ordered him to attack at once before Hood flanked him and invaded Ohio.

There had also been a message from Secretary of War Edwin Stanton urging Thomas to attack. He'd said that if Thomas wasn't attacking because it would be hazardous, then he should resign, because all warfare is hazardous. He'd also said that if Thomas waited for Wilson and his cavalry to get prepared, he may as well be waiting on the Day of Judgment.

Thomas began to stew on the situation. He'd had about all the condescending messages he could stand. He said, "Will, send another message to General Grant. Tell him I am almost ready to move. Tell him if he doesn't think I've done enough to prepare this army for the assault then he should just relieve me."

Whipple was taken aback. "Relieve you, sir?"

"You heard me right," Thomas grumbled. "I am doing everything I can to be ready to move. I can't control the weather. Nothing I do is enough for the higher authorities."

Whipple cleared his throat. He dreaded bringing up more problems to Thomas at the moment. He said, "Sir, there's another thing I need to bring to your attention."

Thomas let out a long sigh. "What is it, Will?"

228

"Sir, we've had numerous complaints about the men leaving their commands to go visit brothels and gambling halls." Whipple began to massage his temples. "There's also complaints about drunken soldiers all over the streets."

"Have them arrested," Thomas said. He had enough to deal with already. Hood was practically laying siege to the city. Grant, Stanton, and Lincoln were talking about relieving Thomas for not attacking. He sat there and began to mumble under his breath. He gave serious thought to just resigning. *Hell, I need a break, he thought.*

There was another courier at the door with another message. Thomas dreaded hearing what this would be about. Whipple retrieved the message and said, "Sir, it's another telegram from General Grant."

"Great," Thomas said.

"He says he has full confidence in you, but finds you extremely slow. He says he hasn't had a good explanation yet as to why we haven't already attacked Hood. He says Halleck has written out an order relieving you, but he has postponed that order. He wants to know what your plans are. He says he doesn't want to have to repeat the order for you to advance. Only your past good service has prevented him from having you relieved for not attacking on the seventh."

Whipple handed Thomas the telegram. Thomas threw it on the table without reading it. He wished Grant could see the weather conditions here.

Thomas said, "Whipple, write Halleck another message. Tell him the sleet and snow makes any movement here impossible. Tell him as soon as we have a thaw, I will attack Hood."

He wanted to add 'whether I'm prepared or not,' but decided that would be going too far.

He sat back down at the window without saying a word to anyone all afternoon. It was almost four when another message arrived from General Grant.

Whipple read the telegram to him. "It says, uh, if you delay any longer, we will see the Rebel army marching for Ohio, and you will be forced to act regardless of the weather. Let there be no further delay. Hood is far from his supplies and ordnance. Delay no longer for weather or reinforcements."

Thomas sat there for several minutes without replying. Finally, he said, "Will, write General Grant and tell him I will obey the order as soon as possible, however much I may regret it. The attack will be made under a heavy disadvantage. The entire country here is covered with a blanket of ice and sleet. It is difficult for the troops to walk on level ground, much less attack Hood on the heights south of town."

Whipple furiously scribbled the message out. Thomas waited until he was through writing and said, "Order General Wilson to get his cavalry back over the river and into town tomorrow whether they are mounted or not."

229

December 12, 1864, 3:00 p.m.

USA

Major General George Thomas had called a council of war in his room at the St. Cloud Hotel. Major General James Wilson had finally gotten his cavalry back across the Cumberland River, but they weren't in position to advance yet.

Thomas began the meeting by standing and saying, "I have a telegram from General Grant. He says that we can delay our attack no longer for reinforcements or the weather. I've already replied to the commanding general that I will move immediately." Thomas held his head high as he talked. His tone seemed to indicate that he felt like he understood more about the situation here than Grant, which he did. He continued, "I just called you all here to get your opinions on the matter."

It was traditional for the junior officer present to speak first. Thomas nodded at Wilson as he sat back down. Thomas realized that Wilson was a Grant man. He owed his rank to General Grant. He was already dreading hearing what Wilson would say.

Wilson cleared his throat. "I fully approve of waiting for the weather to clear. Hood will have no problem defending his works if our men can't even stand up. His men won't even need rifles. You saw how bad it was just getting my cavalry across the river. It took all day, and there were numerous wrecks. I have several horses and riders disabled from falling on the icy streets."

Thomas smiled and relaxed a little. He could hardly believe Wilson had just taken his side over Grant's. Wilson had realized that Grant wasn't here and didn't understand the true situation.

Thomas motioned for Brigadier General Thomas Wood who had taken over command of the Fourth Corps when Stanley had been wounded at Franklin. Wood's statement was short. He said, "The only thing I can do is concur with everything that General Wilson has just said."

Thomas's old friend Major General Steedman was next. Ever since the meeting had begun, Steedman had been eyeing General Schofield with a look of disdain. Thomas wondered what had happened between the two of them. Steedman said, "We must wait for the ice to thaw."

Major General Andrew Smith agreed with Wilson also. He said he was in total agreement with Thomas to wait for a thaw.

The only person left was Major General Schofield. Though he knew perfectly well it was his turn to give his opinion, Schofield sat in silence. Thomas cleared his throat and Schofield looked up. He said, "The only thing I can say is that I will follow whatever orders are given me."

With that, Thomas ended the meeting. He told them they would have another meeting before an order to attack would be given. The men began moving toward the door. Thomas caught Wilson by the arm and asked, "Wilson, would you mind staying behind and having a word with me?"

Wilson looked shocked. He wondered what Thomas wanted with him. He nodded his head and waited until the last officer had left the room.

After the door closed, Thomas motioned for Wilson to sit. Wilson had a puzzled look on his face. Thomas said, "Wilson, the Washington authorities are treating me like I'm just a schoolboy. For some reason, they think I'm incapable of fighting a battle or leading an army. If they'd just leave me alone until we get a thaw, I will show them what I'm capable of."

Wilson was shaking his head. "I assure you that I have full confidence in your ability. The Washington authorities are just nervous. You know how they are up there. They don't understand what the true situation is here."

Thomas pulled a cigar from his pocket and lit it. He sat in silence a long moment. Wilson was watching him closely. He hoped he had help soothe Thomas's feeling of being mistreated. Thomas looked up as if something had just dawned on him. He asked, "Would you like to stay and have supper with me?"

"I'd love to, sir," Wilson smiled.

The main course was beef steak. The servants set the table and politely excused themselves. Thomas watched Wilson tear into his food. He said, "I feel like I've been treated like an ugly stepchild by superiors because I'm from Virginia. Sherman has gone through Georgia on a holiday excursion and taken the best parts of the army with him. All he left me were reserves, recruits, and combat-depleted units to face a veteran Confederate army, and he's not even facing an army. Now they are about to fire me because I can't have this so-called army of mine organized at the snap of a finger. Smith and Steedman just arrived a few days ago."

"I'm sure things aren't as bad as they seem," Wilson spoke between chews. "I was serious when I said I have complete confidence in you, sir."

Thomas finally took a bite. He chewed slowly as he thought. "I know Grant is your friend, Wilson. Don't take what I'm about to say personally."

Wilson held up a hand. "Grant is my friend, but you're my commander now. Please, speak freely."

Thomas laid the fork on his plate. "Grant is rushing me to take action. He is deadlocked with Lee in Petersburg at the moment but is shouting for me to move. It's a bit hypocritical when you think about it."

"Yes, I have to admit it does sound that way," Wilson took another bite. He continued talking with his mouth full. The words came out slurred. "You know he has Stanton and Lincoln and Halleck sending him telegrams to make us move. Washington panics over the smallest things." Wilson stopped and swallowed hard. "He's under a lot of pressure, and I guess that pressure rolls downhill to you."

"They may relieve me," Thomas spoke with confidence, "but, I'm not about to send my men into slaughter the way Grant would. I'm not about to lose a lot of men just because Washington thinks I should hurry."

They finished eating, and for the first time, Thomas had gained respect for his cavalryman. The man had agreed with him on everything. *Sure, he's cocky, Thomas thought; but he's young. His ego could be an asset for the cavalry. Troops are usually a reflection of their commander.*

After they were finished eating, Thomas walked Wilson to the door. Wilson started to salute, but Thomas extended his hand. As they shook hands, Thomas said, "I do appreciate the kind words and the vote of confidence."

"Sir, you are one of the finest commanders I've served under. We will whip John Bell Hood when it thaws, and there will be no more questions from Washington about your ability." Wilson also found he had gained quite a bit of respect for George Thomas. Few people had confided in Wilson the way this man had tonight.

Thomas went back to the table and moved his plate aside so he could study the map again. He'd been looking at this map for three weeks now. He had made marks in pencil where Hood's lines were. This campaign was coming down to a race against time. He wouldn't have any trouble whipping Hood if he could just keep Washington and Grant at bay.

Soon Whipple was back. Thomas never looked up from the map. He was in deep thought. Normally, Whipple wouldn't interrupt him when he was working, but something was obviously on his mind tonight. He sat across the table and stared hard at Thomas. Thomas looked up and asked, "What's on your mind, Will?"

"After the meeting, I went outside and had an interesting conversation with General Steedman." Whipple held his head back in a way that suggested he'd learned something of vast importance. "Did you not think it strange that John Schofield had nothing to add at the meeting this afternoon?"

Thomas shrugged. He'd thought nothing of it at the time. He asked, "Is he not in agreement with the rest of us?"

"I don't think so," Whipple replied. "There is something I think you should know about the man."

"I'm waiting, Will," Thomas sighed. Sometimes when Whipple had some information that he thought was important, Thomas had to work it out of the man. It was almost like pulling teeth. He hadn't slept well last night and wasn't in the mood for theatrics at the moment.

"Sir," Whipple didn't feel like he'd built up enough suspense just yet, "it appears you have a Judas in your army."

"A Judas?" Thomas repeated.

Whipple gave Thomas a grim smile. "General Steedman says that one of his aides, Captain Marshall Davis, has proof that Schofield is telegraphing secret messages to General Grant about how all your subordinates want to attack, but you are dragging your feet. He told Grant that no one has confidence in you because you are too slow to move. General Steedman says he's seen one of these messages, and it's definitely Schofield's handwriting."

Thomas was shocked. His face bore an expression of bewilderment. He almost couldn't believe his ears. He asked, "Why would he do that?"

Whipple smiled at the naivety of George Thomas. Whipple knew he was genuinely surprised. That was the type of person George Thomas was. He believed every man was generally a good person or tried to be, and when he met someone that acted otherwise, he was often shocked. "Sir, think a moment. If you are relieved, who will take command?"

"Oh, I see," Thomas said and shook his head. It was all suddenly clear to him. A week ago, Schofield was in a race for his life and begging Thomas for help. Now, the man was trying to get Thomas fired so he could take his job. Everything started coming together in Thomas's mind. He could see why Washington was threatening to fire him now. He said, "You know, Will, the war's not going to last much longer. Schofield hasn't gotten as much recognition as he would have liked. I suppose this is his one gambit to try and get it before the war ends."

Whipple nodded in agreement. He asked, "So how did your little dinner with Wilson go?"

"Very well," Thomas said, "Very well, indeed. He actually agrees with me over his good friend, General Grant. He believes if General Grant were to come here, he would say we need to wait for a thaw. Wilson doesn't want to send his men into combat in this mess any more than I want to."

"I'm glad to hear that," Whipple smiled. "I was pleasantly surprised at his comments during the meeting. He was the one I was most worried about."

"As was I, Will," Thomas pulled a cigar from his pocket and lit it. "I need you to send a message to Halleck. Explain to him that I have my troops in position for the assault. As soon as the ice and snow are gone, I will move. Tell him it has taken the entire day just to get the cavalry across the river. There were many accidents today with the horses slipping on the icy roads. Many horses are lame now, and many cavalrymen out of action because of their falling mounts. All my commanders agree with me that an attack under these conditions will be an utter failure and a useless loss of life."

December 12, 1864, 10:00 p.m.

CSA

John Bell Hood couldn't sleep. He rose from the bed and grabbed the crutches. He left the wooden leg propped against the wall. Misses Overton had been kind to allow him the use of her home. He hobbled into the parlor and sat in a chair next to the window. He wondered why they had named their home 'Traveler's Rest.' He'd meant to ask her but forgot.

He had been utterly confused today by the reports he'd received from the Federal lines. He knew Wilson's cavalry was back on this side of the river now. Things appeared to be working out just as he planned. When they'd first

233

given him the information, he'd almost smiled. Thomas would move toward Hood's right flank and try to relieve Rosseau at Murfreesboro, and he would crush his flank and rear.

That was the first report. The second report stated that Wilson and his cavalry were trying to move into position on his far left. *That doesn't make any sense at all, he thought. I wonder why things never seem to work the way I plan them. This entire time, I've been strengthening my right flank, and now they're moving toward my left.*

At least there were the redoubts. He'd been so concerned about his right flank, that he'd ordered General Stewart to build five redoubts on the hills on his left flank. The tiny forts were designed to be self-supporting. They would contain artillery and about two hundred infantry. Made of dirt and logs, they were designed to hold out against a large enemy force.

Hood was so concerned about these forts; he'd actually given Stewart orders to personally oversee their construction. He hadn't wanted the job left to some junior officer. He'd told Stewart he wanted the redoubts built so that when Thomas came out of his works and moved toward Murfreesboro, Stewart could send two of his divisions to the right in support of Cheatham. The other division would hold these redoubts just in case.

Now, after the report, Hood was left in a quandary. Thomas just wasn't doing what a rational commander would do. Hood began to worry about his left flank now, and that's the reason he couldn't sleep tonight. Something was up, and John Bell Hood needed to know what that something was.

Colonel Mason had heard Hood leave the room. He quickly dressed and stepped into the parlor. "Do you need anything, sir?"

"Colonel, I'm not going to keep you up all night because I can't sleep." Hood moved his paralyzed arm onto his lap so that it didn't hang limply by his side. "However, I do need you to write an order for me. Have Colonel Coleman, commander of Ector's brigade, move to the extreme left flank. That brigade missed the battle of Franklin and should be in fair shape."

"Right, sir," Mason struck a match and lit a lamp. He walked to the table that Misses Overton had offered him to use as a desk.

"Bate is back from Murfreesboro." Hood continued staring out into the darkness. "Is he back on line with Cheatham's corps?"

"Yes, sir," Mason replied as he began writing out the order.

Hood shook his head and asked, "Is it true? The report I saw that one quarter of Bate's men are shoeless?"

"That's correct, sir," Mason replied. He never looked up from his writing.

Hood wondered how those men could survive barefoot in weather like this. The army was back together now, except for Forrest's cavalry. He wondered for a moment if he should recall them to Nashville before the Federal army attacked but decided against it. If Forrest returned, that would leave Rosseau loose in his rear.

Out on the lawn, Hood could see a group of horsemen approaching the house. He watched the shadowy figures dismount. One of the figures moved toward the front door. Hood turned to Mason and said, "Get the door before whoever is out there wakes the entire house."

Mason stood and walked to the door. He managed to open it just as the man was about to knock. The man identified himself as Brigadier General James Argyle Smith. Mason stepped aside and let the dark-haired, thick-bearded officer inside.

The man stepped inside the door. He saw General Hood and saluted. Hood could tell the man was cold and trying hard not to shiver. He said, "General Hood, I've successfully brought the supply train up from Florence. I just came by to see where you wanted me to place my brigade."

"If I'm not mistaken, you're the ranking brigade commander in Cleburne's division." Hood watched General Smith nod his head. "Well, you know you're in command of the division now."

"Right sir," Smith was surprised at the way Hood made the promotion sound so simple.

Hood asked, "Who will that leave commanding your brigade?"

"Charles Olmstead is my senior colonel, sir," Smith replied.

Hood began to rub his temples. He'd been suffering from a nagging headache all afternoon. The stress was getting to him. He said, "Have Olmstead move the brigade toward Murfreesboro."

"Murfreesboro, sir?" Smith asked.

"Yeah," Hood replied, "that's right. Tell him to report to General Forrest there. I have the cavalry watching Rosseau's troops at Murfreesboro."

Smith stood there a long moment. He wanted to remind General Hood that his brigade was the only fresh troops in the entire division. They'd been busy escorting the supply train up and had missed the battle at Franklin. After a long, awkward pause, he said, "I will pass the order to Olmstead, and then I'll take command of the division."

Hood watched the man show himself out the door and then turned to Mason. "Who's in command of Cockrell's brigade now?"

Mason was forced to look on a piece of paper where he had all the commands listed. "That would be Colonel Peter Flournoy. Sir, that unit was pretty much destroyed at Franklin. I'm afraid they're not gonna be worth much in a fight."

"I know that," Hood had his eyes closed. He continued to rub his temples. "Send Colonel Flournoy an order to take his brigade to Johnsonville, Tennessee."

"Johnsonville, sir?" Mason asked. His voice betrayed his surprise. He saw Hood look up. "Begging the General's pardon, sir, but what in the hell is in Johnsonville?"

Hood smiled at the way Mason had asked the question. "Tell him to construct a fort on the heights there overlooking the Tennessee River. Send some artillery along with him. I want him to prevent the Federal gunboats from passing up the river and interfering with my supply line."

Mason nodded his head. "I see now."

Hood watched him write the order and leave the house to find a courier. He sat looking out into the darkness and thought about the message he had gotten from Beauregard this morning. It said that he could expect no reinforcements from Texas because General Kirby Smith said he couldn't risk sending troops across the Mississippi River.

Hood wouldn't have needed those troops if things would have gone according to plan. He'd expected to find plenty of recruits here in Tennessee, but that hadn't happened. Nothing seemed to happen the way he planned. His mood was beginning to grow dark. He began to worry again.

Mason walked back into the room. He asked, "Is there anything else you need General, before I retire for the night?"

"How many recruits have we gotten since we entered Tennessee?" Hood asked.

"By the latest count…" Mason looked toward the ceiling as he dug around in his mind to pull the number out. "It's one hundred and sixty-four men, sir."

Hood shook his head in frustration. He just couldn't fathom why men would not fight for their very freedom when they were so close to losing this war.

"Another thing," Mason suppressed a smile, "those two hundred and ninety-six cavalry you ordered to serve as infantry in Johnson's division…" He waited for Hood to answer. Hood simply nodded his head. "Well, sir, they've all deserted except for forty-two."

Hood lowered his head. He did a few quick calculations. "So, let me get this straight. We march all the way from Atlanta to Northern Tennessee. We gain a hundred and sixty-four men, and in the process, we lose two hundred and fifty-four."

Mason wanted to remind Hood that they'd lost about ten thousand at Franklin, but he knew better. It wouldn't be the wise thing to say at the moment.

Hood grew angrier by the second. He couldn't believe what he was hearing. He was disappointed in the patriotism of his countrymen. He turned to Mason and said, "Any able-bodied man should be brought into the army at the point of the bayonet. If they won't join, we'll conscript them."

Mason asked, "Should I write up an order, sir?"

"Yeah," Hood nodded his head, "that's an order."

"I was talking to S.D. Lee this morning," Mason didn't want Hood to get his hopes up about this idea successfully bringing a lot of men into the army. "He says that an estimated seven thousand men had fled ahead of our army to Nashville to avoid being forced to serve. It really is a shame, sir."

"How many infantry we got on line now?" Hood asked.

"About twenty-three thousand," Mason had just looked at the numbers this afternoon. "We're stretched pretty thin."

Hood turned back to the window and began to think about his present situation. He thought back to the map he'd been studying for days. His flanks were pulled back because there was nothing to anchor them on. There just weren't enough troops to stretch the line from the river east of town to the river west of town. He'd been preparing for Thomas to strike his right, but now it was appearing he would hit the left.

He excused Mason so the man could get a little sleep. Hood continued to stare out into the night. His mind began to take him back to Richmond where Buck Preston was waiting. *She's the belle of Richmond, he thought, perhaps of the entire Confederacy—her throat so soft and white, her feet so small and dainty.*

The night he'd met her hadn't gone over the way he'd planned. Doctor Darby, Hood's personal physician, was engaged to Buck's sister Mary and had promised to introduce the general and the belle. They were there for a night of playing cards, but Buck had refused to come out of her room and meet him. She was beautiful, but she was also very moody.

He'd met women like her before. She was the type that just couldn't seem to make up her mind what she wanted in a man. He finally got to meet the woman on the streets of Richmond while his division was passing through. It was like a giant military parade. Thousands of people were on the streets cheering his division on. It was love at first sight for General Hood.

Everyone accused her of being a flirt. She always seemed to lure the man in and then keep him at arm's length. The more she tried to push Hood away, the more he wanted her. They had been an odd couple. She was sophisticated, speaking proper English. She'd come from the planter class. Hood was raw, unsophisticated, and spoke without proper grammar. He was just a country boy, although his father had been a doctor.

Then there was the rumor about the Buck Preston curse. It seemed that every one of her suitors would be killed or seriously maimed in battle. Hood had scoffed at the idea. He still didn't put much faith in there being a curse, but sometimes he had to wonder. After calling on Buck, he'd lost the use of his arm at Gettysburg and then his entire leg at Chickamauga. Still, he didn't worry much; he'd always had the premonition that he would survive this war.

Some of the best days of his life were spent during his recovery in Richmond. The first time she had seen him following the amputation, she looked as though she would burst into tears. It made him feel good that she cared for him. They'd often gone for carriage rides through the streets of Richmond, sometimes taking along Mary Chesnut. Buck would be looking her best, wearing her black velvet and ermine dress. She reminded him of a princess.

After he'd lost the leg, he was sure that Buck wouldn't marry him. Surprisingly, she had shown renewed interest. Of course, it hadn't hurt that

237

everyone in Richmond toasted him a great hero. She'd told Hood his wounds were not detracting from him but made him appear glorious.

That was before the falling out they had on Christmas Eve. The roads had been icy then also. Her servant had been half helping Hood from the carriage and had accidentally dropped him on the ground. It had been extremely embarrassing for the general. He had lost his temper and cursed the poor man, even as he was apologizing. Buck had grown upset at his behavior and told him there would be no way she would ever marry him. He'd admitted to Mary Chesnut later that his courtship of Buck Preston had been the hardest battle he'd ever fought.

He'd known the wedding was off before he left Richmond to come back to the army. Just a couple of nights before he left, he'd been seated at the table talking with President Davis's wife, Varina. He could hear Buck in the next room flirting with another man. They had poked fun at her about being engaged to Hood. Buck's voice was louder than the others. It was if she was intentionally speaking loud so Hood could hear. The words were burned into his soul, though he didn't act as though he heard them. She had said, "Marry that man, never! What do you take me for?"

He didn't blame Buck. Deep down it wasn't her fault. Her parents were to blame. They'd been against the marriage from the outset. They were from the aristocratic class. Hood was just a country bumpkin in their eyes—a man who spoke with a country accent would be nothing but an embarrassment to them. He lacked refinement.

It puzzled him the way they had treated him. Before the engagement, they treated him as a war hero. He was invited to dinner often, to tea, and even out on carriage rides. After he became engaged to Buck, they refused to even speak to him. Every time he would visit Buck, they would make sure there was a house full of guests so the two of them wouldn't be alone.

He wondered why there were people like that. *These are the same people that were toasting me a hero before the engagement. I'm good enough to give my life in battle for them but not to marry their daughter.* He shook his head and decided to go back to bed and try to get some sleep.

December 14, 3:00 p.m.

USA

George Thomas had called this meeting to make sure his commanders understood what was expected of them in the morning. The snow had finally melted, turning the ground to mud. He had to admit, it would be better than fighting on ice. It had been foggy this morning, and that weighed heavily on the mind of General Thomas. Once everyone was seated, he cleared his throat and began. "Gentlemen, if it's not too foggy in the morning, I would like for us to move out as early as possible."

A thought crossed his mind. It had been something he had completely forgotten about until now. He turned to Whipple, said, "Will, send a message to the gunboat commanders and let them know. Ask them if they can lob a couple of shells toward the Confederate lines at first light and try and soften them up for our assault."

Whipple began to scribble the message on a piece of paper. Thomas turned back to his commanders seated around the table. "I have received another nasty telegram from General Halleck. We must move tomorrow. Washington will permit no more delays. I've held them off as long as possible. So, let's try and get this thing right."

General Steedman was nodding his head in agreement. Schofield stared at the table, his long flowing beard resting on his chest; the light from the window made his bald head shine.

Thomas looked at Wilson and continued. "Now, it is my intention to sweep around Hood's western flank with Wilson's three cavalry divisions."

"Sir, I'll get in his rear," Wilson smiled at the thought. "He's sent Forrest off toward Murfreesboro. It was a mistake to send his cavalry away with both flanks in the air. Reminds me of what Hooker did at Chancellorsville, and look how Lee made him pay for that mistake."

"We'll make Hood pay for his mistake tomorrow." Thomas pulled out a cigar but didn't light it. He began to tap the table with it as he thought about what he would say next.

Wilson quickly added, "My dismounted cavalry are going in as infantry."

"Very good," Thomas nodded and turned to General Smith. "Andrew, your corps will advance with Wilson's in a grand left wheel against Stewart's exposed left flank. You should actually hit the flank, while Wilson continues moving into Hood's rear, cutting off his retreat route. General Wood will move against Stewart's front, keeping him from shifting troops out of line to meet you. I can't tell you gentlemen how important it is for your movements to be in concert."

Thomas looked at Wood. "If you attack too soon, you'll be facing abatis, breastworks, and plenty of rifles behind them."

Wood nodded his head in agreement, his forked beard bounced as he did so.

Thomas looked back at Smith. "Andrew, make sure you are far enough out to be on his flank. Drive your men down his line and roll him up like a wet rag."

"General Schofield," Thomas stared hard at the man who was conspiring behind his back to get him fired. "You will remain behind in the works and wait for me to call you up in reserve."

Schofield said nothing. He stared back at the table, his face growing red.

239

Thomas looked at Steedman. "James, I'm placing all the garrison troops under your command."

Schofield cleared his throat and interrupted. "Might I make a suggestion, sir?"

The way he said 'sir' sounded to Thomas like it galled the man. Thomas replied, "You may speak freely."

Schofield didn't like the idea of being held in reserve and missing the action. He wondered why Thomas was punishing him. He hadn't liked Thomas since West Point, and now he disliked the man even more. He'd practically saved Nashville and defeat by delaying Hood's army as long as possible. Yet, Thomas hadn't even commended him one time. After a long pause, he said, "If the entire right wing is making a left wheel, wouldn't it be better if I shifted my troops to the right also? If needed, we would be much closer and lose little time going in."

Thomas thought about that a moment. It actually wasn't a bad idea. He said, "That's fine, Schofield, but I will call you if you're needed. You are the general reserve for tomorrow's battle."

Schofield lowered his head and stared at the table. It didn't appear to him that Thomas was smart enough to look ahead in the campaign and understand the best disposition of the troops. Schofield didn't believe Thomas had the capacity to command an army.

Thomas turned back to Steedman. "James, I don't mean to leave you out of the action, but do you think your colored troops will fight?"

"They'll fight," Steedman replied without hesitation.

Thomas looked at Steedman. He was considered an ugly man. He had large mutton chop whiskers, and his mouth and chin were clean shaven. He looked older than his years from hard drinking and womanizing. His hair was still curly brown with a few streaks of gray. Most of his fellow commanders didn't like him because he was a politician. He'd had no military experience at all before the war. Thomas actually liked the man. Steedman had been an orphan who had worked hard to make something of himself. He'd put that same work ethic to good use in the army. Thomas believed him to be the best division commander he'd ever had.

Thomas said, "I trust them behind breastworks, but I'm just not so sure they'll fight in the open. I have reservations about sending them in."

Steedman was shaking his head while Thomas spoke. "Sir, I trained those boys myself. They'll fight like hell anywhere I lead them."

"Alright," Thomas waved him off. "You may go forward in the morning and make a large demonstration against Hood's eastern flank. Make him think the main assault is coming from the east. Hopefully, he will strip troops from his left to his right. With his left weakened, Wilson and Smith will have little stopping them from rolling up that flank. Now, James, what do you intend to use in the morning?"

"I'll take two brigades of colored troops and one of my white brigades." Steedman began to chuckle. "I think it'll do the Rebs good to see their former slaves fighting against them."

"I hope you're right," Thomas didn't smile. He didn't trust these ex-slaves in combat. *If they can just make a demonstration, he thought, that will be good enough for me.*

"Sir, one of my officers has made several nighttime reconnaissances." Steedman added. "He says the Rebel campfires extend to near Rain's Hill on the Nolensville Pike, about a quarter mile from the railroad. The lines appear to end abruptly at that hill. If I can move out the Murfreesboro Pike and sweep around that hill, I believe I can take the Confederate line in reverse and capture their rifle pits. This should be enough to convince Hood he's in trouble on his right."

Thomas thought about it a long moment. It was the same move he was making on the western flank on a smaller scale. He said, "Pass along my compliments to that officer. That is good work indeed. You understand when you do that, you're going to stir up a hornet's nest over there. Hood will be sending massive amounts of troops against you, and you're not going to have a reserve. At least that's what we're hoping he'll do."

"We'll fortify as soon as we take it," Steedman wasn't afraid. "I'll use my white brigade to take the hill. Thompson's black brigade will make a demonstration in front to prevent them from shifting troops to meet us. The other black brigade will sweep around and get in their rear. After we fortify, all hell can storm that hill if it wants."

"Very well," Thomas lowered his head in thought a moment. He still didn't trust those black soldiers to do much against veteran Confederate infantry. Thomas hoped he could time things to where he rolled up Hood's flank before he sent so many men to the right that he managed to chase Steedman's troops back into the Nashville works. It was a dangerous gamble, but he was full of confidence in the results.

"Does everyone understand their part of the plan?" Thomas asked. No one said a word. "If not, now is the time to ask. Don't wait until you've gotten yourself in a bind tomorrow because you're not sure of your part of the plan."

Still no one had any questions. Thomas said, "The meeting is concluded. Good luck tomorrow, gentlemen. I just hope the fog doesn't delay our movements."

Smith had been sitting throughout the meeting with his arms crossed. He stood up first and took Thomas's hand. His gray hair was almost white in the rays of light that managed to penetrate the room. His large, prominent nose cast a shadow across one side of his face. He said, "I have full confidence in the results tomorrow, General. It's an excellent plan."

Thomas thanked him. Schofield simply left the room. He'd gained something anyway. No matter what happens tomorrow, his ass would be covered. If it's a great victory because of his being called into action, he can claim credit with the last-minute change in plans. If the battle ended in failure, it wouldn't be his fault. After all, he was just playing a small role as the reserve.

General Thomas actually slept well that night. He awoke before daylight and checked out of the hotel. Men were moving up the dark streets. The only sound was their footsteps on the melting snow and mud. The fog was so thick; he couldn't see a hundred feet. He mounted his brown mare and turned up the street. He could hear hushed voices and chains clanking behind him. He'd been in the army long enough to recognize the sound of an artillery battery moving up the road. He felt as though he were watching phantoms moving past—the long lines of men disappearing into the mist. It was hard to imagine thousands of men in this vicinity as quiet as things were.

Part 7

Death of a Nation

"The greatest test of courage on earth is to bear defeat without losing heart."

Robert Green Ingersoll

December 15, 7:00 a.m.

CSA

John Bell Hood had awakened early in the morning. He was anxious to find out what the Federal army was doing. A move appeared imminent over the past few days. The day was becoming surprisingly warm compared to the harsh weather they'd had. Hood sat in his favorite chair staring out the window.

The sky was overcast. A day like this would normally be a dismal one, if not for the fact that he was busy. The sun was up somewhere in the east, but couldn't be seen through the clouds. Fog was so thick that Hood couldn't see his staff officers' tents pitched on the front lawn of Misses Overton's home.

Mason came in from the fog and handed Hood a captured Federal newspaper. He looked at the front page and began to read the article about the Battle of Franklin. Schofield was claiming a total victory with thirty regimental colors captured. He said Hood's army had endured a virtual blood bath.

If I've got this journal, he thought, then I'm sure the authorities in Richmond will have a copy soon. He turned to Mason and said, "Colonel, write to Secretary of War James Seddon, and tell him that we have lost thirteen regimental banners at Franklin and captured about the same number. Tell him our captured colors fell inside Federal lines. When you're finished, I will sign it."

"Will that be all, sir?" Mason asked.

"When you're done," Hood reached up with his good arm and began to rub his eyes, "write a request for General Beauregard. Tell him I need all the available troops he can gather sent here as soon as possible."

Just after eight, Misses Overton brought Hood a plate of eggs and ham. He finished with his meal and was signing the letter to James Seddon, when he heard firing from the front. He cocked his head to try and determine the direction, but he'd been exposed to so much gunfire in this war, he was having trouble with his hearing already. He began to grow concerned. He told Mason, "Colonel, have someone saddle our horses. I'm riding to the front to see what's going on."

He looked out the window and noticed the fog clearing away. In about twenty minutes' time, it was all gone. The sun was breaking through the clouds, and the sky was the color of sapphire.

After the horses were ready, several aides helped Hood onto his mount. There was a crisp air blowing this morning. They were just about to ride north, when a courier arrived with a message from General Cheatham. Mason took the message and read it. He turned to Hood and said, "General Cheatham believes the enemy is only probing the lines this morning looking for a weakness."

244

Hood was worried about his flanks. He decided to ride to the left first and see how General Stewart's position was looking. It was obvious that General Cheatham was in control of whatever was going on with his front at the moment.

They were riding up the Granny White Pike on the way to Stewart's headquarters, when they met another courier riding to find Hood. Heavy artillery had opened fire on Hood's lines. The noise was deafening, even this far to the rear.

The man had been riding at breakneck speed and was out of breath. He said, "General Hood, beg to report, sir."

Hood watched the man panting from the hard ride. "Take your time, corporal."

"Sir," the man was still out of breath, "General Cheatham sends his compliments. His skirmishers were pushed in on his right flank. Two brigades attempted to get in his rear. One brigade was Negro troops. Whoever was in charge of the black brigade didn't have a clue what he was doing. He drove those men into the railroad cut. We got a redoubt on the hill over there, and they sprayed canister fire down that cut. Brigadier General James Smith, commander of Cleburne's division, shifted Granbury's brigade over there and made it a perfect slaughter pen. I don't think we'll have to worry about that group of Negros anymore. They ran like hell. Anyway, General Cheatham thinks the movement you expected toward Murfreesboro is under way and wants to know if you'll send him some of Stewart's men to help him hold his flank."

"Not yet," Hood held up his hand. "I'm going to see what's going on in front of Stewart and Lee's corps, and then I'll be over to see General Cheatham."

The man saluted and rode back down the road. Hood found General Stewart outside his headquarters tent on his horse. When Stewart saw Hood, he saluted.

"What's the situation?" Hood asked.

"I'm worried about my flank," Stewart replied. "I've been at the front all morning. The men in the redoubts say they've seen heavy Federal movement in the trees out west of here."

Another courier came down the road and shouted, "Where's General Hood?"

"Here," Colonel Mason called out.

The courier rode over, smiled a toothy grin, and saluted. He said, "General Cheatham sends his compliments, sir. He wants me to report that a white brigade charged our redoubt on Rain's Hill. Their commander was shot down on the works, and most of his brigade is trapped in the ditch outside, at least the ones that didn't turn tail and run. Those are raw men they're sending in on the right. Sir, it's Franklin in reverse."

"Very well," Hood replied. "Tell General Cheatham to let me know if he sees anymore troops on his flank."

The man spun the horse and was off. Hood turned to Stewart and said, "Let's ride to the front and see what's going on. Where is the best vantage point?"

"That would be Redoubt Number Four, sir," Stewart replied. "It's the most advanced of the five."

Stewart led the way; Hood followed alongside. He turned to Stewart and said, "They've been banging away all morning across the front and the right flank. The main attack will be against you."

Stewart had a look of concern on his face. He asked, "How do you know that?"

"Because," Hood gave a grim smile, "it's what I would do."

Before they'd reached the fort, Hood was sure of what was happening. He could see it in his mind. Thomas feints at the right and hits the left. It's a beautiful move, a move that Hood had been trying to get this army to make since taking command.

He turned in the saddle and looked at Colonel Mason riding just behind him. "Colonel, send a courier to General Lee. Tell him to send any troops he can spare."

"Right," Mason spun his horse.

Hood told Stewart. "You place those men where you need them when they come up."

The heavy artillery from the gunboats and the works around Nashville were still firing at the Confederate lines. The racket was tremendous, but very little damage was done. It was more annoying than anything.

Hood and Stewart rode into Redoubt Number Four on the heights just west of the Hillsboro Pike. There were one hundred men from the Twenty-Ninth Alabama inside the little fort, along with several of Captain Lumsden's smoothbore cannons. The fort itself was in good condition. There were four cannon embrasures facing west. It was obvious to Hood that an attack from the west could be stopped. The breastworks for the infantry were only about three feet high. It was the best that could be done, having to dig in the frozen ground.

Hood asked Stewart, "How many men are assigned to this position?"

"Forty artillerymen under Captain Lumsden," Stewart replied. He looked toward the infantry. "Along with about a hundred men of the Twenty-Ninth Alabama Infantry."

Captain Lumsden walked over and peered up at Hood strapped to his horse. "Sir, there's been a lot of movement over to our left. If they get around there..."

He left the rest unsaid. Hood understood at once what he was saying. It appeared Thomas was attempting to get in his rear and turn him. *The man probably hopes to capture my entire army, he thought. We'll give him something to think about.*

Hood turned to a courier and said, "Have Ector's brigade brought up here to help Captain Lumsden hold this position."

All eyes were on General Hood. They understood something must be going on for the commanding general to be this far in front. Hood took out his field glasses and scanned the trees to the west. He could see movement in there, all right. He turned and spoke to the troops in the fort. "Men, I want you to hold here as long as possible. I'm bringing up reinforcements as we speak. I expect every man here to do his duty. Can I count on you?"

The men all cheered.

He turned to Stewart and said, "Have Walthall's division move over here and cover your left. Things are about to get dicey here."

Stewart galloped off down the hill to the east.

Hood turned the horse and rode back toward the Hillsboro Pike. He was glad his army was operating on interior lines. With his line shaped like a three-sided square, he could rush troops from one threatened point to another in a hurry. Meade had done this very thing to Lee at Gettysburg. *Say what they want about me, Hood thought, but I am a good commander. I learn from what others have done to be successful—if I could just instill the winning spirit in this poor army the way Lee did his army in Virginia.*

He was looking for the reinforcements that Lee was supposed to be sending over here. They should have arrived by now. Hood paused on the Granny White Pike and waited for the men to begin arriving from Lee.

He'd been waiting there for about twenty minutes, when a courier arrived from General Stewart. The man said, "Sir, General Stewart wishes me to inform you that he has shifted Walthall's division to the left just behind the redoubts. There is a problem, sir."

"What?" Hood yelled. He was tired of having to drag messages out of people. Wars could be lost in seconds.

"Uh," the man stammered at being yelled at. "Walthall's division is so battered, there ain't enough men to reach but to Redoubt Number Four. He needs more troops. He also says that Ector's brigade, which you sent out early this morning on the far left, has fallen back. He placed them in support of Redoubt Number Five. He says there's a gap between number four and number five.

"Tell him to hang on as long as he can." Hood looked over his shoulder to the east, hoping to see reinforcements coming from Lee. He saw nothing. He added, "Reinforcements are on the way."

It was a good thing he'd ordered those redoubts built, but they could only hold against a massive assault for so long. With a couple hundred men and a few artillery pieces, an entire Federal corps would swallow them whole. It wouldn't matter that the Confederate army held the high ground. A hundred men would never stop fifteen thousand.

Another courier came galloping up the road from the south. The man reined up and saluted. He was obviously excited. He yelled, "Sir, General Chalmers is fit to be tied. He sent his wagon train to Colonel Coleman commanding Ector's brigade and asked him to guard it while we were slowing down Wilson's cavalry. Colonel Coleman must have gotten scared, sir. He just up and abandoned the wagon train and retreated. Wilson's cavalry has captured Chalmers's entire wagon train. He wants Colonel Coleman brought up on court martial charges."

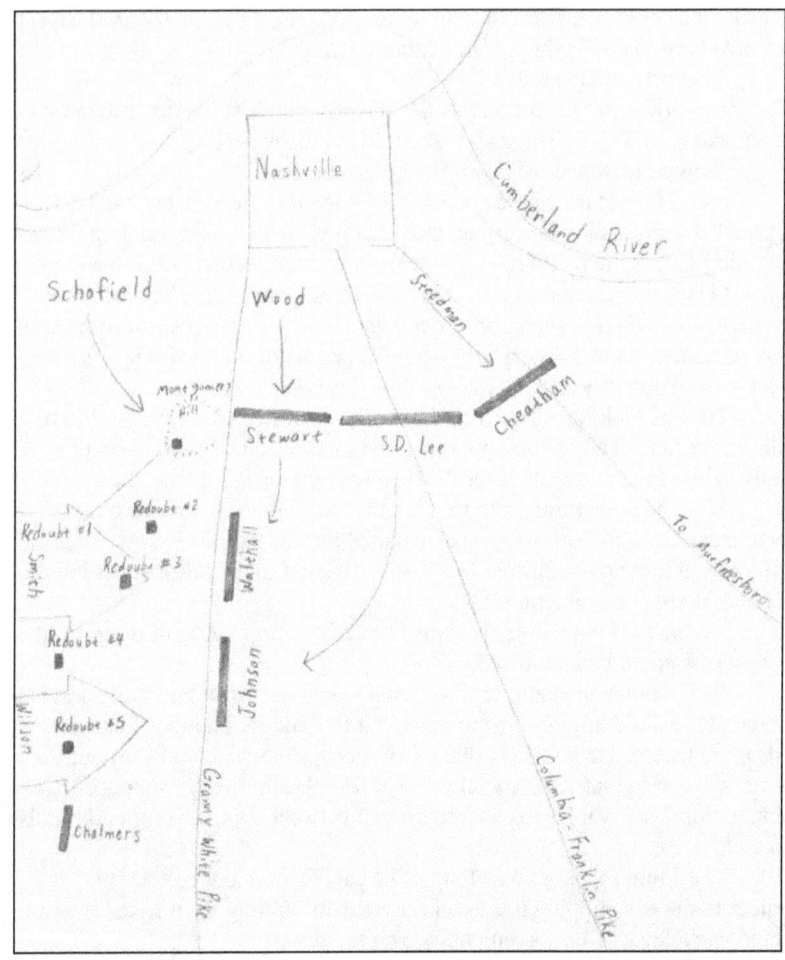

The first day at Nashville. Stewart does everything in his power to prevent the Federal army from turning Hood's left flank.

Another courier came galloping up the road from the south. The man reined up and saluted. He was obviously excited. He yelled, "Sir, General Chalmers is fit to be tied. He sent his wagon train to Colonel Coleman commanding Ector's brigade and asked him to guard it while we were slowing down Wilson's cavalry. Colonel Coleman must have gotten scared, sir. He just up and abandoned the wagon train and retreated. Wilson's cavalry has captured

Chalmers's entire wagon train. He wants Colonel Coleman brought up on court martial charges."

He waited to see what Hood would say. Hood said nothing. He was in deep thought. The entire Federal army is bearing down on my left flank and rear. I haven't the time to deal with this right now. I've got to act here.

He looked at the courier and said, "Tell General Chalmers we'll have to worry about that later. Just now, though, I need his help. Tell him to continue covering my left flank. I need him to hold back Wilson's cavalry until I can get reinforcements up."

"Sir," the man had a worried look in his eyes, "Just so as you know, they's three divisions of cavalry coming at just our one brigade."

"I know, I know," Hood held up a hand. "Help's on the way. I don't expect him to defeat Wilson, just slow him down."

"Right," the man said. He saluted and rode back in the direction he'd come from.

Hood turned the horse to the east and began to ride that way. He said to Mason, "Let's go see what's taking those reinforcements so long."

There had been no action along the center of his line this morning in front of S.D. Lee. This was another lesson he'd learned from General Lee at Sharpsburg. If the enemy is attacking your flanks, shift troops from the center to meet them. If they advance on your center later, simply shift them back. Lee had defeated McClellan at Sharpsburg using this very strategy. McClellan's army had been ninety thousand strong, and yet Lee had won that battle with only thirty-eight thousand men.

They soon found General Lee at his headquarters about midway between the Granny White Pike and the Franklin Pike. Lee saw Hood and saluted. He said, "It's quiet in my front, sir."

"Where are the reinforcements I asked to be sent to Stewart?" Hood didn't have time for small talk.

"Johnson's division is pulling out of line now. I've extended my other two divisions to cover the gap. I didn't want him to just up and leave. If the Federals saw that, they would advance and exploit the gap they left behind." Lee heard a commotion and turned. It was the lead elements of Johnson's division coming up the road.

"Good," Hood said. "Their main assault is coming against our left flank."

"Could've fooled me," Lee shook his head. "I thought it was going to be Cheatham. He had quite a little scrap over there this morning."

"It was just a bluff, Stephen," Hood tugged at the reins on the horse. "Just as I predicted."

A courier came galloping up on a lathered horse. The man didn't bother to salute. He said, "General Hood, sir, General Stewart says that Redoubt Number Five has been overrun by about two thousand Federal infantry and cavalry. There were only a hundred men and two artillery pieces in the fort; there was just no way they could hold against that size a force. At the

249

moment, they are having an artillery duel between the captured guns in Redoubt Number Five and our guns in Number Four. We're getting the best of them right now, but he says if that force advances, he doubts Number Four will hold long."

Hood said, "I'm coming back now. I'll talk to General Stewart personally."

Hood followed the man back west. He found General Stewart near the Hillsboro Pike behind Walthall's division. The artillery was still banging away to the southwest of their position.

Stewart saw Hood and said, "General, they look to be pretty disorganized after taking the fort over there. Our artillery in Number Four is giving them hell at the moment. We may have an opportunity here. If I can get some reinforcements, I might can go crashing back into them and retake Number Five."

"Reinforcements are on the way," Hood jerked his thumb back over his shoulder. "I just left there. They should be arriving in the next ten minutes."

A courier rode up, saluted and said, "General Stewart, the Federals have left Redoubt Number Five and are charging Number Four as we speak."

Stewart asked, "How long does Captain Lumsden think he can hold?"

"Not sure, sir," the man thought a moment. "Them damned Yankee cavalrymen have repeating rifles. How we supposed to defend against that?"

Stewart didn't answer the question. Hood sat on his horse staring toward Redoubt Number Four but couldn't see what was happening from where he was.

After a long pause, Stewart said, "Go back and give the Captain my compliments, and tell him to hold out as long as possible."

They watched the man gallop away. Heavy musket fire opened up in the direction he was going.

Hood said, "So much for the retaking of Number Five. I don't guess they were as disorganized as they appeared."

Stewart turned to Captain Gale of his staff. "Captain, stay here and handle all dispatches for me. I'm gonna ride up to Number Four and see what the situation is for myself."

Gale started to object but saw that Stewart was serious. If Number Four was under attack, it was no place for a corps commander to be with just a hundred and fifty men defending it.

Stewart rode west past General Walthall's division. The men were building fires and preparing what little they had for breakfast. A little farther on, he encountered Brigadier General Reynolds, commander of the Arkansas brigade. He rode up to Reynolds and returned the man's sloppy salute. He said, "My compliments, Daniel, please have your men placed under arms and prepared to move. I'm riding forward to survey the situation myself. I'll send orders when I have assessed things."

250

A courier caught up to Stewart just before he started up the hill to the fort. The man said, "Captain Gale sent me here to inform you that the majority of the Federal army is in our front and on our flank."

No shit, Stewart thought. He said, "Take a message to Walthall to move his division to the left. Have General Reynolds form his brigade behind that little stone wall back there. Can you handle that?"

A smile spread across the man's face. A lieutenant general had just given him some serious responsibility. "You can count on me, sir."

Stewart said nothing. He turned his horse and rode on up the hill toward Redoubt Number Four. When he entered the rear of the fort, he expected to see Ector's brigade there. Hood had ordered it up there. Still, the fort only contained a hundred and fifty men. He saw Captain Lumsden and rode that way. He yelled above the din of the cannons. "Captain, where in hell is Ector's brigade?"

Lumsden turned around and was shocked to see his corps commander. He quickly saluted, obviously caught off guard at the sight of a lieutenant general in a position like this. "They came up, sir, but, uh, when they took Redoubt Five, they were afraid they would be captured and pulled out."

"Damn," Stewart said.

"I pleaded with him to stay," Lumsden shook his head. "He told me this position is untenable, that there's a whole army in my front. I don't know the man, sir, some colonel is in command."

"I know," Stewart said. He looked toward the rear. "Hold as long as you can, I'm going back and try to get you some help."

"Right, sir," Lumsden turned back to his cannons. "Keep it hot, boys; help is on the way."

At that moment, an enemy shell struck a log on the embrasure and sent a flying piece of wood careening into the ribs of Corporal King. Lumsden saw the man sink to his knees. He walked over and asked, "You all right, corporal?"

"Broke some damn ribs, sir," the man said through clenched teeth.

Sergeant Maxwell was a good friend of King. He walked over and bent down beside the poor man. Lieutenant Cole Hargrove shouted, "Maxwell, back to the trail, damn it; back to your place at the gun."

Maxwell patted King on the shoulder as he stood and moved back to his position.

Lumsden said, "When you're able, corporal, go to the rear."

The man nodded and slowly rose to his feet. Lumsden watched the poor man stagger toward the rear. The wound would prove to be a blessing.

He looked to his right and saw a Federal shell land in the midst of the Twenty-Ninth Alabama Infantry. Six men were thrown through the air, all killed with one shell. Things were getting bad. Gun number four had taken such a pounding that he'd been forced to ask the infantry to provide men to help.

A shell exploded just over gun number four. He saw two privates and a lieutenant killed. They were all volunteers from the Alabama Infantry.

251

Lumsden looked down in the valley between this hill and the one that held Redoubt Number Five. It was swarming with Federal soldiers. The snow and mud were slowing them down considerably, but that would only work for a little while. Lumsden shouted at Orderly Sergeant Shivers, "Mack, ride back to General Stewart. Tell him it is evident the enemy is about to charge and overwhelm the fort. If we leave now, we'll lose our guns, but we can save the men. There's probably two, maybe three thousand Federals coming up that hill."

"Right," the man yelled and raced for his horse.

Lumsden heard more artillery fire from his left. The Federals had brought up four guns to within five hundred yards of the redoubt. They were firing in enfilade. Enfilade was a technical term for crossfire. He yelled for his two right guns to pull out of the embrasures and move to the left and return this fire. *We've got to drive them off, he thought. If they get cranked up over there, this little acre of ground is gonna be like hell itself.*

He watched them hand-roll the guns over and begin returning fire. He couldn't help but be proud of his men. They soon had the range right, and the Federal artillerymen had begun to duck and dodge away from their guns. He hoped that would take care of any enfilade fire from the Federal guns.

Mack Shivers came galloping back up the hill. He quickly dismounted. He was panting from the hard ride. Between breaths, he said, "Sir, General Stewart says its necessary to hold the enemy back as long as possible, regardless of the cost."

"Damn," Lumsden shook his head. He walked forward and looked over the embrasure into the valley below. A bullet struck the breastworks, throwing dirt into his face. They were a lot closer, with skirmishers out front firing at anything that appeared. He moved back away from the exposed position. *How long does he consider 'as long as possible,'? he wondered.*

He saw one of his gunners go down with a bullet in the groin. *Damn bad place to take a hit, Lumsden thought. I would rather have one in the head.* The man lay writhing on the muddy ground. Lumsden called for a couple men to help him to the rear. He didn't really have men to spare, but he couldn't very well leave this man lying there in such pain.

Lumsden stepped behind gun number two and watched his men work. He watched Hilen Rosser bring a round to the gunners. Rosser was the youngest of three brothers in his battery. Lumsden liked the boy. He couldn't very well be called a man yet; he was only seventeen. Lumsden thought about that a moment. Yes, he could be considered a man after all he'd been through. The boy was braver than a lot of men Lumsden had seen.

As Rosser handed the shell to Sergeant James Maxwell, a Federal shell came over the embrasure and struck the boy directly in the face. The shell never slowed down or exploded. It went just to the right of Captain Lumsden and buried itself in the ground somewhere behind him. For a moment, Lumsden was blinded. He wondered if he'd been struck also.

He reached up and wiped at his eyes. They were full of blood. His entire face was covered with blood and brain matter. For a moment, he didn't know whose blood it was. In front of Lumsden stood Sergeant Maxwell, in shock, with hands still outstretched waiting for the round to be passed. In front of Maxwell, lay Hilen Rosser. The boy's head was gone. Only a portion of the back of the boy's scalp was still attached with hair.

Maxwell shook himself out of his daze. He ran to Lumsden, "Are you all right, sir?"

"I think so," Lumsden shook his head. "It's not my blood."

Lieutenant Hargrove shouted, "Captain, it looks like they fixin' to charge."

Lumsden walked forward and peered through the embrasure without exposing himself. He turned and yelled, "Go to canister! Give them double canister!"

The enemy was within a hundred yards of the fort, when the guns began to unleash their canister fire. Hundreds of small iron balls about an inch in diameter swept through the Federal ranks. He saw body parts blasted into the air, but still they came on. There were just too many of them. The Federal troops soon reached the breastworks and began climbing over. Lumsden looked around and saw that his infantry support had already run. He watched his gunners fire another round of canister, even as the Federals came over the wall.

Lumsden, still standing behind gun number two, asked, "Are you loaded with canister now?"

Sergeant Maxwell stepped back beside Lumsden, "Yes, sir, but…"

"Fire then, damn it," Lumsden shouted.

"Sir," Maxwell threw up his hands, "the man with the friction primers has run off."

"Take care of yourselves, boys," Lumsden shouted and spun for the rear. It was time to go. To remain any longer would be suicide. To make sure everyone heard him, he shouted over his shoulder again. "Every man for himself!"

As he went over the rear wall of the fort, he glanced back at his fleeing men. Many of them were unable to get away, and he saw them standing back there with their hands in the air. He ran on down the hill toward the pike below. He looked over and saw Sergeant Maxwell race past him.

They soon crossed the pike and climbed over the stone wall that sheltered Brigadier General Reynolds's Arkansas troops. Maxwell and several other men plopped down beside Lumsden. They were all out of breath.

An Arkansas private looked at Sergeant Maxwell and said, "Say, partner, it was pretty hot on that hill over yonder, weren't it? You fellers certainly held 'em back longer than we thought you would."

Maxwell was so out of breath, all he could do was nod at the man. Captain Lumsden only sat there a moment. He said to no one in particular, "I've got to go find General Stewart."

Maxwell decided to follow his commander. He couldn't run any farther, but maybe he could at least walk. The cool air burned his lungs, as sweat dripped down his face. He felt as though he would vomit. The nausea was extreme from the hard run. He got to his feet and staggered along behind Lumsden.

They found General Stewart mounted a few hundred yards farther to the rear. He was talking to his staff officers, and couriers were racing back and forth. Captain Lumsden walked up to General Stewart but didn't salute. His face was still covered with blood, and Stewart hardly recognized the man.

Maxwell noticed that Lumsden was angry. He began to shout at Stewart, "You left my men back there to be butchered! You don't care for your men anymore than that? You just sacrificed us—sent us to the slaughter like a sacrificial lamb!"

Stewart climbed from the saddle. He wasn't the type of man to get upset. He hadn't obtained his rank of lieutenant general by losing his cool but just the opposite. He patted Lumsden on the shoulder. The blood didn't bother Stewart; he'd been in this war long enough, that things like that were quite common.

Stewart spoke in a consoling manner. "Look at the situation, Captain. It couldn't be helped. I hated to leave you and your brave men up there, but look how much time you bought us. I now have a makeshift line along the Hillsboro Pike. I just want to congratulate you and your brave men for the job you've just performed. If I survive this battle, I will make sure your men are recognized for their bravery in my report."

This seemed to disarm the angry artillery captain. Lumsden seemed to be coming off his adrenaline rush. He saw a stump nearby and walked over and sat down. He lowered his head and stared at the ground. Maxwell walked over and pulled off his canteen. "Sir, I'm gonna wash the blood off your face."

Lumsden said nothing. Maxwell took out a rag and began to remove the blood. It took a few minutes. It had begun to dry and was caked in and around his eyes. He hated to be so rough with the man, but that was the only way to get him clean.

When he finished, he sat on the ground beside his commander. There wasn't much to do now. They had lost half their command and all their guns. Lumsden reached up and began picking at his beard. He would pull something gray from the hair and flick it on the ground.

Maxwell asked, "What the hell is that?"

Lumsden looked over at Maxwell with tears in his eyes. "That's poor Rosser's brains."

Maxwell hated that he had asked.

A courier rode up to General Stewart. The man said, "Sir, General Reynolds begs to report. He has halted the Federal advance at the moment. They seem content to hold the hill and Redoubt Number Four, but they've brought up artillery. They're giving us a severe pounding."

Stewart spun the horse and rode that way. He would prefer, under the circumstances, that his men see that he was sharing their fate with them. He got to the stone wall and found Reynolds's men hugging the ground. It reminded him of a postage stamp. Those men couldn't get any closer to the ground than a postage stamp could to an envelope.

Reynolds saw Stewart and walked to him amid the terrible cannonading. "Sir, this is hell on earth."

The artillery bombardment soon ceased. Stewart wasn't sure what it meant. He said, "General, hold this place as long as possible. I'm going back to see what's holding up the reinforcements I was promised."

Stewart rode back and found General Hood near Stewart's temporary headquarters. He said, "They've taken forts four and five. They're on my flank. If we don't get help quickly, my position will be untenable."

"At least it's quiet now," Hood said. He turned and called for Colonel Mason. The aide rode forward. "Send a courier back to hurry General Lee's reinforcements on over. We don't have time to spare. If they don't get here soon, all will be lost."

Hood took out his watch. It was almost three-thirty. Hood said, "Colonel Mason, send a message to General Cheatham. Tell him to send Bate and Brown's divisions this way. Tell him I don't want any excuses about what he is facing over there; I don't have time to argue. Just send them, and send them quick."

Stewart said, "General Hood, I'm going to ride forward and see if I can tell what's happening."

Hood waited where he was. He needed to know those reinforcements would get here in time. Stewart hadn't been gone long before Hood heard artillery and rifle fire open up just northwest of his position. Stewart rode back up, and his eyes betrayed the stress he was under at the moment. He said, "Redoubt Number Three is under attack now. My entire corps is in serious trouble."

Hood said nothing. He didn't need to be told the obvious. He sat looking toward the west through the trees. Mason called out to him. Hood spun in the saddle and saw Major General Edward Johnson approaching.

Hood had never been so happy to see a man in all his life. Johnson placed the large stick he was carrying in his left hand, saluted, and said, "My division is right behind me. Where do you want us?"

"General Stewart will place your division." Hood let out a sigh of relief. Maybe now things could be turned around. "If the two of you can hold out until dark, I'll shift Cheatham's entire corps over here as reinforcements in case they continue the attack in the morning."

Johnson looked at Stewart and said, "Show me the way."

Stewart led Johnson and his men south on the Hillsboro Pike. He wondered why S.D. Lee had sent Johnson's division as reinforcements. It just didn't make any sense. Lee must have been keeping his best troops in case he was attacked later. Johnson's division was the only division of troops engaged at Franklin, and they'd suffered as bad as the rest of the army. Now, he'd sent his weakest division here to protect the army's rear.

Stewart said, "General Johnson, there's a gap between my left and Ector's brigade to the south. Your troops will need to fill that gap."

Johnson said nothing. He just stared at General Stewart with his fast blinking eyes. *He's one strange bird, Stewart thought.* He had the habit of blinking his eyes quickly when he was nervous. While his eyes were blinking, his ears would twitch. It reminded Stewart of a mule trying to scare flies off the back of its head. He knew Johnson despised it out west. He'd been captured at Spotsylvania and exchanged. He'd then been sent here against his will. His men had nicknamed him 'Old Clubby' because he goes into battle with a large hickory club instead of carrying a sword.

They rode out near an open field with a clear view toward Redoubt Number Four. On the east side of the road was a stone wall running south. Stewart said, "You can use that wall for protection."

Johnson swung the club over his head and shouted for his men to get into position. The men of his division came on line pretty fast. Stewart was beginning to breathe a sigh of relief. He could see the nervousness in the eyes of Johnson's men. Federal troops were plainly visible, swarming over the hill just west of them; men were moving in and out of the fort on top. The lowest private could look up there and tell how desperate this was going to be. It appeared they were outnumbered about three to one. It was also a well-known fact that you didn't want to try and defend against an attack when your enemy was on the high ground.

Stewart began to ride back north to see how things were going with Redoubt Number Three, but he already had a pretty good idea of what was happening there. He'd just started up the road, when Federal artillery opened up from the heights to the west. Shells were raining down, plowing giant furrows in the ground and exploding in the sky overhead. He turned and saw Johnson cursing and swinging his club at his fleeing men. The entire division had panicked at the first fire. Stewart couldn't believe his eyes. He couldn't believe they were running from artillery fire. Other than the noise, artillery didn't do much damage from long range. *They miss more times than they hit, he thought. The Federal infantry hasn't even shown any sign of advancing yet.*

Stewart rode out among Johnson's men and attempted to rally them. To the northeast, he saw a battery galloping up. He rode over and asked, "Whose battery is this?"

"Seldon's Alabama Battery," the man looked shocked. "Sir, you don't recognize us?"

Stewart realized they were from his own corps. He said, "I need you to make a stand here."

Just behind the battery, Stewart saw a familiar face. It was Major Mitchell, one of the staff officers of Lieutenant Colonel Samuel Williams, the artillery commander of his corps. Mitchell was one of Stewart's favorites. The man was brave and would attempt to obey any order he's given. This was one of the coolest men Stewart had ever observed under fire. He met Mitchell and returned the man's salute.

Mitchell's red hair and beard were practically glowing in the afternoon light. He asked, "How bad is it, sir?"

"It's damned bad," Stewart jerked a thumb over his shoulder toward the battery that was unlimbering. "I need you to hold this position as long as possible."

"This is Major Trueheart's battalion," Mitchell said. "He's on his way up here now. His other battery was captured up in Redoubt Number Four, and this is all he's got left. I'll see to it he understands the situation, sir."

Stewart nodded and spun back to find Edward Johnson. The man was easy to find. He was swinging the hickory club over his head and swearing at his men. Stewart rode over and saluted. He knew Johnson despised being loaned out to other corps. The man seemed to take everything personally.

Stewart said, "General Johnson, can you move your division over and support that battery of artillery yonder?"

"If these sons-of-bitches don't stand this time," Johnson was still seething at his troops, "I'm gonna shoot every last one of them myself."

Johnson gave the order, and the nervous troops moved that way. Stewart rode along with them. Stewart said, "I want you men to make a stand here or go north."

Several looked up at the lieutenant general. They understood exactly what he was saying. Either stand here and die or be taken prisoner. One ragged private yelled back, "General, we will go north if we stay here."

Stewart ignored the man and rode on. The battery had finished unlimbering their two guns. He could see Major Mitchell and Major Trueheart discussing the situation. Johnson's division was moving over in support of the two artillery pieces. His division was far out of position now, and there was still a huge gap between Walthall's division and Ector's brigade. *They may as well have not come at all, Stewart thought.*

A courier saw the stars on Stewart's collar and rode to him. "Sir, I have a message. Lieutenant Colonel William Butler, who was commanding Manigault's brigade, has been wounded. Lieutenant Colonel Irvine Walker is now in command."

Things were getting bad. Lieutenant colonels were in command of brigades. He pointed toward General Johnson and said to the courier, "You might want to pass that message to General Johnson. He commands this division."

The man looked a little shocked but realized it wouldn't do any good to argue. He had just found the first general he'd come to and delivered his message. Stewart watched him turn the horse and ride toward General Johnson.

Stewart spun his horse to the north to check on Redoubt Number Three. He shook his head as he made his way up the road. He'd definitely earned his living here today. Things had gone far worse than he could have imagined. He sent a courier to find Hood and tell him how things were going.

He found General Walthall behind his division. Walthall said, "I saw what happened. I've shifted Daniel Reynolds's brigade of Arkansas troops over to my left and refused the line so we don't get the entire flank rolled up."

"I don't think that's gonna help," Stewart shook his head. "When they move forward again, they'll get beyond Reynolds's left flank; the entire corps is in danger of being captured. I think we're all right at the moment. If we can just hold our position until dark, General Hood is shifting Frank Cheatham's entire corps over here."

"Good," said Walthall. "That's real good. I hope they're enough."

Stewart nodded toward the west. "How's Redoubt Number Three holding up?"

"It's not," Walthall began to shake his head. "They've captured Number Three, and it won't be long before they have Number Two. The only thing preventing them from breaking through is French's division on my right."

"Damn," Stewart said. He thought about French. The man had come down with a severe eye infection and had been forced to turn command over to Brigadier General Claudius Sears. *I wouldn't mind having some kind of infection at the moment, Stewart smiled to himself.*

There was screaming and firing back to the south in the direction of Johnson's troops. Walthall and Stewart both instinctively looked that way. The Federals were attacking Johnson's division again. Deep down, Stewart knew that Johnson's men weren't going to stand. They'd already run once.

Walthall looked at Stewart with a look of concern. "If they're where they sound like they are…" He left the rest unsaid. It was obvious the Federal army was deep in the Confederate rear.

"Hold here until you hear from me," Stewart shouted as he spun his horse and rode toward the sound of the firing. Up ahead, he could see Johnson's men running across a muddy cornfield. Men were stumbling along, the mud sucking the shoes right off their feet, but they never slowed down. It would have been comical under different circumstances. They'd abandoned Seldon's Alabama Battery. Stewart could see a private spiking one of the guns that had lost all its horses. The other gun was being pulled to the rear when one of its horses was shot down. The limber crashed into a tree and broke the axle on the gun carriage. Stewart watched as the private ran up and spiked that gun, amid all the rifle fire, before continuing toward the rear. The Federals were soon swarming around the captured guns. They seemed a little disorganized from their attack.

Stewart spun his horse back to the west. He had to get his men out of this trap. He sent a courier to tell Sears to get his division out of there. He sent another to Loring with the same message. He rode to tell Walthall himself.

This was the most perilous position his troops had been in during the entire war. It was beginning to look as though Hood was about to lose an entire corps, if not an entire army.

A courier galloped up and saluted. He said, "Sir, General Loring sends his compliments and…"

"Report, damn it," Stewart shouted at the man. He didn't have time for military protocol at a time like this.

The man spat the report out in haste. "General Loring says that the Federals are advancing in his front, and he's seen Sears's division retreating behind us. Our flank's exposed, and he wants to know what you want him to do."

"I want him to run like hell," Stewart shouted. "I sent a courier to him; you must have just passed him. Tell him to fall back east down the line. The entire Federal army is in our rear less than two hundred yards from this spot."

The man's eyes grew wide, and he spun the horse and rode hard back up the road. He had to avoid the retreating men from Walthall's division racing eastward.

Stewart raced the horse to the northwest to see how things were coming there. He found Redoubt Number Two under attack. He shouted at Major Garrett who commanded the two artillery pieces in the fort. "Major, I want you to hold this position to the last man or until I relieve you. Our left flank is breaking, and I need you to buy me some time."

Garrett looked toward the rear and saw Stewart's infantry racing toward the east. He looked back toward his front and saw three solid lines of infantry moving toward his tiny fort of barely a hundred men. He nodded his head at Stewart. Stewart spun his horse and raced off the hill to try and extricate his men.

Garrett walked back over to his men and said, "We've got to cover the retreat regardless of how bad things get. I want everyone here to remember Franklin. It's time we get a little revenge. Wait until they are in canister range and then let's tear them apart. What we do here will be remembered forever."

Waiting for the Federal infantry to get within range was painstaking. He walked up and down the line and continued to encourage his artillerymen and his infantry supports. He'd never felt as alone in his entire life as he did now.

When the enemy reached seventy-five yards of the fort, he gave the command to open fire. The artillery and infantry opened together. He watched the Federals in his front stall. They returned fire but would advance no farther. He heard his men shouting, "Remember Franklin!"

Garrett watched the second and third lines advance and receive the same fate. Their fire was wild; almost all were sailing over the fort. The more canisters his guns poured at the Federals, the lower they hugged the ground. The men in the fort were well protected behind the parapets. He began to think they may be able to hold this position until dark.

Suddenly, things went to hell. He saw the North Carolina infantry to the right of his guns break for the rear. Looking just past them, he understood why. Federal infantry were pouring over the north wall and into his rear.

Garrett spun to the rear of the fort and peered down the hill. He looked in vain for a courier from General Stewart telling him he could fall back now. There was nobody. *My God, he thought, are my men to be sacrificed here? Has*

259

Stewart forgotten about us? It just didn't make any sense. He could see Federal soldiers moving across the bottom of the hill in his rear. He was practically surrounded. The Federal infantry quickly turned and moved against the back of the fort. The position was no longer tenable. There were Federals inside the north wall of the fort and more behind the fort.

A Federal officer on horseback saw the lone Confederate major standing there, and their eyes met. The officer spurred his horse forward to about ten paces from Garrett. He yelled, "Surrender!"

"I think it's about that time," Garrett replied. He looked over his shoulder at his men back there still attempting to resist. "We're completely surrounded."

"Give me your regimental flag," the Federal officer demanded. It was a great honor to capture a flag and usually meant a promotion.

Garrett said, "We're an artillery unit. We have no flag of any kind."

The Federal officer looked disappointed. He said, "Go to your men and order them to lay down their arms, or I will have every damned one of them shot."

Garrett ran back to the other side of the redoubt and ordered his men to cease fire. Bullets were still flying overhead from the men in front. He turned and ran back to the Federal officer. The man was angry now. His face was red, and he was dodging the fire coming over the fort. He screamed, "Why are your men still firing?"

"They're not my men," Garrett yelled back. "That is fire from your infantry on the other side of the fort."

The Federal officer sent word to the troops on the other side of the redoubt to stop firing. His men moved into the fort and began counting prisoners. Confederate artillery fire from the rear began to rain down on the fort amid the prisoners and Federal troops. Every man dove behind the wall of the fort for cover. Federal and Confederate alike lay there waiting for the artillery fire to end.

Garrett saw a Confederate infantryman climb onto the parapet and yell, "Hurray for Hood! Give 'em hell!"

Garrett looked at the man. The last thing he needed was for some idiot to give these Yankees an excuse to shoot them all. He shouted, "Get down from there, you damned fool!"

The man shouted back. "Those are Confederate shells! They won't hurt us!"

Major Mitchell stood up and swatted at the man. The infantryman saw Garrett's "Major" insignia on his collar and dove back in the ditch. Garrett said, "Now stay there and keep your damned mouth shut."

In the confusion back east of the hill, Stewart had made his way to Mister Prater's house. He looked up at the sky. Night was coming on fast now. He needed to find a place to rally his men. It would be dark soon. Stewart could thank God for that at least. He saw a rider approaching. It was Captain William Gale of his staff.

Gale said, "Sir, we've got to get out of here. The Yankees have almost reached the Granny White Pike in our rear. I was back there when Johnson's division broke and ran. Mary Bradford and a young lady were standing on Misses Bradford's front porch begging the men to stand and fight while bullets filled the air all around those two women. I've never seen anything like it. This army is defeated, sir. The men seem lethargic, just barely putting one foot in front of the other. They don't appear to care whether they're captured or not."

Stewart shook his head as they rode eastward. There was nothing he could say.

Gale said, "Sir, General Sears is down. I saw him get hit. A cannonball went through his horse and mangled his leg just below the knee. It looks awful. The most amazing thing happened when he went down. You know his old roan is named 'Billy,' and the general has ridden him throughout the war. Horse and rider both crashed to the snow-covered ground. He just stood right up on the mangled leg and began crying over his poor horse. He was so distraught; he didn't even realize he'd been hit. I jumped off my horse and helped place him in an ambulance. I'm sure they'll amputate. You know Sears is close to sixty. It won't be easy for him to recover from such a wound. Colonel Shotwell has command of the brigade now. He says he only has about a hundred and fifty men left of the entire brigade. He says the rest are either killed or captured."

"William, this is ugly," Stewart managed to say.

"Sir," Gale looked at Stewart, "do you think General Hood will order a retreat tonight?"

Stewart shook his head. "I have no idea."

"I hope he does," Gale said. "It'll just get uglier tomorrow if we stay."

They rode on to the east and away from the advancing Federal army. Ahead, he saw Major Mitchell of his artillery waiting by the roadside. The man had tears in his eyes. He saluted Stewart and said, "We've lost almost all our guns and over half our men."

Mitchell obviously was expecting Stewart to be upset with him. Stewart reached over and patted Mitchell on the arm. He saw the tears making little streams as they flowed into the man's beard.

Stewart said, "I saw everything. You did all that mortal man could accomplish under the circumstances. I can find absolutely no fault with you, Major. Come on back with me, I can use a man like you on my staff."

A Courier came riding down the road, yelling into the darkness. "Has anyone seen General Stewart?"

"This way," Captain Gale shouted.

The courier rode up and said, "Sir, General Reynolds begs to report that his brigade is still intact. He is fighting the advancing Federals now and will hold them back as long as possible."

"Thank you," Stewart replied. He said to Gale and Mitchell, "At least someone's still fighting."

261

They continued their ride eastward until they'd gone far enough to get around the Federal army in their rear. Stewart received word that Hood had changed his headquarters to Judge Lea's house, called 'Lealand.' The Overton home was beyond the right flank of the army now. Judge Lea's house was directly behind the center of the army. It took them about thirty minutes to get there in the dark. They found a lot of activity going on at the house. Couriers were coming and going. Aides were going in and out of the house with messages. Stewart dismounted from his horse and stood there leaning heavily against the animal. He'd been in the saddle all afternoon. His legs and back were stiff. The night was still warm despite the fact the wind had gotten up.

He squatted to the ground trying to loosen his aching legs. It had been a hard day for Stewart, probably the hardest of the war. As exhausted as he was, he realized he wasn't likely to get any rest tonight. His head was beginning to hurt, and he realized he hadn't had anything to eat since breakfast.

Stewart turned to Gale and said, "Go find us something to eat. I'm going to see what Hood's plans are."

He gathered his last bit of energy and walked toward the door. Inside, he found Hood at a table studying a map. He glanced up, saw Stewart, and said, "It's been a bad day, Straight, a bad day indeed."

"I'll have to agree," Stewart walked over and plopped into a chair opposite Hood.

Hood said, "You look like you're about to fall over. You need to get some rest."

"How can I?" Stewart asked. He held up his hands. "My corps is scattered to hell and back. Those damned Yankees will be coming again in the morning."

"They'll be coming at first light," Hood added. He smiled to himself and said, "I was over on a hill just on the other side of the Granny White Pike. Ector's Texans were falling back. They'd gotten cut off from you and Johnson's division. They were running in the wildest confusion. I told them I wanted them to hold that hill regardless of what transpired around them. I reminded them that they were Texans and must fight like Texans. You should have heard them cheer me. It inspired me to believe that we can still win this battle."

"Sir," Stewart said. His eyes betrayed his disbelief.

"It's alright, Straight," Hood smiled and pointed at the map. "I'm placing your corps in the middle here. Cheatham is crossing to the left as we speak. He'll occupy the position you held today. Lee will anchor the right flank. From the center, your corps will only have to act as reserve. I may call on a few of your men if we have problems with the flanks."

"Right," Stewart said. He didn't really know what to say. He wanted to advise Hood to retreat, but then again, he hadn't risen to the rank of lieutenant general by giving advice to superiors.

Hood caught the sound of disbelief in Stewart's voice. It was as though he were reading Stewart's mind. He said, "We lost those redoubts

262

because they weren't quite finished. Your corps got roughed up today, but if we retreat now, all the fighting thus far in the campaign will have been for nothing. All those brave men and officers lost at Franklin will have been in vain, and I cannot allow that. I realize it's a desperate gamble to remain here, but all warfare is a gamble."

Stewart nodded but said nothing.

Hood thought about what Robert E. Lee had done at Gettysburg. He could have ordered a retreat after the second day, but he didn't. He had ordered a desperate charge against the center of the Federal lines because he understood if he retreated, he would never have the opportunity to win the war by invasion again. He continued calling Stewart by his nickname. "Straight, we'll shorten the lines, make them more compact. This new position is stronger. We have two nice hills to anchor our flanks on and plenty of artillery left. Have the men dig in."

Hood thought about how foolish it was to tell Stewart to have the men dig in. It was something they had learned to do without orders. He noticed Stewart staring at the table as if he were a thousand miles away.

Hood said, "Cheatham and Lee's corps are relatively fresh. We'll let them do all the fighting tomorrow. If there is a disaster tomorrow, I want you to retreat down the Franklin Pike and form a rearguard somewhere south of here."

Stewart couldn't help but wonder why Hood would think Cheatham's corps could do any better tomorrow than his had. They had suffered the same fate his corps did at Franklin. He wondered why S.D. Lee's two fresh divisions were being held away from the action.

Hood turned to Colonel Mason and said, "Have a courier ride to General Forrest and tell him to have his cavalry ready to move here at a moment's notice."

Mason repeated the order and began to write. Hood turned around and began to study the map again. Stewart had enough sense to know that the meeting was concluded.

"If you'll excuse me, sir," Stewart slowly rose from the chair. "I've got to find my men and get them on line for tomorrow."

Hood went on looking at the map. He didn't seem to notice when Stewart left.

Out on the lawn, Mitchell and Gale were waiting. Mitchell seemed to have regained his composure, but Gale seemed a little on edge. Gale asked, "So what's the word?"

"Stay and fight it out," Stewart replied. He walked over and leaned heavily on his horse. He didn't know if he had the energy to handle locating and realigning his troops tonight.

"Damn," Gale tossed his kepi on the ground. Stewart was taken aback. Gale was normally a calm person. He'd never seen him get this upset before. Gale continued his rant. "Ever fool in this army knows what's coming tomorrow. I'm just a captain, but I know the best move is to get back behind

Duck River and link up with Forrest. There's no way this disorganized mass he calls an army will be ready for battle tomorrow."

Stewart watched Gale let it all go with a big sigh. *The man is just as exhausted as I am, he thought. I can't blame a man for that. He'll be all right now that he's gotten that off his chest. He'll work as hard as the next staff officer.* There was one thing that bothered Stewart. It was knowing that Captain Gale was right. Every man in this army knew what would happen tomorrow. The only one in denial seemed to be the army commander.

Stewart looked at Gale and said, "I need your help tonight, Captain. I need you to ride with me to the home of Misses Mullins. It's just back of the position Hood wants our corps to occupy. Let all my commanders know that's my headquarters."

It would be Stewart's headquarters, but he would spend the night in the saddle. He turned and practically had to drag himself onto his horse.

December 15, 10:00 p.m.

USA

George Thomas and his staff had claimed an abandoned farmhouse as their headquarters. His staff was busy receiving messages and figuring out what the dispositions of the various units were.

Thomas was reading one of the messages. He turned to Whipple and said, "Will, send a telegram to Washington. Inform General Halleck that we have attacked the Rebel army. We have captured sixteen cannons, a thousand prisoners and driven Hood back about eight miles. Tell them we intend to finish them up in the morning if they haven't retreated first."

"Very good, sir," Whipple saw Thomas give a rare smile. It was good to see his commander with all the pressure of the past few days off of him.

Thomas didn't feel relieved at the moment. Just now he was elated. Things couldn't have gone any better today, except for the lack of enough light to finish the Rebel army off. Thomas held his hand up, his index finger about an inch from his thumb. "We were *that close*, Will…*that close* to capturing Hood's entire army."

A courier came in, saluted Whipple, and handed him a message. Whipple read the note and broke out in a large grin. "Sir, Andrew Smith reports his corps is embedded in Hood's rear like a fat tick. He says he has more prisoners and cannons than he can count. With your permission, he wants to finish things up at first light. He says he's only engaged one division today and will send in his other two fresh divisions tomorrow."

"By all means," Thomas smiled at Whipple. "Permission granted to finish it at first light."

Whipple sent the courier back with the message. Whipple said to Thomas, "Sir, I almost forgot. I have a message here from Wilson. It's about an hour old. He says he is in Hood's rear and attempting to push forward to the Franklin Pike and cut off Hood's escape route."

Thomas shook his head. He didn't like troops moving around in the dark, but it would have to be all right this time. If he could capture Hood's entire army, the war would be all but won.

A few moments later, General Wood walked in the door. Thomas's headquarters was just behind General Wood's line. Wood was an odd-looking man with a black beard cut with two points side by side. His receding hair was gray. He didn't look near as happy as Thomas and his staff.

Thomas asked, "General Wood, what's the word?"

"Disorganization is the word." Wood was shaking his head. "After we moved forward and had to move around that abatis and through the Rebel works in the growing darkness, my men got all jumbled up. It's gonna cost me valuable time to get them sorted back out. I tried to pursue in the dark, but I was afraid of running into some of Smith's men moving across my front. I hate to lose men to friendly fire. I lost a few that way moving through those works. We didn't know that Loring's division had already pulled out."

"It's all right," Thomas smiled and patted Wood on the back. Normally, Thomas would have been upset, but nothing was gonna ruin his night. "Just do the best you can, we'll get back after them at first light."

"Don't worry, sir. Tomorrow we will whip them and do it easily." Wood saluted and excused himself to go finish reorganizing his units. He passed a courier coming in the door.

The man handed a note to Whipple. Whipple read the message and turned to Thomas. "Sir, General Cox has just reported that he's run into a heavy force on a large hill just west of the Granny White Pike. He says he's ordered his men to rest in line of battle until daylight so he can see what he faces."

"That's fine," Thomas said. He didn't need to tell Cox anything. The man was already doing just what Thomas expected of him.

Thomas had finally called up Schofield's troops this afternoon. He planned to use them for mop-up operations. His troops were fresh, along with two of Smith's divisions. If Hood was still there in the morning, the Federal army would make them pay.

Thomas sat down and began to write a letter to his wife in New York. He told her of the day's success and what he expected the morrow to bring. He hadn't been finished with the letter long, when Wilson arrived.

"Sir," Wilson gave a sloppy salute, "I've had to call a halt because of darkness. I can't tell which way we're going; it's so dark. We may be going in circles."

Thomas looked at the skinny little man. Wilson was obviously exhausted. He motioned toward the chair and watched Wilson plop down. "Rebel prisoners confirm that Forrest is still near Murfreesboro."

Wilson suddenly came alive. He was almost shouting, "No wonder Hood's left was so vulnerable. He sent his cavalry away and helped us win the battle."

"I have only one regret," Thomas stopped smiling.

Wilson looked confused. How could the man possibly regret what they had accomplished today? He asked, "What's that, sir?"

"I regret the fog put us so far behind that we couldn't finish it today. We ran out of light, and tomorrow when we wake, General Hood will be gone." Thomas gave a sly grin. "Still, I can't complain."

Wilson called Thomas by his nickname for the first time since being under his command. "Pap, they're demoralized as hell. There's no fight left in 'em. Now, what are the orders?"

Thomas studied the map a long moment. He said, "We finish it tomorrow if Hood's still here. I'm gonna have Steedman try and envelope the eastern flank. Hood's probably weakened that flank by sending his best men to face you and Smith. General Wood will hold the center. Smith and Scofield will continue to hammer the western flank, and you try and get in his rear and cut off the escape route."

"Right," Wilson stood, and instead of saluting, he extended his hand. Thomas shook Wilson's hand. Wilson said, "It's been an honor serving under you, sir."

"We're not through yet," Thomas reminded him and then gave a rare smile.

After Wilson left, Whipple came over and sat across the table. "You're gonna love this, George."

Thomas gave a quizzical look at Whipple and waited.

"Just got this telegram from Washington," Whipple tried to suppress a smile. "General Grant had gone to Washington and was about to get on a train to come here and relieve you himself. After receiving your telegram, he says he will go no farther."

Thomas shook his head. He'd never understood why Grant disliked him so much. "That was a close call."

"I have another telegram from Secretary of War Stanton," Whipple shuffled through the messages in his hand. "He says to accept his congratulations, and please extend them to your men."

Thomas nodded. These were the same men who had been trying to fire him for the past two weeks.

Whipple shuffled through the telegrams again. "Last but not least is this message from President Lincoln."

Thomas sat up and waited.

"His is not as congratulatory as the others," Whipple read the telegram again. "He just says that you're off to a good start, but don't let the Rebels get away."

"That may be impossible," Thomas shook his head. "I'm sure Hood has ordered a retreat already, and we're stuck until daylight. He'll have a good head start on us in the morning."

Whipple said, "Did you know you were performing in front of a large audience today?"

Thomas's eyes narrowed. "What are you talking about, Will?"

"All the hills around Nashville were covered by civilians watching the battle." Whipple smiled a toothy grin. "Most weren't happy with the results. I think they wanted Hood to drive you across the river."

There was a knock at the door, and one of Thomas's aides let General Schofield in. Schofield saw Thomas and saluted. Whipple rose from the chair and moved away. Thomas motioned for Schofield to sit.

Schofield asked, "What do you expect tomorrow?"

"I expect Hood will be gone when we awaken tomorrow," Thomas was still elated. Now that Schofield had been defeated in his bid to replace Thomas, he felt like rubbing it in his face a little, but he was too much of a gentleman to do that. "We will pursue, but he'll have a big jump on us."

"He'll still be here in the morning," Schofield stated flatly. "I know the man. He is aggressive as hell. I wouldn't be surprised if he didn't assault Steedman in the morning. All this fighting and moving around in the dark has gotten our commands all jumbled up. It'd be just like him to try it."

Thomas shook his head in disagreement. "He's whipped. He may stay and fight, but his army is in no condition to take the offensive. We practically destroyed Stewart's corps today. Cheatham's is badly damaged from Franklin, and that only leaves him with Lee's corps. He's probably already ordered a retreat. I fully expect us to wake in the morning and find him gone."

Schofield could see he wasn't making much headway with Thomas. He asked, "May I offer you my opinion, sir?"

Thomas thought that was what Schofield was already doing. He replied, "You may speak freely."

"I talked to General Wilson earlier," Schofield lowered his head. It irritated him to have to submit to Thomas. "He says he is going in pursuit at daylight. I would recommend you wait until you can at least allow us to develop what we have in our front before you send him off. If he's still there, which I believe he will be, then we can capture and destroy his army. He may be bringing Forrest up tonight, and we don't need to allow Wilson to get very far out of place. I've seen firsthand how well Wilson deals with Forrest."

"Very well," Thomas said. "I'll have Wood assault the center at first light to see if Hood's still there. If he's there, I'll have Wilson continue trying to get behind him."

Schofield stood and saluted Thomas, as bad as it galled him to do so. After he'd left, Thomas thought about what he'd said. Perhaps Hood would still be there in the morning. That's just what Thomas wanted him to do. *If he's still here, Thomas thought, we'll capture his entire army and the war will practically be over.*

267

He turned to Whipple and said, "Send a message to Wood to attack whatever is in his front in the morning. Tell him as soon as he finds out whether the enemy is still here to let me know."

Thomas lay down for some much-needed rest. He'd passed some Confederate prisoners being escorted to the rear earlier today. Many of those poor men were barefoot. Some had rags tied around their feet. As they walked, they left blood in the snow from frostbitten feet. Those men were the enemy, but George Thomas couldn't help but feel sorry for them.

December 16, 7:00 a.m.

USA

George Thomas had been forced to modify his plans during the night. Wood was no longer ordered to advance to the attack. His corps was forced to move east and come on line between Smith's corps and Steedman's division on the left. Smith was no longer on the Rebel western flank but facing the left center. Schofield was on the western flank along with Wilson.

He stepped out the door and onto the porch of the small farmhouse. A courier came galloping up and dismounted. The man said, "Sir, General Steedman sends a report."

"Go on," Thomas said as he stepped off the porch and onto the dew-covered grass.

"Sir," the man jerked a thumb back over his shoulder toward the east, "We have recovered the abandoned battlefield of yesterday. All the dead are stripped of clothing—stripped of everything, actually. There are naked corpses all over that hillside. General Steedman is a little perturbed this morning. Colonel William Shafter of the Seventeenth United States Colored Troops has recovered the body of his brother-in-law Captain Job Aldrich. The poor officer was found lying face down without a stitch of clothing. He'd left all his valuables with the Colonel's wife before the campaign because he had a premonition of death. Anyway, Steedman has interviewed one of his wounded black soldiers who says the Rebels were stripping the clothing off the men, and they were still alive. Some men were begging the Rebels for help while they were being wrestled around and stripped of their clothes."

Thomas said nothing. That's one reason he hadn't wanted to send black troops into combat. The Rebels wouldn't treat these former slaves as soldiers. General Forrest had been accused of massacring captured black troops at Fort Pillow just a few months ago. He told the man to return to General Steedman and have him hurry forward and link up with Wood's left flank.

Thomas mounted his brown mare and rode toward the front to see how things were coming along. His staff trailed behind him. They rode south to

Smith's position. The weather was mild. There was a thin mist that hung to the ground, but it was nowhere near as bad as the fog of yesterday. The sky was dotted with beautiful white clouds. The sun was coming up and already beginning to burn the mist away.

He arrived just in time to watch Smith's corps advancing with battle flags flying, the sun glinting off their bayonets. He could see fresh earthworks on the heights to the south. The Confederate artillery immediately opened on Smith's men. Thomas could see men being knocked around by the exploding projectiles. The Confederate artillery was doing some fine work this morning.

The position appeared to be impregnable from back here. The Confederates had obviously spent the night fortifying their new position. It looked like Franklin in reverse, except this time the Confederates occupied the high ground. The advance didn't last long before Smith's men stopped and started throwing up temporary earthworks well short of Confederate rifle range.

Smith saw General Thomas and his staff watching. He rode back to where the General was sitting on his horse. He said, "I've ordered my men to halt about five hundred yards short of the Confederate works. I don't think I'm strong enough to take that position by direct assault. I'm going to order my artillery forward and attempt to soften them up. Schofield will have to flank them the way I did yesterday. He and Wilson ought to be able to get in their rear while I keep them occupied here."

A courier came riding up from the direction of Schofield and Wilson's troops. He saw General Thomas and rode toward him. He said, "Sir, General Schofield begs to report."

"Report," Thomas said.

"Sir," the man was a little nervous reporting in front of all these officers. He paused to catch his breath and then continued. "General Schofield believes he's about to be attacked by a large portion of Hood's army. He says since no one is putting pressure on the Confederate lines, they are massing against him. I believe the word he used was exposed. Yeah, sir, he feels exposed over there by himself."

Thomas watched the young man smile, happy that he had remembered everything. Thomas was shaking his head. Schofield had been begging for reinforcements all night. Thomas had relented and sent him sixteen hundred men. Now he believes he's facing the entire Confederate army alone. The man's obviously nervous after the close brush he had of being captured by Hood.

Thomas said, "Tell General Schofield to hold his position. Wilson is on his right, so he doesn't have to worry about Hood flanking him, just hold his ground until everyone is ready to go in."

The man saluted and wheeled the horse. Thomas looked at Smith and asked, "What do you think, Andrew?"

"I think the man is one curious bird," Smith shook his head. "When you were laying out plans for the coming battle, he was upset that you weren't allowing his men in the fight. Now that he's in the fight, he's about to panic."

269

Thomas turned in the saddle. "Will, send a courier out to see how Wood and Steedman are progressing on the left."

Thomas and Smith sat there making small talk until the courier could get back and report. They were still waiting, when the messenger from Schofield came riding back up.

The man saluted and said, "Sir, General Schofield begs to report."

Thomas wanted to laugh at the man. He was so nervous; he was going to make sure he got the military protocol right. He said, "You may report, young man."

The man stammered trying to remember the right words. "Sir, uh, the, uh, I mean General Schofield says that Hood is going to turn his right flank and regain all he lost yesterday. He doesn't think Wilson is in place on his left. He says Hood is reckless and will attack against the greatest odds."

Thomas interrupted the man. He asked, "What do you think?"

The man's eyes grew wide. He looked at Thomas a long moment trying to see if he was being played with or not. He couldn't believe a major general was asking a private what he thought. Finally, he said, "Sir, I think General Schofield is going to run my poor horse to death today."

Thomas and Smith both broke into laughter. Smith said, "Pap, I think he did a fine job of avoiding your question."

Thomas continued smiling at the man. He said, "Young man, that was a most excellent answer. I think you'll make a general some day."

The man understood now. They had sensed how nervous he was and had lightened the mood by making a joke of him. He began to smile also. He said, "General Schofield says he needs reinforcements to keep from being turned. A division is what he said he needs to prevent a disaster on this flank."

Thomas nodded his head. He turned to Smith and said, "Andrew, can you send Schofield a good division?"

Smith's face went from smiling to anger instantly. He said, "I'll not send him a damned thing. I've already sent him enough. He's probably facing nothing more than a single infantry brigade. To hell with him."

Thomas didn't overrule his subordinate. He told the courier, "I guess General Schofield will have to hold his ground with what he has."

The man saluted and rode away. The courier Whipple had sent soon returned and notified the generals that neither Wood nor Steedman were in position yet.

Thomas decided to ride back to his headquarters and see if there were any dispatches from Washington while they waited. He waited back there until nearly noon. There was still no sound of battle, so he decided to ride back to the front and see what the holdup was.

The sky had become overcast. Ominous gray clouds hung low in the sky. While he was riding back to the front, it began to mist. By the time he got to Smith's position, it had begun to rain. The temperature began to plummet. *Just what I need, he thought, a cold front moving in. He hoped it wouldn't drop below freezing again.*

270

Smith saw Thomas and rode over to meet him. He said, "Schofield has sent that damned courier back here again demanding reinforcements."

Thomas shook his head. He could tell by the look on Smith's face that he hadn't given him any men. As they talked, the rain began to fall in sheets. It was a cold, miserable rain.

Thomas said, "I'm going to ride over and see what Wilson thinks."

He swung wide around Schofield's position. He didn't feel like talking to the man at the moment. He found Wilson behind his lines sitting on a stump with his legs crossed.

Wilson saw Thomas and jumped up. He began shouting before Thomas could dismount. "Sir, I was planning to advance at first light as ordered, but I received word to hold up for Schofield. The man has been in position all night and still he says we're not to move forward. He became upset with me earlier because I sent a reconnaissance force out."

Thomas cut him off. "What did they find?"

Wilson stopped his rant and shook his head. "They went almost all the way to the Granny White Pike and took a handful of prisoners. Cheatham's corps is who I have in my front. I had to pull back my right flank because I got Rebel cavalry over there, and Schofield has me thinking we're about to be turned. Sir, this area over here in these woods is not suitable for cavalry operations. If I can't advance, I request to be moved around to the other flank where we can get in Hood's rear."

Thomas shook his head. "We've wasted far too much time now."

There was a commotion behind Thomas. He and Wilson turned in time to see Schofield and most of his staff riding up. Schofield quickly dismounted. He said to Wilson, "You better stay put, we're about to be attacked by half the Rebel army."

He looked over at Thomas and thought a moment. "...unless General Thomas has other orders for you. You could have caused a disaster when you sent that force forward earlier."

Thomas's face betrayed his frustration. He had planned to assault at first light, and now it's almost two in the afternoon, and nothing seems to be getting done. He looked at Wilson and asked, "James, do you believe you're about to be attacked?"

Wilson looked from Thomas to Schofield. He was aggravated at Schofield at the moment, but he wasn't sure if they were about to be attacked or not. Hood had definitely shifted troops this way, but Wilson wasn't sure for what purpose. He said, "Sir, if I can advance, I can tell you what Hood has up his sleeve. I can't just sit back here inactive and give you a fair answer. If I can't advance from here, I request to be allowed to move to the other flank where I can."

Thomas lowered his head in thought. He was growing extremely irritated that nothing could be done. He said, "Let me ride over and see if Wood and Steedman have gotten into position yet. When they're ready, I will give the order, and we'll all go in at once."

271

He mounted his horse and rode back to the north. It took him about thirty minutes to ride around the army to Wood's position. General Wood seemed happy to see Thomas. He had been given command of Stanley's corps when he'd gotten wounded at Franklin. He wanted the assignment so he could prove himself. The man desperately wanted another star on his shoulder.

Thomas asked, "Is Steedman up yet?"

"No, sir," Wood replied. He looked toward the trees on his left flank as if he were trying to see through them.

Thomas shook his head. "Well, what in hell is taking him so long?"

"Not sure," Wood rubbed his hand through his wet hair. His beard was gray, but his hair was still black. "I think he's being extremely cautious."

Thomas took out his field glasses and studied the hill in Wood's front. He said, "We need to do something soon. What's the name of that hill?"

"Peach Orchard Hill is what my map shows," Wood pulled his glasses out and began to study the hill also. He'd been studying it for the past hour. "Sir, that's the eastern flank of Hood's army."

Thomas could see fresh earthworks on the side of the hill. They ran around the hill as far as he could see to the east. There were a large amount of Confederate battle flags behind those works, which told him the Rebels were in a compact line. It would be a formidable position to assault head on. He looked at the approach. Wood's men would have to cross a muddy cornfield and negotiate uphill through trees the Confederates had chopped down to slow their advance.

Thomas was still looking through his field glasses when he said, "The plan's the same. I want Steedman to turn that hill, and I need you to keep pressure on those troops in your front so they can't shift to meet him. When Steedman gets up, I want you two to work together and organize an attack. Tell Steedman to be sure he doesn't allow the Confederates to turn his flank."

"Right," Wood said. He was feeling better about all this now. To him, it sounded like Thomas had just given him permission to attack. He said, "Sir, with your permission, I would like to send one of my brigade commanders forward to see if he thinks he can take that hill without Steedman. If we can take that hill, I can get my corps behind Hood's army and capture most of it."

Thomas nodded. He was glad someone was thinking of attacking.

Wood told a staff officer to go bring forward Colonel Sidney Post. While they waited, Wood said, "Post is my most aggressive brigade commander. If that hill can be taken, he's the man that can take it."

Thomas wanted action, but he was worried about Wood going in alone. He sent another courier to find Steedman. Wood saw Colonel Post riding up and went to meet him. Thomas watched them talk a few moments. Post took out his field glasses and began to study the hill in his front. He then rode forward alone.

Wood rode back over and said, "He's gonna ride forward and look the situation over."

The courier was soon back. He said, "Sir, Steedman says he is moving up cautiously. He has no cavalry to his left and doesn't want to advance into a trap. He'll be on the field momentarily."

Thomas nodded but said nothing. He was growing more frustrated by the minute.

Post wasn't gone but ten minutes before he returned. He saluted Thomas and Wood and said, "The position is very formidable, but I will attempt to take it if ordered."

Thomas asked, "Do you think you can take it, Colonel?"

"Yes, sir, I do," Post smiled, his drooping mustache rising at the ends.

Wood said, "With your permission, General Thomas, I will send Colonel Post's brigade in with Colonel Abel Streight in support."

Thomas nodded. He said, "Go ahead then; something must be done. If Steedman gets here before dark, tell him to flank that damned hill. I want you to advance with caution. If you can't take the position, don't waste a lot of good men hitting their damned breastworks. I still want the main attack to come from the other flank, unless you and Steedman find an opening over here."

"I'll see to it," Wood saluted.

Thomas turned his horse and rode back to Smith's position. On the way back, he rode through an area being pummeled by Confederate artillery fire. He saw an old man sitting on his front porch smoking a pipe. Stray shells were passing overhead, and a few actually landed fairly close to his home. There were four children playing in the front yard as if it were just a normal day. Thomas shook his head and continued riding.

When he got there, he rode off to a vacant spot and dismounted. His staff recognized his mood and gave him plenty of room. He sat on a log, placed his elbows on his knees, removed his gauntlets, and began rubbing his beard. He was thoroughly aggravated about the day's events. He'd gone from complete elation last night to despair today. It seemed nothing could be done. He'd given orders for everyone to attack this morning as soon as possible, and now it was getting over into the afternoon and nothing had been done. Smith says the position in his front is too formidable to attack. Wood faces the same situation and believes he can successfully take the position. Steedman has got a case of "the slows" this morning. Wilson is fretting to get into action, but Schofield appears to be panicked.

There wasn't much happening besides a stray shell here and there. A carriage came riding up in the field just back of the Federal line. There was a colored man driving. Thomas wondered who was inside. He watched the door open and Tennessee Governor Andrew Johnson stuck his head out of the carriage and peered around. The large head bobbed from side to side. His red face had the same glum expression he always wore. Wrinkles furrowed his brow from years of hard drinking. The man was clean shaven in a day when few men were clean shaven. His eyes were bloodshot, which told Thomas all

273

he needed to know about the man's condition this morning. Thomas wondered where the man had found the horses after Wilson had confiscated the others.

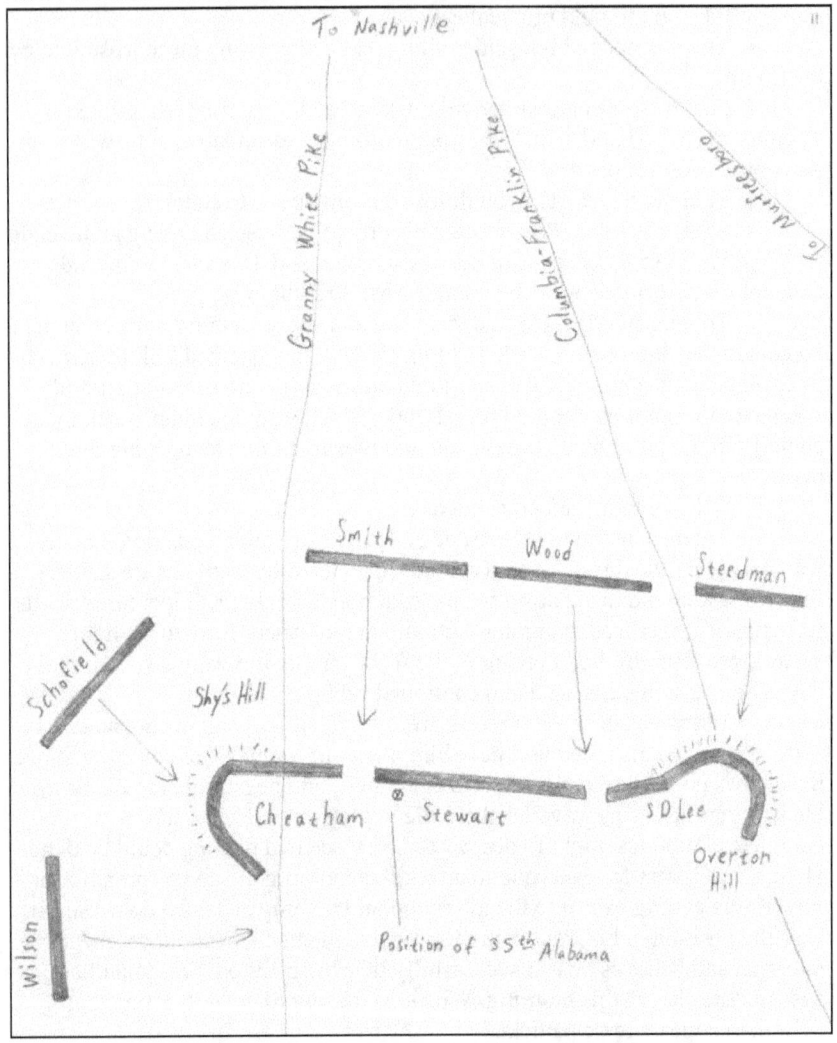

The second day at Nashville. Cheatham's corps is overran on Shy's Hill. The army collapses in full retreat.

Johnson was about to step from the carriage, when a shell exploded overhead. The governor jumped back into the buggy and slammed the door. He yelled at the driver, "Take me back to the capital!"

274

Thomas watched the frightened driver jerk at the horse's reins. He was disgusted with politicians. They never seem to mind asking someone else to die for their beliefs, but they're not about to place themselves in any danger.

A courier came riding up from the east. The man dismounted and said, "Sir, General Wood says General Steedman is arriving on the field at the moment, so he has delayed attacking so they can both go in together."

"Very good," Thomas quietly breathed a sigh of relief. He'd been worried about Wood sending in two brigades against the massed infantry on Peach Orchard Hill. They were not only fortified, but they were facing S.D. Lee's corps. They would be assaulting the freshest troops in Hood's army, the only troops that missed Franklin.

Another courier came riding up, just passing the one who was leaving. It was the same man who had reported for General Steedman this morning. Thomas motioned for the man to report.

The man said, "Sir, General Steedman says an assault on Peach Orchard Hill will be desperate. He says it looks like a large fortified island in the middle of a muddy cornfield."

Thomas shook his head. Now it sounded like Steedman was losing his nerve. He asked, "What does he intend to do?"

"He intends to attack with General Wood's corps," the man replied without hesitation.

Thomas smiled. That's the James Steedman I know, he thought. He said, "Very good."

At that instant, Steedman and Wood's artillery opened fire. Thomas looked that way. They were attempting to soften up the Confederate position. From where Thomas was, he could see the shells bursting in the air over Peach Orchard Hill. He wondered why the Confederate artillery wasn't returning the fire. The smoke from his cannons seemed to envelope the hill in a cloud of smoke. The artillery fire appeared to be hitting the Confederate position. He actually found it quite entertaining watching the spectacle. If he didn't know better, he would think it impossible for anyone to live on that hill.

Soon the firing stopped. Thomas couldn't see from where he was, but he knew that Wood and Steedman were sending their infantry forward at this very moment. He looked at his watch; it was nearly three o'clock. There were about two hours of daylight left.

The hill erupted again. Thomas looked up. This time it was Confederate artillery opening fire. Thomas shook his head. They were withholding their fire waiting for the infantry to advance. He would have to give S.D. Lee credit for that move. It was brilliant.

275

December 16, 3:05 p.m.

CSA

Major General Henry Clayton stood behind his lines on top of Peach Orchard Hill. The Alabamian's short brown hair was receding on top, and his well-trimmed beard and mustache had already turned gray even though he was only thirty-seven years old. He was an attorney before the war. It was moments like these that made him wonder how he'd gotten this far. He'd seen some of the most desperate fighting that had occurred during this war. Like almost all the other commanders here, he'd been wounded and had horses killed from beneath him. He'd lost three horses in one battle alone. Most men promoted to major general have some prior military experience, but that wasn't the case with Henry Clayton.

He'd been promoted because of his cool thinking under pressure. That same cool thinking is what had made him such a success as an attorney. He was also brave to a fault, which surprisingly, hadn't gotten him killed yet. He was a determined man, and that was something that had carried over to his troops. Today, he was determined to hold this hill against the mass of troops moving to assault his front.

The sky had been overcast and then the rain had begun. Normally, Clayton would have felt a bit depressed on a dreary day like this, but not today. However, it was a day of anxiety for the general. The left flank had buckled yesterday, and he'd been expecting the same thing to happen again to day. Now he realized they were coming for this flank.

Clayton propped himself behind a pine tree and surveyed the situation. There didn't appear to be enough troops down there to break his line, but you just never knew.

He watched the Federal soldiers struggle through the muddy field to reach the hill. He could tell that soldiers' shoes were being sucked from their feet down there. *This is going to be beautiful, he thought.* He looked down the line and studied his position. His old Alabama brigade under General Holtzclaw and Gibson's Louisianans held the stone wall to his left, while Stovall's Georgia brigade held the right side of Peach Orchard Hill. They were well entrenched with plenty of artillery. He wished the damned Yankees would advance.

He could see that the troops assaulting Stovall were black troops. Artillery fire was knocking men out of the ranks down there. Still, they closed up and continued their struggle across that sea of mud.

Soon, he saw the brigade of white troops moving toward his front merge with the regiment of black troops coming from the east. The command became jumbled, and confusion set in, as officers tried to sort them out under the punishing artillery fire. Clayton couldn't ask for things to get much better.

Soon, the officers managed to get both units moving forward as one large mass. Clayton didn't have to give the order for his artillery to go to canister fire against the large mob of men. Thousands of tiny balls erupted from the mouth of the cannons. For a moment, Clayton was sure he could hear bones crunching down among the Federal troops above the din of fire.

It was moments like these that Clayton understood what General Robert E. Lee had meant by the words he'd spoken at Fredericksburg. He repeated the words quietly to himself. "It is well that war is so terrible or we would grow too fond of it."

The mob of soldiers worked their way over a rail fence at the bottom of the hill and pressed onward. They worked their way over the fallen trees and rushed for the abatis in his front. He saw them falling by the hundreds with nowhere to go. Bodies hung from the branches of the abatis just like he'd seen at Franklin. The only difference was these bodies were wearing blue. Several of the men could stand the fire no more and broke and ran for the rear.

The ones that remained pulled desperately at the abatis, hoping to throw the treetops aside. Clayton smiled to himself as he watched their futile attempts. He'd thought of this ahead of time and had ordered his men to stake the abatis to the ground. There was no way they could remove that barrier. They soon figured out there was no way to get through and just threw themselves on the ground or scrambled for what little cover there was left there.

They can bring their entire army up here, Clayton thought. As long as I have ammunition, they're not taking this hill. I'll kill them all first.

A hand touched Clayton's shoulder from behind. He spun around and saw a captain saluting. Infantry was coming up the hill behind him.

The man identified himself as Captain Broughton, commander of Granbury's old Texas brigade. He said he had Lowrey's Mississippi brigade with him also. General Hood had thought Clayton was in danger of being flanked and sent reinforcements.

I'm not about to waste the extra firepower, he thought. I need all the lead in the air I can possibly get. Clayton said, "My men are spread pretty thin here, but we're still giving them hell. Captain, place your two brigades in the works alongside my men, and kill every son-of-a-bitch that comes within rifle range."

The captain saluted and turned to order his men forward. *Let the killing continue, Clayton thought. We'll punish the bastards for this mistake. He wondered who'd been foolish enough to send troops against an entrenched foe on high ground.*

The two brigades of Cleburne's old division had just gotten into the works, when a mounted Federal officer was regrouping his men for another charge up the hill. As they surged forward, the fresh troops opened fire alongside Clayton's men. The brave officer on horseback was leading the assault. At that moment, a blast of canister exploded from a cannon near Clayton. He saw horse and rider both go down. The horse never moved again,

277

but the officer had evidently been struck in the leg. He was attempting to crawl toward the rear.

There was another brigade to the left of this one that had stopped about halfway across the field and opened a long range musket fire toward Holtzclaw's Alabama brigade. The black troops to his right had fallen back before the horrific fire.

Clayton had seen many battlefields. He did some quick calculations in his mind and figured there were over a thousand casualties in his front. He walked down the hill to check on General Holtzclaw. General Holtzclaw was behind his lines watching the troops in his front falling back.

He turned and saw Clayton approaching. He said, "In this entire war, I've never seen dead men lay so thick."

Clayton smiled at the heavyset officer. He rubbed his rain-soaked black hair backwards. The thick, drooping mustache covered his lips. Holtzclaw's eyes were set farther apart than normal, and he had a conspicuous double chin. He too had been a lawyer before the war and had risen from major to brigadier general on merit alone.

Clayton said, "It's not over yet, James."

Holtzclaw spun around and saw what Clayton was talking about. There was a lone regiment of black troops moving from east to west. It appeared they were moving directly toward Holtzclaw's position.

Clayton looked at Holtzclaw. The man was standing there with his mouth gaped open in awe. He looked at Clayton and said, "This won't take long."

They were the only enemy in front of Clayton's division at the moment, and all his men concentrated their fire on these six hundred men. A few began to break from the severe fire they were receiving, but most kept moving. It looked like a suicide mission to Clayton. He wondered who was allowing this mistake to occur.

They struck the breastworks to the right of Holtzclaw's position. Every gun on the hill was aimed at this small group of men. They burst forth with a yell and attempted to charge through the abatis. Men were caught in the branches. A color sergeant stood just in front of the treetops defiantly waving the colors at the Rebel line. Clayton watched the man get riddled with bullets and collapse. Another member of the color guard grabbed the colors and raised them back in the air. He was immediately hit.

Those poor men were shot down without a chance to fight back. Mounted white officers rode in front of their men encouraging them to fight. Most were shot down along with their horses. He was impressed as five men picked up the Federal colors, only to be shot down.

The regiment had suffered about fifty percent casualties. They'd taken all they could endure. It seemed to happen all at once. The entire mob turned and raced for the rear.

Holtzclaw turned to Clayton and said, "They came only to die."

"You'd better look to your men," Clayton shouted back.

Holtzclaw spun and saw his junior officers about to order a charge against the retreating Federal troops. Their blood was up, and they wanted to finish what had been started here.

Holtzclaw raced down his line, shouting, "Hold up! Cancel that order! We go charging across that field, and we'll get the same treatment we just gave them!"

A young lieutenant came back from beyond the lines with the captured battle flag that so many men had died trying to carry forward. He presented the flag to Holtzclaw, who thanked him and carried it over to General Clayton.

The front of the banner was stained with the blood of those brave men. Together they read the words sewn on the front of the banner. "Thirteenth Regiment U.S. Colored Infantry, presented by the colored ladies of Murfreesboro."

Holtzclaw handed the banner to Clayton and said, "Got to give them credit; they fought like veterans. Those were some very brave men."

Clayton nodded his head in agreement. "Stupid charge, but brave men."

3:30 p.m.

USA

George Thomas was still sitting on the log watching the smoke covering Peach Orchard Hill. The firing had just died down. He was pretty sure he knew what the result was over there without receiving a report.

Across the field, he saw a courier approaching as fast as possible, his horse struggling through the muddy field. The man rode up and identified himself as coming from General Wood.

Thomas said nothing and waited.

The man said, "Sir, we failed to take the heights. Streight's brigade didn't even reach the other side of the field. Post's brigade took a pounding. Colonel Post himself is down, probably gonna lose a leg. Steedman's black troops have been repulsed with heavy losses also. It was, uh, ugly, sir."

Thomas lowered his head for a moment. He'd asked them to turn the position with caution. Instead, they had advanced recklessly and made a frontal assault against an entrenched foe. The troops on his right can't seem to do anything. He began to shake his head.

Whipple walked over to Thomas and said, "Sir, I just got word from Wilson. He's moving around the flank of that large hill over there. He says the going is rough. There are rolling hills with thickets and forest. It's not an ideal area for cavalry operations. He says all his cavalry are fighting dismounted and

279

attacking a small knoll in Hood's rear near the Granny White Pike. The knoll is defended by Confederate cavalry under James Chalmers."

Thomas stood up. It was about time someone did something. He had gained renewed respect for the cocky young cavalryman General Grant had sent him. He asked, "Is that all?"

"No, sir," Whipple smiled. "He attacked Chalmers's entire brigade of cavalry with only a regiment. It appears the Seventh Illinois Cavalry is armed with Spencer repeating rifles. They took the knoll, but just after that, a Confederate infantry brigade came back and retook it. They almost destroyed the Seventh. After that, he brought up some artillery and drove the Confederate infantry off the hill. He says that he now has possession of the Granny White Pike in Hood's rear. He thinks it's time for the infantry to do their job."

"It is indeed," Thomas replied. He slapped his thigh with his glove. "Send orders to Smith and Schofield. Tell them to attack at once."

4:00 p.m.

CSA

Brigadier General Thomas Benton Smith was young, just twenty-six years old. He was a striking man, tall and attractive to the ladies. He thought about Tod Carter, his assistant quartermaster who'd been killed back at Franklin. Tod had always kidded him about sharing a few ladies with him.

Like General Gordon, who'd been captured at Franklin, Smith had graduated from the Nashville Military Institute. He'd become a railroad conductor after graduation. People just didn't seem to understand that he liked to ride trains.

The rain was coming down in torrents now. Like his men, he was cold, tired, and hungry. They'd gotten little sleep last night. At the moment, Smith was frustrated over his position. They'd been placed here in the dark on the crest of this hill. Instead of being on the military crest, they were on the actual crest itself. What all this meant was, when the Federals advanced, they couldn't fire on them until they came over the ledge just twenty yards in front of his position. This situation made his line extremely weak.

He had cannons, but they couldn't depress their muzzles to fire on the advancing Yankees until they were on top of them. It wasn't his fault either, but that wasn't any consolation to him at the moment. Ector's Texans had occupied the position in the dark last evening. They hadn't even bothered to throw up breastworks or place abatis in front of the lines. His brigade had been brought up here later in the night, and they'd had to dig all night to be prepared. By the time it had gotten to be daylight, he realized the fragility of his situation, but by then it was too late. Bate had instructed him to throw up breastworks. He had told Smith that the entire position of the army may rest on his brigade on top of this hill.

The ground had been frozen last night and made the digging difficult. To add to the problem, he had very few picks and shovels. Most of his men were forced to dig with their bayonets. Others would sneak out into the dark and gather branches and logs. They threw anything that would stop a bullet into their breastworks. Rocks were piled up and covered over with dirt. All night long he had listened to the enemy voices in the cool night air near the base of the hill. He could see their fires through the trees.

His adjutant, Captain Jones, and James Cooper, one of his aides, walked up. Cooper said, "Sir, a six-foot man could get within twenty feet of our works, and we wouldn't know it."

Captain Jones added, "This is the poorest position we've ever been placed in."

"I agree," Smith replied, "but it's too late to change our dispositions now, gentlemen."

"That's not all the good news, sir," Cooper jerked a thumb over his shoulder toward the rear. "Cheatham has ordered off Ector's brigade. That's the only reserves we have, and we keep stretching the line left. We ain't much more than a skirmish line now."

Smith shook his head, making no reply.

Cooper added. "I'm sure, when darkness gets here, we'll be ordered to retreat. By the sound in our rear, we may already be surrounded."

He looked to his right and noticed how thin Finley's Florida brigade had become. Ector's Texas brigade had been pulled out of line about an hour ago to go face Wilson's cavalry on some knoll in their rear. He and Strahl's old brigade had been forced to extend their already thin lines to cover the gap Ector's men left behind. He thought about poor old Otho Strahl. He was a good man. He'll be severely missed. Strahl's brigade and Smith's were all Tennesseans fighting for their homes.

By the sound of the firing behind him, he wondered if his brigade would see any fighting at all. It was becoming unnerving. The Federal cavalry was definitely getting in their rear, and he began to wonder if they wouldn't be forced to surrender without a fight. The firing in rear of their position soon stopped. He wished he knew what was happening.

Suddenly, Thomas Smith's world erupted in flame and smoke. Federal batteries to the west and north of the hill all opened fire at once. It felt as though they were concentrating their fire on Smith's one brigade. It probably felt that way to everyone on the hill. With that much artillery being poured on this hill, it could only mean one thing—an infantry assault was coming.

He watched James Cooper sit down behind a tree for shelter. Within a minute's time, six cannonballs had struck the tree and ricocheted away at an angle. Cooper didn't seem to notice. Smith walked over and bent close to his aide's ear. "I think they're aiming at you, James. You better find another tree."

Cooper looked around. His face betrayed a look of concern. He jumped up and dashed to another tree a few yards away. Smith couldn't help but smile. He turned and walked back toward his line. The rain was still falling, and the ground was slippery with mud.

There was a light tap on his shoulder. Smith turned and saw General Bate standing behind him. Bate scratched at his long, black beard. He said, "I've been complaining to Cheatham all morning about the position. I knew something was coming sooner or later, and all the while, he's been pulling troops out of line and sending them elsewhere. The man just won't listen. He keeps repeating the same statement. He says he can't overrule General Hood."

Thomas Smith shook his head. "We're about to be up to our necks in Yankees, and there's not a thing we can do about it."

Bate limped forward to Smith's line of troops and attempted to peer over the crest of the hill beyond. He'd been hit in the leg at Shiloh, and it had been a miracle it hadn't required amputation. It was painfully obvious now that the limp would remain for the rest of his life. Smith walked up beside him. Down beyond the hill, they could see two heavy lines of infantry moving forward with a line of skirmishers out front. Their skirmish line appeared to contain more men than Bate had in the works on the hill. Bate spoke aloud to himself. "Things are about to get ugly."

He limped back up the hill with Smith. He motioned for one of his staff officers. The man walked forward, and Bate said, "Send a courier to Cheatham. Tell him they're coming now, and we must have reinforcements if he wants this hill held."

Bate turned to Smith and said, "Did you notice the skirmishers are carrying repeating rifles?"

"Didn't pay that much attention," Smith replied. He was pulling at the small tuft of hair below his bottom lip. The hair on his top lip wasn't much more than peach fuzz.

The artillery fire suddenly stopped. Bate had a quizzical look on his face. He limped forward and stared into the trees beyond the line. He felt like he was watching himself being led to the gallows. The line crossed the field and into the timber near the base of the hill. Bate then lost sight of them because they had dropped below the curvature of the hill.

The staff officer had returned with a message from Cheatham. He said, "Sir, General Cheatham says if you think you're in danger of being turned, you should extend your line to the left. He has no troops to spare."

"Damn," Bate said to no one in particular. He looked at Smith again. "Do you believe that arrogant bastard? We're stretched to the breaking point now. Hell, he won't even come up here to share our fate."

Smith said nothing. He didn't have time for small talk at the moment. He began to move down his line. He shouted, "Gentlemen, take good aim, and make every shot count!"

He called for Captain Jones and James Cooper. Both men came running up to him. Smith said, "Jones, I want you to go to the right flank and hold things together."

Jones saluted and turned that way. Smith patted his friend and aide Cooper on the shoulder. "James, you go to the left and take care of yourself."

"Right," James Cooper saluted. He began to hurry away but looked over his shoulder and said, "I'll be praying for nightfall."

Smith soon came to the position occupied by Colonel William Shy's regiment. He said, "Bill, things are gonna get desperate when they come over that rise."

Shy simply nodded in reply. He was a quiet man, modest to a fault, but he always took good care of his men. Smith didn't think he'd ever seen a cooler man in combat than William Shy. He smiled at the thought of Shy's parents. His father was a Union sympathizer, while his mother was a Confederate through and through. Smith looked at Shy. They were both the same age. Shy always combed his hair back but wore a small mustache and goatee similar to Smith's.

The man looked resolute standing there waiting for the inevitable. He had the squarest chin Smith had ever seen on a man.

The enemy was long gone from view. Smith knew they were climbing the hill, coming for them. He hoped they would be winded when they reached the top. He shouted to his men. "Hold your fire until they come over that ridge, and pour it into their very faces!"

It took them longer than he had thought to climb the steep hill. They burst over the crest in a rush. Smith's men unleashed a deadly volley at point-blank range. Many were shot down, but there were just too many of them. They were soon coming over the parapet, and the fighting became hand to hand. Smith saw a Federal colonel shot down on top of the works. A Federal flag bearer was standing on the works waving his banner frantically. The man seemed oblivious to all the chaos happening around him.

It didn't take long for Smith to realize he was being hit head-on by a Federal brigade at full strength. The scene around him was pure bedlam. Men were firing in all directions, swinging muskets like clubs and bayoneting each other. Men looked to Thomas Smith to see what they should do next. He shouted, "Keep firing!"

We may all be killed, he thought, but we'll do our duty. Smith looked to his right and saw Federal troops overrunning the hill to the north. Bullets seemed to be striking his men from all directions now. He saw Finley's Florida brigade break and race for the rear before they were even assaulted. Smith spun around and noticed they weren't the only ones breaking. It seemed the entire division had melted away.

General Bate rode just behind General Smith at this moment. He shouted, "Thomas, if it's possible, get your men out of here."

Smith saw him ride on toward the rear. He turned around and noticed all the Federal soldiers pouring over the wall and around his right flank. There was no way he could extricate them from this mess.

He looked to his right and saw Colonel William Shy and his gallant regiment. The young man was bending over to pick up a dropped musket, when a Federal soldier stuck the barrel of his rifle almost against the top of his head. The bullet entered the hairline just above the right eye and exploded from his skull just behind the left ear. The man was standing so close that powder burns were visible around the entrance wound.

Just as suddenly as it had all began, it was over. Smith gave the order for his men to throw down their weapons. Further fighting would just result in more casualties with the same outcome. The only reason they were still alive now was because there were Federal troops on all sides of them. The Yankees had stopped firing, for fear of hitting their own men.

All his men had thrown down their weapons and raised their hands in the air. Some of the Federals weren't quite finished fighting just yet. Smith saw the flag bearer who had been standing on the parapet bravely waving his flag strike a surrendering soldier over the head with the flag staff. The banner was bulky, and the man couldn't get enough force behind his swing to do any good. Another Federal soldier walked over with his rifle and said, "Let me show you how to do that."

He swung the musket high in the air and struck the man on top of the head. The man fell to the ground. Surprisingly, he slowly got back to his feet and stared at the man with the rifle with defiance in his eyes.

Thomas Smith shouted, "Enough! I demand you treat my men as prisoners, or let us pick our muskets back up and fight to the death!"

Federal Colonel William McMillan walked out into the crowd of prisoners. He walked up to General Smith and said, "Give me your damned sword, you Rebel son-of-a-bitch!"

Smith stood looking at the man for a long moment. He could smell whiskey on the man's breath. *A man in this condition could be dangerous, he thought. He wondered what he should do next.*

McMillan shouted, "Are you deaf or just plain ignorant?"

Smith realized the man was putting on a show for his troops. He looked around and noticed his men watching him. They too were wondering what he'd do. He reached down and slowly pulled the sword from its scabbard. Holding the sword flat in both hands, he held it out to the intoxicated enemy colonel.

McMillan took the sword with his left hand, and at the same time brought his own sword over his head with his right hand. The swing was a frantic one and not well aimed. It struck Smith on the head at an odd angle. The blow knocked the Confederate general backwards. As soon as he regained his balance, McMillan swung again. This time, his aim was more deliberate and struck in almost the same spot. Had the blade been sharp, it would have cut Smith's head in two.

284

General Smith went to his knees. McMillan quickly swung again, and this time, Smith fell facedown on the ground. After a few long moments, the brave Confederate General slowly rose to his feet. Everyone present was amazed the man was still alive. He looked at McMillan and said, "I'm an unarmed prisoner and demand to be treated as such."

McMillan raised the sword over his head again, but this time, several Federal officers intervened. Some grabbed at the sword, while others pushed Thomas Smith out of range. One Federal officer said, "This is a brave officer, who stood here and suffered the same fate as his men. He deserves to be treated with respect."

Smith stood there defiantly looking at the drunken Federal. Blood ran off his forehead, through his right eye and dripped off his chin.

McMillan realized he was losing the respect of his men by his actions. He turned in his drunken stupor and pointed at several Confederate prisoners. He shouted, "Follow me, you sons-of-bitches!"

The prisoners just stood there eyeing the drunken enemy officer. McMillan began to grow frustrated. It seemed every eye on that hill was watching him make a fool of himself. He spun and yelled at his own men. "Will you let these Rebel bastards and their general live while your own colonel lies over there on the breastworks dying?"

No one spoke a word. McMillan feared his men had lost all respect for him. He wondered what he would do if he could get none of them to obey another order. He lowered his head in thought. At the moment, he really wished everyone would stop staring at him. He raised his head and shouted again, "Are you listening to me?"

Again, no one said a word. No one in his entire command made a move to do his bidding. These men had fought hard and surrendered. The killing was over. It was one thing to kill a man in combat, but to kill an unarmed prisoner was beyond human decency. There wasn't even one crackpot in the entire outfit who would raise his weapon and kill one of these brave men.

McMillan turned to a captain and said, "You and your company escort these prisoners to the rear, damn it."

The officer saluted and ordered his men to secure all the prisoners on the hill. There were almost sixteen hundred men who needed to be escorted to Nashville. As they got them in line, the captain gave the order to move off the bloody hill. McMillan gave the captain another order with sarcastic emphasis. "Captain, if one of these damned Rebs falls behind, I want you to shoot him down like a mangy dog."

The captain ignored the man but gave the order for the group to move out. Several Confederate prisoners helped Thomas Smith down the hill and toward the Federal rear. Over half the brigade were casualties. As they moved toward Nashville, black women and children lined the sides of the streets shouting all manners of vituperations at the prisoners. One Confederate soldier replied, "Them Yanks won't always be here, you know."

285

They soon found a Federal field hospital and took Smith to one of the surgeons there. Smith practically collapsed on the ground. The surgeon inspected the wound. The skull had been fractured, and brain matter was visible in the grooves the sword had cut.

The surgeon said, "There is no way this man can possibly live. All we can do is make him as comfortable as possible and wait for the inevitable."

4:15 p.m.

CSA

It had been a dark, cold, miserable day for Mack Keenum and the rest of the boys of Company B. There had been occasional rain showers all day long. Their command was part of Stewart's corps, which occupied the center of the Confederate army. The Thirty-Fifth Alabama was under Colonel Snodgrass's command, which was just east of the large hill anchoring Hood's western flank. They were lucky. Their position contained a nice stone wall which ran east to west with their line.

Everyone wanted to know what was happening. The men asked each other if they would stay and fight or retreat. Of course, no one knew, and each answer was pure speculation.

Keenum sat down and rolled up his pant leg and inspected his knee. The skin around the wound was black from all the strain he placed on it yesterday. Sergeant Downs saw Mack's knee and asked, "You gone be all right?"

"I can fight as well as I ever could," Mack rolled the pant leg back down. "My knee's stiff from the cold. If we retreat, I'm gonna be in big trouble. You'd better let me get a head start."

Dan Downs reached over and patted Mack on the shoulder. "I heard Colonel Snodgrass say we are gonna stay right here and fight it out."

Mack Keenum turned to Tom Barrett and said, "I'm out of water. Want to walk back to the little stream and get some more?"

Barrett jumped to his feet. He was always ready to do something. The man got bored sitting around. They made their way back along the tree line toward the little stream where they'd gotten water last night. At the stream, they found a dead Confederate soldier with his head and arm in the water. He'd crawled there sometime yesterday and died. It had been so dark last night that they hadn't seen the body.

Tom turned and tried not to vomit. Mack just stared at the man. He wanted to believe the body hadn't been there last night. He said, "Come on, Tom, let's go upstream a little ways and get water."

Just after noon was when the artillery fire started. It had been nerve-wracking, because they had to sit and endure it without being able to fight back. Mack had seen men almost go mad waiting for the projectiles to stop coming. Some would explode overhead, raining shrapnel down all around them. Others would actually strike the stone wall, hurling rocks everywhere. Some would slice through the trees overhead, and limbs would crash down among the men. It was sad to see a man get killed by a falling limb. Mack could hear men cursing over the explosions. The waiting for it to end was the most demoralizing part of being shelled.

The amazing thing was the birds. Mack peeked over the top of the stone wall and watched, as the concussion of the exploding shells actually knocked birds from the sky. They didn't even have to be close to the explosion. It was amazing—a shell would explode, and birds would just stop flying and fall to the ground.

In the morning, after it warmed up, the mist had dispelled. Beyond the field in their front were masses of Federal infantry in the tree line a half mile away. The artillery was somewhere behind that line of infantry. Mack looked down the long, thin Confederate line. The position was strong, but the line was thin. It looked more like a skirmish line than a line of battle. It didn't take a genius to know that, when the enemy advanced, there would be no stopping them.

By now, the artillery fire had been coming in for over six hours. Mack couldn't remember enduring quite so bad a shelling during the entire war. Unlike the Confederate artillery, the Yankees seemed to have an endless supply of ammunition. He began to wish the infantry would just come on and get this thing over with. To reach the Confederate lines, the Federals would have to cross a muddy field over three hundred yards wide. That would slow them down and expose them to more rifle fire.

Between lulls in the cannon fire, they'd been listening to the firing coming from their rear between Confederates and Wilson's Federal cavalry. It was beginning to sound like a repeat of what happened yesterday. They'd been held in position until their escape route was almost completely cut off. They had to run like hell to escape capture.

The artillery had just stopped firing again. Mack was behind the stone wall waiting. He heard cheering to the front. Every Confederate behind the stone wall stood and looked that way. Everyone knew what that meant. The bombardment was over; the infantry was coming. He heard men breathe a sigh of relief.

Mack Keenum's best friend, Tom Barrett, said, "That's the longest artillery fire I've had to endure during this entire war."

Mack nodded in agreement. His ears were ringing from all the explosions.

Sergeant Downs muttered to himself, "Let the bastards come on."

The blue line seemed to spring from the trees across the field. They were coming at the double-quick. There were three solid lines of blue infantry moving toward their thinly-held stone wall. *They're coming fast, Mack thought. They're hoping to get in close quarters with us before we can shred them with rifle fire.* Some Confederate artillery to their right opened fire with canister. Thousands of tiny iron balls began to create large gaps in their lines.

"Fire!" Colonel Snodgrass screamed.

Mack had his rifle resting on the stone wall for better aim. All the men did. After they fired, each man began to quickly reload. Federal soldiers in the front line had crashed to the ground, slowing those behind. The rebel yell rose from somewhere on the left and traveled down the line.

This may be the last time we're able to give that yell, Mack thought, so he put some extra emphasis in it. He knew they would be here soon, and things would get ugly when they crossed the wall. Mack didn't have a bayonet. He would have to use his musket as a club when they arrived. It wouldn't matter, there were just too many of them to stop. The Thirty-Fifth would be swallowed up in no time.

Every man was reloading and firing as fast as possible. Mack had managed to get off four shots before the Federal line stopped. They were still a good fifty yards away. He could see panic spread down the Federal line. The rapid fire and rebel yell had convinced them there were more Confederates behind this wall than what were actually here. It was sudden. The Federal line broke for the rear almost as one. The panic was contagious. He'd seen it before. All the men behind the wall were yelling again. They could hardly believe their eyes.

He looked out at the dead and wounded Federals in the muddy field. He wondered if any of those had fallen to his rifle. With so many men firing at once, there was just no possible way to know. Mack would be justified if he had killed someone. Those men had had every intention of killing him.

Mack had just reloaded his rifle and began to relax, when he saw the Federal line move out of the trees again. The Yankee officers had done a good job of reforming them and urging them back across the field. When Colonel Snodgrass gave the command, the Rebel line opened fire again with deadly effect. The cannons on the right were still throwing canister at them. This assault ended the same way the other had. The Federal officers could prod their men no further.

This time, instead of retreating in panic, they simply fell back a few yards and lay down in the mud. Those men were content to lay there over two hundred yards away and fire at long range. *Smart men, Mack thought.*

Someone cried out to his left. "Come on! Come on, you miserable sons-of-bitches!"

Mack looked at Tom, and they both burst into laughter. Soon, every one of them was screaming at the Federals across the field, begging them to come again. They cursed them as cowards for staying out of range.

Mack began to feel confident again. It seemed as though they may actually win this battle. Their thin line had stopped a force almost four times as large. It inspired him. For the first time in a while, Mack Keenum felt glorious.

That feeling didn't last very long. There was yelling and screaming to their rear. Every man in the command spun in unison. Confederate soldiers were racing off the hill to their left. Men were running as fast as they could downhill. Some tripped and turned flips, while others were actually so panicked they bounced off the trees.

Mack wondered how those men could have been driven off that massive hill. *We're down here in the lowest portion of the battlefield, and we held against four times our number. Those boys had the high ground.* Not two hundred yards away, on top of the hill, were swarms of Federal soldiers. They were firing down at the fleeing troops.

It was obvious to everyone present that the army was collapsing. Men were racing in all directions off the hill. The United States flag was visible on top of the hill. Their position behind this stone wall was no longer tenable. To remain here meant they would be enveloped. There was an enemy firing at them from the front, and those Yankees on that hill would soon move down and be in their rear. Still, no one ordered a retreat. Mack wondered what the officers were thinking just now.

The regimental adjutant walked up and held a message in his hand. He'd been to the right of the line and hadn't seen what they were all watching. He said in a loud voice, "I have a proclamation to read from General Hood. The commanding general takes great pleasure in announcing to his troops that victory and success are within our grasp..."

"Look yonder!" Waddy Mosely shouted at the man.

The adjutant stopped reading and spun toward the rear. Federals were a mere fifty yards away and rolling up the Confederate left flank. The adjutant yelled, "Forget the proclamation, boys! It's every man for himself!"

It would have been comical under different circumstances. The four cannons to their right spun their tubes to the left and waited for the Confederate infantry to get clear. The Federals were within twenty yards, when they opened fire with canister. At this range, canister was devastating. Federal troops simply ceased to exist from the tiny iron balls. Body parts flew through the air. Mack looked over his shoulder and saw an arm sail thirty feet behind the enemy line. If it hadn't been for those cannons, not one of them would have escaped. It had bought them just enough time. Mack Keenum ran as hard as possible on the stiff knee.

Now, it was the Confederates' turn to run across a muddy field under fire. It was a half mile to a tree-covered hill in their rear. If a man could just make it to those trees, his chances of survival would go way up. He expected to get hit any moment. He saw Tom Barrett and Waddy Mosely up ahead of him. Waddy's ankle had about healed, which was lucky for him. Mack's knee wasn't healing that fast. It had been an uglier wound.

To the right of them was Steve Harmon. The man was moving pretty quick. He'd caught up to Tom and Joe and was about to pass them, when he stumbled and fell on the ground. Mack glanced back and saw the man grab at his ankle. There was no blood, which told Mack that the boy either sprained or

289

broke his ankle. There was no doubt in his mind that the boy would be captured.

About two hundred yards farther, Mack began to tire. Having to limp in the mud had caused his good leg to wear out. He paused and thought about dropping to the ground for a rest, when a bullet passed close by his head. Someone had taken a deliberate shot at him. This gave him a new burst of energy, and off he went again.

It seemed to take forever for him to reach the tree line, but once he did, he felt better. He paused with his back to the first tree he came to. He could hear the bullets striking the other side of the tree. *There's no way I can get to the top of this hill with a bad leg, he thought, as he stared up the steep slope.*

He peeked back into the field behind him and saw the Federals advancing across the mud. They would pause, fire, and advance as they reloaded. To stay here any longer would mean certain capture. He began to dodge from tree to tree as he made his way up the hill. At least the thick woods made him feel secure. He was about halfway up and limping along, when a bullet traveled through the back of his frock coat and through his pants, just grazing the skin on the inside of his thigh.

The slight wound was just a scratch, but it burned and itched at the same time. Mack dove behind a tree and inspected the wound through the hole in his pants. He was lucky. At least it was in the same leg as his bad knee. At least it wouldn't slow him down anymore.

He peeked around the tree and saw the Federals moving from the field into the trees below. It appeared to him that there were a thousand of them. All of them were firing uphill into the retreating Confederate soldiers. Bullets struck the trees all around his position. He began to feel like every one of them was aiming at him. He wondered if he'd ever reach the top.

He struggled on upward and finally did reach the top. As he made his way over the crest, he sat down on a log to rest. Confederates were continuously coming over the hill. One ragged barefoot soldier struggled over and sat on the log beside him. He was exhausted and seemed to have trouble getting his breath.

Mack recognized him as a man from Company A who used to play cards with them. He asked, "Are they still coming?"

"No," the man replied between pants. "They content to stand at the bottom of the hill and just shoot at us."

A thought worried Mack. He asked, "Do you know Tom Barrett?"

"Company B?" the man gasped. "I think so; I'm in Company A, but I think I know the man—big cutup all the time?"

"That's him. He's my best friend," Mack's face betrayed his concern. "We got separated."

"I think I saw him at the base of the hill," the man frowned and panted a few more times. "I think he gave out, couldn't go no farther."

"Damn," Mack said to himself. "We need to move from here. They won't stay down there long, and I got a bum knee. I can't be running like I did before."

The man took a deep breath and stood up. "I'll stay with you until we find our unit."

They limped off the hill and onto the road below. It was soon dark, and a storm was approaching on the horizon. He could see lightning streak across the night air. It looked like another miserable night ahead.

Ahead was a large fire beside the road. The glare of the fire was almost blinding. As they approached the fire, a familiar voice called out. "Mack, I thought you was a goner."

Mack looked at the man in the muddy uniform. He almost broke down, tears streaming down his face. He said, "Tom, I thought you was gone up the spout also."

Tom walked over and held Mack tight. Both were crying. They cried because the other had survived. They cried from the strain of what they had just gone through. They cried just because.

They held each other for a long moment. Finally, Tom said, "Come over here and get warm."

He practically pulled Mack over to the fire. He said, "I have no idea where everybody else is."

"Scattered to hell and back," said the man from Company A.

"Steve Harmon was captured," Mack added. "I lost you and Waddy."

"Waddy's fine," Tom patted his friend on the back. "I gave out. The last I saw, he was still making good time. We got down here on the road, and I had to stop and rest, but he kept going."

"We can't stay here," Mack began to limp toward the road again. "I'm exhausted, but we got to keep moving. I can't take anymore close calls on this bad leg."

The man from Company A decided he was going to rest here with the other men by the fire and start out early in the morning. Tom helped Mack out into the road. Just stopping for a few moments had made his knee stiffen up even more.

They staggered on southward into the cold, wet night. When the thunderstorm hit, still they continued. They walked until two in the morning, until the fatigue finally caught up with them. They found an old barn just off the road. It was full of stragglers, but it was also full of hay. It would make a comfortable bed for the night.

4:30 p.m.

USA

George Thomas watched the mass of Confederate soldiers pour down the north and west flank of the large hill. A look of concern spread across his face. It appeared that Smith and Schofield's attack had failed, just like Steedman and Wood's attack on the other flank. This looked bad. From the appearance of things, the Confederates hadn't been content to let them fall back but were counterattacking instead.

Thomas spurred the horse forward to Smith's position. Smith was sitting on his horse beneath a large oak tree. His face bore a grim expression. It looked to Thomas like the man was frozen, too afraid to act.

Thomas practically screamed. "Andrew, what's happened? Have your men been captured by a counterattack?"

"Hell no," Smith glared at Thomas. "Not by a damned sight. My men are capturing them. Those are my prisoners being herded to the rear."

Thomas let out a sigh of relief. He studied the grim look on Smith's face. If he hadn't known better, he would think the man was sad. Thomas threw his head back and roared with laughter. Smith looked confused as he continued to stare at his commander. It was the first time Smith had ever seen the man laugh. After a long moment, he allowed a smile to appear at the corner of his lips.

Thomas asked, "Have Schofield's men gone in with yours?"

"Not yet," Smith replied.

Thomas spun in the saddle and called to Whipple. "Send a message to Schofield. Tell him to pursue the broken Confederate army."

Thomas reached over and patted Smith on the shoulder. "I'll be at my headquarters if you need me."

About nine that night, Whipple approached Thomas with a situation report. Thomas had lay down and taken a short nap. Whipple said, "Sir, General Wood reports he went in hard and attempted to pursue but was forced to stop and reform his men. He's afraid of running into friendly fire in the dark. General Steedman has advanced nowhere. He says his men are out of everything except ammunition and wants to know what you expect of him at this point."

Thomas interrupted. "What about Schofield? His men were idle most of the day, and I gave him orders to pursue."

Whipple was shaking his head. "General Schofield reports that things haven't gone as planned. He attempted to pursue, but Smith's troops were blocking the road. He has put his troops in bivouac for the night."

Thomas slapped his knee. He was growing aggravated at Schofield. It seemed the man intentionally tried to derail his every plan. "I tell you what,

Will, have Schofield move to the rear and escort the supply trains. Surely, he can get that right. He doesn't seem to want to do anything else."

Whipple said, "You have a message here from Doctor Brinton, the superintendent of military hospitals in Nashville."

"What's he need?" Thomas grunted. He could only imagine what the doctor wanted.

"He doesn't need anything," Whipple shook his head. "He just wants to inform you that the Confederate and Federal wounded were being treated side by side without preference to allegiance."

Thomas was nodding in agreement. Whipple continued, "He wishes to inform you that he has sent the black soldiers to an old warehouse downtown. He doesn't think it's proper to have blacks share the hospital with the white soldiers."

"That's fine," Thomas nodded again. It may not sound right, but he hadn't been in favor of putting those men in uniform to begin with. He really didn't believe the Negro was near as smart as the white man. No one in this army believed that. He just wondered why the politicians in Washington couldn't see that. *Someday they may be our equals, but that day is far away. If we hadn't been losing this war, Lincoln would have never allowed them to fight either. The draft dodgers and substitute hiring had forced this move on the country.*

"There's another thing," Whipple smiled at Thomas. "About a third of the Confederate prisoners are barefoot. They seem to be in good spirits though. Several were being escorted to the rear and were laughing about how John Bell Hood had kept his word and gotten them in Nashville."

Thomas smiled at the thought. "I guess he did, didn't he?"

A courier entered the door and handed a wet message to Whipple. Whipple thanked the drenched man and began reading. He said, "It's a message from Schofield, sir. He says he's been interrogating prisoners and believes the Confederate army is all but destroyed."

No shit, Thomas thought. We could have captured them all if Schofield would have been as busy pursuing as he'd been interrogating prisoners.

Whipple tried to hide the smile on his face. He asked, "You still want to order the man to the rear escorting the trains?"

Thomas almost laughed. "Yes, place his men in charge of the trains, and place him in charge of all prisoner interrogations."

"Right," Whipple could contain the smile no longer.

"I'm riding to the front to see Wilson," Thomas pulled his boots back on. "I need to see how things are coming. If I have a commander left that will pursue, he's my man."

"Sir, it's been coming a storm for the past hour." Whipple knew better than to try and talk his commander out of going, but at least he could warn him. "Do you think you can find Wilson out there on a dark, stormy night?"

"I'll find him," Thomas said almost to himself. He reached and got the rain coat off the coat rack by the door. "You stay here and hold the fort."

Thomas rode south. The night was dark, and rain was falling in sheets. The only visibility occurred when the lightening flashed. The roar of the thunder was almost as loud as the cannons had been earlier. Already, he could feel the temperature dropping. He thought about how miserable the night was going to be for his men in this weather.

He wondered why there always seemed to be a storm following a battle. He wondered if there was a scientific explanation. One man had told him that cannon fire causes thunderstorms. Thomas hardly believed that, but then again, he could hardly just dismiss the theory either. He'd heard one man explain that God sent a storm after a battle to cleanse man's blood from his pure land. Thomas couldn't very well argue with that theory either.

He thought about his family back in Virginia. Of course, they weren't his family any longer. He'd been told that when Virginia seceded, and he went with the northern states in this war, they had disowned him. His sisters had turned his pictures to the wall. They even refused to speak his name. If a visitor asked about him, they would pretend they didn't know a George Thomas. At least his wife would be by his side. He could be thankful she was loyal.

He asked several troopers where General Wilson could be found, and they had finally gotten him to the cavalry commander. George saw him by the flash of lightening. He was standing in the road ahead talking to members of his staff. Thomas rode the horse up and peered down on his skinny cavalryman.

Wilson looked up at the silhouette of a large man on horseback in the flashes of lightening. The heavy raincoat made Thomas look larger than he was. Thomas yelled over the noise of rain and thunder. "Dang it to hell, Wilson. Didn't I tell you we could whip them? I told you, didn't I?"

Wilson was nodding his head. He smiled at the thought of George Thomas cursing. The man never cursed, and to him, 'dang' and 'hell' were curse words. Wilson shouted back. "This has been a splendid day—a glorious day."

Thomas dismounted and grabbed Wilson in a giant bear hug. It was an extremely rare display of emotion from George Thomas.

He quickly composed himself and asked, "How does it look on pursuit?"

"My horses are far in the rear," Wilson shook his head. "I've been working my ass off to get everything ready to pursue at first light. The terrain is not suited for cavalry operations at all. My men have become scattered to hell and back. I hope to have everyone reformed and the horses brought through those thickets back there and to be chasing the Rebs at daylight."

"Very well," Thomas reached out and patted his cavalryman on the shoulder. "You do realize you'll be running into Bedford Forrest down there somewhere."

Wilson nodded in the dark. He said, "Can't wait; I owe the man."

294

5:00 p.m.

CSA

General Hood sat in the road watching his army fall apart around him. General Stewart rode up and paused beside Hood.

Stewart asked, "What are the orders, sir?"

"I think if I can disengage my army here," Hood stared straight ahead as if in deep thought, "we can swing around Thomas's flank and strike him in his rear in the morning."

"Sir," Stewart said. His voice betrayed what he was thinking. Hood seemed to be losing touch with reality. He just couldn't admit the campaign had become a dismal failure.

General Cheatham came galloping down the road. The short, heavyset general bounced in the saddle. He reined up and yelled from excitement. "Sir, my men have been shifted around so much today, they think the officers are confused. They've broken without much of a fight. I was worrying over the left flank, when a bullet struck a tree beside me from behind. I looked around and saw Bate's entire division in flight. The area behind me was full of Yankees."

Hood's face betrayed an expression of shock. He asked, "Has the army broken?"

"All to hell," Cheatham replied.

Hood swung in the saddle and yelled, "Colonel Mason, send a courier to General Lee. Tell him he must hold the enemy back while the army regroups in the rear."

Hood turned back to Cheatham and Stewart. "Gentlemen, let's ride forward and rally the men. The battle's not lost yet."

The three men rode into the frightened mob and attempted to stop the panic. It didn't take Hood long to see it was useless. All hope of making a stand quickly left his mind. He'd never seen Confederate troops this panicked.

He saw General Bate trying to rally his men. The man was riding along as cool as if he were on dress parade, begging his men to turn and fight. It was all to no avail. They streamed right on past him heading south, away from the enemy. It was the most shameful thing he had ever seen. The worst part was watching the junior officers going right along with them.

Hood rode up beside General Bate, but the man didn't seem to notice him there. A staff officer came running up. Bate yelled, "Cooper, where is General Smith?"

The staff officer replied, "Captured, I think."

"James," Bate called the man by his first name. "I need you to help me here. Stop every man you can and form a line here."

Cooper looked around at the panicked mob racing for the rear. He knew it was a waste of time to attempt to rally this mob, but that's not something you tell a general. He said, "I'll do my best, sir."

Bate looked toward the hill where all the enemy soldiers were racing down after his men. He mumbled something to himself and rode toward the right to try and make a stand.

General Cheatham was in the middle of the road waving his sword in the air. A ragged barefoot Confederate private passed him heading to the rear. The poor man was covered in mud. Cheatham yelled at the man. "Where are you going? We must turn and fight. There's no danger back there."

The man turned and looked at the general in the neat, clean uniform. Without slowing down he said, "You go to hell. I've been back there."

Before long, Colonel Mason rode forward and found General Hood. He said, "The courier's back from Lee. He says his corps has all but broken also. Only Clayton's division remains intact. He is forming a rearguard with that lone division now."

Hood nodded his head in approval. Anything would have to do at the moment.

Mason continued, "The man says General Lee was in the middle of the road waving a regimental flag and rallying his men. He said Lee looked like a very god of war out there trying to lead his men."

"Very good," Hood was still nodding. "That's very good; we need good, brave men just now."

"Sir, General Ed Johnson has been captured," Mason said.

Hood thought about 'Old Clubby' being captured again. The man had just been captured last May and now here again. He won't be very happy about that. After his last capture, Robert E. Lee had sent him west. Johnson had felt as though he were being demoted. This had to feel like the ultimate insult. Hood asked, "What happened?"

"He was running for the rear across a muddy field," Mason thought about Johnson running, and it almost seemed comical. He fought back the urge to smile. "Anyway, he's a little overweight and couldn't reach his horse in time."

Hood turned the horse and rode south. He looked at Mason and said, "We'll make Misses Maney's home our headquarters until forced to retreat farther."

"Right," Mason said. They rode on in silence. Mason looked at Hood in the fading light and noticed how sad he looked. Tears coursed down his face and into his beard. The man's career would be over following such a disaster. He watched his commander rubbing his hand through his hair over and over.

At the Maney house, they tried to persuade Hood to eat, but the man was just too depressed. He finally worked up the courage to ask Colonel Mason how bad things were.

Mason shook his head. He dreaded telling his commander and friend just how bad things really were. He said, "I got a report that Colonel Rucker, commanding one of Chalmers's cavalry brigades, is wounded and captured. He'll probably lose an arm."

Hood said nothing. Mason was putting off the inevitable, telling the small problems first. Hood nodded his head and said, "Go on."

"General Sears, of course you know, was wounded yesterday and will probably lose a leg." Mason rubbed his eyes. When he talked, he avoided eye contact with his commander. "General Thomas Smith was captured, and we have a report that he was struck over the head with a sword after surrendering. They say that wound is feared mortal. Henry Jackson, commanding the Georgia brigade, has been captured. Like Johnson, he was running across a muddy field, and so much mud became caked on his riding boots, he just couldn't go any father."

Hood struck the table with his fist but not in anger. It was more frustration than anything. He asked, "What about casualties?"

"I won't have any numbers until sometime tomorrow." Mason shook his head again. "Everyone is so scattered in retreat, no one knows who is captured, wounded, or just missing as they race for the rear."

Hood heard a commotion on the front lawn of the house. There were several horses on the lawn, and men were talking in a loud voice. In a moment, the front door swung open and in walked General Forrest. Hood breathed a sigh of relief.

Forrest walked over and gave a sloppy salute. It irked him to salute this man that he truly didn't care for very much. Mason rose from the chair and offered it to Forrest.

Forrest sat down and waited.

"I need your help, General Forrest." Hood looked Forrest in the eyes. He didn't want anymore confrontations with this wild man, but he also was going to let his subordinate know who was truly in command here. "Can your cavalry provide a rearguard until I can get the army safely back to Alabama?"

"No, I can't," Forrest replied. He stared back into Hood's eyes. His own eyes showed nothing but coldness. "I can't do it with my cavalry alone. I ain't got but about three thousand men."

Forrest watched Hood lower his head in thought. Forrest said, "If I can have a good infantry division, with a commander of my choosing, I believe I can hold them off."

Hood looked up, and for the first time, there was hope in his melancholy face. He said, "Colonel Mason, which troops are the freshest we have?"

Mason stepped back to the table. "Sir, Quarles's Alabama and Tennessee brigade, commanded by General George Johnson, Reynolds's Arkansas brigade, Ector's Texas brigade, commanded by Colonel David Coleman, and Featherston's Mississippi brigade from Stewart's corps are capable. Maney's Tennessee brigade, commanded by Colonel Hume Field, Smith's brigade of Georgia troops, commanded by Colonel Charles Olmstead, and Strahl's Tennessee brigade, commanded by Colonel Andrew Kellar from

Cheatham's corps are in fairly descent shape. Palmer's Tennessee brigade from Lee's corps is also in good shape. These men have missed the worst of the fighting here at Nashville and should be battle ready."

"How many men do those eight brigades contain?" Hood asked.

Mason did a quick calculation in his head. "About nineteen hundred men, sir."

Hood looked at Forrest and asked, "Will that be enough?"

"Maybe," Forrest replied. "It's according to whether or not I get the commander I want for those men."

Hood was about to ask who Forrest wanted, when Mason interrupted. "Sir, I'm sorry, but four hundred of those nineteen hundred are without shoes."

Forrest glared at Mason. "Hell, I don't need men without shoes. Send them on with the wagons, and just let me take the fifteen hundred who are prepared for battle." Forrest looked back at General Hood. "With my three thousand cavalry, that'll give me what, forty-five hundred men? That'll be plenty."

Hood nodded in agreement. He asked, "General, who do you want to command that infantry?"

Forrest didn't hesitate. "I want Major General Edward Walthall."

Hood was taken aback. Walthall wasn't one of the bigger names in the army. The man was capable and competent but not as famous as some of the others. Hood turned to Mason. "Colonel, have General Walthall brought here immediately."

Hood offered Forrest something to eat while they waited. Forrest declined. Hood pulled out his map, and together they began to study the retreat route. Hood told Forrest what he wanted, and Forrest agreed to do the best he could. It was the best the two men had worked together to date.

Walthall soon arrived. He looked concerned. Usually, when you were ordered to report to headquarters, it was because you were being blamed for some failure. The man was tall and lanky. He reminded Hood of General Granbury, except his hair was curly instead of waving wildly in the air. He had a thick, brown mustache that completely covered his lips. His eyes drooped at the corners but seemed like they were piercing your very soul when he looked at you. Forrest stood and took Walthall's hand. Mason placed a chair at the table for him to sit.

Walthall looked a bit uncomfortable here before these two famous officers. He couldn't help but wonder what he had done. After he'd taken a seat, Hood said, "I have decided to organize a rearguard. General Forrest says he can't stop the Federal army with just his cavalry. He thinks it can be done with a division of infantry helping him. General Walthall, this position is a post of honor, but it is also a post of great peril. The danger is so great; I cannot bring myself to order it upon you unless you are willing to take it. General Forrest has asked for you personally to command these eight brigades. The army must be saved, come what may, even if it's necessary to sacrifice your command to accomplish this."

Walthall felt proud knowing the great General Forrest had asked for him personally. He glanced over at Forrest, but the man betrayed nothing. He sat patiently, waiting for Walthall's answer.

Walthall began to shake his head. "General Hood, I've never accepted a difficult position for glory, and I've never accepted a soft position for comfort. I take my chances as they come and always endeavor to do my duty. Just give me the orders, and I will do the best I can."

Forrest let out a sigh of relief. He turned to Hood and said, "Now we will hold them back."

The next morning, as Hood rode southward with his broken army, he heard a soldier marching along singing. The song sounded like 'The Yellow Rose of Texas.' Hood spurred the horse forward and rode close behind the man. He thought it might be one of his Texas soldiers. The words were different from the ones in the Texas song, but the tune was definitely the same.

At that point, he could make out the words clearer. The man sang, "So now I'm marching southward, my heart is full of woe. I'm going back to Georgia to see my Uncle Joe. You may talk about your Beauregard and sing of General Lee, but the gallant Hood of Texas played hell in Tennessee."

It galled Hood to think of his army being taken from him and placed back under the command of his enemy, General Joe Johnston. Hood spurred the horse on southward toward Alabama and the end of the war.

December 19, 1864, 4:00 p.m.

CSA

Virginia Cliffe was relieved when the wagon stopped in front of the Compton Home. The trip here from Franklin had been very exhausting in a wagon that practically jarred your teeth out on the rough roads.

James jumped from the wagon and extended a hand to help her down. Together, they'd searched all over the hill where Colonel Shy had been killed, looking for his body or a grave that held some identification. A Federal soldier there on burial detail had told them the body was taken to the home of Felix Compton. The soldier also told her the hill had been renamed Shy's Hill, in honor of the brave officer for whom she was searching.

Virginia's husband was a Union sympathizer, and this had allowed her to pass through Federal lines to retrieve the body for Shy's parents, who were neighbors of hers. She was proud to be the wife of a doctor. The man was a party to healing, instead of killing like the vast majority of people in this country were at the moment.

Doctor Daniel Cliffe had been too busy caring for the wounded at Franklin to see to this himself. He'd sent Virginia and one of his servants. She

299

thought about how ironic things were. He's for the Union, but he owns slaves. He didn't see the war as a war upon slavery but a war over government. Everyone had thought it strange seeing a woman coming for a body. It wasn't quite the way things were in the south. Women were supposed to be protected from such things.

She thought about her dear husband. When the war began, he had sided with the Confederacy because these were his friends and neighbors. The poor man was from Ohio and had moved to Tennessee when he was just thirteen. He'd found himself torn by this war.

He'd begun the war as a Confederate surgeon under General Zollicoffer in East Tennessee. When Zollicoffer had been killed, he'd embalmed the lanky-built officer and escorted his body back to Nashville for burial. Her husband would embalm Colonel Shy also, if they could just find the body.

Daniel Cliffe had become frustrated with the Confederate cause, and when the Federals took Nashville, he'd simply swapped sides, swearing allegiance to the United States. Most men who did this were called traitors and hated by their neighbors, but not Daniel. He'd done everything possible to help his neighbors against wrongs suffered by the invading army, and that's how she had been chosen to travel here and retrieve a body.

Felix Compton and his daughter Emily were standing near one of the square columns of his beautiful white home. Virginia walked toward them, attempting to shake the dust from her dress. Felix Compton bowed politely. Virginia said, "Excuse me, but I'm here to retrieve the body of Colonel William Shy. A Federal soldier said the body has been brought here."

"That's right, ma'am," Felix said. "I thought someone would probably be coming for the body, so I wouldn't allow them to bury him just yet."

Emily stepped forward and pointed to the end of the porch. "That's him down there; I'll take you."

Virginia followed Emily down to where several bodies were covered by gray Confederate army blankets. Emily pointed toward the one that contained Shy's body. She asked, "Are you related to him?"

"No," Virginia stepped forward and knelt near the body. "My husband is a doctor and obtained a pass for me to come and bring the body back to his parents."

Virginia reached for the top of the blanket and pulled it down. William Shy lay with his eyes closed and except for the wounds looked peaceful. His face had been washed of all blood and powder marks. She gasped as she stared at the damage the bullet had done to his head. Hair, scalp and brain matter hung from the exit wound over the right ear.

Emily said, "I couldn't stand to see him in such shape. He was a brave man—a hero. I washed his face and cleaned him up as much as I could."

Virginia replaced the blanket. She was impressed with the young girl. She said, "You did well."

300

"I found the body," Emily said. Her voice betrayed the melancholy she felt. "When the battle was over, I got a neighbor to go with me and help me find some of the Tennessee men who'd been killed. They say he was killed by the shot through the head. Some sick fiends in the Federal army had stripped him of all his clothing and bayoneted his body to a tree. That's the way we found him. He was too good a man to be disgraced in such a way."

Virginia lowered her head. She wondered how long God would allow all this killing to continue. It had to end someday.

Emily said, "Another neighbor of ours was out the night after the battle robbing the dead and wounded. Some soldier still had a loaded rifle and shot him through the thighs. They're saying he may not survive. I can't help but be amazed at the atrocities men are capable of committing on one another."

Virginia said nothing. She had often wondered the same thing.

Felix watched Virginia slowly rise and step away from the body. He said, "I see your trip has been exhausting. You should stay the night, eat a good dinner with us, and start back in the morning. Our home has been turned into a hospital to soldiers of both sides, but we have plenty of room for you."

"I appreciate your hospitality," Virginia gave a slight curtsy. "This trip has been exhausting for me."

Emily took Virginia by the hand and said, "Let's get you inside. You can sleep in my room tonight."

"Thank you," Virginia nodded.

As they reached the door, Emily stopped and turned around. She thought she'd better warn Virginia what the inside of the house was like before they entered. "Misses Cliffe, there are close to a hundred and fifty wounded Confederate soldiers inside. It's not a pretty sight."

"I understand," Virginia smiled at the girl. "My husband's a physician. I'll be fine, but thank you."

Emily opened the door and entered the house. The smell was horrible. The young girl took Virginia up the stairs. She said, "They've allowed my mother and I to give the Confederate soldiers bread, water, and a little milk. That's about all we've had. The Yankees burst down the door of our smokehouse and stole everything. Fanny, our old black mammy, has stolen and begged off the Yankees everything we have now, or we would have starved to death. She's a good woman."

"I'll be glad when this war is over," Virginia was still trying to adjust to the smell. "I will be glad when all wars cease."

Virginia and her servant spent the night, and the next morning, Felix Compton helped the black man load William Shy's body into the wagon. Virginia tried to pay Felix for the food and board, but he, being a southern gentleman, would have none of that.

They returned to Franklin with the body, and her husband embalmed Colonel William Shy with arsenic as he had General Zollicoffer over three years ago. He then dressed him in a tuxedo his parents had brought. He placed the body in a cast iron coffin painted white. The thing looked like something that had come from medieval times. It had four handles bolted on the side and a window in the top so the family could view the body without having to deal with the smell.

He was carried back to his boyhood home and buried in the back yard, where his mother and father could watch over his grave until they joined him in death. His story would not end there. Sometimes, a man comes back a century later.

Epilog

The Confederacy's second most important army was broken, and with it, so was the Confederacy. The war would last until the following spring, but all hope of obtaining independence was gone with that bitter December in Tennessee. Hood did manage to get his army back to Tupelo, but by then, it was a shell of its former self.

This army had almost wrecked Grant at Shiloh. It had invaded Kentucky and put fear in the people north of the Ohio River. It had almost captured Rosecrans's army at Murfreesboro and had broken that same army at Chickamauga.

Of the 38,000 men General Hood took with him into Tennessee, he could muster only 14,211 men in Tupelo. He'd lost 23,789 casualties from the time he entered Tennessee in November until he returned in December. He'd also lost 53 cannons and 3,034 small arms.

In contrast, General Thomas had suffered just over 6,000 casualties.

Still, the campaign remains one of the war's greatest 'what ifs.' What if he had captured Schofield's army at Spring Hill and took Nashville before Smith arrived? We'll never know.

Afterwards

Nathan Bedford Forrest

The fighting didn't end for General Forrest at Nashville. He had to cover the army's retreat back to Alabama. There was an ugly incident at Columbia, Tennessee, that could have been catastrophic. He had just arrived at the Duck River and was preparing to cross his cavalry. General Cheatham came riding up at that moment and told Forrest that he intended to cross his troops first. Forrest naturally took this as an insult. He told Cheatham that he would cross first, as he had gotten there first.

Cheatham, who ranked Forrest, said, "I think not, sir. You are mistaken. I am crossing first and would be obliged if you would move your troops out of my way."

Forrest drew his revolver and rode up beside Cheatham. He aimed his weapon at Frank Cheatham's chest and said, "If you are a better man than me, your troops may cross ahead of mine."

Confederate soldiers from both men's commands raised their rifles in preparation of defending their commanders. Fortunately, General Stephen Lee, who happened to rank both men, arrived on the scene at this moment. He realized that both men were exhausted from the campaign and acted as mediator between the two. Apologies were soon exchanged, and General Lee took Cheatham aside while Forrest got his troops across the river.

He'd again proven himself a military genius by asking General Walthall to help command the rearguard. It was Walthall's best performance of the war.

Bedford Forrest would soon be promoted to lieutenant general. By the close of the war, he'd been wounded four times and had twenty-nine horses shot out from under him. By his own hand, he'd killed thirty Federal soldiers and often claimed that made him one up on them.

A millionaire before the war, he was forced to take bankruptcy in 1868. He would serve as a railroad president and attempt to grow crops. The war had used the man up. He died in Memphis, Tennessee, of diabetes in 1877, at the age of 56. He and his wife are buried beneath a statue of the general in a park in Memphis. Norfolk Southern's Forrest Yard in Memphis is named in his honor. After the war, Confederate President, Jefferson Davis, admitted that his greatest mistake of the war was in not recognizing the genius of Bedford Forrest until it was too late to do any good.

Benjamin Franklin Cheatham

Frank Cheatham would never get his coveted promotion to lieutenant general. He would revert to division commander after the campaign and go with his men to join Joseph Johnston in the Carolina Campaign. He would surrender his command to General William Tecumseh Sherman there.

After the war, the lifelong bachelor returned to Tennessee and married Anna Bell Robertson. He would fail in politics but serve four years as the superintendent of the Tennessee State Prison. He then became postmaster of Nashville until his death in 1886, at the age of 65. He was buried in Nashville's Mount Olivet Cemetery, and his funeral was considered the most imposing Nashville had ever witnessed. He was loved by the men he commanded and by the public.

John Calvin Brown

He would recover from his serious leg wound in time to join his men in the Carolina Campaign. He would surrender there to William Tecumseh Sherman. He was elected to the Tennessee state legislature in 1867. In 1870, he was elected as governor of Tennessee and then re-elected for a second term. After retiring from politics, he became president of the Texas and Pacific Railroad. He would die in 1889, at the age of 62. He was buried in Maplewood Cemetery, Pulaski, Tennessee.

Some historians believe that, shortly before his death, he wrote an apology for his actions of that night at Spring Hill. His family would never allow the report to become public, and it is believed his wife destroyed the damning letter to avoid any type of stain being attached to her husband's memory. What the letter actually contained will likely never be known.

Patrick Ronayne Cleburne

His body would be carried back to St. John's Episcopal Churchyard and buried in the cemetery he had said of, "It is almost worth dying for to be buried in such a beautiful place."

The entire Confederacy would mourn his passing. His own troops would mourn the brave man for months. He is perhaps one of the greatest Confederate generals and should be ranked with Lee, Jackson, and Forrest. He was one of only two foreign-born officers to reach the rank of major general in the Confederate army.

In 1870, his body was disinterred and buried in Maple Hill Cemetery, back in his adopted hometown of Helena, Arkansas.

John Bell Hood

He had been defeated more than any other Confederate general before him. His army was practically destroyed, but it was not all his fault. His physical disabilities had a lot to do with his failures. Problems in the army he commanded were also unfixable by the time he took command. While Bragg had been in command, the army had practically turned against itself.

He would write S.D. Lee after the war, saying, "Injustice has been done me...I have never feared but I would get justice, but expect it to be tardy."

He would be relieved of command after the campaign and would never command in the field again. His engagement with Buck Preston was broken off in 1865. He would marry the beautiful Anna Marie Hennen in 1868 and settle in New Orleans, Louisiana. He worked in the insurance business and as a cotton merchant.

After the war, he was forced to defend himself against numerous allegations by General Joseph Johnston, who blamed Hood for losing north Georgia while Johnston commanded the army. Many of the present-day beliefs about Hood's incompetence come from the writing of Joseph Johnston, who never gained the fame he desired as a great commander.

Hood was living in New Orleans in 1879, struggling with his physical disabilities and poor finances, when tragedy struck. His wife, a daughter, and then General Hood himself, all died of yellow fever within a week. John Bell Hood was 48. He is buried in Metairie Cemetery, New Orleans, Louisiana.

Stephen Dill Lee

Lee was a busy man following the war. He married Regina Harrison of Columbus, Mississippi, and made that place his home. After the war, he would sell insurance, serve in the Mississippi state senate, and become a college president. He was also deeply involved in the preservation of Vicksburg National Military Park. He was the first commander in chief of the United Confederate Veterans, which later became the present-day Sons of Confederate Veterans.

He and John Bell Hood would remain close friends until Hood's death in 1879. Stephen Lee would die of a cerebral hemorrhage in 1908, at the age of 74. He is buried in Friendship Cemetery, Columbus, Mississippi.

Thomas Benton Smith

The young brigadier general, who was struck over the head by the sword of Colonel McMillan, would survive the ugly wound that exposed his brain, despite what the doctors had said. He was taken to Fort Warren in Boston Harbor and held prisoner there until the end of the war. After his release, he would return to Nashville and work as a railroad conductor again. It was only temporary. In 1876, he was committed to the Tennessee State Hospital as a result of the attack after he had surrendered. He would survive there another forty-seven years, dying in 1923, at the age of 85. He is buried in Mount Olivet Cemetery, Nashville, Tennessee.

Alexander Peter Stewart

'Old Straight' would continue to lead his men, serving in the Carolina Campaign under Joseph Johnston. He would surrender there with his men. He would return to the field of education after the war. He taught at Cumberland University and later served as president of the University of Mississippi. He also worked to help preserve what is now the Chickamauga and Chattanooga National Park. He would survive being hit by a train in 1893 and die in 1908, at the age of 86. He is buried in Bellefontaine Cemetery, Saint Louis, Missouri.

George Henry Thomas

The Federal commander with all the colorful nicknames, 'Old Slow Trot,' 'The Rock of Chickamauga,' and 'Pap,' would receive another after the Tennessee Campaign. Some would refer to him as 'The Sledge of Nashville.'

He would continue to serve in the United States Army following the war. President Andrew Johnson did not forget his service in Johnson's home state of Tennessee and would offer him a promotion to lieutenant general. Thomas would decline the appointment, modestly stating that he hadn't earned the promotion.

He was assigned to a military post in San Francisco, California, in 1869. He would die there of a stroke in 1870, at the age of 53. His family, having disowned him for remaining with the Union during the war, would not even attend his funeral. He is buried in Oakwood Cemetery, Troy, New York.

John McAllister Schofield

Though he never got the fame he felt he deserved in the war, he would rise to the rank of lieutenant general in 1895 and command of the entire United States Army. He also served as Secretary of War under President Andrew Johnson.

He would die in St. Augustine, Florida, in 1906, at the age of 74 and is buried in Arlington National Cemetery.

Samuel Emerson Opdycke

The fiery, red-haired colonel would eventually be promoted to brigadier general and placed in command of the state of Texas during reconstruction. He would resign from the army in 1866 and move to New York City, where he operated a dry goods business.

He was very active in veterans' affairs and wrote extensively about the war. His memory seemed to fail during his writing days. Instead of remembering how he'd beaten his own men over the head at the Battle of Franklin, he would now remember how he had broken his pistol over the heads of Confederate soldiers.

He died in New York in 1884, at the age of 54, while cleaning his pistol; it accidentally discharged, shooting him in the abdomen. Opdycke is buried in Oakwood Cemetery, Warren, Ohio.

James Harrison Wilson

The lightweight Federal cavalryman with the large ego would eventually defeat Bedford Forrest in Selma, Alabama, at the close of the war. He and Forrest would remain close friends following the war until Forrest's death in 1877.

He would be promoted to Major General before the close of the war. Wilson would resign from the army in 1870. He would work as a railroad executive and in other business enterprises. In 1898, he would return to the United States Army and fight in the Spanish-American War. He would retire from the army a second time in 1902. Wilson died in Wilmington, Delaware, in 1925, at the age of 87 and is buried there in Old Swedes Churchyard.

William Mabry Shy

The Confederate colonel who was killed, stripped, and bayoneted to a tree on present-day Shy's Hill, would come back into this world a century later. On Christmas Eve in 1977, police would be called to investigate a grave being disturbed. Someone had placed a body on the casket of Colonel Shy. Forensic experts from the University of Tennessee's body farm were called in to investigate and help solve the murder. They found the victim had been dead from two to six months. It was the corpse of a white male with brown hair who stood approximately five-feet-eleven-inches and weighing about a hundred and seventy-five pounds. The man was between the ages of twenty-six and twenty-nine years old. He had been killed by a severe blow to the head. Soon, the truth would come out. Everything the experts had said about the victim was true, except the length of time the man had been dead. He had been killed one hundred and thirteen years before. Now we know what an excellent job Doctor Cliffe had done embalming the young colonel. William Shy would be reburied in a modern coffin. The coffin he rested in for over a hundred years can be viewed today at the Carter House Museum in Franklin, Tennessee.

The men of Company B, 35th Alabama Infantry

Joe Thompson would spend the rest of the war at Camp Chase prisoner of war camp in Ohio. Once released, he would return home and become a doctor in Tuscumbia. He visited the battlefield of Franklin once more and found the graves of the two Missouri soldiers who had crossed the Tennessee River with him. He is buried in Oakwood Cemetery, Tuscumbia, Alabama.

Sometime following the war, flag bearer Robert Wheeler would be exhumed and returned to Alabama for burial. He rests in Oakwood Cemetery, Tuscumbia, Alabama, near the graves of other Confederate dead.

Dick Beaumont would survive the war and return home to live out his life in Tuscumbia, Alabama. He too is buried in Oakwood Cemetery.

Mack Keenum would return home to see his wife and two daughters on his farm in Colbert County, Alabama. He would die sometime before 1870. His daughter, Mary Elizabeth Keenum, would marry John Alexander Osborn, and they would have several children. One child would be a red-haired daughter named Roxie Ann Osborn. She would marry Clarence Hartwell Kent, and they would have four children. The oldest son, named Price Kent, would have a son named Price Harley Kent. Price Harley Kent would marry Leola Lee Stonecipher, and they would have a son named Timothy Harley Kent, the author of this book. His hair is the same color as his great grandmother, and so is that of his son, Chase.

Bluewater Publications is a multi-faceted publishing company capable of meeting all of your reading and publishing needs. Our two-fold aim is to:

1) Provide the market with educationally enlightening and inspiring research and reading materials.

2) Make the opportunity of being published available to any author and or researcher who desires to be published.

We are passionate about preserving history; whether through the re-publishing of an out-of-print classic, or by publishing the research of historians and genealogists. Bluewater Publications is the Peoples' Choice Publisher.

For company information or information about how you can be published through Bluewater Publications, please visit:

www.BluewaterPublications.com

Also check Amazon.com to purchase any of the books that we publish.

Confidently Preserving Our Past,

Bluewater Publications.com

www.ingramcontent.com/pod-product-compliance
Lightning Source LLC
Chambersburg PA
CBHW061515020726
47502CB00006B/2078